The Malthus Pandemic

Terry Morgan

Published by TJM Books.
www.tjmbooks.com
ISBN: 978-0-9569675-6-5

Cover design and illustration by www.samwall.com

CHAPTER 1

My name is Daniel Capelli and, before you ask, I am not Italian. My father was but my mother wasn't. I am English born and bred. Born in Portsmouth and brought up around West London - Chiswick to be precise. I'm forty five years old and until recently I'd never found it hard to stay single. But details of my private life are sure to crop up later anyway so let's cut out the personal stuff right now. There's a lot to cover and I hate wasting time.

I'm writing this for a hundred different reasons but, before we start, I need to get something off my chest.

In the USA, UK and what is humorously called the European Union it is supposed to be a democracy. Right? Individuals can express their opinion freely, they can influence decisions that affect them and they are listened to because politicians need their votes. Correct? The many layers of bureaucracy, frustrating though they are, exist to ensure the necessary checks and balances so that we all live together in some sort of big, happy community. Organisations have been put in place that provide us, the hard working tax-payer, with protection and support when we need protection and support. Those that get paid out of our taxes do as we want not what they want.

So if we want to improve things and can show that it can be done at no extra cost to the public purse it stands to reason that we can point this out, expect immediate action and won't need to wait for an election to come around. And if we showed them that half of this happy community might be dead within a year, then what would you expect?

If I am not badly mistaken, you would expect all of our highly paid political leaders and that teeming mass of salaried and pensioned pen pushers that is their back office support to drop everything and deal with it. Right?

Well, let's hope so because as I write this I'm so concerned for the future of this community of billions that I'm beginning to think a short spell of dictatorship might be better for a while. As far as I can tell, nothing has been learned from what we found and yet another man-made, lethal virus with another fancy name could, right now, be sat in a freezer next door to where you live.

Are you comfortable knowing that? If so, would you like to see someone else, perhaps a scientist, taking decisions for all those politicians who have shown they are too afraid to listen let alone take any action?

1

So why do I start this with a rant? Well, the politicians and bureaucrats had their backs turned or were on their tax payer funded summer holidays at the time. But it only took a handful of us to uncover this ingenious but complicated plot - and we weren't even being paid. The hand wringing and buck-passing started when we tried to explain to them what was going on under their noses and asked them to act. We weren't part of their cosy system you see. We were outside their comfort zone and so they couldn't recognise us, in the official sense of the word. Their system ensures they only deal with each other. That way they keep control and cover each other's backs to keep the cosy system ticking over. But many of us want to see real, dynamic leadership and action. We're fed up with this short-term pandering just to get re-elected. So is it any wonder that some, tired of waiting, decide to take direct action themselves and bypass the system?

But, you know what really hurts? At one stage they thought we were a bunch of fruitcakes. But I forgive them for that last bit. There are lots of fruitcakes out there.

So, yes, I'm Daniel Capelli and now I've got that first rant off my chest, let me tell you what I do and then introduce you to a few other fruitcakes.

In a nutshell I'm a private investigator. That's not what it says in my passport but it's what I sometimes call myself if asked. A business consultant might go a step further and say that I operate in a niche sector. That would be correct.

I like what I do and I'm good at it. If I wasn't any good I wouldn't survive. After all I run a private enterprise not a publicly funded monopoly. I'm a one man band as it's called but my clients are often very big businesses. Most of the companies willing to pay for my services are not easy to please and demand value for their money so if I hadn't been delivering over the last few years then I wouldn't still be around. But I've slowly built a solid reputation for the specialised services I provide. Let's list a few:

Corporate fraud, industrial espionage, theft of intellectual property. That's a start. Satisfying suspicions about how competitors had made money so much more quickly and easily than they did or how the already wealthy have made their sometimes ill-gotten gains are two more. The work does, occasionally, put you at odds with people, so I have to be careful, but I've always believed that life without risk was rather dull, besides being far less lucrative.

I still keep my small pad in West London but I travel around a lot. Airports are a necessity but no country is off limits and so I live mostly out of a suitcase with a few other passports tucked somewhere. Daniel Capelli, you see, also has a few other names he can use from time to time. It makes life so much easier.

But that's enough about me for now.

2

Sometimes I need my own back office support just like those politicians. But my civil service is another one man band, or at least it started out as one. Colin Asher is a mate of mine. We've known each other for years but Colin has also built his business, Asher & Asher, from straight forward private investigation into something that resembles a privately owned SIS - MI5 or MI6. He's got nothing like the same numbers of staff and operates from a little office off the Edgeware Road, but Colin's intelligence gathering service is good enough for my purposes. Colin is important. You'll hear more about Colin.

I'd never heard of Doctor Larry Brown until this case started. This is the way these things go. Larry is American and he's already seen what I've written above about democracy and leadership and the power of individuals. I knew he'd like it. Larry was in Nigeria working for the American Embassy when it started and it was Larry who came across tests on the Malthus A virus being carried out on a hundred or so innocent victims up in the north of Nigeria. Larry is black, of West African descent and mixed well in Nigeria once he'd slipped on a pair of old jeans. I like Larry's gritty determination and frustration with the system. He's left the Embassy now as the frustration got the better of him. But we're staying in touch.

Then there's Kevin Parker. Larry and Kevin are poles apart in many ways but it was Kevin's Malthus Society website that helped us find the technical brains behind the creation of this lethal, human virus, and the plot to release it. Kevin lectures on social and economic history and is a passionate speaker on anything to do with Thomas Malthus, Paul Eyrlich and others you may or may not have heard of. Like them, he holds some very strong views himself on the need for a reduction in the world population and he's full of statistics to show it makes a lot of sense. I learned a lot from Kevin and am now a fully signed up member of his Malthus Society with a growing appreciation of what it wants our sleeping politicians to do. As Kevin says in his usual way, "When the fuckers wake up it'll be too fucking late."

When I spoke to Kevin last week he told me he'd only just started sleeping properly again. Kevin, you see, had been having nightmares about being arrested on suspicion of involvement in a bioterrorism plot.

There are several others I could mention as well but you'll come across them later. But I need to make a special mention of Jimmy 'The Ferret' Banda from Nairobi. Jimmy, my friend - you were brilliant.

But let me start with the afternoon a few months ago when Colin finally tracked me down to the airport in Kuala Lumpur and asked me to fly back to London to meet a new client.

3

I had never heard of the American medical research company, Virex International, let alone its President, Charles Brady. But within twenty four hours of the phone call I had abandoned my private plan to go up to Bangkok for the weekend and flown back to London for two nights and one day. The day was mostly spent waiting for Brady's delayed flight to arrive from Boston. What was left of the day was spent discussing Brady's problem.

By the time Brady arrived, I already knew that Virex International did complicated research on viruses that caused influenza and other human diseases and that they had apparently lost some research material. But Brady turned out to be strong on long, technical words and weak on commercial facts. In exasperation, and as he was already looking at his watch, I finally asked him to be more explicit by defining the importance of his loss in financial terms. At first, Brady appeared embarrassed by my bluntness but eventually put a value of a few million dollars on it. It still wasn't an exact sum but it was big enough to explain why Brady had flown first class to London to meet me and why I had then flown to Bangkok. Bangkok, Brady had suggested, might produce a few leads.

Now, at that point, I would normally have asked for far more detail but time was already running out for Brady's return flight and there was also a neat co-incidence of sorts. There was this other business in Bangkok that I had been planning to deal with just two days before and then postponed. So, armed with a very poor remit, I wished Brady a safe journey back to Boston, told him I'd be in touch and bought myself a ticket to Bangkok for the following night.

So let us now jump twenty four hours.

I woke in my Bangkok hotel room to the faint drone of the air conditioning unit and the pale light of dawn breaking through the window blind. I was tired, had slept deeply and for a few seconds wondered where I was. For someone who travels time zones as much as I do this is a common enough experience but, with my eyes still firmly shut, I tried to put the past few days and hours back into perspective.

I knew I had this vague job to do and had been busy but it had all been fairly plain sailing and normal up until last night.

I had arrived late afternoon and, after a shower and a change of clothing into something more suited to the Bangkok weather, ventured out into the hot, evening air, fought my way along the Sukhumvit Road through the hordes of evening strollers and ended up at a certain place that had become a bit of a habit of mine on recent visits to Bangkok. Up until then, it had been like the start of any other business trip but it then changed into something far more private.

4

The job I was there to do for Virex was, as I've said, unusually vague but as I lay there still half asleep, there was no harm in going over everything in my mind. I am, despite how I might sometimes appear, a very organized man. I am a professional in my field and don't normally make rash decisions. It is just that I occasionally take calculated risks or allow myself to be carried on a whim. Whims are a bit like instincts. I know they sound unprofessional but they are much the safest sort of risk. Last night's whim - the one that had taken me to that place - had looked innocent enough at the time. Nevertheless, I had still given it some thought before setting off. After all, any misjudgement could mean, at the very least, a ruined reputation and a nail in the coffin for a self-employed businessman.

But 'nothing ventured, nothing gained' has been a motto of mine for many years. I think I inherited that one from my Italian father. The other motto, 'muddle through' comes, I like to think, from my English mother to ensure that if life throws up the unexpected, as it often does, you can still find a way to deal with it and not be tied down by procedure or other matters that get in the way.

'Impatience is a virtue' is a motto I invented myself and I value it highly - in fact, it partly explains my rant at the beginning. So, anyway, a sudden retreat from the whim to stroll along Sukhumvit Road so as not to end up in that usual place looked like surrender and this is not my style. To accept my fate - whatever it might be - with a shrug had seemed a far more manly response at the time.

But, I admit I still felt a little uncertainty when I reached the door of that place. I had stopped and stared at the door as a vision of myself hit my conscience like that of a drowning man.

I am sure a drowning man can be forgiven for the flashbacks of his past pleasures or regrets. Perhaps, also, a drowning man with no hope of rescue can also cram an entire life into the short space of time it takes to hold his breath until he could stand it no longer and finally inhales that last, fateful lungful.

But that vision of myself had been just as quick. It was like a fast forwarded video, a packaged version of my life to date, a quick snap shot of how other people might judge me if they had followed me over the last twenty years or so. And I freely admit that I did not like what I saw in the closing moments of the vision. I saw a professional loner, a sad example of a forty five years old single man with no place he could call home except a rented flat over a Turkish restaurant in Queensway, West London. I saw a battered case containing a few bare essentials for personal hygiene - a toothbrush, a razor - and a few shirts and socks and a crumpled suit and blue tie in case there was a need to impress.

5

I also saw an empty notepad that I rarely use but still keep in there because, these days, I use mobile phones an awful lot. I'm buying and throwing them all the time for reasons you will slowly understand. I keep a few essential things on a memory stick hung around my neck until I can find a suitable place to plug the laptop in or visit an internet cafe. Often, too, I leave these technical aids behind in a hotel room or somewhere just in case I find myself in a spot of bother. I have learned a thing or two, you see. I regard a mobile phone as the worst piece of technology for storing private data, which is why I prefer new ones empty of all private data and other information. No-one is ever going to steal Daniel Capelli's intellectual property.

Most things I carry in my head and so mine is a surprisingly light case for a man who lives out of it, uses it as his office and as an occasional pillow and travels around the world with it with a couple of spare passports tucked behind its lining.

Now I don't normally get depressed, but what I saw in that vision was, I admit, a bit dull and depressing. But I had always thought that one day I might find the time to sort myself out. It isn't as though I'm short of money although it has taken a lot longer to accumulate than I ever envisaged. After all, this business of mine is not one that promotes itself via a website or glossy brochures. Using third parties, word of mouth and constantly building a reputation works far better.

My ten o'clock appointment with a guy called Amos Gazit, the Research Director of Virex International was proof of that strategy. And the call in KL that had started it had come from Colin Asher and Colin had got the lead from somewhere else. This is how it works.

Anyway, on my bed I opened my eyes again to check the increasing light from the window to guess the time and then returned to the whim that had taken me to that place last night and that awful vision of myself as a lonely man living out of a battered black case. Finally, I had persuaded myself to push the door open. I left the street with all its heat and noise behind and stepped inside.

Now, seven hours later, I could feel a warm hand resting on my shoulder. It then moved down to my waist and around to my bare stomach. Her name is Anna. I was still a professional businessman with a job to do at ten o'clock but I knew then I was also on a very private slippery slope.

CHAPTER 2

Kevin Parker had just finished another week at the Bristol University School of Sociology, Politics and International Studies. But his regular Friday night drinking session with fellow lecturers and other hangers-on had been postponed because Kevin had an appointment.

He had spent most of the day in the library rather than teaching, so Kevin was even more casually dressed than normal. As he locked the door of his cluttered flat in Clifton he was wearing crumpled brown corduroy trousers and a green, open-necked shirt beneath a bright red sweater that said Liverpool FC on the front.

With six years of trying to teach British Economic and Social History to students with mixed results and very little self satisfaction behind him, Kevin's weekends, most evenings and any other spare time was spent on his real interest - moderating the website of the International Malthus Society.

"Dedicated to exploring the ideas of Thomas Malthus on a theoretical and a practical level" was the somewhat uninspiring strap line of Kevin's website. But it opened the doors for all sorts of comment, opinion, political lobbying or action linked to Thomas Malthus' dire, eighteenth century warnings of the effects of overpopulation.

Kevin was on his way by train to London to give what he thought was a talk to Malthus Society members and any other enthusiasts interested in human population control. Kevin was an expert on the subject. He lectured on it so had all the facts and figures at his fingertips but he also tried hard to temper his lectures to conceal his own views and, even more so, his radical solutions. After all, he told some in private, he was not there to behave like some radical cleric in an Islamic mosque.

But he would often feel comfortable enough to expound on his wish to see direct action to radically reduce the world population so that the quality of life for those remaining improved. That was why he was looking forward to giving the lecture.

But the invitation had come as a surprise to Kevin. It had been a phone call from someone he hadn't even heard of and the man was clearly an Arab if the accent and name of El Badry was anything to go by. He also seemed to be an Arab with money as the flat Kevin had been invited to was overlooking Chelsea Embankment. It would certainly be large enough to hold several other members of the Malthus Society if that was what the caller intended.

On the train, Kevin took out his notes and a yellow marker and, in total innocence of who he was to meet, set about highlighting the points he wanted to make.

Larry Brown had always had a somewhat morbid interest in infectious diseases. He told friends that he could trace it back to watching a video as a boy. While his younger sister played at being a nurse, Larry would sit and watch and then replay the video about leprosy, chagas disease, yellow fever and leptospirosis. His sister had gone on to become a lawyer but it was Larry who became the doctor. But the childhood fascination with infection and tropical disease had never waned and was one reason why he had left New York to travel, first to South America and then to West Africa.

Doctor Larry Brown, now in his late thirties and new to his post with the American Embassy commercial team in Lagos, Nigeria had just spent two nights in the northern State capital of Kano. The smaller city of Jos in neighbouring Plateau State was, according to Larry's calculations, only about 150 miles away so as the Evangel Hospital in Jos had always held top spot in Larry's list of places with especially interesting diseases, the chance for a quick visit was too good to miss.

In 1969, before Larry was born, the Evangel Hospital had been the first centre in West Africa to identify the hemorrhagic, flesh-eating, Lassa Fever virus that still causes around five thousand deaths a year across West Africa. Two missionary nurses at the Evangel Hospital died of the virus and a third fell ill and was flown to the USA. It was here where the virus was isolated and named. A year later, the medical director at the hospital, a missionary surgeon, also caught Lassa Fever after she accidentally cut herself during an autopsy. She was dead within two days.

After his visit and hoping that diplomatic relations between the US and Nigeria had been enhanced by his short and unannounced intrusion, Larry began to consider what he himself had discovered the day before during his time in Kano. The more he thought about it the more he was convinced that he might have discovered another new fever. It had none of the characteristics of Lassa Fever but if the estimated death toll in Kano of more than one hundred was accurate then someone needed to sit up and take notice. But no-one yet had.

Larry's official visit to Kano had been at the request of his Embassy superiors in Abuja, the Nigerian capital, and the line was that it would be useful diplomacy for an American to be seen to be doing something for the ordinary people. All the better if it was handled in a way that could not possibly be interpreted as remotely political or in any shape or form designed to inflame ongoing tensions with the northern Moslem community.

So, someone had organised a debate for two schools in Kano. The topic of discussion was to be "Who is more important to society, the teacher or the doctor" and was designed to encourage students to speak good and correct American English using appropriate American expressions. Who better to run the debate, then, than a real live doctor fresh out of New York - and a black one with ancestral roots in West Africa at that.

But Larry had never been a man who did his job and then went home. He met the students as required, learned far more from them than they did from him, went back to his hotel and then, with time on his hands decided to explore Kano.

Whether he was also naturally drawn to clinics and old mission hospitals he didn't know but as he wandered down the Kofar Wambai Road watching, listening to and smelling the local, Kano life he took off down one of the side streets. And he had hardly walked fifty yards when he found himself looking up at a plastic banner hanging, upside down on a thread of red nylon string. It was flapping in the steady, dusty breeze over the entrance to a single story, concrete building with rusting bars fronting unwashed windows. Perhaps it was because a red cross is never upside down, but it made him stop and, by twisting his head to read the rest of the banner, Larry could see it said, "Kofi Clinic."

Interest sparked, Larry thought he'd take a look inside. Being a black American doctor of West African descent, Larry had started to enjoy his ability to blend in with the locals and, as he also enjoyed checking out run down clinical establishments, this one looked like the best example he'd come across for some time. He pushed open the unlocked, wooden door and stood in a dark and dusty hallway that might, had the electricity been turned on, have been lit by a single bare light bulb hanging from the ceiling. At the far end was another door.

"It is closed, sir." The voice that came from behind was that of an elderly woman Larry had seen sitting and sewing outside on a stool. She was now stood behind him holding an old shirt and with the needle and thread hanging from the corner of her mouth.

Dressed in a long, colourful dress she also wore what Larry had recently learned was known, at least in Lagos, as a "Gele" - a Yoruba word for an ornate female head-dress. Despite the plastic stool, the dust, the trash and the lumps of concrete rubble around her feet, the woman looked clean, smart and educated. Larry introduced himself. "Closed down, you say?"

9

"Yes, sir. Very dirty," she said and removed the needle and thread from between her lips.

"So who owned the clinic?"

"Doctor Mustafa."

"Did he have many patients?" Larry asked peering down the dark hallway. All he could see was a grey metal filing cabinet with empty drawers hanging out.

"No sir."

"Where has he gone?"

"I don't know, sir," the old lady said and started to walk back to her stool.

"Do you live locally?" Larry asked as he followed her. She pointed to a concrete block building opposite with a corrugated tin roof and open doorway.

"Did you see patients arrive here?"

"Yes sir, the doctor brought them in his truck."

"A truck? Do you know what happened to them - his patients?"

"Yes, they died."

"So were they very sick when they arrived here?"

"I don't know sir. I was a teacher but not a doctor."

"Of course," said Larry understandingly. "Do you know how many died?"

The old lady already seemed engrossed in her sewing once again but Larry noticed she looked at him out of the corner of her eye as if unsure whether to say anything. Then she glanced back down to her sewing and said, very quietly, "I heard it was more than one hundred." Then she got up again and started to walk away. Larry followed her.

"So who decided to close the clinic?" asked Larry.

"The State Government sir." Then she hurried across the road.

Back at the Prince Hotel in Kano where he was staying, Larry phoned the American Embassy in Abuja and told them briefly what he had found. Pleased that no-one asked him how his earlier meeting with the students had gone or why he was wasting time wandering around Kano instead of hot footing it back to Lagos, he was given a phone number for the Kano State Government and a department that might be able to answer a few questions about the Kofi Clinic.

CHAPTER 3

I realised my growing personal problem as soon as Anna had accepted my invitation to close her bar earlier than normal and spend the rest of the night with me back at my hotel. In the bar, she had looked at me with those big, black eyes, her black hair in a neat, parted fringe at the front and so long at the back.

"What's your name?" she had said in her delightful accent.

"Daniel. The same as last time," I said. "What's yours?"

"Anna, the same as last time."

"Where you come from?" she said and glanced down to where my hand had, without any permission from me, moved to touch hers.

I paused to take a mouthful of beer from my bottle and give myself time to think. "London," I said, truthfully and then watched the look on her face change. She stared directly at me and I knew exactly what her next words would be.

"How long will you stay?" Then she looked down. "Seem like too long. Where you go? I think you forget me."

I was at this point, looking at the top of her bowed head, faintly smelling a perfumed shampoo. Then I held her hand tighter and said to the top of the head. "I missed you."

Oh, yes, I knew right at that moment that my normal composure had gone and with it most of my professional dignity.

I turned over in the bed to look at what I'd brought back with me. Her long black hair was draped across her face but hidden inside it was my problem. And just to prove it, I found himself fumbling to part the long strands of black hair to see her face. And, yes, I openly admit to liking what I saw.

Her eyes opened and for a moment seemed shocked at the sight of my eyes just inches away. They seemed to soften and turn perhaps a little moist. I, of course, looked away but then found myself looking down at her naked body stretched out beside me. And, as I looked, her hand came up to my rough, unshaven face and a finger ran from beneath my eye to my lips and stayed there.

"How long you stay in Bangkok?" she murmured, moving her hips closer and wrapping a leg over mine. Now I found himself looking deep into her black eyes.

"Maybe a few days," I said knowing it was vague. But I did, nevertheless, manage a smile and, as luck would have it, she returned it. Then she stuck her finger into my mouth as if to stop me saying any more.

"Ooh. Long time, eh?" she joked, giggling in a sad sort of way. And my own thoughts went back to the night we had last parted.

She had been very upset when I left the last time. What's more, I hadn't even had the decency to tell her face to face that I was leaving. We had spoken on a noisy mobile phone link. I had been at the airport and she in the middle of a busy evening in the bar. The last sound I heard was the sound of quiet, wet sniffing. It was she who had then cut me off. This was just not normal. That, more than anything, had left me feeling thoroughly sick with myself and unknown to her I had almost taken a taxi back from the airport. But I had had a job to do. Duty called and I needed to be in Kuala Lumpur that night and it had been urgent. So what was I to do?

"I told you I would be back" I said, though I realise I have said that to a few others in the past. There was no response, just a stare. "So," I added, "here I am".

I admit to being a bit embarrassed by my flippancy. In fact you will find I will admit to a number of other personal weaknesses over the next few pages. I tried to sit up but my punishment for the flippancy was that she got hold of my ear and her mood changed. The look on her face also changed. Dear me, this was no frail woman needing the tender protection of a strong male.

"Where have you been?" she asked and her lips puckered not into a shape designed for kissing but one designed to instil fear into a man. This was a woman in angry tirade mode. She sat up and, still holding onto my ear, said:

"Too long you go away, I not know where you are, you not write to me, you not phone me. I try to forget but cannot. I try new man but he no good. I try another one but he go away and not come back. Like you, you crazy farang. You marry now? Why you not call me? I'm still here. Where you go? Why you come now? You make me sad again. You have other lady now. Sure you have. So why you come back and what your name this time? One time you say Daniel, next time Dan, then say Mike, next time say Steven. I think you joke. Another time you check in hotel in the name John. I say I prefer call you Kun Look-Lap, mean Mister No Name."

12

Thankfully, she then let go of my ear, looked away and sat up in bed holding her knees together with her hands. "Why you come?" she asked again, more quietly this time but speaking as if to the opposite wall. I, Kun Look-Lap as she had just called me, watched her reflection in the mirror but found I lacked any suitable words. Instead I rubbed my sore ear.

"Why have you come?" she repeated. "Why didn't you tell me you were coming back?"

Still no words came to me but I put this down to a general weakness with small talk. So here's another admittance. I am not good at chit-chat. Business discussions yes, but not this sort of conversation. The dreadful silence probably lasted seconds but, to me, Kun Luke-Lap, Mister No Name or whoever I now was, it felt like an hour.

"Oooweee!" she then seemed to say, "Same silence as always. You are a very stupid man. You want some coffee?" And she sprang suddenly from the bed.

"Sorry" I muttered, trying to grab her but only finding thin air. "I think of you a lot, wherever I am. Sorry".

"Ao cafe mai?"

Clearly, she was tiring of communicating in English and fleetingly, I wondered if she was also tired of me. I thought I had better say something.

"No thank you. I have had enough."

"Not beer you stupid man. I asked you if you want coffee?"

"Sorry," I said feeling totally insignificant. Then I waited and watched her in the mirror with a sort of thickness in my throat. I wanted to swallow something but there was nothing there.

"Oooweee! Why you say sorry? Sorry, sorry, sorry - you always say sorry but you still leave me. Why did you come back? Why did you come back?"

She was clearly very upset now but I still had no explanation why I had come. I wondered if I should tell her about a migrating bird theory I had once invented but she was definitely not the right woman for this one. So why had I returned? Privately I knew that I had accepted the job with Virex International largely because it offered a trip back to Bangkok and I wanted to see Anna again. But I couldn't possibly admit that, could I?

I think I may have said, "Umm!" or similar because there was this dreadful silence again. Anna was now watching me in the mirror. I couldn't stand it and glanced away.

"You still do the same business?" she asked, clearly trying to stay calm.

"Yes," I said grabbing a possible excuse as it passed by. But then I spoilt it. "Sort of," I added and felt it necessary to try to touch her shoulder.

"What mean, sort of? What real man says that? Only a man with many names or called Mister Crazy Look-Lap can say thing like that," she said crossly.

"Well, yes," I said rather stupidly but trying hard to think how much I may have told her previously about my work. "I still travel a lot. You know. Live in a suitcase."

Yes, I know, no need to tell me - another flippant remark. It was pathetic and, of course, it failed. So I tried to improve on it. "I have been to several countries since I was last here." Oh yes, this was much better. I even sounded better.

"Did you go to London?" she asked.

"Yes, for two nights and one day." True.

"I think you have a wife you've not told me about. That's why you not like to tell me real name. I think there is a Mrs Look-Lap you don't want to talk about."

"No, no, no, believe me. You know I'm not married. There is no Mrs Look-Lap or whatever you call me," I said hurriedly. I'm always very quick to confirm my unmarried status to women. Then I continued because I was anxious to regain some authority. "And, anyway you also have two names - one is English the other I can't pronounce. That makes me confused as well."

"Mmm, maybe," she said but as she clearly wasn't going to let that upset her attack, she added, "But you know it's Anna – I like Anna. It's always Anna. Never change." Then she continued with her interrogation. "So, then, why did you come back?"

I looked at her and tried smiling and then, with a passing thought that I was back on the slippery slope again, found myself saying, "I came to see if you were still here".

But she was quick and her voice became instantly louder once again.

"Yes, so now you can see I am here. You see? This is me. I am sitting here. But why you come? You want me for your wife now?"

This was a bit blunt and pointed I thought. But I have heard that this is not at all untypical of Thai women. I let it pass but continued to slide down the slope. "I came to see you. I told you I think about you a lot".

She obviously wasn't going to be treated like this.

"Yes, but I'm sure you didn't come just to see me. Something else brings you here. You too much of a big shot and have some big business." And, with that she got up, tugged at the bed sheet, wrapped it around her middle and went to the bathroom. All I could do was watch her. Unusually, she closed the bathroom door and I heard her lock it.

I sat naked on the bed staring at the bathroom door.

She was just the same as I remembered. Her hair was a bit longer. The cheap gold chain with the impression of a Buddhist monk still hung around her neck. Her jeans were of the same slim fit that I like. They were hanging on the back of the chair. She still wore small brown sandals. They sat, neatly together on the floor by my case. Her underwear had been put carefully underneath her white blouse.

Finally, I heard the toilet being flushed and the door unlocked. She walked purposefully across the room, still covered in the bed sheet, and took out a comb from her handbag. Then she turned. There was no smile, no tears, no happiness in her eyes. She stared at me. "Why are you here, Mister Look-Lap?"

I still wasn't sure if I liked being called Mister Look-Lap. To be referred to as Mister No-Name felt a little like mockery. Daniel was better. On the other hand it was perfectly true that I used several aliases from time to time. I held several passports as well but it was all part of my profession. It was useful. Often it was necessary. And yes, I had once been operating as a Stephen Crossman and another time as a Mark Fitzgerald-Spencer - the latter name seemed to fit an investigation I was being paid to carry out on a company selling fake Chinese antiques. But I also knew she was clever with her words and, to be fair, I decided, Look-Lap was not a bad name for someone who kept inventing different names for himself for different reasons. Look-Lap sounded like Luke Lapp. Perhaps I should try it out. I had already used Matthew, Mark and John so Luke would complete the quartet.

But, to get back to her question, why was I here? Whilst she was in the bathroom I had had a few minutes to think about the question, which I knew she would soon repeat. So, I looked at her straight and said, "I still do the same thing as last time."

To be fair, I was trying to make it simple. But it was also very vague because, frankly, she did not know what I did and I should have known better. Anna's lips puckered once more and I knew I was in for another tirade. This one was even longer with hardly a breath taken.

"I do not know what you do. You are a busy man and fly, never stay a long time, always go, come and go. I don't know. You left me last time. I was very sad. Where did you go, I don't know. Last time you had a problem. I know. I tried to help but you said I couldn't. Then you left me. I didn't know where or why you went. You didn't tell me. I worried about you when you went. You said there was a big problem and you had to go. I thought maybe you were a bad man. but I then I thought no, you are too kind in heart, good man. I think someone gave you problem. Why you couldn't tell me, I didn't understand. Sometimes I think of you a lot. Many nights I think where you are and I want you here but that maybe you were with another lady or maybe you have a wife. I don't know. Sometime I get very up-sad. I don't know where you are. Big world out there. Maybe you never come to see me again. So I think. Try to forget and look for another man. Many men come here, but I not like them. I check some, but not so many. They are no good. I always think of you and where you are, why you don't come to see me. I worry a lot. Perhaps you had died. I think maybe you will never come. But now you are here again. I didn't know what to say when I saw you last night. Why did you come? Did you come to see me? Did you come for business? Why?"

Finally she stopped and I saw bright, wet eyes. I hate to see upset women, don't you? My manly, protective urges take over and that can be fateful. I have known women do it on purpose. They are a fearful sex. But I myself, felt a little choked now and it was clear I needed to say something meaningful in response. So I said, "Sorry."

With that, her wet eyes shot another frightening glance so I gave a little cough as if preparing to deliver a speech and continued:

"I came here to see you, Anna. I think about you every day. I did not know if you were still there. I thought maybe you had moved somewhere. If you were not there I think I would have had to try to find you. Believe me. I know I left you in a bad way - do you think I did not feel sad? I was also sad and upset, believe me. You say I am a busy man. I know you do not understand but I had to go. I cannot explain everything to you."

I then found myself staring at her without blinking until my own eyes felt so sore that I then had to blink franticly for a few seconds. Then I continued. "I am not a bad man, Anna. I had some business problems when I was here and I had to go. I went to Malaysia and Singapore and then to Hong Kong. I went to the

Middle East - Israel. Then I came back to Malaysia and back to London. I work all the time. No holiday. No rest. Now I come here again. I arrived yesterday afternoon. And what did I do? I came to find you. I know I made you sad and I know that maybe I should not have come to see you but I want to try to say sorry and that I felt very sad and I am sorry and......."

I admit I am useless in very personal, emotionally charged situations. My unnaturally long and private speech, which I regret having mixed with an unnecessary description of a travel schedule, hadn't started too well and it hadn't finished too well either. In the end it had petered out and so I tried looking at her as if pleading for some help. No, I lie. It wasn't 'as if pleading', I was pleading - stop. Anna was staring back at me. Both of us knew that all I had actually said was what she had once called a 'big sorry'. I like the phrase. I have since used it a lot. But how long the silence lasted I do not know. What I do know is that I had a dreadful feeling that she was going to hit me and walk out. But, as you begin to know and understand Anna, you will find her words are far more constructive.

"Do you have a few more minutes to spare me before you rush off again, Mister Luke-Lap?"

CHAPTER 4

Kevin Parker was on the train to London preparing for his talk to what he thought was a small gathering of those interested in Thomas Malthus and human population control. But without being sure of the likely audience or numbers it was proving difficult. His academic's dilemma was whether to pitch it at ideas for direct action to get politicians to do something or whether to stick to the facts and figures.

Kevin had always advocated positive action but waiting for individual Governments to act was, he now knew, utterly pointless. International co-operation was vital for success but few Governments, except perhaps the Chinese with its one family - one child policy, Singapore, or Iran with its mandatory contraception had faced up to it let alone demanded international co-operation. The political will just wasn't there. It was far too risky to open such a bucket of worms when re-election was always the top priority. Dictatorships were a far better system for imposing the will than democracies. Indeed, it was becoming politically incorrect to even talk about reducing population. It infringed basic human rights, it upset the Catholic Church and was often deemed racist even to mention forcefully ending mass economic migration from destitute and overpopulated war torn countries. The excuses for inaction were endless.

So political action was completely stalled and reasons to sweep the issue under the carpet for future generations to worry about just went on and on. There were even countries that considered population as a source of political, economic and military strength.

Kevin Parker had become a very angry and impatient man although he did his best to conceal it from friends and found it hard to support democracy as a system when it came to enforcing birth control. He had written extensively on the subject under his screen name of 'Thalmus' and had once hoped the UK might provide a world lead on it but he was sure now it would never happen.

The British branch of the Malthus Society rarely, if ever, met together but normally shared their views online. As website moderator and unelected Chairman of the UK branch, Kevin had only ever been able to organise one full meeting of members in the past and that meeting, held in the back room of a public house in Wolverhampton, had not been the success Kevin had hoped. If the group were to move their radical views forward to lobby government then they clearly needed funds from somewhere. Despite Kevin's efforts, no-one had offered either to donate to the group or pay a monthly membership subscription. And Kevin had even had to pick up the bar tab. Undeterred, Kevin had persevered and three years later he was still at it - if anything more motivated than ever and certainly more keen for some direct action.

He sat back in his train seat and put his notes to one side. Despite being the unelected chairman of the UK branch of the Malthus Society, Kevin was unsure where this strange Mr El Badry who he was due to meet stood in relation to the Society. He could well have been a regular reader or even a contributor but because the website only asked for screen names and not anyone's full contact details, there was no way of telling. In fact, Kevin only knew the details of about twelve UK members by their online names and this was only because of the Wolverhampton meeting.

But this Mr El Badry could also have been based somewhere outside the UK because there were many other affiliated groups that Kevin monitored - not least the followers of the American Professor, Paul R Ehrlich. Kevin had also lectured on Ehrlich but Thomas Malthus had preceded Ehrlich by two hundred years and was British. Malthus was the one who had set the ball in motion. But knowing that there were thousands of people out there sharing his views was what Kevin found so encouraging.

Years of lecturing students first thing on a Monday morning had taught him the need to get people's attention right from the start and he wanted to cover as much as possible - conflict over food and water supplies, the misery of war and sickness, economic migration and mass unemployment in the west. He wanted to offer quotes from the great Robert Wallace - the "earth would be overstocked and become unable to support its numerous inhabitants." or, as his even greater hero Thomas Malthus had put it, "the germs of existence contained in this spot of earth, with ample food, and ample room to expand in, would fill millions of worlds, in the course of a few thousand years."

Thomas Malthus a British clergyman and economist had published "An Essay on the Principles of Population" in 1798. Population, when unchecked, he proposed, increases in a geometrical ratio. Subsistence increased only in an arithmetical ratio. Malthus outlined the idea of "positive checks" and "preventative checks" on population. Disease, war, disaster and famine were factors that Malthus considered to increase the death rate. "Preventative checks" were factors that Malthus believed to affect the birth rate such as moral restraint, abstinence and birth control. He predicted that only "positive checks" on exponential population growth would ultimately save humanity from itself. Without these checks, human misery was an "absolute necessary consequence."

Anger and impatience was what had led Kevin to track down the many hundreds of groups with similar opinions on population control dotted across the world. He had found them in North America, South America, right across Europe, Russia, the Middle East and Far East, in Japan and in Australia. Many were closeted individuals operating from bedrooms, others were far better organised. Kevin's list of contacts now ran to thousands.

There was the German group that operated from somewhere in Cologne with a membership claimed to be in the hundreds. Ausser Kontrolle (Out of Control) still advocated extermination of certain ethnic groups that did not match up to a long list of criteria they had published. Moslems were high on this list due, according to Ausser Kontrole, to "their unwillingness to move their culture forward from where it had stagnated since the hay-day of Islamic influence on science and education."

Then there was his Indian group, his Indonesian Group and a Singapore Group that advocated a policy of setting IQ tests with those not reaching the required level being left to fend for themselves. There was the Spanish Group, the Italian group and a very low profile South African group with similar views to Ausser Kontrole.

But Kevin's favourite group was the Nigerian one. Tunje Fayinka, also a college lecturer in Sociology, ran the group from his flat in Barnet, north London. Tunje

19

believed that even the current population of Nigeria of some 166 million - a figure expected to reach 390 million by 2050 - was already totally unsustainable. Increasing ethnic and religious conflict was already proof of the need to reduce the population back to at least the 45.2 million figure it stood at in 1960.

Kevin and Tunje had a lot in common. They were, in fact, good friends and verbal sparring partners. But Tunje had learned to be far more careful with what he said in public or wrote online.

"Big Brother is always watching, Kevin. Go careful. The least you should do is keep the laptop hidden some place where MI6 won't go looking. Alternatively, just appear to be an innocent nutcase."

Until then, Kevin had not thought very much about security.

With good evidence, Kevin Parker knew that his UK Malthus Society website had become a genuine focal point for similar groups and he was proud of all that he had done to achieve that. Kevin now wanted to see some results for all his efforts, but not at any cost.

He sat back as the train rolled into Reading Station and picked up his copy of the Guardian. He read the headlines once again and then dropped the newspaper back on the adjacent, empty seat. Buying a Guardian had become a habit although he rarely read it properly these days. The newspaper was another English institution he now disliked because of the furore that had erupted amongst indignant would-be mothers attending fertility clinics and wealthy politicians with four children after his open letter to the Editor was published. Indeed, he had, afterwards, been summoned to meet the University departments' Professor for an explanation.

But Kevin had personal experience of poor living conditions and overcrowding. As the oldest sibling of eleven brought up on a housing estate in Liverpool he had seen and felt the consequences. His father had left soon after Kevin was born and his ten brothers and sisters had ten different fathers.

Castration or mass sterilisation had once been an attractive and popular idea put on the Malthus Society website and Kevin, with Tunje Fayinka's help, had become an expert on access to water supplies in target countries just in case an opportunity arose. But what was really needed was action on an international scale. A world war with nuclear weapons might have helped but was too indiscriminate. An epidemic of biblical proportions had possibilities but science moved so fast these days that treatments almost always became available before they had any real effect. Mass famine brought on by essential crops like rice and wheat being ruined by widespread resistance to pesticide was another idea.

Kevin had been running out of new, practical ideas until, that is, he reached the Chelsea apartment of Mr El Badry

Larry Brown had been working for the American Embassy in Nigeria for less than six weeks and the cultural shock of life outside its confines had more than lived up to his expectations. But he had come for the interest more than career progression so he was more than ready to do whatever was needed. And, if he found he didn't like the job, he'd just move on somewhere else.

As a New York doctor, who had quickly tired of the daily mix of coughs, colds and backache, Larry had decided to do some overseas volunteering. He went first to Chile and then to Kenya and it was in Nairobi that he was asked if he was interested in looking at the Nigerian health system with a view to - as it eventually explained in his new job description - "assisting American companies to understand how best to win lucrative contracts in the provision of management services. medical supplies and medical equipment."

Larry had been unsure about taking the job at first but the thought of combining it with some travelling around Nigeria and possibly elsewhere on expenses had swung it. He had spent the first few days in Lagos and, if it not been for the hotel he'd been staying at, wasn't sure he if he would have survived the job for long. But the new apartment he now had was making it bearable and he was also starting to make the most of his status with the American Embassy.

It was this status that helped him make the appointment at the Kano State Government office to ask about the closed Kofi Clinic. He was met by a State official whose own status wasn't so well defined.

"Our police don't have time to look for missing Doctors, Doctor Brown," the man said. "More important to our police and security forces is to deal with those murderous Islamist thugs, Boko Haram, who are threatening to disturb our peace."

The man had then seen an opportunity for a joke. He laughed.

"You need to watch out Doctor Brown. They don't like Westerners, especially Americans and in particular black Americans who they think have gone native."

"But I heard there were over one hundred deaths from this disease," said Larry.

The official shrugged. "We had a hundred die in a bomb blast a month ago."

Larry knew he was getting nowhere. But from what the State Government official had gone on to tell him, during their raid of the Kofi Clinic they had found no patient records but a drawer in an otherwise empty desk containing a note book listing the first names of over one hundred patients who seemed to have attended at some time or another.

There were no family names and no addresses for any of the patients but each of them had been given a number. All they knew was that conditions at the clinic were very poor. They had found it empty except for three stretchers, one wheel chair and the empty desk. Locals said they had seen patients arriving in the back of Doctor Mustafa's Toyota pick-up truck and that all the patients had looked very sick and weak and had been coughing when they were led inside by Doctor Mustafa and another man. One man said he'd seen what he thought were two dead bodies under a green cloth being taken out using the same Toyota truck although no-one could back this up. But it was unanimous - those arriving there looked and sounded very sick and some, if not all, of those who left it were already dead. All the official knew was that when they came to inspect the clinic no-one was there and no-one had seen Doctor Mustafa since.

Philippe Fournier's idea to take his new Italian friend, Mara, for a Saturday drive in a rented Jeep to the small town of Kijabe fifty kilometres north west of Nairobi, Kenya was supposed to form part of a relaxing and mildly adventurous weekend away from Philippe's work at the Kenyatta National Hospital. Also, as he was becoming desperate to invite Mara back to his room later, he was rapidly running out of ideas to impress.

He had, in fact, struggled to win the girl over for a week or more as she had seemed far more interested in meeting other foreign students in Nairobi than learning about the valuable and pioneering work he was doing on HIV treatment and prevention.

"This is not just for the benefit of Kenyans," he had stressed. "Work we do here is for the good of all Africa. This is now a seat of excellence."

Having left France and England in order to pursue his childhood ambition to return to his grandparent's roots and work in Africa, Philippe's manner had become, perhaps, a little overbearing when it came to constantly mentioning his work and the low pay that came with it. But he felt strongly about what he was doing and was sure that an Italian nurse being paid generous expenses to learn a bit about tropical diseases in order to further her own career back home could have shown just a little more interest. He was also sure she earned far more than he did which was upsetting.

Philippe had visited Kijabe once before, although on that occasion it had been with a group of about ten others in a mini bus. This time, he was to be both the driver and the tour guide.

Fifty kilometres was no great distance but it was far enough outside the capital to give a feeling of being on a sort of romantic safari. It would also be quick to get back home if things turned out well.

During the journey he had explained once again about the work in his department - that it was there, as he put it, "to find more multi-sectoral and multi-disciplinary partners to reduce HIV transmission, to mitigate the impact of HIV/AIDS on vulnerable populations" and that his role was "especially focussed on training and ways to convey information and advice." And all throughout his explanation he had tried to use occasional Italian words mixed with the English. It had been quite an effort but Mara still seemed more interested in looking out of the window of the Jeep.

Nearing Kijabe, though, he had finally got around to describing where they were actually going. Kijabe, Philippe explained, was Masai for "Place of the Wind" as it stood on the edge of the great rift valley and was over two thousand metres above sea level.

"And it has a railway station," he explained as he swung the steering wheel of the Jeep to avoid a Masai farmer with a cow.

"Where does the train go," Mara asked and Philippe beamed at the show of interest.

"Uganda one way and Mombasa the other," replied Philippe. "And there is a small hospital there. It is called Kijabe Hospital. And there is a guest house for those who get lost or delayed."

Mara looked out of the passenger window.

Philippe, though, had not reckoned on there being a problem at Kijabe Station.

The train driver, fifty six year old Samson Omwenga had taken ill whilst on the footplate. He hadn't felt well for several days but at Kijabe, he had finally given up his efforts to deal with the increasingly nauseous headache, sore throat, dizziness, the tickling cough and the general feeling of weakness. He had struggled to climb down from his engine, collapsed onto the platform and announced, between bouts of coughing that he was unable to continue. A doctor had been called but, when Philippe and Mara arrived to view the historic station and the train that was still known as the Lunatic Express, they were still waiting. Meanwhile, the passengers had disembarked and were either sat waiting for

23

developments or standing in groups discussing the aptness of the train's other name.

Parking the Jeep next to a large puddle of red, muddy water, Phillipe got out and waited while Mara decided it would be safer and certainly cleaner and drier if she clambered over to get out of the driver's door rather than use the passenger door.

By then, Philippe had been approached by someone clearly in charge of railway administration to ask whether he was the doctor. Being black but with facial features suggesting he was not Kenyan but possibly of West African and Francophone origin, Philippe was, nevertheless honoured to be mistaken for the doctor.

"Yes," he said. "I am a doctor, but not a medical doctor. I work at the Kenyatta National Hospital. What is the problem?"

The stationmaster quickly explained everything and began to usher Philippe towards the station waiting room while Mara was still shutting the driver's door of the Jeep.

In the waiting room, a wooden bench had been acquisitioned to use as a temporary bed for the sick engine driver, Samson Omwenga.

With Philippe still trying to confirm his non medical qualifications to an uninterested stationmaster the circle of onlookers surrounding the sick driver parted to allow him to approach.

"This is senior engine driver Samson Omwenga," said the stationmaster.

Philippe got as far as repeating, "Yes, but I'm not......." when the patient suddenly struggled to sit up and then coughed violently. He clearly did not look well. He was sweating profusely, his eyes were red and puffy, his mouth was open and he was clearly having difficulty in breathing. Sitting up was probably making it easier for him to cough or breathe but he looked weak and on the verge of collapse.

"This is the doctor," said the stationmaster.

"But I'm not,,,,,,,,,,,,,"

The patient coughed again, harder and even longer this time, and his eyes widened. Philippe looked at him and felt sorry he was not a real doctor but only had a PhD in microbiology and biochemistry. But he saw patients with AIDS on a regular basis and recognised the look of fear in the eyes. And the sweating suggested that driver Samson Omwenga was running a very high temperature.

"He needs to go to hospital, sir," said Philippe to the stationmaster.

"Do you not have some medicine for him? The train is late."

"Sir," said Philippe. "This man is very sick. He can hardly breath. He has a very high temperature. His lips and eyes are very red. Just look at him. He has no strength.- not even enough to drive the train to Nairobi let alone onwards to Mombasa. He needs a proper doctor. But I am only a......"

"Can you take him sir? We have too many passengers here and they all think he will be OK to start driving the train again soon and we do not have a qualified replacement. If you take him away they will see that the train is going to be delayed."

Mara finally arrived and came to stand alongside Philippe.

"This is Mara," said Philippe. "She is a nurse from Italy. I will ask her what she thinks."

Within fifteen minutes, Philippe was driving back to Nairobi with Mara in the passenger seat still staring silently out of the window. On the back seat lay a sweating, coughing Samson Omwenga, Philippe took him straight to the Kenyatta National Hospital.

Late that night, depressed and very much alone in his room, Philippe decided to phone his American doctor friend, Larry Brown in Nigeria for someone to talk to.

He had once met Larry at a conference on Infectious Diseases in Nairobi and they had struck up a good rapport that had ended in a very memorable evening at a nightclub. As a result, an update on women was always the first subject to discuss and as Mara was still on his mind, he thought he would mention his drive up to Kinjabe and the sick train driver he'd driven back to Nairobi.

It was two days after Larry Brown's trip up north and he had only just arrived back at his apartment when his mobile phone rang.

It was Philippe Fournier a Frenchman he had once befriended at a conference in Nairobi. Philippe was clearly in need of a friend to talk to and whatever the cost of the long distance call from Nairobi seemed to think that he, Larry Brown, would be a good listener.

Larry was trying to get the hang of his new gas cooker and his head was inside the oven. At the same time he tried listening to Philippe.

"How do you find the local women, then, Larry? Any good? Anything must be better than white women back home, eh? They are far too emancipated, man. That's what I think."

"No time, yet, Philippe," said Larry. "Still settling in."

"That being said, Larry, I've got myself an Italian. She's a bit quiet but nice tits - nice lady, Larry - nice legs as well - but didn't get to see much more."

"Why not, Philippe - something you said?"

"No, nothing like that, Larry. I took her to Kijabe."

"That must have been romantic, Philippe."

"Yes, but I still didn't get a chance. I ended up with an extra passenger in the Jeep."

Larry soon learned about the train driver and Philippe's return to Nairobi that had been far quicker than his trip out. He stopped his work on the oven and sat on his new sofa.

"I dropped him off at the Kenyatta National Hospital in Nairobi, Larry. Mon dieu, he was coughing just like a child with the whooping cough. Just like my cat when she had a hair ball stuck. Very high temperature. I called the hospital this evening to check and he died about an hour after Mara and I left him."

Larry logged it, was still thinking about it and would have liked to know more but Philippe was still talking.

".....and women like to be entertained. It's so expensive." Philippe continued.

"Tell me something I don't know already." Larry commiserated.

"Do you have any job vacancies that might pay more?" asked Philippe clearly now on a different tack and, perhaps, Larry realised, the real reason for his call. "I'm beginning to think I should have stayed in France."

"I don't run an employment agency, Philippe. If I did, the American Embassy would sure find out. You desperate?"

"Even bloody nurses earn more than me." Philippe said, using a word he'd often heard British nurses use.

"Sorry I can't help, Philippe," Larry laughed with as much sympathy as he could muster. "Try the bloody French Embassy."

Next morning, Larry phoned the World Health Organisation - the WHO - in Geneva to ask if they were aware of the Nigerian deaths. They weren't. So Larry then explained what he'd found and suggested someone needed to look into it. As a doctor, he said, one hundred unexplained deaths in one small area, even though it hadn't seemed to bother the Nigerian Health authorities, could hardly be ignored.

And while he was on the phone, he decided to mention the Kenyan case and then pointed out that a friend of his currently on a back packing holiday in northern Thailand had seen a report on Thai TV news about some sudden deaths near Bangkok rumoured to be from a kind of 'flu'.

Yes, the WHO knew something about the Thai cases but thanked him nevertheless. Larry Brown was starting to make himself known to the WHO.

Behind her desk, strolling a few steps in one direction and then back again, the diminutive Director General of the World Health Organisation in Geneva read the report she had just been given with growing concern.

Her adviser, Richard Lacey, an Englishman, sat patiently across the DG's desk. He knew she wouldn't take long to get to the core of the problem. The two of them had worked together for several years now and the rapport had always been good. Despite their closeness, he always treated her with the utmost respect for the responsibility she shouldered. Doctor Mary Chu had preceded Richard Lacey by two years and she was already way past her first official term in office. To Richard Lacey the DG was not Doctor Chu, or Mary but ma'am.

"CoV?" Mary Chu said at last. "Coronavirus?" It was a question posed as if she already knew the answer.

"No one yet knows, ma'am."

"If it's not Coronavirus, then what is it?" she then asked.

"Can't be sure, ma'am."

"Because we aren't getting any reliable virology?" This time it was a statement rather than a question.

"Yes, exactly."

"Because the cases are scattered and in rural areas and where doctors are in short supply and where there is no proper health service and no decent laboratory."

"Yes."

"Except Thailand, of course, where we have the highest number of cases or at least, the highest number of cases reported by the authorities."

"That's right. The point about reported cases need underlining," replied Richard Lacey stressing the word reported.

"The clinical symptoms from all the cases in Nigeria and the single case in Kenya are similar?"

"Although we can't be exactly sure, the signs are that they are very similar to the Thai ones. The symptoms are different to the Middle East version - MERS-CoV. It's the type of cough that characterises this one. It was only because the American doctor working in Kano, Northern Nigeria and a Frenchman working in Kenya knew each other that the African cases came to light. It seems the American doctor also had links with Thailand so he had also heard about the few cases there. He thought it was worth mentioning. He reckoned there might have been over one hundred cases in northern Nigeria."

"More than one hundred? How many more?" interrupted the DG, looking at her adviser with visible consternation.

"Well, we're in touch with the American doctor, Larry Brown. We've not got any data from Kenya - just the one case with similar symptoms. But in all cases we have apparently healthy individuals with no evidence of previous health problems. They catch a cold - dismiss it as we might all do as a two day inconvenience but then the symptoms worsen - serious cough - difficulty in breathing - blood in sputum - fever - then loss of consciousness during an unstoppable coughing fit. All dying within approximately three days of taking to their beds. It's the cough that has triggered the attention. But there might be many more cases we don't know about."

"And no laboratory has got a proper fix yet?"

"The Thai lab is working on it but cremations have taken place before sampling. And we have no idea at all what happened in Nigeria."

"So why haven't the Thai authorities reported earlier? Their Health Ministry is usually so efficient and when I was in Bangkok just last February nothing was said. It was still all about HIV, pigs and chickens."

Richard Lacey shrugged."Politics, ma'am? Keen to stamp on rumours of any health risks that might affect the tourism industry?" he suggested.

"Mmm." said the DG. She then sat down and toyed with the watch on her wrist.

"What exactly does the Thai lab say?" she said eventually.

"That it looked like a Coronavirus. They thought it was MERS-CoV - Middle East Respiratory Syndrome Coronavirus - at first but the symptoms seemed different. The current virology suggests something similar, perhaps a variant."

"But they still failed to report it immediately.............?"

It was Richard Lacey's turn to say, "Mmm."

The Director General stood up once more and glanced out of her office window. Then she turned back.

"Can you ask the Regional Director for South East Asia to phone me, please? He has just left to attend the Conference on Virology and Infectious Diseases in Bangkok."

CHAPTER 5

"Can we eat now? You make me very hungry, Mr Luke Lapp." Anna emerged from the bathroom for the second time that morning, this time wrapped in a white towel.

I was still naked except for the bed sheet and put down the new mobile phone I had been checking. Breakfast was not something I was planning. The unscheduled interruption to my timetable had lasted longer than anticipated and my ten o'clock appointment with Virex International looked in danger of being missed if I didn't hurry. I switched the mobile phone off and looked up wondering what excuse to give now.

"You had a phone call just now?"

What is it about women? Eyes, ears everywhere.

"A text," I said as, to my horror, I now watched Anna rummaging in my own, very private, black bag. No-one ever ventured inside there, except me. I watched her open it and peer inside. Then her hand disappeared and came out with a comb.

"OK?" she asked, "Can I? Mine is no good."

"Yes," I said. A comb seemed to pose no real threat.

I then sat watching her comb her hair with my comb and then, as the towel dropped away, I watched her recover her clothes and then dress. I also needed to shower and change urgently if I was to eat breakfast and then make my ten o'clock client. But, something seemed to be stop me rushing.

"So you do your business today? Not stay with me?" she asked, and turned away now fully dressed. I watched her in the mirror. As usual I wasn't sure how to respond. To be honest, I hate mixing business with private intimacy, particularly if it needs an explanation of what I do. With others it's easy. You lie or, at least, you create plausible stories. But that's business. So, how to respond was troubling me and she was now looking at me in the reflection in the mirror, waiting for an answer.

"Some," I said at last. "I have to meet someone at a hotel. I don't know how long it will take. Maybe an hour, maybe longer. It depends. When do you need to go to the bar?"

"At five," she said and then, hunger apparently forgotten, went on, "I think I'll go to my apartment now and eat later. When will I see you? Will you come to the bar tonight? Can I be with you tonight?"

"Yes, I'll see you in the bar," I said, but my stomach churned and not with a need for breakfast. Things might not be so easy tonight. "I want to see you," I said and I meant it.

Thankfully, she seemed to detect my genuine sincerity but, possibly, also the doubt. She came over to me and looked up. I put my arms around her but looked out of the window behind. Through the tinted hotel windows, I think I remember it looked cloudy but that the sun was making its way up behind blocks of skyscrapers opposite.

"I'll see you later," I said and put my lips onto the still damp hair hanging over her shoulders.

"OK. I'll make special for when you come tonight." She said it with a clear tinge of doubt and finished her words by looking up at me for a sign of something or other. But instead I turned away and looked out of the window again.

"Mister Luke-Lapp?" I heard her say as if she wanted to ask or say something more.

"Yes," I replied and turned to look at her. Her face was a mixture of sadness and frustration, of patience and perhaps of hopeful tolerance. And, seeing it I then planted both feet stood on the slippery slope and felt myself sliding totally out

30

of control. Whatever it was she might have been going to say, I will never know because words started to form in my head, or in my heart or somewhere.

"Thank you, Anna," I said. "I'm glad I came to see you. Even when I walked out of the hotel last night I was not sure where I was going. But something seemed to take me there. And I know I say sorry too much, Anna, but......it's difficult, you see."

Yes, it was a pretty useless statement but probably significant. And I had used her preferred name, Anna, twice. Anna was the name she had told me she especially liked because it was the name her father had always called her. I normally try very hard not to use familiar names with women if I can possibly help it.

"I'll go now," she said, "I'll see you later".

I followed her to the door and slid the lock.

"My name is Daniel," I said and smiled.

"I know," she said. Then she pushed past me in exactly the way I remembered from the last time. She walked down the corridor without so much as a wave or a backward look. I stood and watched from the doorway as she turned the corner towards the lift. I even stood watching the corner in case she returned. But it was pointless. Instead it was the hotel maid who appeared.

"You check out?" she asked.

"Twenty minutes," I said.

"OK," she replied and wheeled her trolley on past my door.

I turned back into the room, showered, quickly re-packed the few things I had taken out of my case the night before. I replaced the comb that Anna had used, exchanged the jeans I had worn the night before for a pair of light casual trousers, put on a clean, white, short sleeved shirt and a blue tie. Then I returned to the bed, re-read the phone text message from Colin and deleted it. Then I left the room and walked out into the mid-morning heat, hailed a taxi and took off into the Bangkok traffic.

CHAPTER 6

In a cheap hotel room off Gloucester Road in London, Kevin Parker had been unable to sleep. He had left the meeting with Mr El Badry with his mind in turmoil. But, mixed with the sense of finally having found someone with similar

31

views to his own, a ready-made solution and, apparently, the resources to do something about it, Kevin felt very uneasy.

Getting off the tube at Gloucester Road station after his meeting with El Badry, Kevin had been offered something by a black youth stood outside Tesco Express and was tempted. But Kevin had felt high enough already.

Now, six in the morning with a hint of the dawn of a grey, damp London morning seeping through the faded curtains, Kevin felt he was at last starting to grasp what he had been told and what was being offered. Sitting on the edge of the creaking bed in his boxer shorts, he could see the No Smoking sign on the door opposite but ignored it and lit a cigarette.

He had found the red brick apartment block on Chelsea Embankment to be just as he had imagined - plush. He had taken the lift to the second floor and rang the bell. Then he had rung it again and, just as he did so, a big woman in a long black Arab dress with a cream-coloured head scarf opened it.

"I have come to see Mr El Badry," Kevin announced. "For a meeting of the Malthus Society."

"Yes," the woman said, "Come this way."

Kevin followed her across the shiny oak floor. The walls were clean and white with neat row of Arabic prints in ornate wooden frames. They came to a second shiny oak door and the woman pushed it open with a hand that bore large gold rings with blue stones. She beckoned Kevin to enter and then closed the door behind him. Kevin looked around.

It was clearly an office of sorts with a large wooden desk, a few papers scattered, a green desk light and a closed lap top computer. But the sofa and separate chairs, coffee table and Persian carpet (or whatever make it was) that dominated the centre of the floor gave it more of a living room feel. Through the vast plate glass window behind the desk, Kevin could see the river Thames and what he assumed was Battersea Park.

Kevin, clutching the brown folder that contained the notes for his talk, stood and waited, wondering whether other members of the Malthus Society or other foreign groups might also have received invitations and would turn up. For a moment he felt a little let down. Surely, as chairman of the Society, he should, at the very least. have been given more advanced information of the meeting. But, he consoled himself in knowing that all of the Malthus groups on his database operated in a slightly cloak and dagger manner.

Kevin was still wondering if he should go and sit in one of the white leather chairs or, perhaps, the white leather sofa, when he heard the door open behind him and the man he assumed was Mr El Badry walked towards him.

He was a not a big man, certainly not as tall as Kevin, but neatly dressed in a dark navy blue suit, white shirt and blue tie. The greying hair looked gelled and neatly parted but the heavy moustache seemed to have retained its original black colour. As he approached holding out his hand, the other hand removed a pair of rimless spectacles.

Kevin, in his open necked green shirt and red Liverpool sweater, held out his hand.

"Mr Parker, Kevin Parker. I am Mohamed El Badry. Welcome."

Kevin took the hand and got a distinct whiff of aftershave or some other male cosmetic. Kevin had never bothered with such expensive luxuries but already felt he was in the company and in the home of a rich man. He decided to wait to be told what was expected of him.

"Please, be seated," El Badry said and Kevin sat on the edge of the white leather sofa. El Bady relaxed in one of the white chairs and crossed his legs to expose red socks and shiny, patent leather shoes.

"I have been following your work, Kevin - may I call you Kevin?"

"Yes, please do," said Kevin still clutching his folder.

"Your enthusiasm for the group you call the Malthus Society has become known to me. Tell me, Kevin, how many members do you now have on your lists?"

"In the UK we have around fifty," said Kevin, "but I have an international network of groups with similar views that probably adds up to well over a thousand people. "

"That is, indeed, impressive, Kevin. And you deliberately keep everything on a low profile, I believe."

"Yes," said Kevin, "I've already had some bad personal experiences of having my own views published. In fact, I now advise most of my network to deliberately avoid publicity as it seems to anger politicians and others," he paused,"The fertility clinic lot take a very dim view."

Kevin tried the little joke as he was still unsure where all this was leading and Tunje's warning about the CIA or MI6 was already in his mind.

Fortunately, El Badry seemed to like the joke as a smile appeared beneath the moustache. "Yes, there is an unfortunate shortage of people who share our view that we need more urgent and radical solutions, Kevin," he said. Then he continued:

"Tell me, Kevin, do you have a personal view on a solution to the problems of overpopulation?"

Kevin thought about it for a moment. This was dangerous ground. He scratched his chin with the edge of his folder and thought about it. To announce his opinion to someone he had only just met was risky. On the other hand, El Badry didn't quite have the feel or look of someone from a government or an intelligence body. He looked around the room wondering whether he was being secretly filmed or recorded but Kevin was not an expert on such technology. He had no idea. He decided on a cautious approach.

"I have my views, Mr El Badry, but I am not willing to disclose these until I know who I am talking to. Where do you stand on this subject? I came here expecting to give a talk on the views of Thomas Malthus with some additional views on potential solutions thrown in, but only if appropriate to the meeting."

Kevin was pleased with himself.

El Badry smiled again and this time eased himself up from his leather chair. He went over towards his desk and put his glasses back on. Then he sat in the white leather chair behind it and swivelled around to look out towards Battersea Park.

"As I said, Kevin, I have been following your work. You are right in what you say. We cannot wait for talking shops like the United Nations to act, even if one felt they might ever arrive at a consensus. What would you say if you knew that many more thousands of people in influential positions shared your views about overpopulation and wanted a solution now? "

Kevin, sitting in his much lower sofa, looked up towards the balding back of El Badry's head. "I'd say I already know that, Mr El Badry."

"And what would you say if there is a solution being developed that could bypass the political debate that we all know is going nowhere and makes things actually happen?"

"I'd say that there is no political debate taking place, Mr El Badry. There hasn't been anything serious since Thomas Malthus raised the matter way back in 1798. I and members of my groups have been wanting the debate for a very long time. But then we want a solution not just more talk."

El Badry swivelled back to face Kevin.

"We have a solution, Kevin."

"Who is we, Mr El Badry?"

"We, meaning my company, my associates, my researchers, my agents and my distributors. We are ready to move."

Kevin's brain was working overtime. It was like music to his ears but he had no wish to get carried away just yet. "I'm interested, Mr El Badry."

Kevin was trying to adopt a business-like tone to someone he now believed not only looked like but probably was some big shot businessman based somewhere or another, probably the Middle East.

"You have a friend, a Nigerian, who runs a similar group?" said El Badry.

"Yes," said Kevin, very surprised that Tunje was already known. But so as not to lose any initiative, he added, "He is someone who joined my British Malthus group."

"He speaks highly of you."

So he fucking should, thought Kevin. Tunje Fayinke had learned most of his facts and figures and got most of the accumulated evidence by listening to him.

"Yes," El Badry went on, "We have recently been working with Mr. Fayinke to test out a few ideas."

This was news to Kevin. Inside, he raised an eyebrow and continued to listen.

"Tunje has a lot to learn, though. He will have to learn to live with local politics and high local security because of problems with Islamic militants. We will help him overcome all of this nonsense but, as a result, we want to try to find a few other people like Tunje to test out our plans in other countries. This is where you come in."

Kevin said nothing but put his folder on the sofa beside him. Despite all his preparations, clearly he was not required to give a lecture.

El Badry swung his seat around again to face the river view.

"Let us not, what you say, beat about the bush, Kevin. Instead, let's get straight to the point. What, in your view, would be an effective way to forcibly reduce the world population?"

For Kevin, the slippery ground had returned but he decided to go for one of the most radical ideas just to check the reaction. It was one that had been mentioned before, even by Ehrlich. Then he deliberately smiled so as to suggest he was not

35

entirely serious. If there was, indeed, a camera recording him, they might perhaps watch the playback and think he was talking with one tongue firmly planted in his cheek.

"Use public water supplies to disperse anti-fertility compounds."

"Any other ideas?"

El Badry was pushing him. What was he playing at?

"Introduce super-resistant bugs or other plant pathogens that caused essential crops to fail."

El Badry smiled. "Anything else?"

"Start a pandemic with a new virus or bacteria with no known cure."

Kevin smiled once again and looked up at El Badry who had turned back to face him. El Badry then leaned over to open a drawer in his desk.

"Whisky, Kevin? Gin and tonic? Vodka? Arak?"

"Whisky, please."

"Soda? Tonic? Water?"

"Neat, please."

El Badry produced two glasses, came over and placed them on the fancy white lace cloth that covered most of the coffee table. He then poured two big, neat whiskies, offered one to Kevin and returned to his leather chair with the other.

"Cheers," he said and lifted his glass. Kevin lifted his and sipped at the contents.

"We have just that," El Badry said. "We have the means to cause a pandemic. But what we also have is a treatment. If you work with us, Kevin, the treatment will be made available to you."

"Will it be free?" asked Kevin, "My university salary only goes so far."

CHAPTER 7

Less than an hour after checking out of the hotel that Anna and I had stayed in, I checked into a much plusher hotel overlooking the Chaoprya River and found myself a quiet corner seat in the hotel lobby. It was ten thirty and, despite the holdups I was still on schedule.

I checked arrival times at Bangkok Suvarnaphum airport and knew the American Airlines flight had landed on schedule. That meant that my client would be arriving at the hotel, traffic being normal, roughly on schedule.

At ten forty five, I watched a mini bus pull up outside. Those disembarking were clearly American and, although I had never before seen the Virex man, Amos Gazit, before, quickly recognised him. He was much as I had imagined - middle aged and slightly bald but with a pair of glasses hanging on a cord around his neck. He wore a pair of baggy beige trousers, a colourful casual shirt and stood slightly apart from his compatriots.

For the Research Director of Virex International, Boston, USA, Amos Gazit looked every part the scientist. But he clearly had some business acumen I thought or, at least, an intimate knowledge of the company or his boss in USA, Charles Brady, would not have tasked him with this meeting. As the rest of his group dispersed towards the lifts, the American wandered across to stand amongst a forest of large, potted ferns. He put a small white bag between his feet.

As I got up and walked towards him, he clearly saw me coming. By the look on his face, he seemed grateful that what he had been told would happen was actually happening.

"Mr Capelli?" the American asked, lifting his spectacles onto his nose and squinting.

"Mr Gazit, I presume," I replied as if I was Stanley finally finding Doctor Livingstone in the jungle.

"Yes sir," the American said, "I'm pleased to make your acquaintance, sir."

"Shall we have a seat?" I pointed towards the corner where I had been waiting.

"Sure." Gazit picked up his white bag and followed.

"Good trip?"

"Sure. But far too long." He sat down and breathed out, loudly. "I understand you spoke to the President of Virex - Charles Brady. So what's the plan?" Gazit was clearly impatient to get straight to the point.

"We need to talk more," I said. "The remit was far too vague and I didn't get long enough with Mr Brady. So, I suggest you get settled into your room, have a rest and meet me later."

"OK," Gazit nodded but looked hot and stressed.

"Take a taxi to Centre Point. Seven thirty, OK? It's an Asian food centre. The taxi driver will know where it is." I said.

The American nodded again. "Do you want me to bring the other stuff?" he asked.

"Yes, of course. I'll see you later."

Gazit started to get up but then hesitated. He delved into a shirt pocket, pulled out a business card and handed it over. It read Amos Gazit - Head of Virology - Virex International and listed phone numbers, a website and an address in Boston, Massachusetts.

"Thanks," I said, "Sorry I can't reciprocate but I don't normally carry a card. But I can confirm my name is Daniel Capelli."

And so, at seven thirty and on schedule I was seated on a plastic chair at a stained metal table at the back of a busy Asian food centre. I had a glass of iced lime juice in my hand and was facing the crowds walking by outside when, also on schedule, the portly American came into view. Still looking hot and a little disorientated, he was carrying a large brown envelope.

Preliminaries over, I ordered two more fresh lime juices and then sat back. "So, what have you brought?" I asked, eyeing the envelope. The American handed it over but I put it on the table without opening it. Instead, I said, "Tell me more. How worried is your company?"

"Very concerned," replied Amos Gazit. "The loss of a hundred grams of research material has been confirmed. All the initial tests on the new treatment were looking good. Eight years of research, you know? Virex has spent several million dollars so far but we are still some way from clinical use. It's going to take a while yet and then a lot more money for approvals etcetera. But things were looking very positive."

"So, where has it gone?" I asked. Having met Charles Brady in London, I already knew the answer that was coming, but it was worth asking once again.

"We don't know," Gazit said at last. "We suspect an internal problem but, as Charles Brady probably told you, the company is in a difficult position. There are over twenty staff employed directly or indirectly on this project. All of them are skilled in their own way. The company can move some out but, at present, there is no evidence. Also, whoever it is probably has the morals of a rat. Unless we have real evidence, the company can't do a lot if he then decides to move his know-how elsewhere."

Amos Gazit paused, clearly waiting for a response.

"Excuse me for appearing naive here," I said, "But what sort of material are you talking about. Can you describe it?"

"Put simply, it's a protein stored in a clear solution that looks like pink rose water - that's how I describe it to students sometimes. It is then sealed inside glass vials and deep frozen. We have pioneered a lot of work on modifying viruses under controlled conditions for vaccines and new drug treatments. We outsource some of the work to another company but they check clean and I know them well. Everything is fine until it gets back to our facility. Then something happens. Three batches of vials disappeared and replaced by similar ones containing nothing except a culture fluid."

"And how many staff have access to the deep frozen, stored material?"

"They all did. Because of the problem I've recently restricted access to two technicians only. Since then we have had no incidents but no company can go on like this Daniel. This is cutting edge biotechnology. Criminality is unknown. But there is big money involved. Big money. Charles will have told you I'm sure.

"What can anyone do with such small samples?" I asked.

"They could use it for some tests. You only need small amounts. Mix it. Dilute it. Inject it. They could probably treat about twenty patients with it and stand back and look at the results. Then, if it's as good as we think it is, my fear is to suddenly find one or more members of my team, all of whom were hand-picked by me, resigning. I've never heard of anything like it before but anything, I suppose, is a possibility. If I have to put a figure on it I'd say we've already lost several million dollars worth of work. If we lose the technology as well it could finish us. Financial backers will get cold feet. Whoever it is or whoever they are could possibly retire on the proceeds of know-how. Chances are the know-how is already being passed on - God forbid. That's why Charles is desperate for confidentiality. Whoever he is, or they are, millions of dollars of work could be saved by bypassing our work. They could also be only a short time behind us on research and development if the insider has been passing on information regularly over the months."

The American paused again and looked around him.

Then he said, "I sure hope you are the guy I'm supposed to be talking with. All I had was a request from Charles Brady, my President, to meet up with someone with the name Capelli in the hotel. It sounded more like a meeting with the mafia to me. Anyway, this Mr Capelli would be waiting as soon as I arrived. I was told you were a Brit and kept a low profile as a mark of confidentiality and respect and that you'd worked for high tech businesses in the past. And that's all

39

Charles Brady had to go on, too, as far as I'm aware. He said you had good references from someone he already knew and respected. Industrial espionage and theft of intellectual property, if that is what this is, is something I'd read about but never considered relevant to me."

I had been listening intently. "I assume everything I asked for is in this?" I said, pointing at the brown envelope.

"Yes, I dealt with it myself. You are registered as a delegate at the Conference on Virology and Infectious Diseases that I'm here for," he said. Then he added, "And in the name you asked for."

"And there is a trade exhibition going on at the same time, I understand."

"Yes, several companies involved in this research area will be there. Virex is not. We were booked but pulled out a few months ago, largely because we're already tightening up on our budgets. There will be companies in medical diagnostics, pharmaceuticals, laboratory technology, infection control and so on. It's an important conference you know. There will be also be a lot of international press coverage. Since the scares about swine flu and bird flu and worries about other new viruses cropping up the world's press love it. There is nothing like the warning of a pandemic to get the media excited."

Amos Gazit drained his glass of lime juice, sighed and went on.

"You may not know but you sure will hear at this conference about new viruses cropping up. It's partly due to improved technology that enables identification and detection, but, by co-incidence, I understand Thailand has had a few cases of something very recently. But nothing is being made too public at present. But, from what I heard, I reckon by the end of this week there is going to be one hell of a stink - a stink on an international scale. Watch my words.

"Just like we need new antibiotics for bacterial infections - to treat superbugs and the like - so we also have an urgent need for new antiviral drugs and particularly a way to respond to the new variants as quickly as they appear. This is a key part of Virex's work. But it doesn't come cheap, Daniel. Years and years of investment goes in and just as we get close along comes this."

Gazit seemed to be on a roll, The enthusiasm for his work was obvious. I just sat back and let him roll. It was interesting anyway and I learned a lot.

"Did they tell you it was me who was credited with developing an enzyme that works on certain virus particles and upsets their replication? You know, it has taken six years of work to get this far. Most of this was spent in developing the techniques, we now use."

40

"God damn it," he finally said. "I am a scientist Daniel. I'm not used to this sort of thing. It's wrong. It's immoral and I'm still shocked to think there must be someone working for me who is so lacking in commitment to the company and to me that he can do this. "

"Are you sure it's a he?" I asked. I was actually feeling sorry for the American.

"No," said Gazit, "I just assume it is. I am old fashioned enough to think that a woman would show a bit more respect and not be tempted to try to destroy their employer."

"I wouldn't be too sure about that," I said, "But have you any suspicions about who it might be?"

"No," said Gazit. "Sleepless nights? I have had a lot. But as far as putting my finger on who and why, no. I've watched, listened to, talked to them all without letting on I was checking them out - but no, no indication."

I looked at the American with a tinge of affection for the man who was obviously deeply concerned about the company he worked for and personally very hurt by whatever was going on. He was also, probably, far more at home in a laboratory than in the hot, stuffy confines of an Asian food centre in Bangkok. Enough for now, I beckoned the waiter for the bill and said:

"Do you think anyone, a person or a company, who you suspect of involvement in this will be at the conference?" It was the question I had wanted to ask Charles Brady in London.

"I'm not sure," said Gazit, "We think that whoever is behind this must be big enough to be in a position to do something with what they have stolen from us but must also be total crooks. It can't be a big, well known, multinational organization. They would not dare work like this. Would they? If they want know-how or people, they just go in and buy. Money no object."

"When I met Charles Brady, your president, back in the UK he told me something about one of your competitors losing key researchers. Seemed to think there might be a connection. Tell me a bit more."

"Yes, Biox Research International - also with their headquarters in Boston. There was a lot of newspaper interest and even more talk in the industry when David Solomon their director of research, a British guy, disappeared just over a year ago. No-one has seen him since. He was well known for political opinions. He would rail against the power of multinational businesses and was apparently involved with groups that would attack G8 type conferences. Most of us wondered how the hell he had risen to his position in the first place. But he was internationally respected for his research - he was a leading expert.

"Then there was the senior lecturer in immunology at Cambridge who disappeared last fall. He had worked for Biox and knew Solomon, in fact they were good friends from the UK. Name of Guy Williams. Clever scientist. He wrote several papers on viral chemistry. There have also been a few other resignations but we generally know where those guys have gone and we try not to get paranoid.

"You must also have seen the press coverage on infectious diseases, problems of resistance to current treatments and the prices of many of these drugs being out of reach of all except the rich. This controversy is being fuelled by some University and Institute researchers who are against multinational pharmaceutical companies' ability to dictate prices of drugs. They want the funds for themselves. There is a lot of evidence that proves the point but the counter argument is that the big multinationals need the profits to fund research and development and only have short periods before patents run out. I see both sides."

Amos Gazit shrugged as if he had discussed the subject may times.

"Charles Brady had a theory about all this," I prompted. "Tell me your thoughts."

"Yes," Gazit said, "Charles Brady's suspicion, and mine, is that there might be an organisation out there operating illegally and below the radar, trying to capitalise on the gold mine that everyone sees is there."

Gazit looked at his watch.

"I promised to go along to the pre-drinks session with colleagues back at the hotel. I wouldn't want them thinking I chickened out."

"Before you go," I said, "Please tell me what you expect me to do. Charles Brady gave me some background in London and I know he clearly wants some investigations but do you know what he really wants done if we get somewhere."

The American stared at me but I thought I knew what was coming. They wanted to know as much as possible but then they'd keep it quiet. I'd been here before.

"Yes, Mr Capelli. Whoever you are or whatever it is you do, just keep it quiet. Let us know what you find out. I'm sure Charles told you that. We will decide what to do when we know more. We particularly don't want the media jumping up and down at the moment. We still need financing and backers can get very cold feet if they know that their investments are at risk. Keep it quiet Daniel. I am sure Charles told you that. We just want to know what the hell's going on, then we'll decide."

CHAPTER 8

Kevin Parker had checked out of his one star Gloucester Road hotel and was taking his lunch. Sipping at a plastic mug of Coke with a half eaten Macdonalds burger hanging from its polystyrene box, Kevin had his mobile phone in his free hand trying to contact his Nigerian friend Tunje Fayinka. He had been trying all morning and had already left several voice messages and sent a text so Tunje was either at work at Barnet College, which seemed unlikely, or still asleep which seemed far more likely.

While he waited, mobile in hand, he was re-reading his unused notes from the folder that he had carried with him to see Mohamed El Badry the night before. The notes had already become a little greasy but the words of Thomas Malthus were as inspiring as ever.

"The love of independence is a sentiment that surely none would wish to see erased from the breast of man, though the parish law of England, it must be confessed, is a system of all others the most calculated gradually to weaken this sentiment, and in the end may eradicate it completely."

Kevin looked up from his burger. Malthus was a genius and the written English so perfect. Malthus would have hated McDonalds with its brash red and yellow logo and its cheap mass catering for millions of overfed but unhealthy children. Their early deaths from diabetes, heart attacks and lack of exercise would prove Malthus' point.

"To remedy the frequent distresses of the common people, the poor laws of England have been instituted; but it is to be feared that though they may have alleviated a little the intensity of individual misfortune, they have spread the general evil over a much larger surface.

"The transfer of three shillings and sixpence a day to every labourer would not increase the quantity of meat in the country. There is not at present enough for all to have a decent share. What would then be the consequence?"

"Too right," said Kevin to his burger. "Bloody social security, family tax credits and child benefits. The Chinese will find a way to take it all for themselves if things get any tougher. What would fucking McDonalds do then?"

"I feel no doubt whatever that the parish laws of England have contributed to raise the price of provisions and to lower the real price of labour. The labouring poor, to use a vulgar expression, seem always to live from hand to mouth. Their present wants employ their whole attention, and they seldom think of the future. Even when they have an opportunity of saving they seldom exercise it, but go, generally speaking, to the ale house. "

"Or McDonalds," said Kevin to himself. "He puts it in a nutshell."

"Every endeavour should be used to weaken and destroy all those institutions relating to corporations, apprenticeships etc which cause the labours of agriculture to be worse paid than the labours of trade and manufactures. "

"Fucking McDonalds," muttered Kevin and pushed his half eaten burger to one side.

"To prevent the recurrence of misery is, alas! beyond the power of man. The power of population is so superior to the power in the earth to produce subsistence for man, that premature death must in some shape or other visit the human race."

"Then stop the suffering now," said Kevin and almost stood up.

"Though I may not be able to in the present instance to mark the limit at which further improvement will stop, I can very easily mention a point at which it will not arrive."

"Genius," said Kevin.

"I know of no well-directed attempts of this kind, except in the ancient family of the Bickerstaffs, who are said to have been very successful in whitening the skins and increasing the height of their race by prudent marriages, particularly by that very judicious cross with Maud, the milk-maid, by which some capital defects in the constitutions of the family were corrected."

"Steady on Thomas," muttered Kevin, "Nevertheless, Ausser Kontrolle like this bit."

"The lower classes of people in Europe may at some future period be much better instructed then they are at present; they may be taught to employ the little spare time they have in many better ways than at the ale-house; they may live under better and more equal laws than they have hitherto done, perhaps, in any country; and I even conceive it possible, though not probable, that they may have more leisure; but it is not in the nature of things, that they can be awarded such a quantity of money or substance, as will allow them all to marry early, in the full confidence that they shall be able to provide with ease for a numerous family.

"Singapore 2100 liked this, Thomas. Way ahead of your time."

Kevin's mobile phone suddenly rang.

"Hey man, what you want calling me at this hour?"

"It's midday, Tunje," said Kevin. "I thought you might have been lecturing the good students of Barnet and Southgate on population control."

"Yeh, well, tomorrow, Kev. What's up?"

"Met a mate of your last night. Mister El Badry.........."

"Shhhh...... Kev. Not so loud."

"I hear you're helping him with a few ideas."

"Nope, not me, mate."

"Tunj, my friend. Stop fucking me about. What's going?"

"If you want to know, meet me. Don't use any fucking technology, man. OK?"

"But is it true what he said, Tunj? Is he testing something on your patch?"

"Sure. Apparently. Nothing to do with me, my man. He just wanted my future support."

Kevin was not sure he understood. There was a long pause.

"Tunj. Let's meet. I can't get my head around him. The man's a rich, bloody Arab. What's he want with us?"

CHAPTER 9

I don't think I'll ever know why I didn't go to see Anna after Amos Gazit had left? Fear? Uncertainty? I still don't know.

But as I entered the Convention Hall for the Conference on Virology and Infectious Diseases the next morning, the question was bothering me more than what I could possibly do for Virex International, Amos Gazit, the company's Director of Research or Charles Brady, the company's President.

I had called Anna in the bar to say I was tied up in a meeting and could not make it but would call again. But I could have found the time. It had not been so late when I had returned to the hotel down by the river. She had sounded upset again, as I knew she would, but I suppose it was that old familiar thought of starting another commitment that would end in more heartache, that had fuelled my doubts. But my own heartache was already in full swing.

For the moment, I tried to brush it aside and clutching the envelope Amos Gazit had given me the night before, made my way to the registration desk, took out my official delegate form, handed it over and waited while a girl tapped my name and details into a computer. Seconds later she produced a small name card and slipped it, neatly, into a clear plastic name tag and handed it back.

"Thank you Doctor Stevens, " she said in practiced English.

Temporarily rebranded as Doctor Michael Stevens from the University of Kuala Lumpur, I thanked her, moved away to a quiet corner of the huge hall and examined the rest of the contents of Gazit's envelope.

Inside was a list of delegates - several pages of them with University, Research centre or company names and addresses, a small booklet outlining the lectures, the speakers, their topics and the chairmen for each session. I scanned it all. Then I took out the third booklet - a list of companies exhibiting in the adjacent hall and a list of company-sponsored "poster sessions" for those not officially speaking but who had some research topic to promote. I decided the trade exhibition could wait. I wanted to get a feel for the point of the conference - Virology and Infectious Diseases.

Sitting at the back of the vast lecture theatre I scanned the delegates and thought I could see the back of Gazit's head near the front. There were, I reckon, at least three hundred people present and very mixed nationalities. According to my official notes, the speaker was a local doctor, Dr S Vichai, a small man in a white shirt and dark suit made large on a vast TV screen behind him. The subject, "A new variant of Coronavirus?" It was a question rather than a statement.

Dr Vichai spoke in good but accented English, the accent so familiar and my own thoughts tracked forwards to tonight. Should I or shouldn't I go to see Anna? The unusual distraction was making it hard for me to concentrate on the speaker.

"...........AIDS has been a familiar problem for many years now. The public, worldwide, are mostly fully aware of the disease and how it spreads. They are also aware that it is only now becoming controllable with a mixed but expensive drug cocktail..........."

Doctor Vichai continued for a while and then called up another slide that appeared on the screen behind him.

".........this new variant, currently known by my laboratory in Bangkok as TRS-CoV, is different.............. what we have here is something new..........it appears to start with symptoms like a common cold but it then progresses rapidly to something more like whooping cough...........in the two cases where we have been able to take samples from patients before death, the virus appears new. We do not yet understand how it is transmitted...........we do not know whether some patients may have recovered normally without progressing to the coughing fits and so we have no understanding of the numbers of cases.........the cases notified to us have all centred on just one area around Ayuthaya to the north of Bangkok.......all the males, aged between twenty two and fifty are from this area. All were apparently healthy individuals with no known health problems. The one young woman was the exception and she was from the Bangkok area."

Next to me, a young man with a tablet phone stuck his pen in his mouth and got up. "Excuse me," he said in an English accent and brushed past towards the exit. A few others near the front of the room did the same. The press contingent were clearly picking up a story, but Doctor Vichai was still speaking.

"...........I understand from the WHO that there are reports coming from Nigeria and a possible case in Kenya.......if these are, indeed, all caused by the same virus then this is very unusual as most new respiratory infections are very localised......"

I too got up and followed the English reporter outside. He was now on the phone probably to a London paper.

"Yeh,..........got that? Believe me this is a good story. The implications are horrendous. What? Yes, the speaker -Doctor Vichai - Thai. Look I'll email something right now. Sorry to call you at this hour, Peter, but this has all the appearances of another new influenza or something. Were you still in bed? Sorry. I'll call later."

I remember pulling my own phone out of my pocket on an impulse to phone Anna but then I stopped. No - I'd phone her later. There were things I had to do.

CHAPTER 10

In Nairobi, Philippe Fournier, PhD, leaned back as far as was safe to do so in his broken swing chair, and stared at the papers on his battered wooden desk.

Despite his qualifications as a microbiologist and biochemist, he was, at the request of someone far higher up, designing some leaflets for a sexually transmitted diseases poster. But his computer had, as usual, been going slow. Now it had stopped altogether.

"Merde! he said aloud. Then, "Fils de salope."

Then, deciding it sounded far better in English, he said, "Fucking, crap machine."

He got up, kicked the chair and went out, and because there was nowhere else to go, wandered along the depressingly long corridor that smelled of disinfectant and body fluids. Leaning on the ledge of an open window looking out towards the rest of the Kenyatta National Hospital site, he looked down at the ground below and felt a mouthful of saliva building up in his mouth as if he was going to be sick. He wasn't, but instead he let a large glob of the spit fall from his mouth. He watched it's slimy progress all the way until it nestled in the weeds below. Then his mobile phone rang.

He pulled it from his trouser pocket and checked to see if it was Mara's mobile, but no. He didn't recognise the number.

"Jambo," he muttered although he knew full well that it would suggest to anyone who was calling that he was just a foreigner or tourist practising their Swahili. Philippe was past caring.

"Monsieur Fournier?"

"Oui" he said, now thinking in French because of the title he'd just been given.

"We are recruiting highly qualified scientists for a new laboratory. Your name cropped up," the voice said.

Philippe's eyes lit up despite the speaker having already resorted to English. "Yes?" he said, not wanting to appear too enthusiastic.

"We are looking for someone to lead a group doing research in virology. Your name was mentioned."

"Yes," Philippe said, "I have a PhD from an English University but I also studied in Paris."

"Yes, we know," said the voice.

"How do you know?" asked Philippe, naively.

The caller ignored the question. "It would mean an immediate start for the right person. We can probably at least double your current salary. Are you interested in a meeting to discuss the position?"

"Uh, perhaps, " said Philippe, smiling down to where his spit had landed.

"The Oakwood Hotel at 7pm." said the voice. "I will be waiting for you."

"How do I know you?"

"Don't worry Philippe, I'll find you."

CHAPTER 11

It was the trade exhibition at the Conference that really interested me. But I still had no idea how, or if, it would be of any use for my new client, Virex International. That Anna was constantly on my mind was a reflection of how involved in the job I was being paid to do I actually felt. I was in a dreadful state for a grown man. I felt like a teenage boy who thought a girl fancied him because she'd said she'd wait for him after school by the lamp post.

So, picking up a list of trade exhibitors, I took a deep breath and, adopting as manly a walk as I could muster strolled up and down the three main aisles. It was not a large exhibition by some standards but a mix of high tech medical diagnostics companies, laboratory equipment manufacturers and pharmaceutical companies. But on the corner end of the third aisle I found exactly what I was looking for - Biox Research International - the company that, according to Amos Gazit had lost its research director and an ex employee. I stopped, went forward and picked up a sales leaflet.

"Can I help you sir?" I heard an American accent. "I'm John Wardley."

"I'm not sure," I said looking up. "Perhaps some general product information."

"Doctor Stevens," Wardley said, eyeing my neat nametag. "Where you from, sir?"

"Currently in Kuala Lumpur. Local you might say. University. Molecular genetics. Passing interest in viral biochemistry." Hearing my invented story out loud for the first time it sounded passable.

"British though, eh?" joked Wardley, detecting the accent. "Any clinical involvement Doctor Stevens?"

"Peripheral." I said, vaguely, as I was unsure exactly what that meant. "Actually," I continued in as British a way as I could, "I used to know one of your researchers a few years ago. Chap by the name of Solomon. He and I met at Cambridge. Last I heard he was head of research - done well for himself. I lost touch when I came out here. He went west, I went east." I paused to test the response."

"Dave Solomon," John Wardley said immediately. "I'm surprised you hadn't heard. He disappeared. Last year. Strange story. You say you knew him?"

"Yes, Cambridge. I spent a year there before coming out here but then lost touch with many former colleagues. I've tried to involve myself here as much as I could and my work went in a different direction."

Wardley seemed happy to continue. "Yup," he said, "Disappeared. Just walked out of his downtown apartment, left a girlfriend without even a note and disappeared. There was a lot of talk. He was well respected. In the middle of some very interesting research. Valuable to a competitor, perhaps, but he never surfaced. I know top management in the company were concerned. He was privy to a lot of company information. But I haven't heard him mentioned for a while."

"He was always very political," I said, trying to encourage Wardley to say a bit more. "I seem to remember he was very left wing. Anti-capitalist, environmentalist."

"So I believe, but I didn't know him that well," Wardley said.

"Seems strange how he got on so well with Biox," I went on, pushing it as far as I could. "Although I heard he had toned down a lot after going to USA. Globalization and multinational corporations were always his big hate."

"I don't know a lot," admitted Wardley, "But Jack did." He pointed to an older colleague talking to another visitor. "Jack moved out of the labs into international marketing last year. He knew him well." Then: "Can I get you a coffee Doctor Stevens? We have a system around the back which is designed for guests but mainly to keep us on our feet for the next three days."

His colleague, Jack, was finishing with his visitor and came over.

"Walt Daniels," he said looking straight at me. He put out a big hand to be shaken. "Jack, to many people, I can't imagine why but I admit to liking a drop with the same name from time to time." He laughed at his little joke, but I am very cruel. I recognised it as his usual self-introduction to complete strangers.

Walt took me to a small plastic table covered in empty plastic cups by holding my elbow as if I was his son and my dinner was getting cold. "So," Walt leaned back in his plastic chair, "You interested in diagnostics, Doctor Stevens? Where are you based? Just come for the conference? From England are you?"

Walt was a big man, overweight, probably in his late fifties, balding and looking as though a walk in the Bangkok sun outside might cause problems. I took the cup of coffee and nodded a thank you at John Wardley.

"I'm based in KL, Kuala Lumpur - the University," I repeated for Walt Daniels' benefit. "I'm doing some lecturing and research in molecular genetics. Not really in to your specialist area, I admit, but I had a few days leave and it's quite a quick flight up here from KL. I don't think you will sell me much but, as I was telling your colleague, the name Biox International was familiar. We were discussing David Solomon. I knew him at Cambridge but lost touch. I hear he disappeared."

Walt took a mouthful of coffee and wiped his lips. "Weird, that's what I call it. I worked under him in the virology department. He was head of one of the research divisions so he controlled a lot. My department was working on some second generation tests, those that will come in after all these." Walt waved towards the sales brochures that lay in neat piles on the exhibition stand. "Dave Solomon was more directly involved in virus genetics. He had worked on HIV some years back and was looking at new treatments, enzymes and other things. A very highly respected young man was Dave."

"So how long have you been with Biox?" I asked him.

"I've been there ten years - joined just after it was set up. Biox has pioneered a lot of this type of virus research. Made a lot of money for the backers and for Josh Ornstein the Vice President though not much has come this way." He laughed, drained his cup, and then asked, "So how is Malaysia. How long you been there?"

"Two years, but I also worked in Perth and Singapore after leaving UK."

By this time, I had already used up most of my invented CV and hoped the questions wouldn't linger. I usually think up my stories in advance but it can depend how complicated the subject matter is. Without a PhD in virus genetics I knew I would quickly start to struggle here. I hate the bullshit that sometimes comes with this job. I usually try to divert conversations away as quickly as possible. I tried it this time. "I've been around a bit, you might say, but I like this part of the world," I said, hoping this would divert things away from the deeper aspects of molecular biology. I also wanted to bring another matter into the conversation.

51

"Tell me, didn't Guy Williams also work for Biox?" I asked. "He was another ex Cambridge graduate. Someone told me that he was back in Cambridge but then I heard he hadn't stayed long either. What is it about Biox? When are you going to disappear, Walt?"

"My wife would find me wherever I went," Walt grinned. I pushed a bit more.

"Did you know Guy, Walt? He and I shared a girl friend once in Cambridge. Every Friday night she used to decide who she preferred and we would have to accept her decision. Very civilized English behaviour really."

This was nothing like up to my usual standard of bullshitted probing and I knew it. But my own girlfriend was standing there at the back of my brain. I just couldn't get her to move away. Walt smiled politely and looked at me. His look bothered me and I wondered if I'd just lost a point or two. I was later to be proved right but hindsight, however quickly it comes, is no use in the bullshitting game

"Oh, yeh?" he said. "Guy Williams. Yeh. He worked for Dave Solomon for about a year. They were good friends. Guy went back to Cambridge. He had his eye on a Professorship I think. And yep, apparently he also disappeared late last year. Perhaps you should go back now and find that girl friend. You could have first picking every Friday night."

I remember telling Walt I was trying to stay single, which was sort of true. But then I saw John Wardley cozying up on the other side of the trade stand to a couple of young Japanese girls, nurses I think. I decided I'd better move on. The Biox ice was now broken and I could always come back. Walt and his brochures would be around for a couple more days.

"I must be going," I said, "Thanks for the coffee."

"No problem," said Walt as I got up. But then he added, "How about joining us this evening? We have a small company drinks reception for some delegates at eight. Afterwards, I'm told the nightlife gets interesting and we haven't had a chance to look around yet."

"Good idea," I replied. "I'd be very pleased to join you." Which would have been true a few days ago. But Anna was still lurking there. I could almost hear her winding herself up for another telling off.

I then left the Convention Centre, called a taxi and sat in the back looking out of the window, seeing nothing of the traffic jam around me but thinking about the lectures I'd just listened to. It's surprising how quickly you can become an expert on flu epidemics and epidemiology. But Amos Gazit's words were proving right. I definitely sensed some genuine concern amongst these leading specialists. It was not only the growing bacterial resistance to antibiotics that we all get told about but the regular and apparently spontaneous arrival on the scene of new viruses with quick and fatal consequences and no effective treatment available.

But Virex International had engaged me to help with their own particular problem of losing research material. Was there a connection with what I'd just learned rubbing shoulders with all these white coats? Both Charles Brady and Amos Gazit from Virex seemed to think so but they had provided me with very little evidence - none in fact.

I had never met these two disappeared scientists, David Solomon and Guy Williams, of course, but my made-up stories of having known them were having an effect on me. It was often like that. I can understand how actors playing a character can't just instantly drop the character when the acting's finished.

I started to think about Gazit and Brady. Perhaps they knew a few things about these two guys that they were not letting on. I was, in fact, damn sure of it. I had tried to extract more but they had both been vague and had conveyed nothing factual. I tried to recall exactly what Charles Brady had told me back in London? Talking about Solomon, who, let's not forget, had never worked for Virex but for the other Boston based company, Biox, Brady had said:

"I met him several times. He was good. We were thinking of getting him to join Virex. We used to meet at seminars. But then I started to lose confidence in him. Always trying to suggest we should change our emphasis. Always trying to suggest that medical research should be heavily subsidized on an international basis. Always suggesting that the new drugs we were looking for should be available to all and not just the rich countries of the West. He didn't seem to understand that specialised drugs needed highly trained doctors and facilities. Just look at modern cancer therapy in the West and then compare it to Africa. It's a sad fact that in some places there is still only one doctor to several thousands of people let alone specialists available. It didn't seem to affect him. To him it was still wrong."

Yes. I can go with all that, I thought. Nothing particularly wrong there. Solomon talks some sense at least some of the time.

And why had Brady suggested I come to this Conference? He genuinely seemed to think it would help lead to some answers if I mixed with people and companies. But he hadn't given me anything more specific.

I was still deep in thought when my taxi arrived near the river. Close to the bank of the wide and muddy water, rafts of green lotus weed floated past.

Ploughing its way upstream was a long barge being pulled by a single noisy tug and amongst it all, was the throaty roar of river taxis. I love Bangkok. Every free space beside the road at this point was taken up by food carts and the pavements was crammed with rickety tables, chairs and people eating.

I suddenly felt very hungry. Something hot and spicy eaten at one of these hawker stalls appealed. But alone? No. I'm always alone. Relaxing company was what I suddenly craved. Someone I could sit with, in total un-pressured comfort, and absorb the heat, the sound, the smells and the views of one of my favourite cities. So what should I do about that other burning question? Goddamn it, Anna was bothering me every few minutes and she wasn't even there. My life recently seemed to be a perpetual battle between conscience, duty, desire, the excitement of my job and the fear of personal commitment. I was becoming as pathetic as that vision I'd seen.

The taxi turned down another side street and within minutes I was back in the hotel. Now the next question?

Should I stay there or check out and return to my normal hotel off Sukhumvit Road? I had only moved to the river side hotel because Virex had booked me the room so I could meet Amos Gazit. I hadn't spoken to Gazit at the Conference because I'd been complying with my arrangement with them. Virex did not want to be seen by anyone to be in any way connected to this guy Doctor Mike Stevens from Kuala Lumpur.

I hate being indecisive. I took the lift to my room. An hour later, showered and changed, I sat on the bed and phoned Anna. But there was no answer. Somewhat dejected, I went down to the hotel bar, ordered a cold beer and sat in the corner. I suppose I could have got drunk and forgotten about everything. I could have got up, taken a taxi to the airport and flown back to London and my mate Colin. I could have ditched Virex and dumped.........no. I just couldn't do any of that. Not now.

Anyway I don't drink much alcohol and I actually hate beer. I do not link beer with jovial, social gatherings in English pubs or American bars. I may have done when much younger but I now link beer with lone drinking in dark corners.

CHAPTER 12

In Nairobi, Philippe had arrived at the Oakwood Hotel by 6.15, three quarters of an hour before his appointment with the mysterious caller.

Meeting people like this was not something Philippe was used to although he knew where the Oakwood Hotel was. Sandwiched between some high-rise buildings, it looked out of place and as it seemed to specialise in organising safaris for tourists. Philippe sat in the corner listening to conversations to try to get a fix on the cost of various safari packages. One group was wanting to go climbing, but thinking that Mara was unlikely to want to climb Mount Kilimanjaro, he dismissed it and focussed on the relevant costs of two day and four day safaris to the Masai Mara instead.

By 7pm, though, he was getting anxious as no-one had yet approached him about the job interview. By 7.15pm he started to stroll around the small lobby and finally went to ask the receptionist if anyone had asked to speak to him. It was then that he felt the tap on his shoulder.

"Monsieur Fournier?"

Philippe jumped and turned, a little nervously, to find a man in a suit holding out his hand apparently expecting it to be shaken. Philippe said, "Yes," and took hold of the hand whilst looking into a slightly tanned face with a large smile across it.

"Shall we go up to the bar and balcony," said the man and, without waiting, led the way. "The Oakwood is typical old Kenya, I think," the man said as Philippe followed behind.

The small balcony next to the bar was a great vantage point to watch the Nairobi street life below. Looking towards the Stanley Hotel and the Thorn Tree Cafe, Philippe took the seat next to the small table he was directed to and looked around him. The tanned face man was ordering drinks.

"Whisky," he said to the barman. "You take ice?"

"Uh, yes," said Philippe, a complete stranger to anything stronger than Kenyan Tusker. Cider had been his favourite when at Reading University but only because he liked apples. Meanwhile, the man sat down across the table, loosened his tie and sat back. "I told you I'd recognise you," he said, still smiling. "So you are interested in a job?"

"Yes, sir," said Philippe. "Perhaps," he added, trying not to show too much early enthusiasm.

"You studied at a place called Reading, right?"

"Yes, sir. The Faculty of Biological Sciences."

"And you obtained a PhD, I understand." The accent may have been slightly French but Philippe did not question it.

"Yes, sir, on molecular virology, molecular pathogenesis and evolution and mechanisms of virus structure and replication - especially Coronavirus and arenavirus infection. I studied under Doctor Mark Cavendish, sir."

"That is very important Philippe. I, also, am an expert on Coronaviruses but what the fuck are arenaviruses?"

The language was now Americanised French or something similar, but Philippe only heard the word fuck. He was surprised by it being used during an interview but one of the senior researchers at Reading had been prone to mix his sentences with expletives so he decided not to let this put him off.

"Well sir, it is complicated. Do you want me to explain in some detail?"

"Yes, go ahead, Philippe. Ah, here is the whisky - sante."

"Well," Philippe began, "Arenaviruses have a bisegmented negative-strand RNA genome, which encodes four viral proteins: GP and NP by the S segment and L and Z by the L segment. These four proteins possess multiple functions in infection, replication and release of progeny viruses from infected cells. The small Ring finger protein, Z protein is a matrix protein that plays a central role in viral assembly and budding.............."

"OK, Philippe, I see you know your arenaviruses - boire - drink your whisky - sante."

"Thank you," Philippe put his glass to his lips and sipped. It was like drinking fire.

"So, time for a career move, then, Philippe." The man peeled off his tie completely and then took his jacket off, hung it over the back of his chair and pulled out a mobile phone. He then looked out over the balcony towards the Stanley Hotel opposite. "One minute, Philippe. I need to make a call." With that the man got up and walked away leaving Philippe staring at the empty chair with the discarded red tie and jacket. While he waited, Philippe tried his drink again and wondered, briefly, if Mara liked whisky. He hoped not.

But Philippe was pleased that the man pronounced his name so well and not Fillip like so many Kenyans and British. The man suddenly returned and Philippe jumped out of his fleeting dream.

"Well," the man said. "The job is yours if you want it. You'll work for two of our senior scientists at our new laboratory. Private company. Funding is no problem. Virology, infectious diseases, that sort of thing - you know, you've done it before. Pioneering research, a new laboratory and the facilities are superb." He pronounced superb as if it had a 'e' at the end and then held up his thumb and first finger to make a perfect circle. "Are you interested? Do you have any questions?"

Philippe was overwhelmed by how quick it was. He'd expected a much longer interview, perhaps a second or even a third interview, aptitude testing, a tour of the laboratory even. "Uh, yes," he said, trying to think up sensible questions as fast as he could but also hanging onto the word superb pronounced just as a Frenchman would. Everything sounded superbe. "How much will I be paid?"

"You'll be paid seventy five thousand dollars a year plus a bonus if all goes well. All living expenses."

Philippe's eyes widened. "Uh, is the laboratory far from here?"

"We will arrange transport. But you'll live on site. Luxury villa."

Philippe thought about Mara. Surely he'd get weekends off. And a luxury villa? With a swimming pool, perhaps?

"Can you start immediately?"

"Uh, yes sir."

"Good, I'll pick you up here at 8pm tomorrow night. Come with a suitcase as if going away for a long weekend. And bring your passport. Ca va?"

"Oui. Yes, sir."

"And one last thing. Don't tell anyone just yet. Plenty of time to notify your friends and family. It's the company policy - ne t'inquiète pas!"

"Yes, sir."

Philippe left in a dream. It was only at midnight as he was going over and over the interview in his sleepless mind that it struck him. He had no idea who the man was or what the company was called. But he now remembered the man's French accent so perhaps he was being recruited by a French company. And why the need for a passport? Perhaps he would be going to France for training. Philippe was both nervous and excited but he couldn't recall the man's face.

CHAPTER 13

I think I drank half a bottle of beer in the hotel before phoning Anna again but her phone seemed to be switched off. Thinking that perhaps I was now getting the silent tirade, I headed back to the Convention Centre and then found I was far too early for the drinks reception, courtesy of Biox International. So I sat in a corner waiting and playing with my phone until the start time.

For a while I mingled and listened to others, sipping at orange juice but saying nothing about myself. You know what it's like at these dos. If you're quiet and keep yourself to yourself you can quickly spot those who are comfortable and those who feel out of place. It's always a good opportunity to spot an out of place female, make her feel less out of place and see how things develop but I wasn't even in the mood for that. So I generally hung around, nodding, smiling and sipping my juice. At nine, as people started to wander away, John Wardley tapped me on the shoulder. "Time to go have some fun," he said.

So, nothing ventured, nothing gained as my dad used to say, I took a deep breath and re-confirmed my willingness to act as their bar crawl guide. As I waited for Walt and John to close down the Biox trade stand for the night, I wandered off through the hall still clutching my orange juice.

The Livingstone Pharmaceuticals trade stand was in a corner where two of their salesmen were, like John and Walt, also packing up for the night. I watched them until they went away and then walked over to their stand. The Livingstone in-house company "news sheet" was lying on a coffee table and I picked it up for no other reason than passing interest.

The front page showed a picture of a small group of what I took to be Livingstone staff giving a cheque to someone for some good community cause - the caring, compassionate and charitable side of Livingstone. I flipped it open to the second page and to an article inside and read:

"Livingstone Pharmaceuticals have recently appointed Shah Medicals to market the new Histocytex range in parts of East Africa. This has followed two years of successful co-operation with in marketing Clarion Hand Creams, Clarion Skin Care and Mentha decongestants range.

"Shah Medicals is fast becoming a well known name in international pharmaceutical sales and distribution under its banner of Shah Corporation. Already well established in the Middle East, the company has several branches in South East Asia and plans to increase its marketing activity in East and West Africa. The tie in with Livingstone will enable Shah Corporation to grow its African operation from its base in Nairobi where it now has its own research facility and regional base for all types of medical product licensing and trials."

The article closed with a wish for success to Shah Medicals and showed a photograph of the Shah Corporation chief executive, a smiling Mr Mohamed Kader seen shaking hands with someone from Livingstone Pharmaceuticals..

I'm usually good at remembering faces and I was sure I had seen the man before, or at least a photograph of him. The similarity to that old tyrant, Saddam Hussein, had struck me before although this man was dressed in a good business suit, not an army uniform, and there were other, obvious, differences. But the smile and the heavy black moustache were strikingly similar.

On the other hand, the man looked similar to thousands of middle aged men from the Jordan or Iraq area. Yes, I could pin-point the man to that specific area. It's another of my many talents acquired from too much travelling and too much time spent watching others. I pocketed the company's newspaper and wandered on past the emptying trade stands to find John and Walt for an evening in the Bangkok bars.

It was past midnight when we got back to Walt's hotel. That's not late for Bangkok but Walt had been showing signs of exhaustion before the evening had even started. After three hours of noisy bars he was all in. John though, was still going. But it was in one particular bar that Walt had spotted someone he knew and, above the loud music, had shouted something into my ear:

"Say, Mike. See those guys over there," he had nodded towards the other end of the bar where two Europeans or Americans were engaged with two attentive young ladies. "On the trade stand near ours - Livingstone Pharmaceuticals - you know the company?"

I shook my head but was, nevertheless, interested in what might come next. Walt looked as if he had more to say. He took a breath and shouted into my ear again.

"Those two guys. I think the older one must be the owner, Greg O'Brian. I've only ever seen a photo of him. By reputation he's a rogue and normally keeps a very low profile. I've no idea of his background but I believe he just stepped in and bought Livingstone when it was up for sale. Must have seen an opportunity. But Livingstone is a strange American company. It's an old business that started off doing consumer type products. Rumours have it they are moving into more high tech stuff. I suppose that's why they're here. Perhaps I'll have a sniff around sometime. Headquarters in New York I think but someone told me yesterday they're doing something in East Africa - Kenya, I think he said. I think the other guy is their international sales manager. But if that's O'Brian then it's interesting. He rarely shows his face in public."

Walt had then stopped and tried sitting back on a stool that was far too small for his size and weight. "Hell. I'm getting too old for this," he had shouted. "Can't hear yourself think." He paused, nodding towards his colleague John Wardley who was clearly enjoying the night. "But I suppose you don't come in here for serious discussions."

"Why don't we leave John here, Walt," I said."He's a big boy and should know all about the risks he might be taking. How about a drink somewhere more quiet?"

"Sure thing, Mike," Walt replied, before draining his glass and edging off the stool. Then he tapped John on the shoulder. "We're off. The English doctor says you are to be a good boy. OK?"

I was pleased to leave. Anna was not there but she was spoiling my night if you get my drift. I hailed a taxi. With Walt slumped into the well-worn rear seats and with the taxi's air conditioning appearing to slowly revive him, we both stayed silent and looked out of the window. You'll know what was on my mind. But, suddenly, just as it seemed Walt may have fallen asleep, he mumbled something. I turned to look at him.

"Funny you should know Guy Williams and David Solomon," Walt said, still looking out of the window on his side. "No-one has mentioned either of them for quite a while."

Then, as I was wondering what to say Walt went on, "You're not really a doctor are you?" Walt continued looking out of the window.

I was just a little taken aback but tried not to show it. I paused and replied in a way I've used before when trying to step around awkward questions. I've used it with women in the past but I won't ever try it on Anna. "What makes you say that?"

The weakness of the words was a real give away. Inwardly, I cringed. I am a man with a few years of experience in dealing with people of so many different nationalities and in circumstances that almost always required tact, diplomacy and, sometimes, to be a good liar. Surely, I thought, I could have done better than that. I resigned himself to the obvious next questions but, frankly, was not too bothered. Walt and I had only met that morning but I already felt comfortable with him and decided it may not be such a bad thing to come clean.

As I've said, I hate bullshit. Believe it or not I prefer total honesty. If bullshit can be avoided, then I'll avoid it. If it is shown to be total bullshit then I'll come clean and admit it. This was a clear cut case of the latter.

Walt's reply came after only a slight pause. He was still looking out of the window but obviously far from asleep.

"Several things really," he muttered. "For one thing Guy Williams was openly gay." Walt stopped to wait for the point to sink in. "You shared a girl friend, Doctor Stevens?" Then: "Gut feeling. You don't quite have the right image for your job. Most of us in this game, the lab ones anyway, are a boring lot, you know. We don't move around that much. You've been around."

Walt now turned to look directly at me. "You're not a doctor. Am I right?"

The guilty deceiver had been found out, so quickly. I wanted to smile but, for a moment, tried to retain the facial expression of an innocent one who was not being believed. But I couldn't hold the expression for long. I looked over at Walt and said: "Yes, you're right."

"Then what the fuck are you up to?"

I looked away from Walt and it was my turn to look at the passing scenery, not that there was much. We were in a late night traffic jam. I then looked back at Walt to find Walt's face very, very close. He was looking straight up at me, his chin resting on his chest and his eyes pointing up - a sweaty and greasy brow with horizontal wrinkles of accusation and inquisition.

"Frankly, Walt," I said, "I am trying to help a friend who has lost something. I can't tell you too much. It's an industrial secret - that sort of thing. But my friend and I think there might somehow be a connection between those two missing characters and what they have lost." I stopped and handed the initiative back to Walt. It was his turn.

"So what's your real name?"

"Just call me Mike, for now. OK? Sorry but I can't divulge more than that about myself. But, listen Walt. I'm trying to be honest here. I could do with some help."

I stopped right there and looked out of the taxi window again. I was doing a bit of my regular self-analysing, asking questions of myself, checking my direction and strategy. What sort of help was I after? And here I was, sat there in the back of a Bangkok taxi about to pour my honest soul out to a competitor of my client. I asked myself if I had gone raving mad and the answer I got back from myself was no. What else should I do at this stage? I still had a good feeling about Walt. If Walt was OK then Biox was OK. Did that make sense? No. But I needed help, some leads, some ideas, some pointers to which way I should go.

61

So I said, "Are you awake enough to share a last beer or something with me, Walt?"

And to prove my judgement was spot on, Walt said, "Suddenly, I feel wide awake again."

CHAPTER 14

It was clear to Kevin Parker that Tunje Fayinke was far too hung up about being monitored by a Big Brother somewhere for any meaningful mobile phone discussion.

"OK, if the CIA and MI6 are definitely on your trail, Tunj, we'd better meet up for a pint. I assume you're not doing anything else today and as you've already had your eighteen hours sleep, how about a pint or two at the One Tun, Tottenham Court Road. Just use a tortuous route from Barnet via Brixton - that'll throw them off. And, by the way, it's your bloody turn to pay.

But, for all his efforts, Kevin had been sitting at the One Tun public house for nearly an hour before Tunje arrived. He was already onto his third pint.

"Just given you up, Tunj. Thought the CIA had got you."

"Sorry, my man. Got delayed. Mine's a pint - best bitter."

They settled into the corner that Kevin had already made his own.

"Now then, what the bloody hell is going on with this guy Mohamed El Badry?" Kevin asked. "I got interrogated like I was one of his staff last night. I never got to give the talk I'd spent hours preparing and he seemed to know more about me than I did."

"Ah, that'll be me," Tunje said. "I told him about the networks."

"So much for your strict security measures, then Tunj? You keep talking about being scared of Big Brother. Well, I actually think you'll find you've been talking direct to Big Brother himself. El Badry is Big Brother personified. "

"Fuck," said Tunje. "But he's keen to do something, Kev. He's Action Man personified."

"Yes, Tunj, but I still don't fully understand what he's up to or why, where he comes from or even the how, if, what or when. Do you, Tunj?"

"Yeh, he's also Big Shot personified. He has this business - pharmaceuticals. Got research places dotted all over. Worth a mega fortune. Got a company in Nigeria, Kenya - all over the fucking place."

" And how do you know all that, Tunj?"

"He told me, Kev."

"So why does your Mister Big Shot personified come asking one Little Shot Tunje Fayinke for all the details of the Malthus Society, chairman of which is a slightly bigger Little Shot called Kevin Parker who's sitting right here next to you. Answer me that, Tunj, please."

"Clinical trials, man."

"Yes, I got wind of something along those lines last night. But you're hardly going to give him the names of all twenty eight members of the Nigerian Malthus Society for him to contact and ask if they'd be interested in helping them with his clinical trials are you, Tunj?"

"Fuck sake, Kev. Show a bit of confidence in me."

"Listen to me, Tunj. This is serious. If I recall El Badry's words from last night it went something like: 'We have been working with Mr. Fayinke to test out a few ideas.' What the bloody hell is that, Tunj?"

"Search me, Kev."

"Then he said something like 'Tunje has a lot to learn, though.' Then something about the need for security because of problems with Islamic militants."

"Ah yes, I mentioned it wasn't easy moving around up there because of Boko Haram."

"And what the bloody hell has Boko Haram got to do with it, Tunj? I'm rapidly losing the plot here."

"Yeh, Boko Haram, the Islamic insurgents, are up in the north of Nigeria. Don't you read the Guardian any more Kev? I think he wants to focus his activity on the north to start with. He may even have already started."

"He's started already?"

"I don't know, Kev. Sorry. But he seemed to have thought it all through. Very professional like."

"You mean a professional eradicator of half a million of your fellow Nigerians?"

"It'll never be that many Kev. He's only at the testing stage."

"Tunj. Listen to me. What the bloody hell is he up to? Do we or don't we know exactly what he's playing at? And who the fuck is he?"

"Yeh, I admit there are a few gaps in our knowledge at present."

"Gaps? A few gaps?" Kevin almost screamed and heads in the otherwise quiet pub turned to look. "Do you realise the potential seriousness of this? Yes, we've been demanding action for years but we've always said we wanted action by legitimate governments not by a fucking individual operating like he's a terrorist who's suddenly found a stock of nerve gas."

"Mmm," said Tunje, "Mmm, I see."

"And when did you see him?" asked Kevin trying desperately to stay calm.

"I got invited to his flat. Kev. Just like you. Nice place."

"Mmm," said Kevin deliberately copying Tunje. "So you beat a path to his luxury pad before me." He took a swig of his beer as he felt the tension inside him growing again. With beer dripping off his lower lip Kevin then said, "He said he wanted me to help him find other people like you to help out. What does that mean?"

"Calm it, Kev. It's nothing, man. All I did was tell him about the website, which he seemed to know about anyway and that if he wanted any help, leave a message or something - anyone interested could get back to him."

"Via whom, Tunj? How is he going to contact Malthus group activists without contacting me. I'm the only one who keeps a rough tab on their personal details and even I struggle to know who most of them really are."

"But that's it, Kev. That's why he asked to see you. He needs contacts - not just Nigeria but anywhere."

"What?" yelled Kevin. "Everywhere?" He took another mouthful of his beer. "Why, Tunj? Why does he need the contacts? What the bloody hell is he up to? Who the fuck is he? What does he really want, Tunj? Because, I can tell you I came away last night one minute so excited I could shit myself thinking we'd at last found a threat we could use for direct action and the next minute coming out in a cold sweat because we, or mostly you, had given away so much that we risked losing all control to some Big Shot Arab who could, unlike you and me, probably pay over the odds for a get out of jail card if it all went pear shaped."

Kevin felt so out of breath now that he swallowed the remaining half of his pint in one go. "Your bloody turn. Mine's a pint - best bitter."

CHAPTER 15

At Walt Daniel's hotel, we were waiting for the bar hostess to finish serving a Jack Daniels whisky for Walt and a coffee for me. We had hardly spoken since the taxi ride back. As soon as the hostess had finished, Walt leaned forward and helped himself from a bowl of peanuts.

"So, what sort of help do you want?" he asked.

"More facts," I said. "Far more than you will be able to give me, Walt. But understanding those disappearances might help. I need a few pointers to the whole scene."

"So, are you FBI or something?" Walt asked, looking me directly in the face. "But you're English aren't you. What's the English equivalent?"

"I'm nothing like that, Walt," I replied. "As I said, I have been asked to investigate a few problems on behalf of another company. There's not a lot I can tell you for reasons of confidentiality. On the other hand there's not a lot I know yet."

I stopped for a moment and helped myself to the same peanuts but decided that peanuts and coffee don't mix. I then went on, deciding to come clean.

"I'm a private investigator, Walt. I specialise mostly in international business problems - industrial espionage, theft of intellectual property , that sort of thing. But I'm new to your type of business. I've read a bit and I know how businesses operate – big ones, small ones. Frankly you must have been asleep if you don't know about outbreaks of disease, resistance to antibiotics, health risks from eating everything from beef to, well, peanuts these days. Everyone from school age up seems to have an opinion on the subject. You only had to sit in on the seminar this morning to know that this business is headlines. A new virus. No known cures. Outbreaks of what looks like the same virus in odd places like Thailand and Nigeria. New drugs, getting more and more expensive to find and produce. Bacteria and viruses getting the better of what is available. Then you get top scientists, scientists with reputations in this field just disappearing."

I paused for a moment. "So what sort of business is it these days Walt? You've been around a while."

Walt looked at me with tired, red eyes. "And why should I tell you anything," he said. "Most likely you're working for a competitor. Is that right? Sure, I've been in the pharmaceuticals and medical technology industry for a long time now. How I ended up on sales God knows, but they seem to need scientists to sell to other scientists these days. Green, raw salesmen straight out of college are not enough. The industry still gets a bad press from time to time but things have improved. I remember a time when there was a lot of media pressure. You know, business being bought by unethical incentives to doctors, that sort of thing. You had it in UK at one time. Then there are a lot of multinationals joining other multinationals. Some of these organizations make annual profits bigger than the income of some entire countries. But a lot of the good research and innovation is still being done by the smaller companies, universities and hospital research departments. Biox is one of them. We've had some successes but it takes a long time to get anything licensed and ready to use these days even though we can sometimes get early licensing for special circumstances."

He stopped. "I'm rambling. What exactly do you want to know?"

"Tell me about David Solomon and Guy Williams. What's your gut feeling, Walt?"

"I dunno. For sure, both were a bit alike. They used to socialise together but don't get me wrong, this was not a liaison as far as I know. Dave was as straight as a die. Both had similar political leanings – that's what they had in common. Environmental issues and such like. That and they were both were from the UK. Both with some weird notions about everyone should get free drugs, everyone was equal and no-one should have a priority on treatments just because they were better off than the next man. Dave was real hung up on this if you got him talking. Fall backs to state run enterprise stuff. It just don't work, man, and everyone 'cept those two knew it."

Walt took a drink from his glass, wiped his mouth and continued. "Course they both had fall outs with Josh Ornstein, the Biox Vice President. But both were good scientists, working long hours and both were productive.

"Dave Solomon was given his top post because he could motivate others. In the lab he would keep his private thoughts to himself. Outside, in the bar or wherever, it was different. I don't know what he got up to. But, first thing, Guy Williams left. Went back to UK. He'd been offered a place at Cambridge where he had started out from. We got news he also disappeared last fall. Dave Solomon just went home one night from the lab - this must be over a year ago now - seemed to spend the night with a girl friend who shared his apartment. Next morning she goes her way, left him at the apartment. What he did after that no-one knows. But he didn't turn up for work that day. His girlfriend called the lab next day to ask if anyone knew where he was. None of us did. We were starting to wonder ourselves. Anyway, turns out he had packed a case after his girlfriend had left, said nothing and just disappeared. His girlfriend was interviewed by the police and I know Josh Ornstein and others went to see her. But - nothing. Apparently she had not sensed anything wrong and was naturally a bit upset about everything. There was a bit of newspaper talk for a while but the company deliberately tried to keep it a quiet and, like everything, life goes on."

Walt stopped again, drained his glass and then said, "And that's about it. None of us have bothered too much about it for quite a while. Any the wiser?" He grinned and slumped back into his seat, clutching his glass of whisky and another handful of peanuts.

"No, but thanks, Walt," I smiled. "It's a slightly clearer picture now. I think you should get some sleep, Walt. Thanks again for the information. If it's all right with you I'll call round by your trade stand again in the morning." I made a move to leave and Walt eased himself out of his chair.

"One last thing, Walt. Do you think these two guys may be together somewhere?"

"I know that's what Josh Ornstein thinks. You bet. It's a possibility. But where? Who with? They're keeping a low profile wherever they are."

I thanked Walt, wished him a good night's sleep and said I'd see him the next morning. Ten minutes later - it was now one in the morning - I asked my taxi driver to take a detour along some side streets. Then I told him to stop. I got out, paid him and then tried the door of the bar. It was still open and I walked in. Dimly lit as usual, the only drinkers left were two Europeans, already well oiled and about to leave. They pushed past me, through the door and went off into the night.

Anna was standing alone behind the bar. I went over, leaned on the stained bar and she smiled at me from a distance.

"Sorry, Anna" he said, "I was busy. But I did try to phone you."

She said nothing but continued to clear the empty glasses. She then came over and stood, hands on the bar, and faced me.

"Where are you staying, now? I called the hotel but they said you'd checked out."

I think I sighed. I know I said: "Come on, Anna, take me to your apartment. Tell me about all about the lady-boy who lives in the next apartment again. I don't want serious, OK?"

"Why not the nice hotel?" she asked. "I have no air conditioning in my apartment. Better in hotel. Where did you stay last night?"

I shrugged. "I was busy. Business. Sorry."

Some six hours later I found I was lying on my back on a low bed, the dim grey light of dawn just appearing through a small corner window covered in mosquito netting. I was watching a large brown cockroach making its way in rapid movements across the top of a wooden closet. On the floor, boxes, cases and other belongings were piled high. Space here was very limited and it had been very hot all night although the fan had helped in directing a breeze of air at the two of us on the bed. I didn't mind.

I leaned over and looked at Anna as she slept as usual with her long black hair across her face. I then turned on my side and put my arm around her. It was even hotter but it felt the right thing to do. No, in actual fact, I couldn't resist it. She stirred slightly but stayed asleep.

Wherever I am, the hours around dawn are my best thinking hours and my biological clock seems to self adjust. I suppose it's got used to all the travelling by now.

I ran over the events of yesterday and wondered if I should talk to Amos Gazit again today. But my thoughts then switched to the noisy bar where Walt and I had left John Wardley and to Walt's comment about the two other drinkers from Livingstone Pharmaceuticals sat opposite us.

Suddenly, I sat up. It happens like that sometimes especially when I've suddenly put a name to a face. I now knew where I had seen that man in the picture in the Livingstone magazine - the man called Mohamed Kader. Mohamed Abdul Kader was an Arab, probably Egyptian, with a string of companies in Kuwait and the Gulf States - mainly agency businesses in baby food and basic medicines for pharmacies. I remembered being in Abu Dhabi about two years ago when the man's picture had appeared in the business section of the Gulf Times. A multi-millionaire, he had just acquired yet another agency, this time for a much bigger, higher profile, international pharmaceutical company and was pictured in the same sort of pose as the one in the Livingstone publication.

If my memory was serving me right, Mohamed Kader's business had spread from the Gulf base and gone international. Many Arab businessmen from his background had stayed local there being, at least at one time, enough money to

68

be made in the Gulf without expanding further afield. But this man was different.

I was sat on the edge of the low bed. The cockroach had vanished and I wondered where. Having now remembered the man's name from the Livingstone photograph, another piece of information from my memory slotted into place. This was, most likely, the same Mohamed Kader I had heard about in Hong Kong recently. There had been a scare caused by some contaminated batches of baby food sold by a distribution company owned by Kader. Health officials had inspected the company that had made the food in Hong Kong but had been unable to decide what had caused the problem. While I was there, the story had been a paragraph on an inside page but it was enough to log itself into my memory.

But, and it is times like this when I like to think my self-analysis comes into play again, perhaps I was wrong. Even if I was right, perhaps it was irrelevant. I lay back onto the pillow and found that Anna was now fully awake and watching me. I had nothing on and the fan was blowing the few hairs on my chest. Whether this was especially interesting for her or not I don't know but she suddenly cried out: "Crazy farang, I thought you'd fallen off the bed. What are you doing now?"

"Sorry. But I suddenly remembered something," I said and I pulled Anna towards me, pressing the side of her cheek onto my chest. If she wanted to get close to my chest hairs then she was now as close as she could get. But I also had another devious little plan. I wanted to say a few things without her staring at me.

"I'm always saying sorry to you, Anna." I said, "But....but, you're very good for me you know?"

That was it. It was rather meaningless, I know. But I'm a bloke, OK? Don't criticise when I'm just getting going. I half regretted it anyway and had second thoughts about continuing. Instead, I hugged her even closer. It was hot, but she stayed there for a moment before wriggling free. She then sat astride me, looking down.

"Yes, I agree. I am very, very good for you," she said and smiled. "You want to shower? I'll make coffee."

She wrapped a towel around her waist and went to the corner of the little room where she sat crouched over a low shelf to find two cups. She busied herself while I wandered into the separate, small tiled area that she called the bathroom. I showered, washed my hair and pondered again on whether I was getting somewhere for Virex or chasing unconnected coincidences. But my thoughts then turned back to Anna. I began to think about her real, much longer name and tried to say it to myself. It was a pretty name and I liked it. But Anna was easier.

As I picked up a towel from the floor to dry my hair, Anna's face appeared through the plastic curtain. "Don't use that. Very dirty. I use that to clean the floor. I find good one."

She returned with a clean towel with pink floral decoration and stood there, still smiling, watching me. As I finished she took my hand and looked up at me, the towel dropping from her slim waist. Then she led me from the shower.

"Drink coffee later."

CHAPTER 16

At the World Health Organisation HQ office in Geneva, the Director General was in a meeting with the South African Minister of Health. It had turned out to be a very formal meeting with pleasantries and dignified acknowledgements of the important status of each other. The politics was obvious. The DG was showing no outward signs of the impatience she was feeling but her adviser, Richard Lacey saw it. He glanced at his own deputy, Claire Sodano to check if she, too, had spotted it.

Besides the DG, Richard Lacey and Claire Sodano, the Minister had brought along his own Deputy Minister and secretary.

"Yes," the Minister was saying, "New infections among mature age groups in South Africa remain high but, most thankfully, new infections among teenagers seem to be on the decline. Regretfully, KwaZulu-Natal rates are still very high and so are those in Mpumalanga but the Government is continuing to pledge funding and support for educational campaigns and so on. We must..........."

The DG was well aware of the dreadful South African statistics. She probably knew the actual figures better than the Minister. But still she remained impassive and listened intently.

Richard Lacey's phone, though, buzzed in his pocket. He quickly glanced at the caller, saw it was his own secretary and knew it as a sign to speed up the meeting if possible as either something important had cropped up or someone else was waiting to speak to the DG. Furtively, he pressed a couple of keys and waited. Instantly, the three letter return message was "SEA". Lacey knew what this meant. The WHO's Regional Director for South East Asia was waiting on the phone.

70

"Excuse me, ma'am - sir" he said to the DG and bowed his head to the Minister. He then got up and left the room.

"Doctor Pradit, Richard." the secretary said as he returned to his office.

"OK, transfer it to my office. Tell him the DG's with a Minister and I'll deal with it."

It took just seconds for Richard Lacey to digest the information from the Regional Director for South East Asia.

"Ah, Richard, ah. It's Pradit. I'm in Bangkok. We're getting some, ah, vital information now on the Bangkok respiratory outbreak. First, ah, viral tests show it's, ah, a new one. They're calling it TRS-CoV. What we need now are, ah, samples from the Nigerian cases to check if there is any, ah, similarity. Any chance of some urgent, ah, what you say, ah, arm twisting?"

"Not much of a hope, Pradit. I'll try but as far as Nigeria is concerned, it sounds as if it's too late."

Doctor Larry Brown had been summoned to Abuja, to meet the US Ambassador next morning. He was a single man but, so far at least, was finding that the evenings dragged. Yes, there had been a few noisy night clubs and a few women who had liked his American accent but, with the stress of Nigerian Airways and Nigerian taxis, he was finding his energy levels after 6pm far lower than he would have liked. Being a doctor he diagnosed physical and mental acclimatisation - patience was needed and his energy levels would soon return to normal.

Alone and sprawled on the sofa with his feet up on the coffee table in an Abuja flat he was able to use when in the capital, he was engrossed in what he knew had become a bad habit - playing with his mobile phone. In fact, he was checking logs and trying to build some sort of contacts list that might come in useful. For a minute or two, he couldn't place the phone call he'd received several days before that showed no caller's number. Then he remembered it had been from Philippe in Kenya. Philippe was sharing a serviced apartment with another Frenchman, a lecturer at the University.

Being bored, Larry tried the Nairobi number.

"Oui, uh, yes. This is Charles."

Larry asked to speak to Philippe.

"Uh, sorry. May I ask who is calling?"

"Larry - a friend - Nigeria."

"Mr Larry?"

"Larry Brown, US Embassy, Abuja. Philippe phoned me several days ago. He had a problem."

"Ah, yes. Philippe is not here. I am worried. I have not seen him for three days. He left on Monday. Took a small bag. He is not at the Hospital either. No-one has seen him. It is very strange. You say he had a problem? Do you know his family in Paris? I think they should know."

Larry apologised for being unable to help. Neither did he have any other contact details. Feeling sure Philippe would turn up somewhere, sooner or later, Larry forgot about it and instead started to think about his meeting with his boss, the American Ambassador. next morning.

CHAPTER 17

I was back at the trade show at the Bangkok Convention Centre and Walt Daniels was standing, arms folded at his stand like a sergeant major watching the troops go by. Had I been a potential customer I think I would have walked on past, but let us not digress into the dos and don'ts of body language when running a successful exhibition.

"Ah," Walt said, "The man of mystery returns. Fancy a coffee?"

I accepted and thanked him for last night. John Wardley then emerged from somewhere, looking jaded from the night before.

"John is feeling a little unwell this morning, aren't you John?"

Wardley nodded and said, "I need to visit the men's room, Walt. I might be gone a while."

"Go ahead, young man," he waved John away. "What goes down either comes back up very quickly or travels further on down. Whichever route it chooses, it'll soon be out." He turned to me. "Told you didn't I? Not sure if he got his end away last night or not but, either way, it hasn't done him a lot of good. Had a job raising him this morning." Walt poured coffee into two plastic mugs.

"Thanks for being so understanding, last night, Walt," I said.

"You mean understanding about John or understanding about you?"

"Me, Walt. But I've still got a few questions. Do you mind?"

Walt took a mouthful of black coffee and swirled it around his teeth. "Go ahead."

"What sort of research was David Solomon doing before he disappeared?"

"New treatments for viral infections as we all were. Specifically, looking at systems that acted on the surfaces of viruses. Certain enzymes were looking useful. He was also an expert on virus replication and was looking at the ways in which viruses changed. It's called 'gain of function' - GOF - research in our jargon. You change something, like a virus, and see how it then behaves. Controversial, but it's what we do. And he had done a lot of work on Influenza before he joined us."

"Did you know his girlfriend?"

"I met her once but he kept his private life to himself. Josh Ornstein spoke to her after he disappeared and, of course the police did. Why don't you ask Josh? You should probably talk to him anyway. Phone numbers are on my business card. Call him. He's away a lot but you can probably track him down."

"How co-operative will he be?"

"He's OK. I should tell him about you, anyway. I owe it to the company."

I thought, briefly, before replying."Perhaps I'll call him and tell him that you and I have spoken. OK?"

"Sure, no problem. Good luck," said Walt. Then, seeing a possible customer approaching, he got up. "Must see to this guy."

I wandered out to the Convention Centre concourse, stood in a corner and, following my hunch of earlier that morning, phoned Hong Kong.

CHAPTER 18

At the American Embassy In Diplomatic Drive, Abuja, Doctor Larry Brown was waiting for his first chat with the American Ambassador since he'd started work. He'd already waited an hour. But at last he was called in.

"Larry, good to see you. Settling in?"

"Yes, thanks."

"I hear you've spent a lot of your first few weeks travelling and in and around Lagos. Good idea. Get a good feeling of the problem there. Up here in Abuja, there's a bit more fresh air to breathe. How do you find it?"

"Lagos, sir? I'm still trying to get my head around the place, let alone travel around it."

"It's a challenge, Larry. That's what it is - a challenge. But you know the US position on healthcare. The only health care worth having here is private. Even these fall short of what we would expect in USA - and the quality of doctors? - makes me want to cry, Larry. Officially it's rated as poor to fair and as for the use of modern procedures - I wouldn't let them treat my dog.

"And as you know most of their medicines are imported from Europe. That's OK, I suppose, Larry, but we need to change that. More stuff needs to come out of USA. That's partly why you're here - to find ways to get our exports in. Met the guys in charge? Takes a while.

"As for their blood supplies - keep a pint or two of your own in the 'fridge, Larry. And never have a car accident out of town. And make sure you're nowhere near the scene if there's a civil disaster. The military couldn't cope and would probably only scrape up their own folk. And don't just stand there watching, Larry. Oh, dear me no. Make yourself scarce Larry - you wouldn't want to get the blame."

"Yes, sir. I'm learning all that," said Larry.

"Too many of them anyway, Larry. Breed like rabbits. Nice rabbits I hasten to say. I like Nigerians, don't get me wrong. Lot of character. I've been here long enough to make a lot of friends. But it's one hell of a mess out there. Shoulder to shoulder - especially Lagos."

"Yes, sir, I noticed."

"Now, Harry. Reason for getting you back up here. I understand you uncovered a bout of sickness up north. WHO are keen to know more. They phoned. What did you find? We need to get back to WHO with something. They're easily panicked."

"Kano, sir. I came across a closed private clinic in a back street. Seems the Kano State government had been trying to clear things up......"

"Told you, Larry. It's all about standards. At last they're taking note. Go on."

"Well, it seems there was a doctor operating out of the clinic who was bringing sick patients in, in the back of a Toyota pick-up and........."

"Christ! Go on."

".....and carrying them out in the same pick-up................"

"Cured, Larry? Cured?"

"Dead, sir."

"Dear Lord. How many?"

"I spoke to a State Government official. They reckon a hundred or more. More than a hundred records found anyway. No names, just numbers."

"Jeez.....go on."

"Seems like they all came in with the same sort of infection - fever, serious respiratory, coughing. That's why I called WHO. Things like that need reporting."

"Dead right, Larry. So have they arrested the doctor?"

"No, he's disappeared."

"Disappeared? Where?"

"No idea sir."

"So what is the State Government doing about it?"

"Nothing. Too busy with the Boko Haram Islamic insurgency. They uncovered another bomb stock yesterday, I understand. It was on CNN..........."

"Yes, I know - we're keeping our fingers crossed, Larry - don't want to get involved but don't want another Iraq or Syria, either. Go on."

"Then I heard about a similar case in Kenya - from a French guy I know. Then there are some cases in Thailand. Have you read the New York Times, today?"

"No time, yet. Why you ask?"

"There was a conference in Bangkok. Could be a new virus. "

"And you, an American, discovered it, Larry?"

"Not exactly, sir. We must leave it to the WHO, but let me know if you start sneezing or coughing, sir."

"Ha! Where's my handkerchief? Keep me posted, Larry."

Later that day, Larry, logged onto the WHO website to find a new 'Disease Outbreak Notification' - a DON - had just been posted.

"The Ministry of Public Health in Thailand has announced three laboratory-confirmed cases of a Respiratory Infection caused by a virus similar to, but not identical to, the Middle East Coronavirus MERS-CoV.

The first case patient was a 42-year-old man from Ayuttaya, the second a 28-year-old man from the same area. The third patient was a twenty one year old woman from Bangkok. All three patients have died.

It is known that at least four more patients have also died following similar symptoms. The Ministry is currently investigating all cases.

WHO is currently investigating reports of an outbreak of a respiratory infections with similar symptoms to the Thai cases in Kano State, Northern Nigeria and one similar case in Kenya. The number of associated deaths in Nigeria is unknown. The Kenyan patient is known to have died.

WHO is monitoring the situation, particularly in relation to identifying the virus."

"So what are the Nigerian Health authorities themselves saying, then?" Larry asked himself out loud. He answered it himself. "Nothing by the look of it."

CHAPTER 19

Kay Choon was an old friend and a client of mine from my early days as an investigator. Standing outside the Bangkok convention centre, I phoned Kay's mobile in Hong Kong. There was a short pause after the ring tone finished and then a strong Chinese accent. "Hey, Choon, how are you?" I said, "Did you get anywhere with your commission problem?"

"Hey, man. Where are you? In Hong Kong again?"

"No, Bangkok. How's it going? Everything resolved now? Did the guy eventually pay up?"

"Got half so far. The money went direct into the company account from a bank in Manila. I don't know who paid but I've been told to expect the rest this week. Thanks for all your help on that. Your own commission will be on its way as soon as we get ours. Is that why you called?"

"No," I admitted. "I needed a favour. You remember that baby food scandal when I was in HK? The supplier was a competitor of yours, right? Are they anywhere near solving the mystery?"

"Ah, Ching Seng," said Kay Choon. "The Public Health people were investigating Sun Foods who made the product but, as far as I know, got nowhere. Why do you ask?"

I had already got what I wanted - the name Ching Seng was what had been missing from my mental filing system. "Big competitor are they?" I asked.

"Not really. They are more into pharmacy supplies, not baby foods. Why?"

"Who owns Ching Seng, do you know?"

"It used to be Ed Ling but he recently sold out to an Arab company. Their chief was here, in person, a while ago, just after he bought them. He is based in Cairo or somewhere. It seems as if it will become part of the Shah Corporation, whatever that is."

"The Shah Corporation." I repeated it for my own benefit. "Do you know anything about the Arab company?"

"Not a lot. I spoke to Ed Ling some time ago. He is retiring soon and he sold out to fund his retirement. He had an incredible offer. More than he thought the company was worth."

"What's the Arab planning to do with Ching Seng, do you know?"

"Change its name for one thing. But it's in dire need of some change. Sales dropped a lot in the last year or so as Ed was losing interest. But what the Arab was thinking of in buying it I can't imagine. Ed had a few good agency lines but I think most of the sales went to other agents selling in China. His margins were small and his local sales were dropping if anything."

"So, no real idea of the Arab's motive for buying?" I probed.

"No, sorry, Dan. You called me just for that? What are you up to now. Into something connected with the Arab?"

"I just thought you might help, Choon, and you just have. Thanks for that. Keep in touch, OK?"

It was just a small piece of the jigsaw, but enough for now. I pocketed my phone and returned to the trade exhibition.

At the Livingstone Pharmaceuticals stand two men were talking to delegates I thought one was the sales manager Walt and I had seen through the dim light of the bar. The other, Greg O'Brian, the owner according to Walt, was nowhere to be seen. I loitered a while until the visitors had moved on and then approached the sales manager. The tall American was quick to introduce himself.

"Sam Marshall." he introduced himself. "Pleased to meet you, Doctor Stevens. "Where are you from, sir?"

"Kuala Lumpur," I replied sticking to my story line. But before the subject could move on or went in the wrong direction I said, "I wanted a word with Greg O'Brian. Is he here?"

"Sure, sitting in on the proceedings - should be here any minute. The conference finishes about now. Can I help you, in any way?"

"No problem," I said, "I'll come back."

Ten minutes later, watching from another exhibitor's stand, I saw O'Brian ushering a small group of doctors towards the Livingstone stand. I loitered a bit more. I was just a few yards away.

This was my first real look at Greg O'Brian, a man destined to affect me, what I was doing for Virex and a lot of other people for quite a while. I put his age at late fifties or early sixties. He was as tall as me at nearly six feet but I'm quite slim. O'Brian was not overweight but a noticeably bigger build than me. He was dressed in an expensive dark suit, white shirt and tie. The black shoes were very shiny. But there were signs of balding amongst the otherwise well groomed and greying hair.

Eventually the visitors moved off and, judged by the hand shaking between O'Brian and Marshall, it appeared that Greg O'Brian had just made a sale and needed to show the younger man how it was all done. I saw my chance and walked over.

"Mr O'Brian?"

"Yeh?" O'Brian tried to see my lapel badge but the smile from his apparent recent success was still lingering. "Can I help you?" He didn't offer to shake my hand.

He hadn't uttered many words but, for me, the accent was recognisable and, with a name like that, perhaps I should have guessed. O'Brian was Irish American.

"I heard about your company. Mr O'Brian," I said. "I'm currently in KL, Kuala Lumpur, you know, and I was wondering if you could help me in some way. I'm going to Nairobi on secondment to the University there in about two months time. I will also be doing a bit of teaching. Someone told me you were setting up there and I was wondering if there would be any chance of some co-operation. I would be looking to give a few students some work experience in microbiology or anything. Expenses paid so it'd cost you nothing. Anything you could offer would be very welcome."

The made up story, invented during my spell of loitering, sounded OK to me so I stood back to test the response.

"So who told you that?" said O'Brian. "And what's your business?" The accent could now be pinpointed to time spent in or around New York. He'd said 'business', too. Jack or Amos Gazit, both scientists, would have said 'what's your interest' or 'what's your field." O'Brian was a man who's thoughts went straight to the bottom line.

"Bacteriology," I said, deliberately ignoring his first question, "But the University is keen to get involved with other local public health matters. There might even be some possible reciprocal arrangements - Kenyan students working in KL?"

Aloud, it sounded pompous but I had said it, so there was nothing more I could do. Clearly, though, O'Brian was not in the least interested and, frankly, I didn't care a toss.

"Well, I dunno," O'Brian said and I could tell he was already being distracted by something or other over my shoulder "It's nothing like that, you know - just a distribution agreement and we don't have plans for research." The Belfast accent was now showing through. He went on: "There is a lab of sorts but we'll use it for product registration work." The distraction behind me, whatever it was, was obvious. O'Brian moved as if to get away. I was ready for it.

"Anyone else who might help me?" I asked.

O'Brian groped inside a top pocket of his dark suit and withdrew a business card. He handed it not to me but to Marshall. "Here, Sam, write down Luther's name, or whatever his name is, and give it to this guy will you. I need to go."

Then, without another word, O'Brian wandered off, clearly conveying the impression that I had been a total inconvenience. O'Brian had far more important things to do than talk to some English prat from Kuala Lumpur. But I got a name, Luther Jasman, and another possible lead. And I'd also met Greg O'Brian although I hadn't shaken his hand.

With that I took a taxi back to the hotel and, en route phoned Colin Asher in London.

Colin had apparently just left his office off the Edgeware Road in London to get a breath of fresh air and buy a sandwich for his lunch when his phone rang.

"Colin, it's me - 007. I need your help again." I said.

"Typical - just as I was en route to lunch. Where the hell are you? In Bangkok again or somewhere else this time?"

"In the vicinity of Bangkok," I replied.

"What's up?" Colin said, the sound of London traffic clearly audible in the background.

"I need some information on a Kuwaiti company, Colin - the usual stuff, subsidiaries, associated companies and the like. Also, I think they may have something going in Nairobi and Hong Kong. Any information on the guy at the top as well. The name is Mohamed Kader so that'll be a challenge - like checking on Smiths and Browns. Can you make a start now? I'll email you some more information right away as I can hear you are not where you should be at this time of day - sat at your desk. "

"That's all very considerate of you, 007. Also very astute. I'm actually strolling towards Marble Arch at present. Can't you hear it? Can't you smell the exhaust fumes?"

"I can certainly hear something, Colin. Just get back to your bloody office will you? The world can't stop just because you're going out for a sandwich."

"So where do I send the stuff?"

"Just hit the reply button on my email, Colin. I'll use the Dan Dare email.

"So does Dan Dare dare to tell me exactly where in the world he is or is it a secret?"

"Bangkok, Colin. Your guess was spot on."

CHAPTER 20

Early morning in Geneva and the Director General of the WHO was, once again, trying to understand the nature of the respiratory infections being reported from places as widely separated as Nigeria, Kenya and Thailand.

What was worrying her was that the symptoms appeared similar yet the cases were so far apart. And the virology information coming out of Thailand suggested something new. But it was her role to stay calm, establish the facts and not make connections where there weren't any. Only after that could the WHO give advice and recommend a plan of action. The problem was the lack of facts.

They had not yet even published a DON (Disease Outbreak Notification) on the website for fear of it being either alarmist or inaccurate. But the media had already got wind of something during the Bangkok Conference and if more scare stories were whipped up, everything could get out of control. So the WHO was already being pressed for comment and would, very soon, need to say something. But what?

There was useful information coming from Thailand although the detail about the virus needed far more work. But the real unknown was the extent of infection in Africa.

The WHO Regional Director for Africa had been advised about some outbreaks of respiratory infection in Nigeria but the DG knew that it was not a priority for him at present. Neither did it appear to be a priority for the Nigerian Health Ministry. And the Regional Director for Africa was in Kinshasa dealing with a yellow fever outbreak in the Congo whilst also trying to cope with widespread publicity that had followed a BBC TV documentary on violence against women in parts of West Africa. Added to his other top responsibilities for improving the health of mothers and children and dealing with all the ongoing problems surrounding HIV/AIDS, malaria and tuberculosis, Doctor Pedro Lopez from Angola was a busy man.

By midday, though, the DG felt more confident that, by collating information from Pedro Lopez, the Nigerian Ministry of Health, the Kano State Government and the original source of information - Doctor Larry Brown at the US Embassy in Lagos - some facts might start to emerge.

CHAPTER 21

These days, Colin has a couple of women in his office to help. Both of them are ex Metropolitan Police but the speed at which Asher and Asher works sometimes astounds me. The SIS could learn a few things from Colin but don't tell him I said so. It was 11.30 pm in Bangkok when I thought I'd check my emails. I don't get many and I was only looking for one. But it was there already and must have been sent around 5 pm GMT. Colin's little team had produced this report within six hours. Some civil service.

"007," the email began. "As promised - see attached - a few notes for which you need to thank Karen in my office for the speed, not me. I've been pounding the streets of London most of the day and night. And it's cold and it's bloody raining. Colin."

I smiled to myself, opened the attachment and read:

"Report on Shah Corporation:

Shah Corporation - established 2001 - international trading arm for Al Zafar Agencies Ltd, a company originally registered in Jordan in 1998. Al Zafar is solely owned by Mohamed Abdul Rahman Kader - nationality uncertain but either Egyptian or Jordanian.

Al Zafar is mainly an agency for a long list of international companies in baby foods, health foods and pharmaceuticals.

The organisation has offices bearing the name Al Zafar in Saudi Arabia, Kuwait, Bahrain, Qatar and Abu Dhabi. Latest figures suggest a profitable company - turnover end of 2009 USD 60 million - but unlikely to be accurate.

Our Kuwaiti agent says Mohamed Kader is a multi millionaire with business interests in several other companies - am trying to obtain more detail.

Shah Corporation was set up as Shah Medicals in Egypt in 2005. No information on the Egyptian company. Al Zafar/Mohamed Kader is involved somehow - perhaps owns it.

Shah Medicals Pte. Ltd is based in Singapore - small - Al Zafar is involved somehow - perhaps owns it - sells to pharmacies in Singapore and Malaysia. Our Malaysian agent says it is unusual for an Arab to set up a company like this in South East Asia. Local manager - David Chua.

Al Zafar/Mohamed Kader recently bought Hong Kong company, Chin Seng Trading - no detail.

Shah Medicals (Nairobi) set up very recently - no detail but thought to be a takeover of a local pharmaceutical distribution company also going by the name Shah, which may have been a useful reason for buying the company. Al Zafar/Mohamed Kader is involved somehow.

Shah Medicals may include Shah Pharmaceuticals, Shah Technick, Shah Africa, Shah Trading - still trying to unravel this.

Our Kenyan agent Jimmy Banda is out of town but his secretary Louise says the company was in the news recently - apparently expanding into manufacture.

Mohamed Kader was there. He was interviewed on the radio. Personal note: Louise says she used to buy hand cream from old Mr Shah's pharmacy and her mother used to buy sore throat pills and other Indian and African remedies. Suggests Shah has long history.

Mr Shah (he was already 82) retired on the proceeds of the buy-out but he was well respected - a prominent pharmacist of the old school - ex President of the Pharmaceutical Society etc.

Other information:

Mohamed Kader may (unconfirmed) also have offices or agents in Jakarta, Bangkok, Jeddah, Cairo, Athens, Istanbul and Lagos, Nigeria.

Al Zafar name is officially registered in several countries.

According to our Kuwaiti agent Mohamed Kader trained as a doctor in Cairo but failed or was thrown out of University (unconfirmed). Started as a medical salesman in Amman before setting up Al Zafar agencies."

I logged off and laid back on the bed.

Colin and his team had, as usual, performed brilliantly but there was not much more about Mohamed Kader than I had already dredged from my memory except, perhaps, a few pointers to suggest the company was more widely spread than I thought and worth more investigation. But I knew I could still be chasing something that was totally unconnected to Virex's problem. Except that - and I kept returning to this - both Amos Gazit and Charles Brady seemed to have suspicions about one or more companies who were at the trade show. Which one? And why?

The origins of Greg O'Brian were also starting to interest me. So what should I do next?

It was now midnight and as I lay there thinking I'd better go and find Anna, the main hotel telephone next to my bed rang and startled me. Hesitant, but thinking it might be Anna checking on my whereabouts, I rolled over and picked it up.

"Daniel?"

"Yes?" I said and immediately recognised the voice of Amos Gazit.

"It's Amos Gazit. Sorry to call you but I think you should know something. I just had a call from Boston - Charles Brady. He told me to inform you, in strictest confidence."

Gazit paused as if uncertain how to put it.

"We seem to have lost one of our own senior researchers. He's a guy called Jan De Jonge. He failed to turn up on Monday morning. We've checked it out and he appears to have just disappeared. I told you we were worried about an inside connection, but this guy was not one of my suspects. He's a Dutch guy. Been with us three years. Worked in my department, for God's sake. Know him well. Nothing to suspect. Single guy. Most worrying thing is he was closely involved in the development of the material we lost. In fact he had been responsible for modifying an electrophoresis technique we were using."

I moved the phone to my other ear and sat up.

"Go on," I said.

"Charles thinks there's a connection. Asked me if you had anything yet. I told him it was far too early. Police not told yet, nor his family in Holland. Reckon to give it a day to see if he turns up. But, I can tell you, we are not confident. There's a chance he might show up but things are too coincidental to be anything else."

Gazit rambled on a while longer, clearly shocked by the news. Eventually he stopped. "Well," he said, "What do you think?"

Gazit was clearly clutching at straws and I, Daniel Capelli was the only straw within grabbing distance. But I had no idea what I thought. It was obvious that Virex did not want any publicity about this. But families and others had a right to know and needed an explanation. That meant the police should know. The public may then get to know. Everyone might get to know.

"I assume you're in the hotel, Amos. Meet me downstairs in the lobby."

I left the room and found Amos Gazit already waiting amongst the potted ferns. Together we walked through the hotel, past the closed souvenir and gift shops and through the restaurant bordering the river where a pianist was still playing in the midst of tables surrounded by a few late diners. We stood at the iron railings bordering the ten feet fall into the river flowing silently below. Gazit leaned on the railings and was the first to speak.

"So what can we do?"

"I really don't yet know," I admitted. "It seems likely there is a connection here with what you've lost but we still can't be sure. There are too many unknowns. It's difficult to know where to start. Tell me, Amos, how much were the police, FBI etcetera involved with the Biox disappearances? Did Biox deliberately keep it quiet for corporate reasons just like you? Did they just adopt the stance of this being adults deciding on a career move somewhere unknown, but nothing suspicious? Is that what you should do with this Dutch guy? For the sake of your financial situation, stay cool, treat it as unimportant - just an ordinary employee deciding to move on? Can you do that?"

"I don't think we should make a big public issue out of it, that's for sure."

"I spoke to Biox about their disappearances," I admitted. I expected a shocked response and got it.

"You did what? Why?" Gazit almost shouted.

"Don't worry. I didn't tell them about Virex or what you have lost, but I had to dig a bit more to find out about their own problems. It was useful but I still haven't got enough to go on." I put my hand on Gazit's shoulder. "Don't worry. Let's take a stroll down there. I like the river at night."

It's true. I like rivers at night. But there are ways to make the experience a little nicer. One way is not to go strolling with a stocky American in his fifties who's sweating with nerves.

We strolled slowly on the raised walkway. Moths and a thick concentration of other exotic insect life circled the streetlights. Water slopped against the wall beneath us adding to the throaty roar of late river taxis drifting across on the warm, windless air. Am I getting the mood?

"Tell me more about this Dutch guy," I said. "Putting the problem of theft aside for a moment, can you think of any reason why he should suddenly take off like that?"

"He was just a very quiet guy," said Amos Gazit. "Like I said, he'd worked for a Dutch pharmaceutical company for two years and joined us on a recommendation - poached if you like - by consultants we sometimes use. He was first rate. He had already done some virology in Boston before going back to Holland. Then he came back again. As I said he worked under me. Obviously he knew a lot about what we were looking for. Spent a lot of time getting some of the extraction and purification techniques right. Used to work late, often in the lab after most everybody else had gone. I was often still there of course and we used to chat a bit. Mostly about work. He was always interested in the business side. Often checking with me on the time scale we had been set. Not that there was a fixed one, but it showed his concern for quick results."

Gazit paused. He looked across the river but was seeing nothing.

"I'm beginning to see he may have had another reason. He also used to talk politics a bit. But we all do, don't we? He didn't like the way Europe was going.

85

Too centralized for him. Kept saying that Britain was the only place that seemed to think things through and ask questions. There were too many people, the world was overpopulated. He was a biologist who cared about world resources but conversations were never long. Sort of short bursts."

"Did he know the two guys from Biox?"

"Yeh, I was wondering if you were about to ask that. Thinking about it, the answer is yes - probably. We were all in and around Boston a lot. The scientific community is quite close. And we all used to meet up at congresses and so on but I don't think it was anything more than that. On the other hand I don't know what he did in his spare time. He liked to go to the gym a lot. He played tennis at a club that several other staff frequented. Other than that work was his main interest. He had written a few papers on Herpes virus with some people from the company in Holland. Useful for what he was doing for us but only because understood the research methods. I think he also mixed with students from Boston University - but where is the harm in that? He probably crossed paths with David Solomon who I know also spent time at the University. He used to complain about pay a bit but I can't think why. He was well paid, like everyone at Virex although he did ask me about part-time lecturing once. I told him to forget it. Focus on his real job."

"So, why would he go? Sounds a bit like politics with the two from Biox but why has your man gone. Can you pin it down more firmly?"

"I really can't say. Unless he was promised a lot of money to reveal what we were up to." He paused. "Yeh," he continued as if he might have hit on something, "Money might be the reason. He genuinely seemed to think he was worth a lot more than we were paying. He was being paid more than he would have got in Europe and the cost of living in the US is no higher. I must admit I couldn't understand him on that point."

"So, money," I concluded, "It was a real hang up of his was it?"

"Real hang up? Not sure. An issue? Maybe. But maybe there was something else biting him."

Gazit turned to face me. "Whatever, Jan's problems were, if this proves to be connected to the other disappearances, then I think you must agree, there is something amiss here. These guys are going somewhere and, unless they're dead, they are going to surface somewhere, sometime. But where? Who is it? What's going on?"

Because of Gazit and his problem I had spent another night in the hotel and not spent it with Anna. Gazit and I finished chatting around 2pm and after I'd phoned Anna to say sorry again I had lain on the bed thinking. I then fell asleep fully dressed. But at six thirty I was awake, showered, dressed and so hungry that I called room service and ordered a full American breakfast. As Virex were paying I didn't give it too much thought.

But by seven thirty I had checked out and was in a taxi heading for Anna's side street apartment. At eight I knocked on the door of room 118 and waited. The door was unbolted from inside and opened just a fraction on the chain. Anna's sleepy eyes peered through the small opening.

An hour later, we were lying on the low bed, she, on her elbows, peering down into my eyes.

Now, let me explain that I am not always the tongue tied, apologetic wimp you may think. Now and again, conditions being perfect, I can perform like any male lead in a black and white, post-war film drama. I don't need a neat, greased-up haircut, a dark suit or a cigarette and my leading lady does not need to be wearing long, flowing skirts, petticoats and red lipstick and to be smoking her cigarette on a silver holder. But I can still talk like Cary Grant if I want to.

We were lying on Anna's bed and, at the height of my dialogue, two cockroaches had been watching and, presumably, learning. I had started cautiously enough but soon got into the swing. The start was all about my business, the travelling and the risks I sometimes took when investigating criminal activity. It was very romantic.

"Perhaps, Anna," I said, finally, "I should not be telling you this but I need to share my life with someone."

That's when my nerves started. Could I trust her I asked himself. But you had to trust someone. Could I mix my business with a companion and share my most private feelings? Could I make it work? Finally, I said, "So, will you come with me?"

And in saying that I knew I had made one huge decision. Anna fell onto my chest, the long hair flowing over me. "When are you going?"

"Today." I whispered in her ear.

Anna sat upright, the smile first evaporating then replaced by an expression of surprise and doubt mingled with excitement. "Today?" She repeated it to check what she had heard.

87

"Yes, I need to buy air tickets. You won't need a visa for the first part. But I need to go today - later this evening."

Anna looked at me. She was probably still trying to fathom me out. I knew I'd been a bit of a challenge. But I think it went OK. Anna's life is beautifully simple. Mine is just too damned complicated. But perhaps that is the attraction. "I must go now, Anna," I said. "I've got a lot of things to do today. Do you want to come with me?"

She smiled and nodded energetically. For once she said nothing. But no words were necessary. I was convinced.

"Then, while I'm out, go, pack your case. Take enough for a few days. Tell the apartment office you are going away for a while. I'll come for you around six this evening."

"Where are we going?" Anna asked.

"Singapore," I said.

It was late evening when we arrived at Changi Airport, Singapore. After going through my normal routine of buying a new phone and local SIM card, we took a taxi to a hotel I often stay at just off Orchard Road. Tired from a long day, we both slept soundly until at six, my usual waking time, I heard the rustling sound of a newspaper being slipped under the door.

Although given second place to a speech by the Singapore Prime Minister, the other front page story was about the Bangkok Conference. And, just to prove Amos Gazit's comment about a media frenzy the headline read: "New Influenza Fear - WHO concerns." Below it was a small photograph of the Thai speaker Doctor Vichai.

I showed it to Anna. "So, why did you go to this meeting?" she asked.

It was a good question. I had attended the meeting at the suggestion of Charles Brady, Virex's President. But why? I still had no clear idea except that Brady had suggested it and that I still harboured a gut feeling that there was something that I hadn't yet been told. I re-read the article and then the quote from the WHO:

"............WHO is currently investigating reports of an outbreak of respiratory infections with similar symptoms to the Thai cases in Kano State, Northern

Nigeria and one case in Kenya. The number of associated deaths in Nigeria is unknown. The Kenyan patient is known to have died................."

So, no longer was it just about Thailand but Nigeria and Kenya. This was news to me.

Breakfast over and with Anna still apparently content to look out of the window of the twelve story hotel window at the panoramic view of Singapore in daylight, I decided to make a few phone calls. Shah Medicals was top of my list. I asked to speak to David Chua.

"Sorry, he's out on a sales visit. Who is calling please?"

I'd quite liked being Doctor Mike Stevens for two days so I decided to continue. "My name is Mike Stevens, from the UK. When will he be back?"

"I think about one hour. Can I ask him to call you?"

"No, thank you. I'll call him.."

I then called another number. This time, the accent was clear and definitely English "Good Morning, British High Commission."

"Good morning. May I speak to Caroline - trade and investment - please?"

"Can I have your name, please?"

"It's a private call. Just say it's Rupert Bear from the Henley Regatta. She'll understand."

The response was quick. "Rupert Bear uh! Still wearing your little scarf in this weather are you? Hang on a moment."

There was a minute of silence and Anna again looked at me. I was still smiling at Anna when a plummy, female English voice answered.

"Is that really you Rupert, dear?"

"Hello, Caroline. How are you? Still keeping the wheels of British industry spinning from your tropical hideaway?"

I put the phone on "speaker" for Anna to hear.

"How nice to hear from you, dear. It's been so long. Thought you might have caught your death when you fell out of the boat last time we met. Too much champers you know. Not good for a man with your weak will. Bit warmer here, though, isn't it? Where are you, darling? In town are you? Coming to see me?

Hope so. What's it this time? Catching big time foreign fraudsters again are you? Or is it something more refined?"

"I'm holed up here for a day or so but wondered if you could fill me in on a couple of local companies," I replied. "Medical industry to be precise. Not normally my speciality, but then, what is, you might ask. Please don't ask me why I'm into this particular business at the moment - I don't want to have to spin you too many yarns. Can I pop in and see you? Only keep you a few minutes."

"Better still, Rupert, dear, you can take me to lunch. Just had a cancellation. Seems they don't want me at their official lunch today after all. I'm beginning to put that sort of thing down to budget constraints so that I don't feel too personally insulted."

"Love to. Shall I pick you up or meet you somewhere."

"Meet me at the Mandarin Hotel, OK? Say about one."

"I'll be there. See you later."

I turned to Anna and smiled again. "I shall be out for lunch today. I'm taking a lady out."

"Who did you talk to?" Anna asked, with just a hint of hurt. "And why does she call you Rupert?"

"She's someone I know, Anna. Don't worry. This lady is fun for ten minutes and then she's hard work. But she might help." She calls me Rupert because it is her nick name for me."

"Nick name?"

"She gets confused about what my real name is."

"Yes," said Anna. "I understand."

An hour later I tried Shah Medicals again. This time, David Chua was there.

"My name is Michael Stevens - I'm from UK - an export agency - Asher & Asher. We work for a group of companies manufacturing over-the-counter medicines for marketing in South East Asia. I'm here to meet some local distributors for possible co-operation."

"We may be - very competitive lah - not so easy, lah. What have you got? It needs to be better or cheaper than the competition, lah."

"I can't say much at this stage," I said, "but the group is quite big - industrial chemicals, toiletries, that sort of thing - big European market share, also in the Middle East - now looking towards South East Asia."

I paused, waiting for a sign of interest from the other end of the line. "We might be," David Chua said, "We are just getting organised with a better sales team in Singapore and Malaysia."

I finally fixed my meeting for late afternoon at the Hyatt Hotel and, business side of things organised, asked Anna if she'd like to go shopping. "You might need more than one bag of clothes," I said, realising that I, myself, could, when necessary, live out of a single bag for weeks on end. And, frankly, I have never gone shopping in my life.

CHAPTER 22

Kevin Parker and Tunje Fayinka were still sitting in the One Tun public house in Tottenham Court Road in London. It was nearly 4pm and they had been analysing the motives of Mohamed El Badry for nearly three hours and had still got nowhere.

Kevin looked at his watch but could barely see it. He was on his sixth or seventh pint already although he had lost count. But he already knew that Tunje had apparently left most of his loose change in his Barnet flat and his, Kevin's, bar tab was mounting up.

Kevin had also not wanted to pay for another hotel for the night. He either wanted to go back to Bristol on the train or get Tunje to at least offer to put him on the floor of his flat for the night.

"I need a piss, Tunj. Then I must make a move. Liverpool are playing tonight."

"Liverpool? Liverpool? That is some genuine crap team, Kev. Come up and watch Arsenal some time."

"Why, Tunj? Are you offering me a seat in the main stand, paid for out of the salary Barnet College pay you?"

"Nah, mate, I meant watch them on my wide screen, like you do Liverpool."

"For your information, I do not possess a wide screen, Tunj - it wouldn't fit in my bloody flat. Anyway, I need a piss. I won't be a minute." Kevin wobbled his way towards where he thought the toilet was.

He was gone for perhaps slightly more than a minute but when he returned, Tunje was reading a crumpled newspaper someone had left on the next table.

"Seen this, Kev?" Tunje's arms were outstretched reading something on one of the inside pages.

"What is it, Tunj?" Kevin asked, impatiently.

"Shh," said Tunje, "I'm reading."

While Kevin sat with his arms folded, Tunje's black eyes raced left to right, left to right. Then they moved up as if he was now reading the next column. Kevin had had enough.

"Right, I'm off," said Kevin and stood up, knocking the table as he did so. Tunje's empty beer mug rattled. Kevin's was still half full and stayed upright and rock steady.

"Here," Tunje said. "Before you go, check it out, man. This proves what I've been saying. I reckon Big Shot El Badry has already started his clinical trials."

"What?" Kevin said. "Give it here."

"Just a minute, man. Nearly finished."

Kevin sat down again and then snatched the paper.

"Don't you know it's rude to read at table? Didn't mummy Fayinke teach you any table manners?"

Tunje shrugged. Kevin read.

"What do you think, Kev?"

"I haven't finished yet. Quiet. "

"Now what do you think, Kev?"

"Bloody hell," said Kevin. "But who's to say El Badry has got anything to do with it?"

"Nigeria, Kev. A hundred cases in Nigeria says the WHO. Aren't you able to read or do you want me to read it to you? Didn't mummy Parker ever read to you in bed?"

"Shut up about my mother, Tunje. She had ten others to deal with."

"Sorry, Kev, but a hundred cases of an unknown respiratory disease in northern Nigeria? Doesn't that sound like too much of a co-incidence?"

"Mmm," said Kevin, "I know what you mean."

Both of them were quiet for a few moments. Tunje looked into his empty beer glass. Kevin stared at the ceiling thinking about what he'd read but also hoping Tunje would not want another drink.

"I think we need to keep this to ourselves a while, Tunj," Kevin finally said. "We haven't got any proof of a link. It might be just you and your vivid imagination. I'll dig around a bit - see if any of my networks have had similar approaches. But I still don't understand what the bloody hell a rich Arab like El Badry would want with the Malthus Society. It still bothers me, Tunj."

"To put the blame onto us?" said Tunje thoughtfully.

"Christ," said Kevin, "I hope not. If so both you are I already implicated, Tunj. Perhaps he videoed us at his apartment. You always said we needed to go careful."

"Yeh, that's still my gut feeling. Anyway, I got to go. I'm meeting some mates in Watford."

"Watford branch of the Malthus Society is it Tunj?" said Kevin already resigning himself to getting the train back to Bristol as well as settling the bar bill. "Perhaps El Badry will turn up."

CHAPTER 23

Twelve thirty, shopping done and with Anna sorting bags, I left the hotel. I walked down Emerald Hill in hot, midday sun, past the renovated and picturesque old Chinese houses, back onto Orchard Road where we had just shopped, then the short distance to the Mandarin Hotel. Inside the darker, air conditioned lobby I found a seat where I could see but not be seen. Before long, I saw the tall, gangly form of Caroline Mason coming my way. But despite my efforts, she had clearly seen me first.

Caroline always walks as if she is on a long distance hike. I can barely keep up with her. On this occasion, the long strides made her flowery skirt billow in the passing air. Today she had topped the skirt with a white blouse tied with a black bow at the neck. In her hand was a brown handbag cum briefcase, which she dropped noisily onto the table by my side.

I rose to my feet and held out my hand but it was quickly apparent that Caroline planned a public display of affection in the form of a kiss. She planted it firmly on my left cheek, followed by a similar one on my right one. She also took my hand.

"Rupert, my dear, how lovely to see you. Long time. How are you?"

"Hello, Caroline. It's good to see you too. Come and sit down or would you prefer to go straight through for a gin and tonic."

"I think a G and T sounds splendid. Mustn't have too many though. Got a few things to do when I get back." She laughed and, taking my hand again, pulled me towards the reception desk of the restaurant. The pretty, young Chinese girl asked if we had a reservation.

"Yes, dear," said Caroline, "For two. I phoned earlier. Caroline Mason. Table by the window. Thanks."

We were escorted to Caroline's preferred window table, ordered gin and tonics to be delivered at once and took the proffered menus. Caroline had, as I expected, plenty to say.

"So, what have you been up to. I know I shouldn't call you Rupert but it suits you so much. You do remember don't you what a fabulous day that was. Pity about the bloody British weather - spoils everything - can't plan a thing - but that didn't stop us did it?"

I cringed inwardly but let Caroline continue.

"Heard you were involved behind the scenes in the Stewart Insurance fraud. Got a bad bit of publicity in the end didn't he - Stewart I mean - but I never really understood what you actually did. Was it listening devices or plain old fashioned hiding under the bed in the Frankfurt Sheraton?" She laughed again and, as usual. I felt it necessary to join in.

The gin and tonics arrived and Caroline's enthusiasm in toasting our renewed acquaintance was almost enough to smash the crystal glasses. By now I felt it was my turn to say something. "It's nice to see you also Caroline. I only flew in last night and I made you my first meeting."

"Flatterer!"

"I was at a conference on Infectious Diseases in Bangkok. Have you seen the papers in the last couple of days? Quite a stir."

"Scary - at least you could have some fun before catching AIDS. So what or who sent you there?"

"A client - the trade show was useful to meet a few people - I'm now following up some things that cropped up while I was there. That's why I wondered if you could help, Caroline - in the name of trying to ensure industrial harmony around the globe - British fair play and all that."

"You are a naughty boy, but I'll try."

The waiter arrived for our order and Caroline took a pair of thick rimmed glasses from her bag. "Sign of old age I'm afraid, dear. Catches up even with the sprightly - can barely read anything unless its inches from my eyes."

She put them on, scanned the menu and then said, "I must admit I'm a bit of an old bore really - always want the same thing - what about you?" she put the menu down, removed her glasses and looked at me.

"So, what are you having?". I thought I'd check before committing myself. I'm none too fussy about food. I'll eat anything I've seen others eating.

"Fillet steak, they do a good one, chips, the works really."

"Very oriental, I must say - I'll join you."

Order taken, Caroline said, "So, what can Her Majesty's services do to help?"

"Easy really," I said. "Some information on a local company - name of Shah Medicals. It was set up a few years ago by an Arab gentleman so I understand. So, information on the company background - anything really."

Caroline nodded but before she had a chance to say anything I asked another. "There's something else, Caroline. Is Clive Tasker still in Jordan? You remember someone mentioning him back in the UK? I haven't been to Amman for about two years but he was due to retire last time we spoke."

"Good old Clive," said Caroline. "Yes, retired at Christmas - got a card - retired to Cyprus. He knew it well when he was in Beirut and Jordan. He even put his address on the card. Do you want it?"

"Please," I said.

And so the conversation continued until: "So where are you staying, Rupert, dear? I could drop the stuff around if you like."

"Secret, Caroline. Running incognito as usual. But I bet with your connections you could soon track me down. Please don't try. Innocent British citizen trying to earn an honest crust by tracking down dishonest foreigners and all that. You know me well enough to know that I sometimes need a bit of cover. Better I call you tomorrow morning if I may. Meantime, I'd be very grateful for anything about this Shah Medicals company. Can I call round at the High Commission tomorrow morning. I may well move on from Singapore tomorrow afternoon."

Later, after lunch and after Caroline had drunk the best part of a bottle of red wine, we made our way out onto Orchard Road again. Caroline found it necessary to give me another big kiss, said "Until tomorrow", and beckoned a taxi. I watched her fall in, catch her bag in the door, open it again to retrieve it, shut it once more and, with a wave, through the rear window disappear into the traffic. I admit to still having a soft spot for Caroline.

It was now seven thirty and I was in the Singapore Hyatt Hotel. I had no difficulty in recognising David Chua. The small, middle-aged, Chinese man wore a whitish shirt with a greasy-looking, loose grey tie around the open neck. He shuffled in looking worried and stressed. He was clearly looking for someone. I tapped him on the shoulder. "David Chua?"

"Ah yes, yes - sorry, sorry - so late, lah - too many problems today - everything go wrong. Mr Stevens is it? My card."

"Pleased to meet you. Thank you for seeing me. Would you like a drink - tea or something?"

I apologised that I couldn't reciprocate with my own business card to offer. "So sorry - I ran out of business cards in Manila."

Over Chinese tea, served in delicate white cups sitting around a low, glass-topped table, we talked although I was as deliberately vague as I had been on the phone earlier until: "My client thinks the hand cleansers and antiseptic soaps are likely to be of most interest here. Would this fit into your marketing plans?" I was very pleased with the way that came out. It made me sound like a genuine business consultant.

"Ah, yes, ah," Chua replied encouragingly. He then seemed to relax. "We have grown a lot in the last few years. We now have a new branch in Malaysia and are a market leader in some products. It's taken a lot of work, lah. Singapore, Malaysia very stressful you know." He drained his small cup of green tea with his still sweaty hands. Then he went on: "But I need more information, lah - cannot do anything without information."

Just like any genuine business consultant I was ready for this. "No problem," I said, "If you can give me more information on your organisation, I'll report back and we can take matters further. We are keen to move ahead quickly with the right partner."

It was quite clear that David Chua had not come with anything in written format but he was definitely the man in charge locally. I saw through it all. But there was still a bigger boss somewhere who might think well of him if he could pull off a good deal. I was now pushing him for the missing background.

"OK, lah. I started as a salesman for medical companies - then worked for Suzuki Pharmaceuticals - good business, lah, but the company decided to open their own office here - at same time, lah, I met Mr Kader - he owns Shah Medicals - he was in Singapore looking for agencies to buy up - very wealthy man, lah.............."

David Chua's tongue was loosening. I ordered more tea.

".....well, lah, Mr Kader asked me if I wanted to set up on my own - I said of course, lah, who doesn't, lah? Well, to make a long story shorter, he put up some money - we found an office - he sent me some stock and we started - all very good business, but you have to work hard here, lah - I've now got three salesmen here, two in Malaysia and several sub distributors. I opened our office in KL late last year. Very fast, lah. "

Chua looked genuinely out of breath with the speed of things. He looked up from his sixth cup of tea apparently wondering if that was sufficient. It was. But unfortunately for the poor guy I now had some additional questions.

"Your business looks very compatible with what we are looking for - right size, right set up - we could grow things together. How are you placed for raising money for investment in a venture like this? Bear in mind my client is a well established brand in UK and Europe. "

David Chua looked impressed but fidgeted in his chair. The second lot of tea was finished. "Ah yes, of course, lah - I would need to sort things out - talk to Mr Kader, lah."

"Tell me a bit about Mr Kader," I said noticing that David Chua was showing no signs of being under any instructions to keep quiet.

"He's from the Middle East. Offices all over. He recently set up in Hong Kong and he has a lot of business interests in Africa and other places. Rich man, lah, very rich."

"Is Al Zafar part of his organisation?" I asked innocently.

"Oh yes - forgot to say, lah. Mr Kader owns Al Zafar. It's a holding company. Very ambitious man is Mr Kader. Wants us to take on many new products. I keep telling him - slow down, lah - we are not ready for all this yet. But he is very keen, very keen. Push, push."

I now saw another opportunity. It was what I call, for my own purposes, the negative prompt. I use it often.

"So, perhaps our proposal may not be so interesting for him if he has ambitions in another direction."

David Chua clearly saw this might be the case. I pushed him further. "If Mr Kader has plans for marketing highly specialised drugs in Singapore would he have told you?"

Chua's look changed to one of even greater disappointment.

"Ah, maybe no. He keeps many things to himself. But I know he has some big plans in Africa. He is setting up some sort of research facility there, which is somehow connected to his business in Egypt. Very complicated but he is a very busy man - a lot going on - very dynamic."

There was a moment's pause as I allowed David Chua to self digest what he'd just said. The positive pause. Then I pushed for action. "So, how do we proceed with this?"

David Chua glanced up from his pondering of the tabletop and empty cups. "I'll try to speak to Mr Kader or email him. He likes to be involved with things like this." He said it proudly as if wanting to dispel any thoughts that he was desperate to earn a medal from Kader for his efforts. I encouraged him - the positive support.

"Which way would you take the company if you owned it outright?" I asked.

David Chua looked directly at me as if suspecting I might have something else up my sleeve that might be to his financial advantage.

"I think we should stay in the business we know," he said. "Expand and grow slowly, lah. We've not done badly since I started. What you propose may be very interesting. but I need more information."

It was enough. I moved as if to stand up and that seemed to loosen David Chua up. His face visibly relaxed. Always try to finish on a lighter note - it is often the only part remembered.

""So, life here still as hectic as ever?" I said, looking around the hectic hotel concourse. David Chua seemed relieved at a less searching question. He even sat back in his chair.

"Sure, lah - everything still big pressure. But we got to maintain kiasu or we wouldn't be Singaporean would we?" At last he chuckled slightly and lifted his cup to his lips only to find it bone dry. But then he said something which I was to remember over and over again during the coming weeks.

"Just too many people here," he said looking around. "Singapore is very prosperous but too many people, too crowded, too much stress, not enough time to relax." Then, he fidgeted again and glanced at a bare wrist as though it normally bore a watch. "You must excuse me, Mr Stevens, got to go now. The American I was supposed to meet here was delayed. All my schedule now big problem, lah."

"Americans, all the same, eh?" I grinned and then added, "Is he on his way in or on his way out?"

"Arriving late from a conference in Bangkok. Infection Control. You read about it? On TV news this morning, lah. In newspaper also."

"Oh, yes," I said. "I read about it. The American - another supplier of yours?"

"Livingstone. You know them? Another rich man - Greg O'Brian. He's booked to stay here. I promised to pick him up from Changi. You know the company?" he asked again.

"The name is familiar," I said, although my tone in no way revealed an urgent need to glean as much information as quickly as possible. "Livingstone Pharmaceuticals?"

"Yes. It's linked to Al Zafar somehow. I usually meet their salesman, Mr Marshall, but this time the CEO himself is coming."

"So, what do they want, any idea?"

"Mr O'Brian and Mr Kader have a project in Africa but I'm really only interested in products such as yours, Mr Stevens."

I had, over the course of our conversation, noticed a change in his tone. David Chua now seemed to be falling over backwards to find reasons not to follow Kader into new ventures. I got up from the table, retrieved the bill lying under the tray and beckoned the waitress. "Thank you very much for your time. I'll take care of this and I'll be in touch as soon as possible."

CHAPTER 24

Kevin Parker arrived home at his Clifton, Bristol flat with a headache from the afternoon in the One Tun with Tunje Fayinke. He was also feeling hungry. No food had passed his lips since the half-eaten burger at lunchtime. But, knowing he wouldn't be able to sleep if he turned in, he walked to a late night local Indian take-away, bought himself a chicken biriani and rice and, as he sat on the kitchen floor eating it, logged onto the internet on his laptop.

He checked a few emails, deleted them all and then logged onto the WHO, Geneva website. And, yes, there it was - a so-called Disease Outbreak Notification - a DON. And, just as he and Tunje had read earlier in the discarded and crumpled copy of the Daily Mail, there was the confirmation.

"...........WHO is currently investigating reports of an outbreak of respiratory infections with similar symptoms to the Thai cases in Kano State, Northern Nigeria and one case in Kenya. The number of associated deaths in Nigeria is unknown. The Kenyan patient is known to have died.................."

The only difference was that the Daily Mail seemed to know the deaths in Nigeria amounted to over a hundred. The WHO, on the other hand, seemed unwilling to put a figure on it.

Kevin, spooned in the last mouthful of chicken biriani, wiped his mouth and then logged onto his Malthus Society website.

Nothing much had happened since the day before. There was only one message from the Boston USA group announcing their next meeting and giving details of a lecture on drought in Sub Saharan Africa to be given at Boston University. Someone calling themselves "day-owl" - Kevin had no idea who it was - had left a message. "Don't go - let there be drought" Kevin smiled.

Using his own sign of "Thalmus" he typed: "Check out WHO DON. Anyone know anything?"

Then he logged off.

The American Embassy in Nigeria was based in Abuja, but Lagos was still the centre of US Commercial Services. Larry Brown, a fresher in consular circles, was still struggling to understand how, as a black, American doctor, he could best serve the commercial services team.

It was only mid morning and he was already staring out of the window looking for inspiration. Yes, he had the job description which provided for a good deal of freedom to do what he liked and he also had the salary. What Larry was missing was focus. Not only that but his energy had started to return and Larry wanted some action.

Behind him, staring at computer screens, sat three commercial specialists - Nigerian nationals who were divided up into industry sectors and did their best to answer queries from US companies, guide them through Nigerian bureaucracy and organise meetings and trade shows.

On Larry's healthcare sector was Joseph Eke. But Joseph also had franchising, printing and consumer electronics to deal with and Joseph had come straight out of University with a degree in IT. Larry already knew that Joseph only liked the consumer electronics part of his job. He was also probably angling for a future job with an American IT company.

"Joseph," Larry called out, still looking out of the window and with his back to the room, "Can't we run a healthcare trade exhibition some time? The Ambassador says he wouldn't even send his dog to see a doctor in Nigeria. Can't we bring in a few good US companies, focus on the private sector, show them some decent equipment, proper medicines. Perhaps even bring in an American vet or two?"

Larry turned. As it seemed Joseph had not heard him, he coughed deliberately and pretended to be choking. At last, Joseph and the two other commercial specialists looked up.

"Got any medicine for a bad cough, Joseph? Do I need a chest X ray? Was that a first sign of TB? What hospital should I go to in Lagos and know I was being taken good care of?"

Joseph grinned over the top of his computer screen.

"Did you hear me just then, Joseph? Jo?"

"Yes, Larry, you said something about trade exhibitions."

"Good man. So what about it?"

"They don't like coming here, Larry. It's not a priority. They prefer to focus on China, Brazil, Russia and India. Nigeria is not on their radar."

Larry turned to look out of the window again but then turned just his head around. Joseph had already returned to staring at his screen. "That's exactly what I thought, Jo. Carry on."

Two minutes later, Larry coughed again. "Got a decent directory of US pharmaceutical companies, Jo? And please don't point me towards Google."

Joseph pointed towards a book-shelf with his thumb whilst still staring at his screen.

Larry found the directory, went across the room for a cup of water from the machine, sat behind his allocated desk and, in an hour, had circled in red pen, thirty US healthcare companies. Then he checked their websites.

At five, Joseph and the others got up to go home. Larry, with no particular place to go, stayed. He sent a few emails, telling the companies who he was and what he wanted. Then he went out for a coffee and came back to check for any replies. As there weren't any and it was still midday or earlier in the USA he went through his list again and directly phoned companies in New York, Atlanta, San Francisco, Los Angeles and Boston.

Finally, by 9pm Larry had some names.

CHAPTER 25

Anna was watching a Tom and Jerry cartoon on TV when I got back to the hotel. I'd seen it before and knew the outcome so I sat with a piece of hotel notepaper trying to make sense of what I currently knew. It wasn't much.

I wrote down all the individual names and company names and tried connecting them with hard lines or dotted lines. There were still too may gaps. I wrote the name Mohamed Kader and connecting lines to a list of his company names that was becoming longer and longer. I wrote the name Livingstone Pharmaceuticals and then Greg O'Brian. Already I didn't he like the man but knew I mustn't let this get in the way just yet. I drew a thick line between Livingstone, Greg O'Brian and Mohamed Kader.

Then there was Ching Seng, Hong Kong, owned now by Shah Corporation or Al Zafar, which meant Mohamed Kader. There was Shah Medicals, Singapore - owned by Mohamed Kader through Al Zafar and O'Brian was probably in Singapore right now talking to David Chua.

To me it looked as if some sort of distribution network was being created. Nothing wrong with that, of course, but the parties did not have quite the sophisticated look of other multinational organisations I have dealt with. This one didn't look right and didn't smell right.

And, if my intuition was right then I should have been able to draw a line between the Al Zafar/Kader/Livingstone group and the Biox/Virex group but I couldn't. And so I was right back to the gut feeling that there was something that Charles Brady and, or, Amos Gazit had not yet told me.

Short of any further inspiration, I drafted an email to Colin in London.

"I know it's Saturday but I'm assuming you were not planning to watch that dismal team of yours - Chelsea FC - today. On that assumption, can I please have a breakdown (usual stuff) on the following: Livingstone Pharmaceuticals and their C/E Greg O'Brian. It's urgent, of course..Yours, Dan Dare."

I hit "send" and lay back to watch Tom chasing Jerry. But as I said, I'd seen it before and knew how it ended. Jerry won. And I was hungry.

"Lunch, Anna? I've got no other lady to take out today."

"Mmm," said Anna. "Thai, please."

Two thirty, Thai lunch in Clarke Quay over and it was time to meet Caroline again. I got the taxi to drop off Anna at the hotel and then went on to the British High Commission. In the commercial section I asked for Caroline and she emerged carrying a thin, buff coloured folder.

"Come," she beckoned to me. "Sorry I can't give you a kiss here, dear. Not the thing to do with pictures of Her Majesty looking down on one. Shame really. Had a bit of a hangover last night."

"So, did you dig up anything useful about Shah Medicals?" I asked as we walked into a small, empty meeting room. A coffee pot with two cups was already on a tray.

"A little. But I found Clive Tasker's address in Cyprus. I re-read his Christmas card, bless him. I always keep them a while. I've written it on here for you." She handed me a neatly typed scrap of paper. "Give him a call," Caroline continued. He's probably bored to death, poor soul. You could help liven him up a bit."

She then opened her buff folder.

"I always keep these reports on local distributors - sector by sector. This piece on Shah Medicals was updated only six months ago. Here, have a look while I pour you a coffee."

I browsed the contents for a while in silence but it told me little more than I knew already about the background and Arab involvement. Al Zafar Agencies was mentioned. An address in Cairo was noted. But my eye was drawn to some scribbled notes at the bottom. Presumably Caroline's, it read: "Company looking for new principals manufacturing anti-virals and antibiotics etc........."

I looked up to find Caroline's eyes staring at me through her glasses. "Did you meet David Chua?" I asked.

"Yes," Caroline said. "Wiry little chap. Bundle of nervous energy. Made me feel stressed and I was only with him a short time." Then she went on: "This wiry little chap, Chua, has history, though - you might be interested. He's just your sort of chap, Rupert dear. He came up through some rather sordid roots - his family were criminals - Chinese mafia - this was before the really tough clampdowns. He was also arrested a year or so back for being involved in a group called Singapore 2100. But just your type of character, I thought when I read it this morning."

"So is he a good boy, now?"

"How do I know, dear. I could probably delve a bit if you wanted but it's unlikely we could come up with anything - not our business - but, once a crook, always a crook, eh?" Caroline laughed heartily.

"And what is this group Singapore 2100?" I asked.

"Search me dear. Something to do with right wing extremism and authoritarian rule if I recall. Wouldn't have thought that bothered the government here though, would you.......?" Caroline stopped. "Sorry, shouldn't have said that. Slap my hand. Wash my mouth out with Dettol." She grinned.

"What did you find out about the Arab connection, Al Zafar?"

"That they were the financial backers. I got the impression that Chua was nervous of him - or impressed by his money - I couldn't tell which - it's the Chinese inscrutable nature."

I thought about the "nervous" bit for a second. It hadn't struck me last night but maybe what I had interpreted as admiration was, in fact, fear.

"So, is that it?" I said, and handed the report back to Caroline.

"Sorry if you're not impressed, Rupert dear. But there are limitations. Anything else I can do before I throw you out into the humidity again?" She smiled at me - rather affectionately, I thought. "Missed you a bit you know," she added. "And I'm still not sure what your real name is, but I always had a liking for men of mystery. When are you leaving?"

"Tonight," I replied. "I've got to move on, but thanks for everything Caroline, much appreciated. I'll certainly try to catch up with Clive. He calls me Ian, by the way."

Caroline looked confused but we shook hands formally and she saw me to the door. But then she looked furtively around and suddenly planted another kiss. Almost as tall as my six feet and so not having to reach very far, her gesture was quick and discreet. I thanked her once again and then walked off down the driveway between lawns and trees, looking back as I went. Caroline had already gone.

As I walked, I took out the typed note with Clive Tasker's address and telephone number. So Clive was living in Troodos, Cyprus. I recalled a weekend there several years ago - two days of escape into the cool hills of fragrant pine trees and away from the hot and humid coastal sun. It would be nice to go back sometime.

CHAPTER 26

Larry Brown was still working through his list of American pharmaceutical companies but, as he was drawing blanks at every stage, he decided to broaden it out to cover medical research companies.

It was as he checked out the Biox, Boston, Massachusetts website that he remembered something about two of their researchers going missing. Not only that but he had once met the Biox president, Josh Ornstein. He phoned Boston.

Larry was beginning to be impressed by the reaction to phone calls if he said he was calling from the American Embassy, Lagos. If he had just been Doctor Larry Brown from the Mount Sinai Hospital, New York, it was highly likely that the most any company boss would have done would have been to get his secretary to take a message.

As it was, he got straight through to Josh Ornstein and, pleasantries and introduction over, reminded him of when they'd met before. "The infection control conference in Seattle, Mr Ornstein. March last year. Remember?"

With more ice broken, Larry went on to briefly explain his new job. For a man heading a medical research company, not a manufacturer, Ornstein seemed unusually interested.

"Nigeria is where that outbreak of respiratory infections is being looked into, right Larry?"

That wasn't really why Larry had phoned but he said, "Yes, in fact it was me who notified WHO."

"You? Jesus. How did that happen then Larry?"

Larry briefly explained and added, "Right up your street isn't it, Josh - respiratory viruses?"

"That's why I asked. Any news on the virus, Larry? Is it a virus? I heard WHO were still waiting on tests. We asked as well but so far we've had nothing. The Thailand laboratory was leading on the virology - samples were going to London. All predictably slow. So what's happening in Nigeria?"

"Forget it, Josh. They're not that interested. I'm in touch with the Kano State government. If they hear of any more similar cases they've said they'll contact me. But a hundred deaths from what they regard as just a fever and a cough and cold are not exactly top priority. The Ministry obviously knows but what can anyone do after deaths. Sampling for tests for Flu virus needs to be done far sooner than that. So I'm also acting as a link to the WHO's Africa Regional Director."

"Have the very localised cases in Nigeria petered out, then Larry?"

"I assume so," said Larry, "But your guess is as good as mine. And there have been no more cases in Thailand either, as far as I'm aware. But we have a good description of the progress of the disease from Thailand. It seems to start as a simple cold but develops rapidly into this fever and cough. Patients don't even get to hospital. It could be they're still contracting it and dying out in the countryside. Local doctors have been asked to keep a look out but....."

"A very localised outbreak in Nigeria, then Larry?"

Again, Larry noticed Josh Ornstein's unusual interest in Nigeria. He decided not to tell him that a doctor was implicated but had disappeared. Let WHO announce that if they wished. Instead, Larry said, "But of course there was also a single case in Nairobi. It's probably unconnected but WHO have logged it."

"Of course," said Josh Ornstein. "We must all keep an eye on it."

Larry still sensed an interest that went beyond a scientific one. It looked personal. He noted it but decided to talk about his real reason for the call.

"So, Josh, I'm sat here in Lagos with the US Government breathing down my neck wanting more healthcare exports to Nigeria. What's your strategy in Africa?"

"We do research, Larry. Once we have found something we sell it to others. Exports is not our thing."

Larry Brown was still without his focus.

CHAPTER 27

Rather than fly to Cyprus as I might have done, normally, I decided to phone Clive Tasker instead. We had, at one time, been good friends but a phone call was still not ideal. I have always found direct, eye to eye, contact is best and this would have been my much preferred option with Clive.

Clive's job had, officially, been a 'commercial officer' at the British Embassy in Amman but I knew full well that Clive had other, unspecified roles as well. Clive was also a man who probably knew that Ian McCann was really Daniel Capelli, but nothing has ever been said.

Taking the next available flight out of Bangkok or Singapore to Cyprus - as I might have done in the past - now seemed out of the question. My business has evolved to be run by a single man or someone with no ties. At the very least it is for someone with a very understanding wife or partner. But I needed to learn to change my ways.

So Anna and I returned to Bangkok and checked into my normal hotel off of Sukhumvit Road. Then I phoned Cyprus, reminding myself that Clive had always known me as Ian McCann.

"Tasker," said the abrupt but almost forgotten voice.

"Hello, Clive. Ian McCann. I'm in Bangkok. Long time - I heard you've retired."

"Yes, I was expecting you, Ian. Caroline phoned me earlier to say she'd met you. I knew it was you even though she called you Rupert." I merely laughed.

Pleasantries over and, within the constraints of a mobile phone conversation about something both complicated and sensitive, I started to explain.

"I need your help, Clive," I began as Anna curled an arm around my waist and squeezed me. It was nice but untimely. I smiled at her but beckoned her to go away. "I can't tell you too much at this stage," I went on, "but I need some information about one particular company and the man behind it. He's a Jordanian or possibly Egyptian, which is why I thought you might help.

"He started small, but has companies all over the Middle East and now in Hong Kong and Singapore where I have just come from. He has, I believe, also got something going on in Kenya and Egypt."

I paused.

"Also, Clive, when you've been in this business for a while you get a strange gut feeling in the pit of your stomach. That gut feeling is telling me there is something going on that may, at the very least, enable me to help my client. Evidence is flimsy, to say the least, so I don't want to go in like a bull in a china shop. But I need some more information on this man."

"What's his name?" Clive asked.

"Mohamed Abdul Rahman Kader. He started business in Jordan in about 1974. The company is called Al Zafar and mostly into pharmaceuticals and healthcare products. He's a very wealthy man and seems to like a bit of positive publicity when he can get it. I remember reading a newspaper report about him when I was in Hong Kong recently. He had just opened up something there."

I stopped to see if there was any reaction. There was.

"Sure I know him," Clive said. "I even met him a couple of times at official British Embassy functions. He was well known. Al Zafar is well known. It represents several UK companies. What do you want to know?"

"Any personal opinions you can share?"

"Yes." Clive seemed to be sipping at something - perhaps it was a glass of something. I knew Clive was a wine buff. "The sort of man to want to be the best at everything," he said and I then heard the chink of a bottle as if Clive was topping up. "He wants to make a big name for himself," he continued. "You could say he already has. Failed doctor out of Cairo so the story went, so sort of rags to riches but knows what he wants and usually gets it."

I let Clive continue for a while. Then, the prompt.

"I believe he may be funding a research company somewhere. By all accounts he may have some sort of laboratory in Nairobi or Cairo. Anything on this?"

"Sorry, Ian. However, it wouldn't surprise me."

"Is he married, Clive?"

"Yes, to an Egyptian woman. They have at least two children to my knowledge. Last I heard they were living in London - children at school while he travelled."

Clive was definitely sipping from a glass of something. There was another pause before he went on:

"Here's an interesting point. Kader claimed to be an environmentalist. Now you don't hear that said much in the Middle East where crude oil gets pumped out of the desert and others fight over land.

"He also hated crowds of people. For someone who liked his share of publicity, that struck me as strange. He hated Cairo by all accounts. I saw him once waving his hands at a crowd of reporters who had gathered in the Amman Sheraton. They hadn't come to see him, of course, but the King was expected to arrive at any minute. But Kader seemed frustrated, overwhelmed if you like. Strange.

"He was also quite outspoken sometimes about so-called corrupt Western influences. All hypocritical rubbish of course and probably deliberately designed to keep him onside with others and I suspect he knew that. He's quite astute. If he thought so badly about the West then why send your wife and kids to live in London? I think he probably knows that most Islamic radicalism comes from a sense of injustice and envy for the West - religion is just the excuse. Mass unemployment, especially amongst youth, provides the resource for the increasing terrorism.

"Just look at Europe, Ian. How many unemployed young people are there now? What is the percentage out of work and with no chance of ever finding a job? Might they soon start to get just a little bit impatient and angry? And what would happen if someone with the right communication skills or resources comes along and starts to organise them? I'm glad I'm past 65, Ian. The future looks bleak whatever way you look at it.

"So Kader is dead right about overcrowding and the environment and I agree with him. Why the hell have I decided to retire to the top of a mountain amongst the fragrant pine trees of Cyprus if it's not to get away from people. In the end, Ian, Mohamed Kader might surprise us all."

I had listened intently and would always remember Clive's words. It was time for pleasantries.

"Thank you, Clive. That'll do me for now. A lot of food for thought but very useful."

"No problem, Ian. Who's your client?"

"An American medical research company - I can't say more."

I heard Clive's glass being filled once more.

"How's Helene," I asked.

"Helene, my dear wife and patient companion for thirty years? The woman I found amongst the concrete rubble of Beirut all those years ago? Still patient and a comfort to me as always, Ian. She's right here. Filling my glass by my side. She says hello."

I suddenly felt touched by Clive's words.

"Not married, yet then Ian? Still too busy? You need to settle down, my boy. Get to know another side to life. Making money is the way to survive, Ian. Love and marriage is the way to live."

I glanced over to Anna. She was still sat, listening. Then she smiled at me and came over to put her arms around me yet again.

CHAPTER 28

Kevin Parker was not a churchgoer. His Sunday ritual, if indeed there was one, included digging around and uploading any fresh information onto the Malthus Society website, lunching at the Royal Oak, perhaps watching football on the wide screen in one of the bars in Bristol Docks and evenings in another of the many Clifton bars. All of it was intended to distract him from remembering it was Monday the next day.

It was in the Richmond that he often met up with Tom Weston, one of the founder members of the Malthus Society. Tom was a retired biology teacher, a Paul Ehrlich fan and, despite his age, still ran a dusty little second hand book shop in Clifton that specialised in books on the environment. He had a whole shelf with a sign over it saying "Paul Ehrlich." In fact, copies of Ehrlich's book, "The Population Bomb" were always on the shelf and had been selling since soon after the book was published.

In it, Ehrlich had argued that the human population was too high already, and that while the level of disaster could be mitigated, humanity could not prevent severe famines, the spread of disease, social unrest, and other negative consequences of overpopulation. Ehrlich's views on the situation had evolved over time but he was always a strong advocate of government intervention into population control.

And Tom also had collections of other books and papers dating back to 1948 - the time of the "neo-Malthusian" debate. His collection included Fairfield Osborn's "Our Plundered Planet" and William Vogt's "Road to Survival." Tom had, at one time or another, read it all. But, alongside Thomas Malthus, Ehrlich was the man who had inspired Tom.

In turn, Tom was the man who had inspired Kevin and widened his understanding of the subject and, despite the age gap of over forty years, Tom was still the same old man who Kevin relaxed with, the man he listened to and the man who Kevin most respected.

But Tom was not a man of the internet. He was someone who appeared frightened by technology and preferred books. But Kevin often had his laptop with him in the pub and Tom could be persuaded to put on his glasses and read whatever subject of mutual interest Kevin found. Tom had even learned how to press the scroll down button.

"What do you make of this then, Tom?" Kevin slid the laptop between the beer glasses towards Tom.

"Woss that then? Tom said in his Bristol accent.

"A posting on the Malthus Society website."

"Woss it say then?"

"Here, read it," said Kevin and Tom donned his glasses and peered at the screen.

"Can't read it for love nor money. Too dark for me."

Kevin leaned over, brightened the screen and increased the font size. "Try that."

Tom squinted at it. Then he scrolled down with an arthritic finger. "Bless my soul," he said and adjusted his glasses. "I know that fellow."

"What do you mean you know him?" Kevin said, "It's only a screen name."

"Yes, but he's written stuff before. I mean real stuff, not on computers. Big fan of Ehrlich. In fact he was at Stanford. "

"Got anything of his on your shelves, then Tom?"

"Probably, " said Tom. "His name is Solomon."

"Yes," said Kevin, "That's his screen name, Tom. But I think I've seen stuff from him before - admittedly it was a while ago. He's a Boston group member. What's his real name?"

"Solomon, you young fool - David Solomon."

"How the hell do you know him, then Tom?"

"Someone brought in a pile of old Journals of Clinical Microbiology - interesting journal - you've probably got it up at the University. He had written something on viruses that caused respiratory tract infections. I read it - it was during the bird flu scare - thought I'd better know something just in case. I've still got the journals somewhere - not a popular item."

111

Kevin looked at Tom, marvelling at both the old man's memory and the amount of uninspiring literature he seemed to find time to read while waiting for customers. But, Kevin reminded himself, Tom was still a biologist at heart and understood a thing or two about what he read.

He pulled the laptop back towards him and re-read the posting from "Solomon" - "Agree, with day-owl - Sub Saharan Africa drought insoluble but the day of reckoning is fast approaching."

It was the Mohamed El Badry effect - any mention of Africa was starting to interest Kevin. He'd even spent the entire morning researching facts, figures and maps of Nigeria. He then did his own scroll, going a long way back but could only find one post from Solomon. It was a year before and it said simply: "Tired of waiting, friends. Moving on." Kevin now remembered it but, like so many others it seemed, Solomon had decided he had better things to do than follow pointless chatter on the Malthus website. So why, then, had he suddenly made a return?

"So what else do you know about Solomon, Tom?" asked Kevin, as Tom started to put away his glasses.

"He was a microbiologist," Tom said, "Just like Ehrlich. I checked some of the other things he had written and he sounded just as controversial and political as Ehrlich. He mentioned Marxism a lot in one article, then stated he had become a Green, then an environmentalist. He wrote an article about destruction of rain forests and said, quite rightly, that it was being driven by commercial demand - where there's market demand someone will exploit it and to hell with the long term. Clever scientist, very sensible and logical but also crazy and a bit mixed up as well I reckoned."

CHAPTER 29

Anna had gone out. I was in the Bangkok hotel with the laptop open on the bed checking emails. Colin had not yet replied to my latest request but there was another email from him.

"Daniel: Phone Clive, Cyprus. He's trying to track you down. Colin. PS Other stuff on its way."

Anxious to know what it was Clive wanted but with the time difference against me, I decided to phone later and turned back to the internet. It was something that Caroline said about David Chua that had sparked my interest: ".......he was

112

arrested a year back for being involved in a group called Singapore 2100 - just your type of character," she had said.

With no difficulty, I found several mentions of the group. They sat amongst other links that had mentioned Singapore and 2100 together and alongside a United Nations report predicting that Singapore's population would hit 10 million by 2100. There was another site with cartoons of traffic jams, of cars packed one on top of the other and people fighting for space and falling from the tops of skyscrapers.

The report said that the world's population would hit 10.9 billion by 2100 with most of the growth a result of high birth-rates in the developing world. The number of inhabitants in the world's least developed countries, especially Africa, it said, was projected to double to 1.8 billion by 2050 and soar to 2.9 billion by 2100.

Then I came to a Straits Times report about the arrest of three Chinese men for "plotting to undermine the Government's policy on population control." No names were given and no details on the so-called plot, either. But was David Chua one of them?

I continued to delve further and several pages down I found something else:

".....And the sea level around the city state could increase by 24 to 65 centimetres by 2100...Malthus Society....Singapore 2100. Temperatures around the city could increase........".

I clicked on Malthus Society and up it came - a website with an ancient picture of Thomas Malthus on its front page, with facts and figures on population, links to books, papers and reports about Thomas Malthus, Paul Ehrlich and others and a message board for anyone who wanted to join a worldwide network of Malthus societies or groups with interests in population control. Singapore 2100 was listed amongst the members.

Deciding it might be interesting to delve further, I entered a few details and instantly found I had become a member - no questions asked about who I was or where I was. I joined as Dan Dare and then began looking at recent messages.

And it was the one from "Solomon" that caught my eye. "Agree, with day-owl - Sub Sahara Africa drought insoluble. But the day of reckoning fast approaches."

I tracked back a few messages and saw one from "day-owl" - "Don't go - let there be drought".

Then I tracked this one back to a message from "popstat" - "Sub Sahara drought again - yeh, I know - don't shoot the messenger - but anyone interested in another lecture to learn what we already know - MIT Friday 14th 2pm - Boston group."

For the first time in a week I had a feeling I was on to something but from a completely different angle.

The message from "Solomon" - could it be David Solomon? And the Boston, MIT - Massachusetts Institute of Technology - link? Had Solomon perhaps disappeared from his employer, Biox, only to move somewhere else in Boston? But the web was a big place and "Solomon" could have been anywhere. It may not even be David Solomon.

I continued to scroll through the message board - all innocent looking stuff from highly opinionated individuals and possibly a few nutcases responding to something or other that someone had posted earlier. In places there were signs that certain individuals were demanding action - they sounded impatient - but no specific types of action were mentioned.

It was as though someone, somewhere owned the site but was monitoring content to keep an angry mob at bay lest someone else started asking too many questions and the group was put under surveillance. It was likely that someone was watching it anyway. Driven by the terrorism threat, there were many governments with facilities that tracked individuals or looked for key words in emails.

The Malthus message board was divided into topics as if inviting serious and sensible debate - destruction of the environment, water shortages, food shortages, contraception, unemployment, over-crowding, health.

One on IVF treatment had clearly sparked a lively debate with someone called "Thalmus" calling for it to be made illegal. The posting was long, much longer than most.

"They want everything - all the food they can eat, nice, clean, well-paid jobs, big houses, TVs, computers, all the gadgets, education, healthcare, welfare protection, unemployment benefit. They even expect the state to provide solutions to their own infertility. Governments should stop this never ending pandering to the whining rich - one minute they complain there aren't any jobs for themselves or their kids, next minute they want to bring more kids into the world, even when nature clearly intended that they shouldn't have any. Someone needs to start accepting responsibility, introduce strict population control methods aimed at a reduction in world population by 2100 ......" And so it went on. I scanned most of it.

"You're right, Thalmus," replied "Antidote", "Trouble is politicians only give - they rarely take away. Taking away something they've already given is political suicide."

"It's time for direct action, Thalmus," said "Nopussyfooting", "We need better co-ordination. I thought this site was for just that. Come on, Thalmus."

I scrolled back up to "General" to find a mixed bag of stuff where rudeness, bad language, extremist views and poor spelling started to take over. Thalmus cropped up several times, correcting errors of fact and suggesting writers toned down their language. Then I saw another, very recent one from the same name: "Check out WHO DON. Anyone know anything?"

So who was "Thalmus" and why would he have picked up on the WHO's Disease Outbreak Notification - the WHO DON? It was also quite clear that "Thalmus" was an anagram of Malthus. So was Thalmus a kingpin in the Malthus Society website and, if so, who was he?

But, as I pondered, there was a knock on the hotel door - Anna had returned. I checked my watch. It was now early morning in Cyprus and a good time to call Clive.

"Breakfasting on the veranda," Clive said. "Fresh orange juice, bacon, eggs, the full works. Lovely morning and fantastic view, Ian. Come and visit us sometime."

"Love to, Clive - I'll see if I can find time."

"I called a friend in Amman last night," Clive said. "As we discussed, it seems your friend Mohamed Kader is expanding. According to my contact, he has been importing a lot of scientific equipment into Jordan as if it's for a laboratory but then he re-exports it. No-one knows exactly where it's going - it's almost certainly Cairo - but I'm trying to find out. The Arab Bank is said to be the consignee. But there is no reason to suspect he is doing anything more than what he said he was going to do - setting up a research facility, that is."

Clive paused. "There is something else you should know. This man has been interesting the intelligence organisations, or at least the CIA and SIS - MI6 to you and me. I mentioned yesterday his interest in Iraq - we think this is purely commercial - but he has also been visiting Pakistan and West Africa - Nigeria I suspect.

"I assume he was being watched for any links to radical Islamic groups. If so, in my opinion they are barking up the wrong tree - he's not like that. There is something going on but if the Intelligence Services know any more then they're not saying. There may be nothing in any of it and I'm rapidly getting out of date, but it seems his business is a complicated web of intrigue.

"So, is that enough to keep you going, young man?" Clive ended.

"Very useful, Clive. Sorry I can't divulge any more from my side except to say I'm dealing with missing scientists.- three to be precise. It was two but three days ago it became three. No-one knows where they're gone but it did cross my mind that Mohamed Kader or someone within the spiders' web of companies he runs might know something."

Clive then revealed more:

"Then I have something else for you, Ian. The University in Amman lost two microbiology technicians last year and a small pharmaceutical manufacturer in Beirut - a French owned company - lost their French production engineer. Also the head of the main government controlled supplier of sterile fluids for hospitals in Syria also departed, ostensibly to escape the problems there. He said he'd been offered a government job in Saudi Arabia but we know he never turned up."

CHAPTER 30

In Lagos, Larry Brown woke well before dawn and couldn't get back to sleep. He often slept badly if the day before had dragged or he felt he hadn't achieved enough. But what had woken him this time was a dream and what was keeping him awake was trying to resolve the problem the dream had thrown up.

In his dream, Joseph, Ibrahim and Olafemi in the office had all phoned in sick. But then Joseph had phoned in again to say he was now better but that Ibrahim and Olafemi were dead.

"Coughing fits, Larry," the dream Joseph said sounding perfectly fit and well.

"What time will you be in, then Jo?" Larry had asked the dream Joseph.

Never," said the dream Joseph, "I need to look after my mom and my dad - they're sick, too."

Larry had woken up, looked at the clock radio, saw it was only 3am and put the pillow over his head. But it was far too hot and he slung the sheet off and lay there, staring into the darkness. The hundred, unexplained, respiratory infection deaths were still troubling him far more than his real, paid job for the Embassy.

What was bothering him was the apparent silence around the Kano deaths - or alleged deaths as he kept reminding himself. The problem was that no records existed and no bodies had been found. It was just rumour from locals about bodies being carried away from the Kofi clinic. What was it about some countries that could accept such a situation without question?

The State Government, probably because he was from the US Embassy, had promised him an update despite their obvious disinterest in tracking down the missing doctor whose clinic they had closed. He understood that bureaucracy sometimes got in the way - the USA had its fair share - but one hundred or more deaths and no names? Nothing except numbers on sheets of paper found in an otherwise empty filing cabinet? At least in the USA someone would have asked questions and then there would have been a public outcry. Here, local people who had witnessed the comings and goings at the clinic appeared disinterested. Neither had he seen anything in the Nigerian press except a low key item in the Daily Independent on the WHO report and a mention that some "isolated" cases of a respiratory "bug" in Kano were being investigated.

Larry got up, made himself a coffee and logged onto the internet. He checked out the Kano State government website to try to understand how it operated - he was none the wiser. He double-checked the WHO website for any updates on the DON - there wasn't one. He checked the Kenyan Ministry of Health website for something - there was nothing. He checked the Thailand Ministry of Public Health site and there was nothing, Larry closed the lid of his laptop.

One thing was for sure - he wasn't going to spend another day looking out of the office window. He decided to fly back up to Kano and do his own checking.

CHAPTER 31

As I've said, Colin Asher's business methods are still a mystery to me. An ex London cop, he started his own private investigation company but has turned it into one that operates more like the back office support for a number of other small, private investigators. But much of Colin's work is local, UK based. For Colin to be of any use to me, Colin had had to change the way he worked. And with my business growing so did Colin's. Colin now has a network of what he calls "sub agents" in far flung places. For me, Colin has become invaluable.

His report on Livingstone Pharmaceuticals arrived on my laptop just as I finished speaking to Clive Tasker.

The report began by giving a date of formation of 1947 when one Josiah Livingstone had started manufacturing hand creams in New York, USA.

Livingstone Skincare Products had grown by slowly adding more and more products and had become a well known brand on the back of marketing itself not just as yet another cosmetics company but as a pharmaceutical company with its own "Dermatology Research" centre also in New York. It continued to develop new products but soon after, in 1991, old Josiah Livingstone died and the business had fallen into the less driven hands of his two sons.

They had sold it to the company's main distributor in New York. That company, realising the asset it had bought for a song, changed its own name to Livingstone Pharmaceuticals. The business had grown by adding painkillers, common cold remedies and other simple treatments and by 2005, Livingstone Pharmaceuticals had become a household name for family type medicines. But again, due to unspecified problems, it was put up for sale.

Colin's report went on and I'll give it to you just as it came:

"The buyer: Daire Capital Investments (DCI) - a company registered in the Cayman Islands. We are seeking more on DCI - initial information suggests Gregory O'Brian is the majority shareholder. DCI Finance Ltd is a company registered with UK Companies House but is not trading. Directors are Gregory John O'Brian, Keith Alan Donovan, Kevin Stephen Mallory. We can delve more if needed.

[Note: Daire is the Irish spelling for Derry or Londonderry - Gregory O'Brian gives this as his place of birth although now a US citizen]

Livingstone Pharmaceuticals: Last information - 65 employees, seems profitable but domestic USA market share is static or falling. Export markets are apparently growing at about 25 percent annually. One report says it is looking at investments in developing countries overseas.

Personal: O'Brian is an Irish American from Boston. Tracking him back shows he originally ran a company trading in fertilizers and animal feed from offices in New York, Dublin and Belfast. No information traceable on Daire Capital Investments. It is probably a holding name that is used for all sorts of business activities. We also found Daire Insurance, Daire Chemicals and Daire Property with O'Brian's name linked somewhere. As a result, the financial picture is currently impossible to track as everything appears to go via the Cayman Islands.

Livingstone Pharmaceuticals Business Strategy (information obtained from business publications): Said to be looking at increasing product registrations and approvals in Africa and the Middle East. There was an expressed interest (information obtained from a copy of an official enquiry to the commercial interests section of the US Embassy in Japan) in taking on agency lines in more specialised pharmaceuticals."

That was it. I read it twice. Then I switched to Colin's final sentence.

"If, as I suspect, it's Greg O'Brian - GOB - that really interests you, Daniel, then phone me. I don't want to put everything in an email."

I looked at Anna. She was sat cross-legged on the bed reading a Thai cookery book but looked up when she realised I was smiling. I smile a lot when I look at Anna.

"Kamun gai, my Mister Look Lap - I think you will like Kamun gai. I'll go and buy some in the street. Bring lunch to our room, yes?"

"Sounds very good to me, Anna," I said. "I've got another phone call to make. You go ahead."

In England it was early morning, seven-thirty, but Colin answered the phone as if he was expecting me to call at any moment. "Morning, 007," he said. "You got the notes I assume? OK, here's more and so I don't prejudice things with my own interpretation, I'll read it to you, verbatim so to speak. As it was given to me. Direct from the horse's mouth, as it were. No frills, you understand. No glossy highlighters and no asterisks......."

"Get on with it, Colin."

"OK. Gregory O'Brian. Age 62. Confirmed links with the Provisional IRA in the seventies and early eighties but avoided arrest or extradition from USA through insufficient evidence. An IRA fund raiser in Boston.

"Linked with several major frauds in USA, UK and Ireland. These including insurance and property with suspicion around embezzlement and money laundering.

"Grew up in Londonderry, father a quarryman and explosives expert. Not short of luck, he won a lot of money doing the "football pools" as betting on football results was once called. Money used to start his business selling animal feed and fertilizer through a business called Daire Agriculture.

"Moved to Boston, USA, married the daughter of a local Irish Republican physician in Boston, childless as far as we can tell and now spends little if any time with his wife. She now lives near Cape Cod. He ran Daire Agriculture from Boston but it was a front for all sorts of illegal activity. Alleged to have made millions through a medical insurance fraud but no-one seemed able to prove anything. This is the likely explanation for the Cayman Islands account and how he found the money to buy Livingstone Pharmaceuticals. Owns several properties including one - estimated value three million dollars - near Newport, Rhode Island. Currently rented out for so called leisure activities. Used by congressmen, film and TV people. Probably earns enough in rent in one year to buy a similar property down the road. Regarded as a high octane but secretive operator. Livingstone Pharmaceuticals appears to run itself as O'Brian takes a back seat. But Livingstone is probably a facade for other things."

Colin stopped as if he was waiting for things to sink in. "What other things?" I asked.

"GOB's other life is the same as his current life. He makes money by whatever devious means he can dream up or comes his way. But I suspect a criminal psychiatrist able to get him to lie still on his coach for an hour might also link it back to failed political ambitions. He never got his dreamed-of unified Ireland with a job in a new Irish Government. Since then he's dabbled in other ways to change the system - any radical idea gets his attention, especially if it involves causing a few headaches for democratically elected politicians in US, UK or anywhere. You got an extreme plan that might upset someone he dislikes? GOB will go for it. A bit of money for National Front? GOB's there. A few living expenses for someone falling foul of the system? GOB's on hand. Fighting fund for anything extreme that might yield a profit in return however many years into the future? GOB's definitely your man. GOB seeks power to influence, power to blackmail, power to get whatever it is he wants. Trouble is he's getting old now - 62 is way too late and past it for some professions and he might be getting impatient."

Six thousand miles away, Colin probably realised from the long pause that I was thinking hard. I was. I was also getting excited. I like this sort of thing. It's what I do. And this case had needed livening up. GOB sounded just like the Malaysian guy I'd met only a month ago. This guy's exclusive holiday resort tucked away near the white sandy beach was for drugs, prostitution and money laundering. But for certain politicians, media people, so-called celebrities and other low life it was a tropical paradise. But let's not stray.

"How do you know all this, Colin?"

"It's my job to know, Daniel. Also, I once did a job for a private investigator who had a client seriously out of pocket after investing in one of GOB's health insurance schemes. GOB was the architect but he hid behind a system he'd deliberately put in place. No-one got arrested. No charges were brought and the only other people to benefit from the work were the trading officers from the local council. But his scam went far wider than the UK. Australia and New Zealand got a taste of him as well.

"But you won't find his name mentioned too loudly, Daniel. He's a nasty piece of work when it comes to revenge."

"Such as?" I asked.

"Such as the client of my client. He was found dead in his garden shed in Bracknell with a garden fork stuck in his chest. It's still an unsolved murder. Needless to say I didn't invoice my client."

"Christ!" I said and I don't normally swear.

"So, Daniel, my friend," said Colin at last. "Food for thought? Will that be all for the time being? Moving on from Bangkok are we or are you finding life comfortable there at present?"

"Comfortable, Colin, thanks for asking," I said thoughtfully as I was still thinking about garden forks stuck in chests. There was then a knock on the hotel room door. Anna came in carrying lunch in several plastic bags.

"Lunch," Anna said and then noticed I was on the phone. "Sorry." She was getting used to me already. The food smelled good.

"GOB as you call him is linked with Mohamed Kader, Colin," I said. "How does that sound?"

"Wow, Daniel, that's something that is. And you are there in the middle of it - whatever it is?"

"They are co-operating on something or another - officially it's a distribution agreement but...."

"But it might not be?" Colin interrupted. "Is that what you're saying?"

"I don't know what I'm saying at present, Colin. I think I'll have some lunch and think about it."

CHAPTER 31

Kevin Parker was just dropping off to sleep on his sofa when his mobile rang and made him jump. It had to be someone to whom time meant nothing. It was.

"Kev, it's Tunje."

"I'd never have guessed it was you, Tunj. What's up?"

"Have you checked out the Malthus Nigeria message board today?"

"No, Tunj, I usually check out the boards where something useful happens or someone has something interesting to say."

"That's very unkind, Kev. You might have missed something."

"No chance, Tunj, you'd have been the first to tell me."

"And so I am Kev. You want to know?"

"Try me."

"Joseph phoned me."

"And who the hell is Joseph?"

"Mate of mine who works at the USA Embassy in Lagos."

"Is he a member, Tunj?"

"Sometimes, Kev. He got interested in the Malthus site when he was doing his computing degree at Wolverhampton University. They were set a project to look at message boards and how they operate. I suggested he check out ours."

"Ours, Tunj, ours? Anyway, did he sign up and contribute anything of use?"

"Yeh, he signed up and I gave him a summary of population control methods from 1786 to 2012."

"So you taught him how to put on a condom, am I right, Tunj?"

"Ha, ha! Comedian tonight, Kev?"

"Get a move on Tunj, I was just dropping off. So why did this Joseph phone you?"

"His boss is an American doctor, Kev. He's the one who reported the Kano deaths to the WHO."

"So how did he know we were interested in these deaths then Tunj?"

"Because of your post, Kev? Remember now? You can't blame me, this time, Kev."

"Ah, yes," Kevin said, remembering his own post of a few days ago.

"So this friend of yours, Joseph, who works at the American Embassy in Lagos and has a degree from that higher education facility known as Wolverhampton University still checks out the Malthus Society website then. Have I got it straight, Tunj?"

"Looks like it, Kev."

"And why did he choose to attend Wolverhampton University then, Tunj? Was it because he had a thousand other Nigerian friends already living in and around that area of England that someone with enormous foresight once called the Black Country?"

There was a mystified pause from Tunje.

"Now don't get all racist again Kev, otherwise I'll start reminding you about Bristol docks, Whiteladies Road, Blackboy Hill and the rest of Bristol's dubious history. Anyway, what the fuck has Wolverhampton University got to do with it, Kev?"

"Because they turned me down when I applied for a job as Head of Faculty, that's why. Anyway, what did Joseph have to say?"

"That he'd seen a message from 'Thalmus' saying 'Check out WHO DON. Anyone know anything?'"

"And his higher education at Wolverhampton University enabled him to work out what WHO and DON meant, Tunj? Their computer course must be better than I thought."

"The lack of sleep is doing your comedy act a world of good, Kev. You should try staying up late every night."

Kevin sighed. "What about this friend Joseph? Why have you phoned me?"

"Ah yes, Joseph. He checked out the WHO site, then saw the DON. And in case you are about to ask, yes, they taught him all about acronyms as well at Wolverhampton."

"And what did he think or do about this information, Tunj?"

"Joseph agrees that Nigeria is a mess, it's still an economic disaster area and totally overpopulated - most of his ex university mates - that includes me of course - agree. That's why he still checks out the Malthus site. And that's why Big Shot Mohamed El Badry contacted him."

"El Badry has spoken to this guy as well?" Kevin almost exploded.

"Yes. About six months ago. But it was nothing to do with me, Kev."

"And what did El Badry want?"

"Let me explain, Kev. It's like this. Joseph works for the American Embassy's commercial team. El Badry phoned to say he was interested in finding

123

somewhere to conduct some customer satisfaction surveys on some medicine his company was introducing. They wanted somewhere small in the north of Nigeria. He was put through to Joseph as Joseph does healthcare. Then, as Joseph comes from Kano, Joseph suggested he try an area called Dala Hill."

Tunje stopped suddenly. Kevin wondered if Tunje still had more to say. As there was silence, Kevin said, "Is that it, Tunj?"

"Yes."

"So what happened next, Tunj? Did El Badry say thank you very much, I'll get back to you once I've done my customer satisfaction survey, or anything?

"No, but Joseph phoned me because it was his boss, the American doctor, who had reported the deaths to WHO. And, according to Joseph, the place where the people who died came from was near Dala Hill. You see now, Kev?"

"Fuck," said Kevin.

"Yes, fuck it is, Kev."

"Call from Bangkok, Richard."

Richard Lacey had just arrived in his office at the WHO Headquarters in Geneva.

"OK - my office," he said. He dumped a brief case on his desk, lifted the phone and immediately recognised the voice of the WHO South East Asia Regional Director.

"Pradit - good morning," said Richard.

"Ah, Richard - morning ah. It's Pradit. I'm in Bangkok. We're now getting some more, ah, information on the respiratory outbreak."

"Good, about time."

"It's truck drivers, Richard."

"Truck drivers, Pradit?"

"Yes, Richard. It appears that all except one of the cases were truck drivers. That accounts for only men, ah - healthy, young, middle aged. They were all delivering water melons to a big fruit wholesaler in Bangkok."

"Are you saying there is a link with water melons, Pradit?"

 No, ah. The common link is the fruit wholesaler. It's near a big bus terminal and train station, ah. Very crowded, ah."

"So why truck drivers and not ordinary bus or train passengers?"

"Good question, ah."

"You mean you don't know yet?"

"Yes, ah, I mean no ah. The Ministry is looking at where they parked the trucks. They, ah, deliver overnight and sleep in the daytime. But they like sleeping in the big shed where, ah, the water melons are sorted. It has air-conditioning."

"So - the air-conditioner?"

"Don't think so, ah."

"And the single female case from Bangkok, Pradit?"

"Yes, ah. She was sleeping with one of the drivers we think."

"So what is the conclusion, Pradit?

"Don't know yet, ah but we found something very strange outside the door of the place where they sleep, ah."

"Yes, Pradit - go on."

"Some mini inhalers, ah, like the ones used by people with asthma. You know the sort, Richard? Made of blue plastic with a mouthpiece. They have a miniature pressurised cylinder for the drug - like salbutamol. One or two puffs - asthma attack gone, ah."

"So are you testing the inhalers, Pradit."

"Ah, yes and no. They don't have the cylinder, ah. Just the blue plastic part. You know what I'm talking about, Richard?"

"Yes," said Richard, "I know them very well. In fact, my son uses one. How many inhalers?"

"Two in a box big enough to hold ten or more. But no labels, no marks. Probably irrelevant but the Ministry say they can probably trace them back to the manufacturer if necessary - but they would need to involve the police, ah, and, anyway, perhaps no connection with the respiratory cases - but very strange, no?"

"Mmm," said Richard, "very strange."

"Anything from Nigeria?" Pradit asked.

"Nothing, Pradit."

Kevin found it impossible to sleep after his conversation with Tunje. He would almost drop off but then hear the voice of Mohamed El Badry echoing in his mind.

"I have been following your work, Kevin - may I call you Kevin? Tell me, Kevin, do you have a personal view on a solution to the problems of overpopulation? And what would you say if there is a solution being developed that could bypass the political debate that we all know is going nowhere and makes things actually happen?"

And he'd then hear his own voice:

"I'd say that there is no political debate taking place, Mr El Badry. There hasn't been any since Thomas Malthus raised the matter way back in 1798. I and members of my groups have been wanting the debate for a very long time. But then we want a solution not yet more talk."

And then he was back to El Badry's voice again:

"We have a solution, Kevin - meaning my company, my associates, my researchers, my agents and my distributors. We are ready to move. We have the means to cause a pandemic. But what we also have is a treatment. If you work with us, Kevin, the treatment will be made available to you."

And then Kevin's own flippant response: "Will it be free? My university salary only goes so far."

But this was no longer a joking matter. A hundred deaths? The World Health Organisation on the case? A place in northern Nigeria called Dala? Did WHO know about El Badry? He, Kevin Parker, had always advocated direct action but what he had always meant was some form of action to force governments to listen, to take the problem more seriously and then to act. Threatening to do something was one thing. Deciding who to test out a disease on in order to start a pandemic was another.

To Kevin, tossing and turning in his bed at three in the morning, it sounded more like an act of terrorism. At four in the morning he called Tunje.

126

"Tunj, it's me."

"Hey Kev, where are you man? If you're in and around St Albans right now, I'm at a party. Come and join us."

"Sorry, Tunj, I'm far away. Home in bed to be precise - where you should be. Aren't you working tomorrow?"

"That's six hours away, Kev. Cool it."

"I've been thinking," said Kevin. "I need to speak to that American doctor - the one your friend, Joseph works for. Got any names or phone numbers?"

"Hang on............," Tunje went quiet. There was a sound of laughing, shouting and general hilarity in the background but Tunje still, apparently, had his wits about him. He was back on in less than thirty seconds. "Here we are, Kev. USA Embassy, commercial section, Victoria Island, Lagos, Nigeria. Here's the number - just texting it. Speak to Joseph - commercial section, healthcare. His boss is one guy called Larry. Doctor Larry what I don't know. OK?"

"Thanks, Tunj. I don't know how I'd manage without you. Have a good night."

The office was empty when Larry arrived at 7.30 but as the flight he'd booked to go to Kano wasn't until 11am, he sat down with a coffee to read a paper he'd bought on the way in. But he had hardly got past the front page headlines when the office phone rang. He got up to answer it and recognised an English accent.

"May I speak to Doctor Larry something or Joseph please."

"Sure," said Larry, "Who's calling? Perhaps I can help."

"Yes, my name is Kevin Parker. I'm a lecturer at Bristol University, England. I understand Doctor Larry was the person who reported the Nigerian deaths from a respiratory virus to the World Health Organisation."

"I believe so," said Larry.

"Then I'd like to discuss this with him, please."

"OK, right. Well, as it happens this is Doctor Larry speaking - Doctor Larry Brown to be precise. How can I help?"

"Firstly, I understand Joseph works for you. Has Joseph spoken to you about this yet?" Kevin asked.

"Joseph? No. Should he have?"

"Can I suggest you ask him what he knows about a request he took from someone wanting to conduct a customer survey on a new medicine as it may be relevant to the deaths you reported."

Suddenly, Larry was interested. If anything he had a bone to pick with Joseph about his communication skills. Kevin was still talking.

"I understand from a Nigerian friend of mine in London that Joseph suggested that a place in Kano called Dala Hill might be suitable. "

"Go on," Larry said.

"Well, I also understand that Joseph suspects that Dala was the centre of the outbreak where the deaths occurred."

Being about to fly to Kano but with no real idea what he might do or where he might go when he got there, Larry's interest grew.

"Has Joseph discussed this with you?" asked Kevin.

"No, goddam it. Listen, Mr Parker............."

"Kevin."

"Listen Kevin, what more do you know? Who the hell are you? What's more do you know? What the hell's going on here?"

Kevin already knew he'd sleep better for sharing something. This was the American Embassy and he was speaking to the Doctor who had reported the outbreak. In a strange way, Kevin felt partly responsible for those deaths. Direct action was supposed to be influential leading to a modicum of democratic accountability, not like this.

"I think you should speak to Joseph first, Doctor, uh Larry. Ask him to confirm the name of the man he spoke to about the customer survey. If he says it was Mohamed El Badry then there's something going on."

"Mohamed El Badry, you say? And do you know this guy, Kevin?"

"I met him once, Larry. And I'm very worried about his motives."

"And how did you meet him?"

"He invited me to his palatial apartment overlooking the River Thames in London," said Kevin and then went on to explain a little about the Malthus Society and its aims.

"................to spread the message that politicians the world over need to wake up to the consequences of overpopulation and the burdens that overpopulation places on the environment.......yes, they talk endlessly about environment, environment, environment but that's because it gives them endless opportunities to raise taxes. But at the bottom of it all is the need not only to control population but to reduce it. And the only way............ " Kevin knew it was always a bad question to ask him anything about population control , but once he'd started he was sometimes unable to stop.

"Hey, hold on Kevin," Larry eventually interrupted. "Let me tell you I agree. One hundred percent I agree. I wish I'd known about the Malthus Club or whatever it is. I might have signed up. But what about this guy, El Badry?"

"You want to know what his last words to me were, Larry?"

"Go ahead, Kevin." Larry said, sensing the concern coming over the phone line from England.

"He asked me what we, the Malthus Society wanted. I said, and these were my exact words - I know because I've used them many times before. I said there is no political debate taking place, Mr El Badry. There hasn't been anything serious since Thomas Malthus raised the matter way back in 1798 - perhaps some debate after Paul Ehrlich's book - but I and members of my groups have been wanting the debate for a very long time. But then we want a solution not yet more talk. That's what I said, Larry."

Kevin went on: "And then he said to me, 'We have a solution, Kevin - my company, my associates, my researchers, my agents and my distributors. We are ready to move. We have the means to cause a pandemic. But what we also have is a treatment."

"Jesus," said Larry, "You sure this guy, El Badry, is serious?"

"Would I call you from England, Larry, if I wasn't concerned. Someone somewhere needs to get to the bottom of this guy. Who is he? Where has he come from?"

"You say you met him at an apartment. Larry?"

"Yes, Chelsea Embankment."

"Aren't there ways to find out who owns the place - a local registry or something?"

"I can try," said Kevin thankful for something that sounded sensible.

"Kevin, let me tell you something," Larry said. "Yes, I'll ask Joseph. But I'm about to leave to fly up to Kano right now. Let's stay in touch."

CHAPTER 32

That I hadn't been given a clear enough starting point and that there were large gaps in what I felt I should have been told by Charles Brady at Virex was beginning to gnaw at me.

I also felt there was something particularly wrong in the way Charles Brady had, in effect, sent a sidekick in the form of Amos Gazit to Bangkok to meet me. It was partly my fault I suppose. I should have refused until better briefed, but returning to Bangkok to resume the long weekend I'd planned for myself with Anna had also been a factor. So I blamed myself a bit. But by early evening in Bangkok - early morning Boston time - the feeling had become too strong to ignore any longer and I phoned Virex HQ in Boston and asked to speak to Amos Gazit.

"Daniel Capelli, Amos, alias Doctor Michael Stevens from the Bangkok conference."

I was building up to a confrontation but didn't yet want to completely ruin the relationship. I had to be careful. Amos Gazit joined in with a few early pleasantries about the conference. Then: "Any news? Charles asked me if I'd heard from you yesterday."

"Well, let's say I'm still following some leads. It's not easy you understand. There wasn't much to go on to start with. I just wanted to report in so to speak. Any more staff gone?" I half joked and then began on the confrontation.

I'd decided to start with Gazit and then, hopefully, be told I needed to speak to Charles Brady. "Frankly speaking," I said, "I think you could do a lot more to help me. Why send me to that Conference? Was there a reason? Are you sure there's not more you can tell me?"

There was a definite pause from Amos Gazit.

"You should speak to Charles Brady. Why didn't you call him? I told him to expect a call."

"I needed something before I phoned him. I've now got a few possible leads but I'm still not sure if it's relevant. Is he there?"

"He's in Chicago. Can I get him to phone you?"

"No, I'll phone him, Amos. In the meantime, can you pass a message? Tell him I need more to go on. You can also tell him I think he could make my job easier if he was a bit more up front with me."

It was pushing a client a bit hard but no harm would come of it. I decided to phone Brady later. Perhaps, by then, Brady might have had time to think about it.

CHAPTER 33

"At least 16 police officers in Nigeria have been killed in an ambush by a local militia outside Kano, officials have said. They were on their way to arrest the leader of an outlawed Islamic group linked to Boko Haram when gunmen opened fire, a State spokesman told CNN.

"The state police chief said that they were forcing local villagers to swear an oath of allegiance to the group and that, besides the 16 dead, 17 officers were still missing.

"One source at the hospital where the bodies were taken told CNN that many more policemen were killed in the attack and the number of dead could rise.

"Nigeria's President has also cut short a visit to Kenya to oversee the response to the latest violence.

"American citizens are reminded of the warnings that are in place for those travelling or working in the areas concerned."

The CNN report on the Embassy TV was a timely, last minute reminder to Larry Brown as he finished speaking to Kevin Parker and prepared to go to the airport to catch the plane to Kano. Having just spoken to Kevin in England, Larry had been in no mood to abandon his plans but knew he would stand out like the affluent American doctor he was if he wore a suit and tie and carried a brief case. Instead, he changed into a pair of worn jeans and plain tee shirt and stuffed everything he might need for an overnight stay into a back pack.

The plane had been almost empty and the airport unexpectedly quiet as Larry arrived. But security was tight and police were on patrol inside and outside the terminal building. Once outside, Larry shopped around for a taxi driver who he could hire for what remained of the day and into the evening if necessary.

"Jonathan" looked the sort he could trust. The young man wore a clean, blue shirt a pair of shoes with the laces tied and a good smile on his face. His car, a Toyota, also looked as if it may recently have been given a wash.

"Where to, sah?"

"Kofar Wambai Road," Larry said, settling himself in the passenger seat next to Jonathan. "Start one end, drive along it and I'll tell you when to stop."

Larry didn't, though, anticipate having to get out and push-start the taxi. But, with the help of an armed policeman, the car eventually fired. Once moving, and with Jonathan's air-conditioning barely working, Larry tried opening the side window only for a truck to blow a cloud of blue exhaust in at him. So started Larry's second experience of travelling around Kano.

The day was hot, dry and still and this time the upside down, plastic banner advertising the Kofi Clinic hung limply outside the door. But the door itself was open.

Larry got out of the taxi, told Jonathan to wait and stood looking at the clinic again. It was the middle building of a row of three. All were single storey with identical, flaking, pale blue paint as if owned or rented out by one person. Whatever had happened in the adjacent, vacant premises was unclear. They were covered in Arabic graffiti but looked as if they might once have been repair shops or perhaps something to do with the local shoe making industry. It was hardly a place for a private medical clinic. The only other change from Larry's last visit a few days before was the wrecked car. Already covered in a fine layer of dust, it had probably once been a Peugeot. It now stood on its axles, its windows gone, its engine gone, its dash board and steering wheel gone - everything was gone except the body. No doubt that would also disappear soon.

But the narrow side street was busier than it had been on his first visit. Three local Hausa men, Moslems in long white gowns sat in a group on broken, wooden chairs next to the car wreck while motorcycles, dusty cars, and pedestrians jostled to pass the parked taxi. Jonathan sat inside his taxi and watched as the men watched Larry get out and look around. They watched him stand outside the clinic doorway and then venture just a few steps inside. Then they watched him come out and stand by the taxi as if he was leaving.

One of the men got up. Larry waited as the tall, almost black-skinned man with grey stubble and wearing a deeply embroidered cap came over.

"Yessah," said the man as if he might be able to help give directions or information on something.

"Sannu," said Larry which was the only Hausa word he knew. "I'm looking for the Doctor who ran this clinic," said Larry trying to conceal his American accent as much as possible and hoping the man might understand."

"Me ya sa," said the man, "Why? Why you want this likita? Bastad."

Larry thought he'd heard bastard so took it as a good start.

"Doctor Mustafa? It was his clinic."

"No good, no good, bastad man. Gone."

"Where?" asked Larry convinced now they were already talking about the same man."

"Not Islam, bastad man." The man's friends then wandered over. Then two more, also wearing long white gowns who happened to be passing by, stopped.

Larry leaned casually on the taxi's open door.

"I'm looking for Doctor Mustafa," said Larry, slightly louder for the benefit of the gathering crowd.

"Gone away," said one," No-one seen him since clinic closed down, man. Why you want to know?"

Larry wasn't sure what to say at first. "Was he at Dala Hill?" he asked.

They looked at one another. "You mean on top of the hill, man?" said one and two others giggled.

"Or near-by, I'm not too familiar with the city."

"You American?"

"Yes," admitted Larry. "I'm a doctor."

"Then you're too late, man. Pity you not come before." The man, younger than the others and clearly with a better command of English, seemed to beckon Larry with his head to come closer. Larry walked a few steps towards him and heard Jonathan in the taxi behind shut the door that Larry had been leaning on.

"You want a coke, man?" the man said in a quiet voice. "No beer here," he then whispered as Larry got closer.

"Sure," Larry said.

"Come," said the younger man and grabbed Larry by his shirt sleeve. He then turned and said something in Hausa over his shoulder to the other men.

Larry followed the younger man.

"My name's Larry Brown," said Larry thinking it polite and possibly safer to introduce himself, "Doctor Larry Brown."

"Abdouleye," said the Nigerian and turned to shake Larry's hand. "Come."

Abdouleye started to lead Larry along the side road back towards Kofar Wambai Road. "You been to Kano before?" he asked.

"Yes, once," said Larry, "Just a few days ago."

"You like this fucking hole?"

"It's interesting," said Larry as they passed a stall selling sweet corn and edged their way past diners and others standing nearby.

Abdouleye stopped at another stall. "Coke or Nescafe?" he asked.

"Coke," said Larry and waited as two cans were produced and handed over.

"400 naira," said Abdouleye. Larry handed over the money and followed Abdouleye once more. They kept walking, drinking from the cans as they went.

"So was Doctor Mustafa anywhere near Dala?"

"Yes."

"Was he living there?"

"He opened an office."

"An office?"

"Yes, his clinic was down there," he pointed towards the Kofi Clinic

"How long was he here?"

"About a year, come and go, come and go."

"Did he have many patients?"

Abdouleye shrugged.

"What do you know about him?"

Abdouleye stopped, pulled Larry to the side and into the shade of another stall. "Why you want to know? What are you doing here? It's not safe you know, even for a black American. Everyone can see you're not Nigerian."

"Yeh, I know," said Larry, "I didn't come here for my safety. I just want to know why this Doctor disappeared, where he is and what he was doing. I've heard stories and I don't like what I've heard. OK?"

Abdouleye looked straight at him for the first time. He pushed his cap back and scratched his head. Larry estimated he was about thirty, Moslem, educated.

"Well known, but no-one says anything. Everyone stays dumb. Typical Nigeria." Abdouleye said.

"What's well known?"

"As a Doctor - he was no good."

"What happened?"

Abdouleye paused as if unsure whether to go on. Then: "He advertised for men to test a new medicine. Could earn a lot of Naira."

"No women?"

"Just men. He seemed to prefer poorer Hausa men from large households where the man is head. Money would go to the wives and children."

"Then what?"

"By all accounts they started to suffer with a cold or influenza but the symptoms worsened. He said they might need to go to hospital for more checks."

"Did many people get paid?"

"Sure. Probably several hundred, especially from the poorer, old sections of town."

"Then what?"

"Some got sick with a fever and coughing. The doctor said it was normal and they'd now need to go to hospital for the checks. More money was given."

"Then what?"

"Men didn't come back. The families went to his office but he was not always there. For a while he told them not to worry - the men were in hospital and still being checked. More money to the family."

"Then?"

"He disappeared. The families didn't know what happened."

Larry scratched his own head.

"And what are the police doing?"

"Nothing."

And the State Government - Health authority?"

"Nothing."

"Why is that?"

Abdouleye looked around him. The area where they were standing was close to the junction with Kofar Wambai Road. It was noisy and filled with cars, trucks, people walking or on motorcycles - the air smelled of smoke, dust and exhaust fumes. Arabic graffiti was everywhere. Arab signs dominated over Hausa or English.

"People are scared, man. They don't say anything. We've got a lot of trouble here. Last night - you saw the news? I'm a Moslem but things aren't good." Abdouleye, finished his can of Coke and slung it towards an overflowing trash bin but it bounced into the gutter. He watched it roll.

"Listen, man," he turned back towards Larry, "I don't know what you want or why you're here but everyone is shit scared. People don't report things any more - they just spread rumours."

"And the rumour is?" asked Larry.

"You want to know why I pulled you away from that crowd just now? One rumour is that Doctor Mustafa, so-called, was an American working for the Nigerian government. Rumour is they were testing a drug to use on terrorists. And why do they say that? A white man was also seen with the doctor six months ago."

Larry almost choked on the last few drops of his can of Coke. Abdouleye was still talking.

"But that wouldn't be a surprise would it? When you have the leader of Boko Haram saying they enjoy killing anyone that God commands them to kill - the way they enjoy killing chickens and rams - that's music to the ears of some people. But it's a declaration of war to others.

"American forces have already lost the struggle on the ground in Iraq, Afghanistan. They know they can't win and they can't afford to continue. That's why the West is reluctant to intervene anymore. The Nigerian army is struggling, the Nigerian police are struggling - insurgents are everywhere.

They're coming in like marching ants, man - the Magreb, Chad, Libya. The place is a mess. The economy is a mess. Who in their right mind would invest here? And it's very easy for insurgents to recruit thousands more. If I was desperate enough, poor enough with no hope of a job and I was angry enough and put no value upon my own life let alone that of others, I'd probably think about it. So, perhaps the army and police are trying something different. If you can't shoot the fuckers, make them sick. That's the rumour."

"But why test it out on innocent Nigerians?" asked Larry. "It doesn't make sense."

"Yeh, I agree. But do you want to try and quell a rumour?"

Standing in the shade of the food stall selling ground corn buns and pepper soup, with a dozen or more people standing or sitting around and others trying to listen to what was being said in English to the black man in jeans and tee shirt who clearly didn't look Nigerian, it was apparent to Larry that Abdouleye was no longer comfortable. Neither was Larry.

He thanked Abdouleye. "OK,," he said, "I get the message. Thanks for the help."

Abdouleye looked him in the eye and nodded.

"You speak good English," said Larry as they parted.

"Yeh," he replied, "I'm a doctor, too. I studied medicine in England."

CHAPTER 34

With Anna telling me she felt hungry again, we left the hotel to find a restaurant. But I wasn't in a good mood. Anna knew something was bothering me.

"Mister Look-Lap - I can see you are not enjoying your dinner. You are very quiet. What is wrong? Don't sit there like that. You make me feel I say something wrong or maybe I not say something right. Maybe I upset you. If something is wrong then you must sort it."

Anna was right. The restaurant was not busy and we were sat at a quiet, corner table overlooking the main Sukhumvit Road and rows of stalls selling everything from crafts and underwear to tee shirts and CDs. Outside it was hot and noisy. Inside, it was cool and peaceful.

"Yes, Anna." I said. "You are right. I have something on my mind. It's spoiling my dinner and I can see it's spoiling yours. I need to phone America."

So that's what I did. Charles Brady's mobile phone in Chicago, or wherever he was, was answered surprisingly quickly.

"Charles, it's Daniel Capelli. I'm still in Bangkok."

"Yes, Amos told me you might phone."

"Can you talk, Charles?"

"Yes. I'm at the airport - the plane is delayed." Yes, I thought. Never book a flight that Charles Brady is already booked on.

"I'm getting nowhere, Charles," I said. "And I hate the feeling I'm not earning my fee."

"Yes, Amos told me."

"I need more from you. I might be wrong but the feeling persists that there is more going on here than just the loss of some research material. And you've now lost a researcher, Charles - just like Biox."

"Yes," said Charles Brady.

"So? Can you let me in on a bit more?"

"What do you suspect?"

"For Christ's sake, Charles. Give me a break. There's more isn't there? What is it about Virex and Biox? I thought you were competitors but from where I'm sitting you look like just one big organisation working in similar fields with similar problems. And you are both located in Boston - a mile away from each other. Don't you talk? Don't you share anything with Josh Ornstein?"

I waited for a response but there was nothing. Silence.

"Then if you don't mind, Charles, I'm going to ditch this very unsatisfactory arrangement with Virex and pursue a few other things that I've uncovered in the last few days. For one thing, I'm going to talk to Biox and when I'm finished there, I'm going to find out a bit more about another company I suspect you are familiar with - namely Livingstone Pharmaceuticals.

"What have you found?" Brady now sounded like a bear with a sore head.

"It's nothing to do with Virex, Charles, so I can't tell you - breaches of confidence and all that."

138

"But......" Charles Brady seemed about to say something else but I didn't give him a chance.

"Why send me to the conference, Charles? Yes, it was interesting but I'm not that keen on becoming an epidemiologist or a virologist at this stage of my life."

"We thought you might find a few leads at the trade exhibition."

"Charles," I said, "Please. Stop messing me about. If you know something, tell me. I'm not inexperienced in this business, you know. I can usually tell if I'm being bluffed or led up a garden path blindfolded. I've had clients who have left it right to the end to tell me something they could have told me right at the start and made it far easier for everyone. I think you're one of them."

Suddenly, Charles Brady seemed to break. I heard a sound as if he may have stood up from where he was sitting.

"It's Livingstone Pharmaceuticals, Daniel, I'm damned sure of it. That's what Josh Ornstein thinks as well."

"So you talk regularly to Biox and Josh Ornstein do you, Charles? I wish I'd known that earlier. How much do you share?"

"We share a lot, Daniel. But some of it is commercially sensitive."

"You mean plans for technical co-operation, merger, acquisition, take over?"

"Remember, Daniel you are subject to the confidentiality agreement you signed." The sore-headed bear had returned.

"Then spill the beans, Charles. Tell me something that will help because I am very tempted, as I've said, to go off on a tangent, on my own, unfettered by confidentiality agreements or other red tape. I am damned sure there is something going on out here which I suspect is far bigger than Virex losing a scientist and few grams of something pink in a test tube."

"It's Livingstone," said Charles Brady. He now sounded like baby bear of Goldilocks and the three bears.

"Yes, you said that. What about Livingstone?"

"The guy who owns them has been the subject of FBI investigations."

"You mean Gregory O'Brian?"

"You know?"

"Get on with it Charles. I want you to tell me something new."

"He's probably developing a new research facility somewhere."

"Yes, I know."

"You know that, too?"

"It's what you're paying me for, Charles. I call it background research. Anything else?"

"I think he's poached David Solomon, Guy Williams and now our guy, Jan."

"Yes, I thought so. Anything else?"

There was another noticeable pause.

"They all think the same - politically."

"Ah," I said. "Progress. What does their shared politics look like?"

"Green issues, the environment."

"Can you be a little more precise?"

"Population control, natural resource - they are all professionals - biologists, virologists and experts on infection control and epidemiology and they belonged to the same club. "

"What club?" I asked.

"Boston University - Malthus Club."

I didn't want to upset Brady too much. I pleaded ignorance.

"It's a society that discusses population control, the environment, international issues, that type of thing." said Brady.

There we have it, I thought. Solomon is still around somewhere and putting messages up onto the Malthus Society website. I smiled at Anna and gave her a thumbs up sign. She smiled back and, at last, tucked into the tom yung kung.

I then decided to cut out some of the crap Brady might have been tempted to introduce before we arrived where I thought we were heading.

"So what could Livingstone Pharmaceuticals, a company whose owner is hardly known for respectable ethical practice, possibly offer a few scientists with interests in the environment?"

"Money?" whimpered Brady.

"Anything else? And let me now ask you the big question, Charles. Do you think Livingstone is the guilty party - the one who has got its sticky little hands on your pink liquid?"

"Could be."

God, this man was a struggle. "Probably?" I pushed.

"Yes, and......" Brady paused, "....an opportunity to do something about their opinions on the environment?"

It was a question from Charles Brady. It was not a statement made with any real conviction.

"And how could Livingstone - or, to be more precise, Gregory O'Brian - offer them an opportunity to do something about the environment? He hardly seems the sort of person to worry about the destruction of rain forests."

I actually thought I already knew the answer and that Charles Brady didn't. It was something that Colin had said about GOB. "A criminal psychiatrist might say it's failed political ambitions," Colin had said. "He never got his dreamed-of job in a new Irish Government. Since then he's dabbled in other ways to change the system - anything radical gets his attention. You've got an extreme plan that might upset someone? GOB will go for it. A fighting fund for anything extreme that might yield a profit years into the future? GOB's definitely your man."

But as I expected, Charles Brady's reply to my last question was another, "I don't know." I decided to help him out.

"How about paying them well, helping them fulfil their ambitions - whatever they are - and, at the same time, channelling everything into making him an even richer man?"

"Yes," said Brady, "I can see that."

At last, I thought. I was still firmly on track.

CHAPTER 35

Larry Brown had no desire to stay on in Kano with police on every corner and a general feeling of insecurity everywhere so he walked back to Jonathan's taxi and headed for the airport and the last flight back to Lagos.

Next morning and before Joseph and the others had turned up for work, Larry found himself looking out of the office window again. Some focus had definitely returned but it had nothing to do with what the US Government was paying him for. He turned to see Joseph and the others settling themselves behind their desks for another day.

"What time do you call this, then Joseph?"

Joseph glanced at his watch. "9am, Larry, time to start work."

Larry turned back to the view from the window. "Is that all it is? How many US healthcare companies have signed up for your trade show, then Joseph?"

"No time, Larry. Still working on the Nigeria Computer Show."

"Well done, Joseph, I'm glad the US computer industry is getting all the support it deserves from the US Embassy " He paused. "Tell me, Joseph, did you ever speak to someone who phoned asking for advice on where he might run consumer tests on a new medicine?"

"No, Larry."

"So who suggested that Kano, Dala Hill to be precise, might be a good place to run these tests?"

"Ah yes, Larry. That was me. It was the first place that came to my mind. He was after somewhere in the north, quite populated, near a city."

"So," said Larry, "now that you've remembered that, can you remember his name or did you write it down somewhere? Office procedure is that we log all this isn't it?"

"Sorry, Larry - no."

Larry looked around for something to throw at Joseph but then thought better of it. "Was his name Mohamed El Badry?"

"Yes, it might have been, Larry."

"So we now offer free commercial advice and guidance for the whole of the Middle East do we?"

"He said he worked for a US company."

"I suppose you've forgotten the name of the US company."

"Yes, Larry."

"So, all along, this Mohamed El Badry might well have been, at least, a bull-shitter or, at worst, a fucking liar. Right?"

"Yes, Larry."

Larry clenched his hands together and looked out of the window again. In his mind he was strangling Joseph. Still looking out he said: "What time is it in England, Joseph?"

"8am, Larry."

Larry went to his desk, found the note he'd made of Kevin Parker's UK phone number and, as he walked out of the office, phoned him.

As it was Tuesday, Kevin was still in bed. He had no students on Tuesdays and so he usually had a lie in before either going up to the University for a subsidised lunch or wandering down to the Richmond to meet Tom Weston or anyone else who happened to be there. When his mobile rang he automatically assumed it was Tunje.

"Been up all night again, Tunj? Couldn't you sleep?"

"Kevin?"

It was not Tunje's North London Nigerian accent but American.

"Sorry, Larry. I thought it was a friend of mine."

"No problem. I was in Kano yesterday. It was very enlightening," said Larry.

"Did you find Mohamed El Badry. Larry?"

"No, but I now know a lot more about what went on leading up to the deaths."

Kevin listened to Larry's story.

"So what can we do, Larry? Clearly the Nigerian authorities don't care."

"I'm going to phone WHO again," Larry said. "It's the only organisation I can think of who might know what to do."

"Did you speak to Joseph?"

"No," said Larry, not wishing to think about Joseph. "You told me as much as I need to know. Joseph was just doing his job."

Ten minutes later, though, Larry spoke to Joseph but not about his conversation with Mohamed El Badry. "What time is it in Geneva, Joseph?"

"Nine fifteen, Larry."

At nine twenty, Larry was speaking to the WHO in Geneva on his mobile phone from outside in the street. There was no way, Joseph was going to hear what he had to say.

At the World Health Organisation, it was Richard Lacey who brought the matter to the attention of his boss, the Director General.

He hadn't spoken directly to Doctor Larry Brown at the US Embassy in Nigeria, he told her, but from the information he had been given it seemed there might well be grounds for thinking that something totally unethical - possibly bordering on criminality - was going on.

Someone needed to get to the bottom of the rumours about the hundred or so Nigerian deaths. It now appeared that not only had the patients themselves disappeared but a mysterious doctor who was being linked to what sounded like a criminal attempt to test out a new drug had also disappeared. To add credence to that, it appeared that all the patients were men and they were being paid to attend the clinic.

"But it's all rumour," Lacey said. "Can we be sure this is not just some lethal medicine made from heaven knows what and a doctor who isn't really a doctor at all? We've heard this sort of thing before from West Africa."

"Yes," said the DG, "I know I keep on about facts but that's what we need - facts."

"Well, it doesn't look as if we're going to get much help from the Nigerian authorities at present. Apparently, they are too pre-occupied with the Islamic insurgency in the north of the country. They are just not taking the cases seriously - it is as if they are willing to believe it was just a local flu epidemic."

The DG got up from behind her desk and paced around her office. Richard Lacey was still trying to summarise the situation.

"Add that to what we have heard from Pradit about the Thai cases all having been in one small area, possibly just one building, and with a mystery surrounding a few inhalers being found, then what are we to make of it all?" he said.

"But we still don't know if the Nigerian virus is the same as the Thai one or the Kenyan one or even if it is a virus," the DG said. "The important thing is to establish whether the Nigerian cases were also TRS-CoV, Richard. And are there more cases coming to light? Are cases just not being reported? Or has it suddenly stopped as quickly as it seemed to appear?"

Richard Lacey nodded. "I'll double-check with Doctor Larry Brown at the US Embassy," he said. "He's the only one who seems to be taking a real interest. His opinion seems to be that this is a virus and not a drug reaction. We'll also have another go at the Nigerian Ministry of Health, perhaps try pushing them harder. And the Regional Director for Africa needs to know but he's now in South Africa."

"And I'll phone the Nigerian Minister of Health, Richard," said the DG. "But I'm beginning to think we're a bit late. If these rumours are true then we may need to consider involving law enforcement agencies."

CHAPTER 36

My private concerns were, of course, all about Anna. Since returning from Singapore we had stayed at the hotel, but I knew I couldn't stay there for much longer. I might need to return to the UK or, whatever eventually happened with the Virex case, perhaps go somewhere else. If Anna was to be with me, and especially if I decided to return to the UK even for a short time, she'd need a visa and that could take time. But sorting out visas was not the only problem.

I was still struggling to know which direction my life was heading. What I knew was that Anna had, in her quiet way, made me think differently. She also had an uncanny ability to understand my feelings and almost hear my thoughts. Not only that but the pathetic vision of myself as a professional loner I had seen in that flashback a week or so ago had vanished. I took the bull by the horns, so to speak, over breakfast.

"Would you like to live in England?" I said.

Anna's eyes with the long black eyelashes widened and a big smile appeared. "Yes. Yes. Can we come back to visit my mother and my father and my sister when we're married?"

So, another decision had been made for me and my slippery slope had just bottomed out.

CHAPTER 37

Being Tuesday, Kevin Parker was still deciding whether to have his lunch at the University or the Richmond pub. He was sitting in his flat reading a book on another of his Victorian heroes - Isambard Kingdom Brunel. But his mind kept wandering - one minute to what Larry Brown had told him earlier and the next minute to what Mohamed El Badry had said about having a solution to over population. To make matters even worse, the latter seemed ready to be launched.

Kevin's vivid imagination had also turned to wondering what could possibly happen if he, directly or through the Malthus Society, was somehow implicated in a plan that might involve deliberately starting a pandemic to reduce the population. Words and phrases like mass murder, annihilation, ethnic cleansing and genocide kept coming into his head. To Kevin it was sounding more and more plausible that El Badry and whoever his associates were, were deliberately planning to carry out one of these crimes and, in doing so, try to implicate the Malthus Society somehow. Could it be that he was trying to divert attention from his own organisation or deliberately use some of the Society's more radical members scattered across the globe?

Could he expect a knock on the door or, worse, the breaking down of the door of his flat by police with battering rams at 3am. Perhaps Tunje was right and word had already got out of something going on and he was already being watched.

It was such a nightmare scenario that he had started to wonder what he should do to avoid the breaking down of the door at 3am. Should he go to the police before they came to him? Warn them in advance and so be able to plead total innocence?

But he, Kevin Parker, had often advocated the use of radical solutions to the problem of overpopulation. If anyone had wanted to check his opinions, all they needed to do was check out the Malthus Society website. The evidence against him was all there.

So, perhaps El Badry was just being supportive. But Kevin was no longer sure he wanted this sort of support and, anyway, he didn't like Mohamed El Badry. The man had made him nervous. He had looked, smelled and sounded like a rogue, just the sort of rich, foreign businessman Kevin had hated in the past, especially in his youth.

And it had all happened too suddenly. Kevin's strategy had always been a patient build up leading eventually to perhaps mass demonstrations by youth across the globe and then the final recognition by politicians that he had been right all along and something needed to be done about the population.

Kevin felt another cold sweat coming on and held his wrist to check how fast his heart was beating. At times like this he often wished he possessed a blood pressure monitor. But Kevin's decision about where to go for his lunch suddenly became clear. He would go to the Richmond. But first he would call Tom Weston to make sure he'd be there.

"How about a pint or two and egg and chips on me, Tom. I need to pick your brains."

CHAPTER 38

"Your bill is mounting up, Dan Dare," said Colin, "I hope you're covering your costs somehow."

"Well, life can get expensive from time to time, Colin, I admit. But now and again we all need to take the plunge - speculate to accumulate so to speak - invest in the future - take a calculated risk."

"Jesus, Daniel, is that really you ?"

"Just trying to be a good businessman, Colin. Anyway - down to business. Malthus Society, Colin. Ever heard of it? It has a website, blog, a message board. Remember your history at school? It supports and promotes many of the views of Thomas Malthus. He wrote a book on population control in 1798 that many feel is now more relevant than ever. The website has facts, figures, references and also a lot of crazy, fanatical views - but a lot of sense, too."

"Never heard of it."

"Then can you check it out, Colin? I need to know who moderates it. He uses the name "Thalmus" - obviously an anagram of Malthus. I'm sure you have the technology so it'll be a quick and simple job for you."

"Yes, we have the means."

"Quick, easy, cheap. - that's what I like."

"So what happened to your plans for taking calculated risks, speculating to accumulate and investing in the future, 007?"

"Oh, I'm doing plenty of that. Colin," I said, "It looks like I'm getting married." Then I switched my phone off.

CHAPTER 39

"Bless my soul," said Tom after Kevin had brought him up to date with everything including his chats with Doctor Larry Brown at the American Embassy in Nigeria.

"So what the bloody hell should I do, Tom?"

"Mmm," said Tom, "Ah........."

While he waited, Kevin wiped the egg from his plate with the last of his chips.

"So," he said, licking his fingers, "Any thoughts?"

"No idea," said Tom, "Go to the police? See your MP?"

"Thought of that. Tom - decided against it. "

"Talk to Larry whatsisname?"

"Yes. I'll definitely talk to Larry Brown again but what the bloody hell can he do to protect the Malthus Society from getting tangled up in all this? What's going on here. Tom? Am I being neurotic? Should I just relax like it's nothing to do with me - sit and watch what happens?"

"Yeh," said Tom, "sit for a bit - see what happens. Something will crop up for sure. Then it'll all become clear. That's what I'd do, young man."

Kevin sat back. "Want another pint?"

"I could be persuaded."

Tom pushed his glass towards Kevin who stood ready to go to the bar. But before he could move, Tom grabbed him by the shirt sleeve. "I checked out that fellow, David Solomon," he said.

Kevin stood, beer glasses in hand. "And?"

"He's a bloody nutcase."

Kevin sat down again.

"Why?"

"Don't ask me why, he just is."

"What I mean is why do you say he's a nutcase?"

"I read some of his stuff."

"Yes, you told me, Tom."

"Not that stuff, other stuff. Stuff he wrote for the club in Boston."

"What club?"

"The Malthus Club in Boston, you young fool."

"Sorry," said Kevin, "I'd forgotten they had a separate one. So what did he write?"

"An article called 'The Day of Reckoning'. I read it again last night."

"Yes, but why does that make him a nutcase?"

"You read it, see what you make of it," Tom fumbled in the inside pocket of the old jacket that he still wore since his teaching days. "Here," he said and handed over a small bundle of folded sheets of paper.

CHAPTER 40

Whim, instinct, hunch. Call it what you like but I was sure that Kenya and Egypt held a few more keys to what was going on here. This business is not like others. In some businesses you can jump in your car and drive off down the road to check a few things out. In my business, I jump on a plane and the distance is not relevant.. Neither is the destination. I once flew from Saudi Arabia to Helsinki. It was January. In Jeddah it was plus 38C, in Helsinki minus 19C. I not only bought myself a new phone at the airport but a thick overcoat and scarf as well.

"I might need to go to Kenya, Anna," I said, trying to break some possibly bad news.

"OK, I'll wait," she replied. "Don't be long."

I wondered if Anna knew where Kenya was. Probably not.

"On the other hand, I might be able to get someone else to help," I said.

"That would be better," she replied. "You work too hard, travel too much - you need to slow down - make others do work."

So, decision made for me, I phoned Colin again. I eventually went to Kenya anyway, but we'll come to that.

"Twice in a day, Dan Dare. And what a shock? After all these years as a single man? What's got into you all of a sudden? What sort of woman is prepared to put up with you? And all the secrecy you liked to adopt - where has it gone? Can I start calling you Daniel regularly?"

"Shut up, Colin. Her name is Anna and she's sat right next to me."

"So does she want to say hello to your best friend - no, let's be blunt - your only friend?"

I handed my phone to Anna. "Say hello to Colin."

"Hello, Colin," said Anna, "I hope to meet you sometime in England. We went to get my visa today." Then she handed the phone back.

"There, Colin. That's the social part. Now the business part........"

Colin interrupted, "I'm on the case. We're looking at that Malthus site as I speak."

"No, there's something else," I said. "Our mutual friend, Jimmy Banda, Nairobi. Is he busy right now?"

"Funny you should ask. He's just been on an assignment for me in Mombasa. He got back today. As usual, he performed brilliantly. Jimmy is my little ferret."

CHAPTER 41

Banda Book-keeping Services was the business Jimmy Banda had started fifteen years ago in the Nairobi suburb of Embakasi. But whenever he arrived late in the office he always felt he needed a good excuse ready in case Louise, his secretary of ten years, started to ask difficult questions about where he had been. On this occasion, Jimmy had been away for two whole days so he had had plenty of time to come up with his explanation.

As expected, Louise looked up from her old computer as he pushed open the door, went straight to the swivel chair behind his own desk and collapsed into it. Then he expelled a lungful of air as if he had just run a marathon. Appearing out of breath was all part of his ready-made excuse.

Unusually though, Louise, the reliable, mainstay of Banda Book-keeping Services, went back to staring at her screen as if he was not there. Jimmy found this even more unnerving as, still breathing heavily, he watched her fingers tapping numbers on the keyboard.

"Did you finish Mr Kalinga's accounts, Louise?"

"Yes, yesterday."

"Did you send them off?"

"Yes, yesterday."

"I've been to Mombasa," Jimmy said, "Looking for new clients."

"We can't cope with the ones we've already got around Embakasi, Mr Banda." Louise said and continued with her typing.

Jimmy relaxed. He pushed a pile of paper and correspondence from one side of his desk to the other, switched on his own computer and then leaned back in his chair so far that his long legs extended half way to Louise's desk. In this almost horizontal position, he closed his eyes and relaxed. Louise glanced at him but then got on with her own work.

Jimmy Banda could relax because he was no longer the book-keeper. Jimmy had passed this job permanently to Louise and now ran Banda Investigation Services. One of his sources of business was Colin Asher. Jimmy was Colin's Kenyan sub agent.

"You're like a little ferret, Jimmy," Colin had once said.

Jimmy had thought he liked that description but had had to look up what a ferret was. He now knew it was a fast little animal with beady eyes and a fascination with going down dark holes. So, relaxing in the knowledge that Louise had no questions today, Jimmy quickly dropped off to sleep. But then his mobile phone rang. He'd just changed the ringtone to something with a heavy drum beat and so it made him jump. When he opened his eyes, Louise was watching him.

He dug into his suit pocket, retrieved it and put it against his ear.

"Banda Investigation Services," he said, "Jimmy Banda speaking."

"Jimmy," said the English accent on the other end of the phone. "It's David Franklin. Long time. How are you?"

Daniel, in Bangkok glanced at Anna, put his forefinger up to his mouth and smiled.

"Hey, long time," said Jimmy, "How are you?" It was a sure sign that Jimmy was struggling to remember David Franklin. Daniel gave him a reminder.

"How's my friend Colin? I hear you've just got back from Mombasa on an assignment."

"Ah, David Franklin, friend of Colin."

"That's me," said Daniel. "Are you busy at present?"

151

Jimmy shuffled the paper on his muddled desk and glanced over at Louise.

"Yes," he said, "Very busy, thank you."

"Could you squeeze in an assignment for me? I've already spoken to Colin about it and he has agreed you can invoice him direct. But it's bit complicated and Colin suggested I phone you direct to discuss it."

"Yes, I can squeeze it in," said Jimmy deciding he'd remember that phrase. It might come in useful sometime.

"But you don't yet know what the assignment is, Jimmy?"

"No, but I can squeeze it in for my friend Colin."

Daniel started to explain what he wanted.

"There is a company in Nairobi called Shah Medicals," he said. "I need someone to go in there, do a bit of ferreting around and try to speak to someone who works there - his name is Luther Jasman."

"OK, I'll go right now." said Jimmy and Daniel thought he heard a chair being pushed back.

"Hang on, Jimmy. Let me give you some background and what to do and say. The company is in Embakasi, close to where you are I think............"

"Yes, we are conveniently located near to many businesses," began Jimmy. Conveniently located was another phrase he'd learned from an Englishman.

".......and you will probably find it is an old established business that has recently started to expand......"

"Ah, yes, old Mr Shah. My mother knew him."

"That'll be him. Jimmy. But it's recently been taken over. I don't want to give you the details over the phone or it might compromise your detective work but...."

"Yes, I don't need too much at this stage or it can compromise my....."

"So try phoning. Ask to speak to Luther Jasman and say that Doctor Michael Stevens from Malaysia recently spoke to......"

"I'll just get some paper - Louise! Pencil."

"Are you ready now? Good. Where was I? Tell him that Doctor Michael Stevens from Malaysia recently met their new chief executive - a man called Mr

O'Brian concerning some possible co-operation on a student exchange for their new laboratory......."

"Mr O'Brian.....students......new laboratory."

"Yes, that's it. Get to know Luther Jasman, perhaps fix a meeting with him. Ask questions. You know how to go from there, Jimmy - you're a natural."

A few more facts from Daniel about Shah Medicals being linked with an organisation called Al Zafar and Livingstone Pharmaceuticals and that they seemed to be recruiting laboratory technicians and Daniel knew that Jimmy had understood. At least, it was enough for him to start. Jimmy had an uncanny knack of uncovering information and information was just what Daniel needed. What's more, Jimmy charged by the hour and as he didn't wear a watch, Jimmy's invoices were never extortionate.

"Haven't you got somewhere more important to go - the University for instance? You've got it far too easy, young man. In my day......"

So saying, eighty year old Tom left Kevin in the Richmond to return to his second hand book shop. Kevin continued to sit and read David Solomon's 'The Day of Reckoning' and was immediately engrossed in it.

It was as if Solomon had used exactly the same introduction to the history of population control that Kevin often gave his students. There were the mentions of the ancient Greeks, Plato and Aristotle, the words of Tertullian and those of Niccola Machiavelli.

"When every province of the world so teems with inhabitants that they can neither subsist where they are nor remove themselves elsewhere, the world will purge itself in floods, plague and famine."

Solomon mentioned Richard Hakluyt with his old English words of warning: "Throughe our longe peace and seldome sickness we are growen more populous than ever heretofore. Many thousandes of idle persons are within this realme, which, havinge no way to be sett on worke, be either mutinous and seeke alteration in the state, or at leaste very burdensome to the commonwealthe. "

There were others but not one reference to any counter arguments. Kevin would normally include at least some. Finally, though, Solomon mentioned Thomas Malthus and Paul Ehrlich.

But then came the science, the molecular genetics, the politics and the plan.

"We can now create new, highly pathogenic and transmissible viruses. We can use them for research to understand infection or we can use them in more practical ways such as for population control."

"But we need to retain our control over the methods we are developing so that we can decide how they should be used. We cannot rely on politicians who do not understand science.

"So we can and must develop a highly resistant bacterium or a virus that can be used to counter the ever-growing threat posed by the effects of overpopulation - the availability of sufficient food, of natural resources, of jobs and the space in which to live a decent and civilised life free of eternal conflict. Scientists must be granted the freedom to use technology to solve social problems of this magnitude. We are granted the freedom to use technology to improve life. But this only has the effect of increasing the population to unsustainable levels. Granting us the freedom to use technology to reduce the population to a balanced and sustainable level has to be the next logical step.

"We cannot allow politicians who do not understand modern molecular biology to continue to perpetuate the status quo for their own shallow, short-term reasons because politicians and religious leaders are to blame for the current situation. They turn their backs on the problem because they are too afraid to act. Scientists and technology must now intervene if the human race is to have a better quality of life in and beyond this overcrowded planet................"

".........but unless we want to destroy everything, we must have an available counter-balance, an effective treatment for our virus - a drug or a vaccine - that is ready and available in advance of the release of the virus to use selectively in order to retain proper scientific control."

Kevin re-folded the papers that Tom had given him and closed his laptop. Then he leaned back in the seat and rubbed his eyes.

Up to a certain point, everything Solomon had written was music to his ears. But then Solomon had gone past the point. What Solomon was advocating was that scientists decide who should live and die. That had never been in Kevin's plan. But perhaps that was because he was not a scientist, a virologist or a molecular biologist, but a teacher of social and economic history.

As he got up to pay for his lengthy lunch, he wondered what Solomon was doing now and it worried him that he might be one of the so-called associates that Mohamed El Badry had spoken of. But as Kevin walked home to his flat, he still did not know what to do.

Kevin's nerves were calmed by Larry Brown's phone call from Lagos that evening.

"I've spoken to WHO," Larry said. "I told them everything I know about the Nigerian deaths, about the doctor who has disappeared and about the fact that he was inviting local men to help test a new medicine for money - everything."

"That's good news, Larry. So when can we expect some proper investigations to start?"

"That is the problem, Kevin. I think it's very optimistic to assume that some sort of international system is in place that will take over and deal with it. You see, the WHO only works through the correct channels, which means it works via governments. And, as we know, the Nigerian government and the Kano State government do not see a few deaths from something that resembled influenza as particularly important - especially when they're dealing with Islamic insurgents from outside Nigeria who come armed with guns and bombs.

"WHO are not even coming clean on the Thai cases, although I think they've uncovered something. If they have, they're not saying what it is. Certainly not to me. I'm a persona non grata you see - an outsider - someone who tipped them off but not someone they are able to deal with on an official basis. The answer might be to get the US or UK government to ask questions but in my case I'd probably need to go via the US Ambassador here. It could all take time."

Kevin's nerves took another turn for the worse and he decided to admit it.

"But I'm becoming very worried now, Larry. My fear is that the Malthus Society will get dragged into this, which means I might get dragged in. I'm starting to fear a knock on my door at midnight."

And then he started a long explanation about the online message from "Solomon" and of tracking down a paper called "The Day of Reckoning" written by David Solomon.

"What was the name?" asked Larry, thinking he'd heard it somewhere.

"David Solomon," confirmed Kevin. "I think he's from Boston."

Larry was trying to place the name but Kevin was still talking. It was not until later that Larry finally made the connection with Biox and Josh Ornstein.

"You see, Larry?" Kevin finally concluded "I think there is far more to this than you and I can deal with. I just don't know where to turn."

"I have an appointment, Louise," Jimmy Banda said. "I might be gone five minutes or five hours."

"Yes, Mr Banda," Louise glanced up from her computer screen for a brief second to see Jimmy removing his tie and undoing the top button of his shirt.

"But I need to make some confidential phone calls first," he added.

"Go ahead. Mr Banda. If you go outside I won't be able to hear."

"Yes," Jimmy said and went out.

On his mobile, Jimmy found the number for Shah Medicals, asked to speak to Luther Jasman and was told to phone another number. This second call was answered by a man who said that he was that person - Luther Jasman. Jimmy knew immediately he was speaking to a Kenyan Asian.

Jimmy span him the yarn about a meeting with a Mr O'Brian and student exchanges

"I see," said Jasman doubtfully, "I would need to check."

"But I already checked with Mr O'Brian," said Jimmy, doing what he often did best - lying through his teeth. "Mr O'Brian said it would be OK. Can we meet?"

"I don't know."

Jimmy now recognised a man with no authority. More made up stories would be well worth trying. "We've also discussed it with your parent company, Al Zafar? Shah Medicals is becoming a very big company now."

"Yes, I see." Jasman resolve was breaking a little.

"Can I come over to see you? I wouldn't keep you long."

"We don't have visitors here. We have tight security."

"Mr O'Brian seemed to think it would be OK."

"He's not my boss."

"But I also heard you were finding it difficult to recruit good technicians."

"Yes, it is making it difficult for us to do what we have to do."

"So use some students - that was Mr O'Brian's idea."

"But he's not my boss."

"But Mr O'Brian had already discussed it with Al Zafar. Who do you report to? I will speak to him directly."

"Well, maybe we should meet."

Jimmy smiled to himself. "Shall I come to your laboratory?"

"Oh, no, no."

"Of course - tight security. Never mind, my friend runs a bed & breakfast house by the social hall - Nyayo B&B. Do you know it?"

"Yes, I have passed it."

"So, this evening after work? At six." said Jimmy. Then he went back inside his office.

"Louise," he said.

"Yes, Mr Banda."

"I remember an article in the Daily Nation about Shah Medicals. Did you see it?"

"Yes, Mr Banda. A takeover. We lost their book-keeping business."

"That's it, Louise. Any chance you could find the paper?"

"It was weeks if not months ago, Mr Banda."

"But do you remember anything?"

"Yes, it was taken over by an Arab company called Al Zafar. Their owner, Mohamed Kader came here. It was he who decided they no longer needed our accountancy services."

"Yes, I remember that, Louise. Anything else?"

"Yes, the boss of Livingstone Pharmaceuticals also came and visited them.."

"Ah, yes," said Jimmy, "Greg O'Brian."

"Yes, Mr Banda. You have a very good memory."

"I'm going out, Louise. I might be gone for an hour - perhaps longer."

Jimmy's car was parked around the corner from the office. Covered in red dust, he had meant to wash it but it would have to wait because he now wanted to find the premises of Shah Medicals. That they had had the audacity to take away the book-keeping business was largely what made Jimmy grind his gears and speed off.

What Jimmy found as he skidded to a halt in a side street of the Bakker Industrial Estate was the same, nondescript double-storied concrete building that he remembered. But it now had rows of dark-green painted windows and a green double door with a shelter made of corrugated steel. And someone had also built a head high chicken wire fence linked by concrete posts around it. But the gate was open so Jimmy got out of his car and walked up to the door. No-one seemed to be around.

The green, hand-painted sign on the door said: "Shah Medicals" and, beneath, in smaller print "Part of Al Zafar Agencies Ltd."

Jimmy took his mobile phone from his pocket and photographed the door with its name-plate. Then he returned to his car and photographed the entire building. No-one had come or gone. Other than a van parked outside an industrial printing company's premises and two men fixing a wheel on a motorcycle, the road was muddy from recent rain and deserted.

But as Jimmy started his engine he noticed that the rear of the building looked as if it had been extended backwards into the side street behind. It had not been there when Banda Book-Keeping Services looked after old Mr Shah's accounts. Deciding it was worth another look, Jimmy drove off, doubled back into the road behind and stopped again.

The building from this side now looked more like a small warehouse. It had a loading area with a wide door open to the inside. And through the door, rows of fluorescent strip lights reflected off white-painted walls, floor and ceiling. And, standing on the floor, were three large, shiny, stainless-steel tanks. Plastic tubing ran along the floor and two men in white coats and hats sat side by side at a desk. Behind them was what looked like an office or laboratory lit by more strip lights. Perhaps, Jimmy thought, this was where Luther Jasman worked.

Jimmy, pretending to use his mobile phone from his car seat, took more photos. No-one seemed to notice him.

Thinking there was nothing to lose, Larry Brown phoned the WHO again. This time he pushed harder and, giving his US Embassy Nigeria credentials, demanded to speak to someone in authority - "Even the Director General herself - this is important." Finally he was told to phone back in an hour to speak to Richard Lacey.

Even so, he then had to wait, holding the line to Geneva while the DG's adviser was traced and came to the phone. Then, after reminding Richard Lacey of the problem he'd identified in Nigeria and listening to what Larry perceived as just polite thanks for his diligence, Larry laid into him.

"That's kind of you, Mr Lacey but what would you say if I suggested that what we have here is blatant criminality? And what would you say if I suggested a conspiracy to deliberately spread a virus like SARS with no known cure with the intention of wiping out hundreds, thousands or perhaps millions of people. If it was a country doing this to another it would be called a declaration of war or genocide. But if it is a private company doing it because they had a treatment or a vaccine ready to launch to make huge profits from, then what would you call it? Good business?"

"I would call it a very unlikely scenario, Doctor Brown. Where is your evidence? And what company would have the resources to do such a thing, let alone be so secretive and unethical as to contemplate doing it?"

"OK, Mr Lacey. Let me put to you another scenario. Infectious disease researchers and virologists are fond of saying that microbes do not respect barriers. So who makes the rules to control researchers who might be tempted to go the extra mile and deliberately engineer a virus for so-called experimental reasons? Does your organisation, The World Health Organisation, have any say? Does it set any safety standards? Does it have an opinion? Do you have an opinion?"

"Yes, Doctor Brown we have had discussions?"

"Where? When? What were the conclusions? I've looked and I can't find them."

"It's very sensitive, Doctor Brown. We have to be careful. We do not publish everything."

"Yes, but don't you have responsibilities as well, and especially a responsibility to protect people. Isn't that precisely what the WHO was set up to do?"

"Yes, of course, and, as I've said, we do discuss the matter."

"With whom? And is it behind closed doors?"

"Doctor Brown, we're very grateful to you for bringing these cases to our attention but I'm not able to explain what we do or how on the telephone. I suggest you talk to the relevant US authorities."

"But this type of work is taking place, Mr Lacey. There are scientists out there right now sat in laboratories changing and modifying viruses for so-called experiments. What I am asking you for is information on the controls placed on someone or an organisation wanting to create a new human virus just for the intellectual challenge? Where are the regulators? What exactly has been put in place to stop an individual or a criminal organisation from engineering such a virus, having a vaccine or drug already available and then releasing the virus to make a huge profit?"

In the end, Larry got nowhere with his discussion - except a small promise and an indication that there were, perhaps, some other things that Larry still didn't know about.

"I'll ensure your views are brought to the attention of the Director General, Doctor Brown. She is already very grateful for the information on the Nigerian cases that you have been providing. We are naturally aware of something going on here but are unable to comment further at present."

CHAPTER 42

"Daniel: The fellow who moderates the Malthus Society website is Kevin Parker and he's British. He's a lecturer in British Social and Economic History at Bristol University and an expert on the history of population control. According to his own description of himself he is, "an advocate of direct action aimed at persuading Governments and the United Nations to accept the need to be pro-active in reducing the world's population." He lives in Bristol and we've got his university email address and a mobile phone number. He is unaware that we have traced him. Over to you. Regards, Colin."

As I finished reading Colin's email, I checked the time. It was evening in Bangkok, early afternoon in UK. I phoned the mobile number of Kevin Parker but it was engaged.

CHAPTER 43

In Nairobi, it was not yet 6pm, but Jimmy Banda had been sitting in the Nyayo Bed and Breakfast for well over an hour waiting for Luther Jasman.

It wasn't that he was always early for appointments but Louise had decided she needed the entire office including Jimmy's desk and chair for a book-keeping meeting with a client. But Jimmy didn't mind. The Nyayo B and B was run by an old school friend, Emmanuel, who not only chatted to him while mopping the kitchen floor but kept Jimmy's coffee mug topped up. When Jimmy returned from a visit to the men's room a short man in a dark suit was ringing the bell in the reception area.

"Ah," said Jimmy still pulling up his zip fastener, "You must be Luther."

"Yes sir," said the man - a short, but neatly presented young man of Indian descent with, as Jimmy noticed, an open necked shirt and no tie. Jimmy tightened his own tie in response.

"Cup of coffee?" Jimmy asked.

"Thank you."

Jimmy led Luther Jasman to the seat he had been warming for the best part of an hour and called out to Emmanuel for two more coffees.

"Yes, I met Greg O'Brian at an Irish Embassy reception." Jimmy said, roughly picking up where he had left off on the phone earlier. "We got chatting. I told him about my part time work at the University - I teach accountancy. Anyway, long story cut short, he asked about students. I said, no problem, how many did he need. He said he had problems recruiting staff and thought students on work experience might help."

Jimmy paused and glanced at Luther Jasman's hands. He was turning and twisting a new and shiny, gold wedding ring on his finger.

"What is your opinion?" Jimmy asked but then gave him no time to reply. "Mr O'Brian gave me your name. You must be very important with Shah Medicals."

"No. I am only in charge of product registration. I am a graduate of the faculty of biology, you see. It is not so complicated, really."

"It sounds very complicated to me,"

"Oh no sir, not for me," admitted Jasman, "The products are quite simple. I've been there for four months."

"So what will you want the students to do?"

"I suppose to help in the laboratory. I have been told we have new products coming very soon."

"So, what sort of students do you need?"

"Perhaps microbiology students, perhaps pharmacists or nurses. We need students who understand infection control. That is my interest. I also understand we need a production engineer."

161

"If I may say so, you seem a bit vague about what the company is planning to do."

Emmanuel brought two mugs of coffee and Luther Jasman lifted one to his lips, decided it was too hot and put it down again. Jimmy drank his.

"It is a new company you see, sir."

"So, if Mr O'Brian isn't your boss, who is?"

"A French man. He reports directly to Mr Mohamed Kader, sir."

"Ah, France," said Jimmy, "I know it well - Eiffel Tower, Champs Elysees, Marble Arch. His name's not Jacques Piquant is it?"

"No sir, it's Dominique Lunneau. We can call him Don."

"So how many people work for you, Luther?"

"Just three, sir. They are from Pakistan. They are allowed here because they are qualified in biotechnology from the University of Karachi."

"Three, did you say? That is a lot."

"Yes, sir, but we are not so busy yet. We are waiting for the new products to come from Egypt."

"Egypt? Pakistan? It is a very international company you work for. Lots of career opportunities I would imagine. I wish you luck."

Luther Jasman started to turn the ring on his finger more rapidly, nervously, and Jimmy knew he had pushed him as far as possible - too far in fact. Hoping Luther would not remember too much about the meeting he'd had in the Nyayo B&B, Jimmy decided to wind it up in case a few more stories came into his mind and he completely overdid it. He stood up.

"Well, thank you, Luther. I'll be in touch as soon as possible. How many students did you say you could use?"

"Perhaps three, Mr, uh......"

"Mr Franklin," said Jimmy and left Luther still drinking his coffee.

From his car, Jimmy sent a text to the other Mr Franklin he knew in Bangkok.

CHAPTER 44

I was still sat waiting for Kevin Parker's call to whoever it was to finish. As I waited, it bleeped. It was a text message from Colin. "Phone Jimmy."

I did and got an excited, fifteen minute summary of what Jimmy had done in the space of the last six hours. There wasn't much there yet but, at least Jimmy had made a start and the Pakistan link was interesting. Perhaps Clive's comment that MI6 and CIA had been watching Mohamed Kader's visits to Pakistan could now be explained as a recruitment drive. But why Pakistan?

"So, Mr Franklin, can I invoice Colin for two hours work?" Jimmy asked.

"Yes," I said. "Make it five hours - after all I'll be paying Colin. And I'll be in touch again, Jimmy. There's more to do on this case. Meanwhile, just keep mum."

"Keep mum?" asked Jimmy.

"Yes, it's an English expression for don't tell anyone."

I knew Jimmy would remember that: A mum ferret.

CHAPTER 45

Kevin was taking his usual long lunch break and as it was a pleasant sunny day he decided to take a casual stroll to clear his mind from thinking about his possible arrest on suspicion of involvement in bioterrorism. With no particular route in mind he walked towards Bristol Zoo, up onto Clifton Downs and then towards Brunel's famous suspension bridge over the Avon Gorge. Here, the sun was warm enough for him to remove his Liverpool FC sweater.

Tunje had phoned him at one point but apologised for having hit a wrong button on his phone and the call had only lasted long enough for Kevin to ask whether Tunje had changed sides to work for MI6 and was monitoring his movements. He had bought a packet of sandwiches and a can of Coke from a local shop and sat down to eat his lunch on a wooden bench overlooking the bridge. As he unwrapped his sandwich, his mobile phone rang yet again.

"My name is Daniel Capelli," the caller said, "Am I speaking to Kevin Parker."

Kevin was very tempted to say no but said yes.

"Forgive me for calling you, Kevin - may I call you Kevin? - but I wondered if you could help me. I am working for a pharmaceutical company in the USA who have reported the loss of some research material they were developing for use in treating virus infections, like influenza. I have reason to believe it may have got into the wrong hands and I am looking for some help."

Kevin was not sure what to say. The man was English, he could tell that. The only question was his name - Capelli sounded Italian and mafia instantly came to Kevin's already paranoid state of mind.

"Well, I'm a lecturer in economic history. How could I possibly help?" Kevin said. He was pleased with his reply but had already lost his appetite for the sandwich lying on his knee.

"Because I've recently logged onto your Malthus Society website and something caught my eye."

Kevin's stomach turned. It wasn't due to hunger but he swallowed anyway. "I see," he said and decided to wait to see what came next.

"Does the name David Solomon mean anything to you, Kevin?"

So, Kevin thought, there is something about this man. "Uh, yes," he replied.

"Do you know much about him?"

"I knew nothing until two days ago," said Kevin thinking that if this was a straw floating past his rapidly sinking body he might, at least, try to grasp it.

"And what happened two days ago?"

"He put something on the message board. It rang a few alarm bells. A friend of mine then checked him out."

"And?"

"Alarm bells are still ringing."

"What did you find out? Can you tell me?"

"I'm not sure who you are."

"I'm a private individual, Kevin, a professional investigator of industrial fraud and I feel we may have uncovered something here - something that borders on serious crime. If you are in any way involved or know anything then please tell me."

Kevin thought about it. The phone call had come out of the blue but he needed a friend in England, not Larry Brown in far away Nigeria or Tunje who never took things seriously enough or Tom who sometimes seemed too old to care. Was this a chance to share the worries he had been carrying around with him since he met Mohamed El Badry? Kevin decided to grab the straw.

"David Solomon is, to use a phrase of my old friend Tom, a nutcase," he began.

"Why?"

"Some of his views are extreme. The Malthus Society and myself in particular advocate action to persuade governments to take population control and the need for population reduction seriously. We do not advocate or support implementation of population control methods that have not been adequately debated and agreed. We might be impatient but we do not do anything without some sort of democratic accountability," said Kevin as if reading from one of his own past writings.

He paused but then went on:

"For example, he wrote in one article, 'unless we want to destroy everyone, we must have an effective drug or vaccine available in advance of the release of the virus - to use selectively in order to retain proper scientific control.' And then came his posting on the Malthus site about the day of reckoning."

For Daniel, this fitted neatly around everything he had imagined and he admitted as much to Kevin. "That's exactly what I thought, Kevin. Will you help me?"

In reply, Kevin described his and Tunje's meeting with Mohamed El Badry. Then:

"A friend of Tunje's works at the American Embassy in Nigeria. A doctor working at the Embassy was the one who reported the Nigerian cases to the WHO. His name is Larry Brown."

They talked for a while longer until it was quite clear, the battery on Kevin's phone was nearly exhausted.

"We need to talk more, Kevin," Daniel said. "I'll phone you again very soon. And I'd like to talk to Larry Brown. Feel free to tell him that you and I have spoken and that I'll call him soon."

"Can we meet?" asked Kevin suddenly anxious to put a face to the caller and perhaps shake his hand.

"Yes, we may need to but I'm calling from Bangkok."

Kevin nearly burst into tears.

Unimpressed by his latest discussion with the WHO, Larry toyed with the idea of raising his concerns with the Ambassador. At least, he thought, he might be able to start a ball rolling somewhere. Unable to contain his impatience any longer he phoned the Embassy in Abuja.

"Larry, how's our discoverer of new diseases? Found any more?"

"Not yet. But I'm uncovering other things which bother me."

"Spill the beans, Larry. I'm all ears. By the way, how's the commercial scene? Anything happening on the healthcare front down there? How's the team supporting you?"

Larry had no wish to go into his other frustrations just at that moment. Joseph was sitting within easy throwing distance and he had no wish to get tangled up in a staffing dispute, just yet at any rate. So he said, "Fine."

"So what's biting you, then Larry? The mosquitoes down there? Hah!"

Larry also didn't want a session of humorous camaraderie just at that moment. He was seething not only with a feeling that things needed putting right in the Embassy's commercial section but in the international system governing control of medical research. That was why he was phoning and he still hadn't worked out where to start. At the end looked a good place in this instance.

"No, the mosquitoes aren't biting but something like a new version of SARS might. It might even get you, too, Mister Ambassador - it'll certainly not care who it decides to infect or how many."

"Yes, you warned me about that Larry. I now keep a clean handkerchief in my pocket. But you sound a bit serious if I may say so."

"How does a million deaths from a SARS-like virus just in the USA sound?"

"You serious?"

"Let me describe a scenario to you. Imagine, if you will, a country that deliberately spreads a virus, like SARS, with no known cure with the intention of wiping out hundreds, thousands or perhaps millions of people in a neighbouring country. Would you call it war using biological weapons, sir?"

166

"Yes, I would, Larry, although wouldn't it kill the aggressors as well? But go on."

"And if it was carried out inside their own country against an ethnic minority for instance it would be called ethnic cleansing or genocide, right?

"Yes, I suppose so. But....."

Larry gave him no chance to butt in.

"But if it is a private company releasing the virus because they had a treatment or a vaccine ready to launch to make huge profits from, what would you call that, sir? Good business practice?"

"I'd call that very unethical, Larry."

"Yes, and what would you say if some of the scientists behind creating that virus and developing the drug or vaccine not only had a commercial interest in it but held some very extreme political views about the need to reduce the world's population for a hundred reasons that they would, if required to, site as indisputable evidence for their actions?"

"But that's ridiculous, Larry. They wouldn't be allowed to get away with it with all the checks and balances in place on research of that sort."

"Are you sure there are any proper checks and balances? Because I'm not and I've looked. There are no international policing systems in place. Any rogue scientist could team up with any rogue businessman with a history of fraud or malpractice and hell bent on making even more money - and what's there to stop it?"

"Are you sure, Larry?"

"Yes, sir. I've checked. And what's more I think we are facing just that scenario out there right now and no-one knows about it or, even if they did, can do anything about it. We might even be too late. I believe those deaths up in Kano were part of what we might call in the world of ethical medical practice a clinical trial. A cleverly chosen place if I may so. A place where the locals have no trust in the system for reporting problems like this, a place where unsubstantiated rumour spreads far faster than facts and just a small corner of a vast area currently fighting a war against Islamic insurgency. And the doctor running the field tests has since disappeared, as you know. "

In Abuja, the Ambassador leaned back in the big leather chair behind his desk. "OK Larry, hang on. Let's test this theory of yours out," he said and picked up the other phone on his desk. Then he pressed a button and Larry heard him say:

"Julie, when they open the shop, can you find me somebody to talk to in the Department of Health and Human Services in Washington. Then do the same thing with the US Federal Drug Administration. We'll take it from there."

Then he turned to Larry again. "Larry, my friend, you've just made the hair on the back of my neck stand up . Give me a while and I'll get back."

CHAPTER 46

With Anna already asleep, I phoned Colin yet again.

"Firstly, Colin, you can expect an invoice from Jimmy. He's done brilliantly. Secondly, can you check another name for me? Clive in Cyprus might help you on this one if you need a lead. There is, or was, a small pharmaceutical manufacturer in Beirut - a French owned company - they lost their French production engineer last year. Can you put a name to him? Better still, can you get a photo?

"Thirdly, have you had any contact with Nagi in Cairo recently?"

There was a noticeable delay from the other side.

"Is that it? I was waiting for a fourth. Answers as follows:

"Jimmy - yes, OK, but I won't hold my breath - for a supposed accountant he really needs to speed up his own invoicing. The missing French chap - I can ask Simone in Paris about that. As far as Nagi is concerned I haven't heard from him for a long while but that doesn't mean he's not operating. For good reasons at present he doesn't like reminders about his old life with the Egyptian Security Forces."

CHAPTER 47

Someone had once told Larry that if you've tried pushing and it fails, try pulling. So, with his efforts to find companies willing to invest in Nigeria failing, he decided to try a new strategy - identify the demand and then meet it. But with Joseph still busy organising his computer show, Larry decided to give himself the rest of the afternoon off to sit and think in the peace of his own apartment. But he had barely arrived when Kevin called with a summary of his conversation with someone called Daniel Capelli.

"He said he'd call you, Larry." Kevin finally concluded. "I don't know much about this guy except he seemed as worried as we are and he's English."

Listening to Kevin's obvious relief at having had a phone conversation with an unheard of English guy based in Bangkok, Larry pondered on whether being English meant anything at all these days. He continued to potter about his apartment and then settled himself in front of the TV with a can of beer and a sandwich to watch CNN or some other US channel. But he had just taken the first bite when his phone rang again.

Daniel introduced himself and began with an explanation of what he did and why he had gone to Bangkok. Larry interrupted. "Is your client, Biox?"

"No," said Daniel, honestly, but intrigued how quickly Larry had mentioned the company. "Why do you ask?"

"They lost a couple of scientists some time back and I know the boss, Josh Ornstein. I happened to speak to him only last week. Respiratory viruses, influenza, SARS are his thing and his company gets a lot of research funding. But I sensed a strange interest in the Nigerian deaths. It was as if he was suspicious of something but couldn't go as far as to admit it."

Larry, by this time, was strolling around his apartment holding the phone."David Solomon was one of the guys they lost. Guy Williams was another."

Large bits of Daniel's jigsaw suddenly started falling rapidly into place. He let Larry continue.

"And Kevin has told me some interesting things about Solomon's background," Larry went on. "Are you aware of this?"

"Yes," said Daniel.

"So is your client Virex?" asked Larry.

"Not allowed to say, Larry, but you've just arrived in Boston, Massachusetts as if by intuition."

Larry gave a short laugh. "Charles Brady," he said. "Good old Charles. He and Josh Ornstein are like two dogs - they bark at one another. One minute they play together, the next minute they are trying to tear each other apart. So does the bickering have any relevance?"

A question like that was what Daniel was trying to answer but the more people he could find like Larry, Kevin, Jimmy in Nigeria and one or two others he was thinking of engaging, the quicker the answers might come.

"The bickering is a side show I suspect, Larry," he said, "Ignore it. But you can add into the equation the fact that Biox are not the only company to have lost scientists and technicians in the last year or so. All were virologists or molecular geneticists or technicians useful to a laboratory hell bent on a bit of, what I understand is called in the trade, gain of function or GOF research. Now add into the equation scientists, like Solomon, with extreme views about the powers that should be granted to themselves to decide what to create and how to use their creations."

For Larry, this was exactly what he had been trying to tell the US Ambassador. But Daniel hadn't finished yet. He then started to touch on an area that Larry had not given much thought to - the money side.

"Then," Daniel said, "Into that tasty soup you need to add something else - funding. Funding need not be a problem for these scientists if they can find one or more rich, private individuals. And if one - or more, or all - of these individuals has stashed away a fortune on the back of a lifetime spent in fraud and embezzlement and other criminality and is only interested in investing it to make more money, then what have you got?"

Daniel stopped, hoping it was sinking in. To Larry, the scenario was like a re-run of one of his recent nightmares. "You want my frank opinion, Larry?" Daniel continued.

"Go ahead, although I think I'm seeing it exactly the same way."

"What we have here is an organised bunch of crooks with money and a motley group of scientists with far more than their fair share of reasons for opting out of the mainstream to pursue their dreams and they are all coming together. But I still suspect that Solomon is the technical wizard behind it all and the one with the extreme views on population control. To be fair on the other scientists and technicians, though, I suspect most of them haven't a clue who they are working for."

"Yes," Larry said, "I'll go with all that."

Jimmy had sent a text message to Daniel from his car and then stopped to buy fuel.

"Jimmy the ferret," Daniel said to Anna as they sat in a Bangkok restaurant. "I'd better phone him right now."

In Nairobi, Jimmy's phone rang just as he was about to pay the garage attendant.

"I phoned Shah Medical's accountant this morning," said Jimmy, "I told him I was from Kenya Revenue Authority and that I needed information on the numbers of employees they had. If he could just tell me on the phone KRA inspectors wouldn't need to call around. They employ sixteen."

"Good work, Jimmy," Daniel smiled across the table at Anna.

"I then asked him if Mr Jomo was still their sales manager - Jomo is an old school friend, Mr Franklin. He said yes, but that Jomo is only working for another three weeks because they no longer need a salesman."

As Daniel listened, there was a noise in the background. "Two thousand shillings? Where is your petrol made, mzee, China? I will go somewhere else next time - here, keep the change.......... Sorry, Mr Franklin. Anyway I met Jomo for a beer last night. We told jokes although Jomo was not wanting to joke too much. He has a wife and four children. ....are you there Mr Franklin?

"Yes," said Daniel, "I'm listening."

"Jomo told me a lot, Mr Franklin. You got plenty of British pounds?

"I can go to the bank, Jimmy"

"OK, I tell you all this before you pay. This is my way."

"Fine, Jimmy. Go on."

"Just a moment, Mr Franklin, I need to stop the car.....OK I have now stopped. Well, Jomo is a very upset man, because he spent fifteen years helping to build Mr Shah's business. According to Jomo, the Frenchman called Don told the staff they are to change everything and start testing some new medicine for infections. So they do not need a Nairobi salesman now. Instead they want to expand to Uganda, Tanzania and Sudan. Jomo doesn't like French people. He prefers British. He can't understand Don's accent and................"

Jimmy's phone stopped but Daniel waited in case the signal was poor.

".........so I bought several beers and said I'd give him a lady and a free condom. Jomo was very depressed last night........"

Daniel listened as the mobile phone signal in Nairobi came and went.

"..........but before Jomo was ready for the lady he saw someone. He saw Don going into the Flamingo Club............but Jomo was impatient for the lady so..........I   waited   outside..................two   hours   I waited.........raining.......then...Don came out..........I took a photo..........followed him to an apartment block ....have address............."

Daniel interrupted him at last.

"Jimmy I can't hear you too well, I'll call you tomorrow."

But Jimmy still hadn't quite finished.

"There's one more thing, Mr Franklin. Jomo says the Shah Medicals headquarters is in Cairo - that's Egypt. Everything comes from Cairo. The big boss is in Cairo and so is Mr O'Brian."

The last snippet from Jimmy made a lot of sense. David Chua in Singapore had mentioned Cairo, he had seen Cairo mentioned in Caroline's Singapore notes, Kay Choon in Hong Kong had mentioned a link with Cairo and Clive Tasker had suggested that Cairo was the ultimate destination for equipment imported into Jordan by Al Zafar and then re-exported.

"And another thing, Mr Franklin. I've got a part......................"

"I can't hear you Jimmy, say that again."

"I have got a part-time job at Shah Medicals."

"You've got what?" yelled Daniel, hoping that at least Jimmy could hear him properly.

"A part-time job at Shah Medicals - two hours every Tuesday and Thursday evening and it's after Luther Jasman has finished work, so don't worry - no-one will recognise me."

"How in God's name did you manage that?"

"I can't hear you, Mr Franklin. I think it is better if you phone me again."

"OK, Jimmy but please, please don't forget - mum's the word."

"Confidentiality is our corporate policy, Mr Franklin............"

CHAPTER 48

"The French guy who disappeared from Beirut. His name is Dominique Lunneau - known as Don by most people. He ran production at a company called Steri-Tech, located in Tripoli in the north of Lebanon, not Beirut as I was originally told."

"That's just what I'd hoped you'd say, Colin. We have a match and I know where he is - good work. Got a photo?"

"Not a good one but it's on its way. And as for our mutual friend Nagi in Cairo I've told him to expect a call from you. Don't forget he knows you as Ian McCann."

I switched the phone off and then looked at Anna.

While I sat thinking or on the phone or scribbling notes that I then tore into shreds, Anna mostly sat patiently reading, sitting cross-legged on the bed. We had now been in the same hotel room for three days. She seemed very content but for me, hotels are a home and an office. For Anna, I wasn't sure if she liked it. I felt a strange longing to take her somewhere, away from the hotel, away from Bangkok, away from what was becoming a routine of sleep, phone, breakfast, phone, lunch, phone, dinner, phone, sleep.

I wanted to show her places I already knew, to relax with her and share more of my thoughts and my past. There were also huge gaps in my understanding of Anna's past life that I wanted to fill.

I was lying on the bed beside her. "Anna, I think we need to go to London soon. Your visa should be ready tomorrow. I think we should leave soon after that."

"But what about your business?"

"The business will travel with us Anna."

"And will we stay in your apartment in London?"

"Yes, but I may need to leave you there for a few days."

"And when will we come back to Thailand to see my family?"

"I think we should visit them tomorrow, Anna. Tell them what is happening and that we will come back very soon."

"And you will come with me?"

"Yes, of course." I said, "I need to meet my new in-laws."

Anna leapt onto me. "We will take the bus. We will start early, maybe at three o'clock."

"In the afternoon?"

"No, in the night time."

Of course. Whatever Anna said eventually made sense.

I had no intention of saying anything more to Charles Brady at Virex, at least for the time being. The investigation had now gone way beyond anything I could possibly have foreseen when I had met him in London. And with Jimmy doing his bit in his own style in Nairobi, I decided to go to Cairo instead. I could always nip down to Kenya from Cairo to join him if necessary So, the travel plan forming in my mind was beginning to look like two more days in Thailand, travel to London, a few days in England to acclimatise Anna and then fly to Cairo.

I rolled over in the bed and put my arm around Anna, drawing her close to me. I was very conscious that I was planning it as if it was an ordinary business trip, but I knew this was no longer the case. I needed to be careful. And I needed to be careful for other reasons that, in the middle of the night, were not difficult to imagine. People like Greg O'Brian, GOB as Colin called him, were not to be messed with.

Cairo was not a problem in itself as I knew the city well and could lean on Nagi El Abdeen with his old Egyptian Security Forces methods for some help. But even Nagi was not essential as there were other methods I had used before and could call upon again. No, the problem that was already starting to bother me was what I should do once I'd got the information. And I was no longer completely alone here. My discussion with Kevin Parker and Larry Brown had shown that they had also arrived at the same conclusion, albeit having started out from different points.

With other cases I would report to the client and then leave it to them to pursue any action. It was entirely up to them whether they involved local law enforcement organisations or dealt with matters in their own way. At that stage, my job would be finished.

But with Virex I saw no possible way for them to proceed. It was looking more certain that Shah Medicals, Al Zafar, Livingstone Pharmaceuticals, Mohamed Kader, GOB, Solomon and any others would just continue with their shady operations as untouchables. And if they were almost ready to launch a new virus through whatever manner or strategy they had planned, who could stop them? Someone, somewhere needed to act. But who? So I was already beginning to ponder on who could take this over once I'd done as much as I could.

If it was all happening on Egyptian soil would the Egyptian authorities act and, if so, how quickly? If Livingstone was an offshore company who would act? If Al Zafar was just a disparate group of companies run by Mohamed Kader from wherever he chose to sit who could act? In the middle of the night, the only fixed and unmoveable object that I saw as an asset that none of the parties could

174

move elsewhere quickly was the stock of virus. And where was that? The choice seemed to be between two - Cairo and Nairobi.

By six thirty and a virtually sleepless night, my plans had come together. First, I needed to speak to Larry Brown again and then find out what Jimmy had been up to.

CHAPTER 49

Larry Brown had also had a sleepless night. So far there had been no word from the American Ambassador but that had not come as a surprise. But going over things in his mind and thinking about Daniel's revelation about missing scientists, Larry suddenly remembered Philippe Fournier.

He phoned the Nairobi private number again but there was no answer. He tried Philippe's mobile number but there was not even a ring tone. He then decided to try Philippe's place of work - the Kenyatta National Hospital. After being passed from one department to another, the answer was clear. Philippe had disappeared with no warning, no notice and no sign of any problems except that he was well known for complaints about his low level of pay. Larry phoned Daniel to report it.

"No word from him at all, Daniel."

"OK, we'll just add him to the growing list then Larry. Any news from the Ambassador?"

"No."

"Would you like to check with him what he thinks about the Biological Weapons Convention? Do they talk to WHO? I've not had time to check but how does the BWC operate anyway. Is it another toothless talking shop?"

"I've already checked, Daniel, and it's the latter. Tinkering with the transmission of microbes is covered by the Biological Weapons Convention but on the bioethics front I've heard they're a miserable bunch only interested in playing with words and seeking personal status. I don't think they'd have a clue what to do if a real situation arose. They'd probably organise a few more meetings."

"Exactly what I thought. Any news from Kevin?"

"No."

"Well, I can't just sit here, Larry. I've decided I'm going to Cairo."

"Why?"

"Only because things seem to point to Cairo. But first I'm going back to UK for a few days I've got some personal affairs to sort out but then I'm off and....." I paused. It had been on my mind for a day or so. "Any chance we could meet in London, Larry? You, me, Kevin? Put faces to the voices?"

We agreed. Larry could make his own decisions, no need to ask permission. Larry would speak to Kevin and Kevin was unlikely to have problems either - apparently he never asked permission either.

As Anna had promised my day started at 3am. We took a taxi to a bus station on the outskirts of Bangkok, then a long bus ride north west towards the provincial capital of Kanchanaburi and then another taxi to Anna's family village way out amongst the hills, besides a lake and surrounded by forest. It was beautiful.

I met her mother, her father, a sister and her sister's two young children and we stayed until late afternoon. During all that time, I just watched and listened from a seat on a hard wooden platform in the shade of mango trees. As Anna's father sat and listened with an occasional nod in my direction, Anna, her mother and her sister talked almost non-stop. I don't know what it was about but I know I was a subject of some particular interest. They probably also talked about London, how cold it might be there and about family matters. I just sat and waited. I ate the lunch that Anna and her sister prepared whilst talking and I drank the iced coconut juice that arrived from somewhere.

It was a day I will never forget. For Anna it was a day that she would eventually look back on with both happiness and sadness but we'll come to that.

By midnight we were back at the hotel in Bangkok. By midday on the following day we were on a flight to London and fourteen hours later I unlocked the door of my apartment for the first time in over six weeks. Quick tour over for Anna's benefit, I had a long phone discussion with Colin and fixed a time to meet up. Anna dusted the flat, tidied it and then sorted things out to her liking. When she'd finished, it looked a whole lot better.

Larry Brown arrived in London from Lagos the following day and Kevin Parker took a train to London and we all met in the Cumberland Hotel on Marble Arch where I also then introduced them to Colin.

For three hours either side of lunch we got to know one another better. We shared views, opinions, exchanged new information and agreed that whilst we had all started from different points and arrived at very similar conclusions, there were still too many unanswered questions. But our conclusion was quite clear - something needed to be done by someone The question was what and who would do it.

Finally, we agreed to split responsibilities between us.

While I flew to Cairo to try to track down the company or companies, Kevin would raise questions with his UK Member of Parliament, push the matter to Government level and try to get some clarification on what powers the UK and EU had to act.

"Don't take no for an answer, Kevin," I said. "If your MP shows signs of doing nothing then raise it direct with the Minister responsible for international trade or someone you think will listen. And whilst you're going with all that fix a meeting with a Member of the European Parliament, a MEP. And if that all gets bogged down and goes nowhere, let's talk again. But we need someone in a powerful position, perhaps even the Prime Minister to sit up and take notice. It's very urgent and I suspect we may be reaching a point where it will be too late."

Larry interrupted. "We were already too late for the hundred Nigerian deaths and the Thai deaths, Daniel. And who the hell was the doctor, Doctor Mustafa and where is he now?"

That question sparked another from me.

"Tell me again, Kevin. What did this Mohamed El Badry look like?"

Kevin described him but Kevin's memory seemed to lack a talent for remembering faces. "Typical Arab, Daniel - big brown face, suit, tie, moustache if I recall." It could have been anyone.

"And the apartment in London?"

"Posh. Chelsea Embankment."

"And a woman was there?"

"Yes, she answered the door."

"Any sign of children around?"

"No, none. Why?"

"Perhaps you met Mohamed Kader, Kevin, not Mohamed El Badry," I said. "And was there anyone who saw your Doctor Mustafa and could describe him, Larry?"

"Plenty of them I suspect but many of them who got a real close-up are now dead. There might be some left like the lady who I spoke to outside the closed clinic in Kano. She saw him come and go in a Toyota pick-up truck. Are you suggesting Mohamed Kader was also Doctor Mustafa?"

"Makes sense doesn't it?" I replied, "He'd fit in quite well in and around Kano, wouldn't he? It might be a reason why he gained their trust. And there is evidence he had travelled to Nigeria - and Pakistan."

We discussed Greg O'Brian - GOB.

"He could be anywhere," I said, "But I'd be surprised if he isn't also dabbling in other things besides Livingstone Pharmaceuticals. I can't imagine a man like GOB in the pharmaceutical industry - it doesn't fit. It just wouldn't be exciting enough. OK, he's hoping to make money out of it but I think there's something more."

Attention then turned to what Larry would do back in Lagos. Unlike Kevin, Larry already knew.

"Phone the Ambassador - push him like crazy for answers, the same as I hope Kevin will do here in UK. I won't wait long for an answer either. I give him a day or so and if he's still too distracted by his diplomatic duties, then I'll speak direct to Washington. I'll chase chairs and committee members on Homeland Securities, Commerce, Science, anyone who'll listen. I'll speak to my own Senator in New York State, see what she has to say. If she wants my vote then I want her ear and then I'll want some action. And if I can't do anything from Lagos, I'll jack the whole fucking job in, push it up the Ambassador's arse and go straight to Washington for a showdown with the Secretary of State."

Kevin clapped. Colin slapped Larry on the back.

"But I've not finished there either," Larry went on, "Who the hell runs the Biological Weapons Convention, I want to know. Last time I looked it was the Division of Peace Studies of the University of Bradford and the website was nearly two years out of date. Where the hell is Bradford anyway, Colin? But it's important because the transmission of a microbe is covered by the Convention. But have they got any teeth? How do they react to evidence of a threat? Is there a system in place? If so what is it and how quick can it react? Who decides?

"I have a thousand questions about that fucking organisation. It's probably run by a bunch of job's worth and failed politicians who get paid to stay in the best hotels, get welcomed to champagne receptions, dress up like penguins for nice big dinners and then put the job on their CVs so they can similar jobs with similar perks. And you and I are paying all their fucking expenses through our tax.

"So, before or after I get on a plane for Washington to see the Secretary of State I'll also jump on one going to Geneva or Bradford or wherever their office is. And, while I'm in Geneva I'll walk into the WHO's office and ask to speak to the Director General and ask her if she really has any powers or is the WHO just a source of basic, common-sense health advice of the sort I normally get by checking the colour of my tonsils, my lumps or looking at myself in the mirror."

That evening, after Larry and Kevin had departed, I took Anna out and Colin joined us. For Anna it was her first taste of Italian food but I knew it was Colin's favourite. For me it was a relaxing interlude with the man who, as Colin himself constantly reminded Anna with only just a hint of tongue in cheek, "It's very sad, Anna but did you know I'm the only friend he's got."

"Well, he now has two, Colin." Anna said, holding my hand. At which point I admit I excused myself to go to the men's room.

"Take care of her please, Colin," I said as we parted later. "I hope not to be gone more than a few days but you never know."

CHAPTER 50

My taxi into Cairo from the airport was an ageing Mercedes. The driver was an ageing Egyptian called Mahmoud. But Mahmoud spoke good English and by the time we arrived at my hotel, I had his mobile phone number and an arrangement that Mahmoud would become my chauffeur if I needed him.

The next morning started hot, clear and sunny and I did my usual bit of shopping - a new mobile phone and a local SIM card - and then spent a few minutes checking it. I emailed Colin to say I was contactable and then phoned Anna on her new English phone to say I had arrived and would be in touch very soon. Domestic duties over, I then phoned Nagi El Abdeen to fix a meeting Then I called Mahmoud.

At twelve o'clock precisely, Mahmoud's Mercedes taxi ground to a halt in a cloud of fine dust outside the wrought iron gates of an older style villa in a quiet, side street of Dokki on the west side of the River Nile.

I got out, told Mahmoud to wait for me in the shade of a palm tree opposite, and walked up to the gate. I remembered the villa well from last time. It lay in a small courtyard marshalled by two Alsation dogs. They weren't barking yet but looked interested enough to start at any second. The big, flat roofed villa lay beyond the dogs and behind two small trees with just a few leaves that offered some small shade.

There was a was a small brass plate saying "Otaiba Business Consultants" on the concrete pillar of the gate and below it a well polished bell. I pressed it.

There was no sound audible to my own ear but the dogs heard something and changed from mild and inquisitive creatures into maniacal beasts the like of which I had not seen since the last time I was there. Dogs and I have never got on and I was happy to remain on the outside for the time being to await human intervention. It was quick in coming.

A well built and stocky woman in a colourful, long dress, her head partially covered in white cloth with gold border emerged, the dogs immediately stopped barking and went timidly to sit in the shade of the trees.

The woman shuffled forward and, without speaking, unlocked the gate. It swung open and I stepped into the courtyard. The gate was closed again and the dogs stood up to watch me. I followed the woman through the front door of the villa into a small, bare concrete floored room, the only furniture a small desk in one corner covered in papers, a white telephone and a rattling air conditioning unit on the wall. There was an empty swivel chair behind the desk and a shelf housing business directories in both Arabic and English. The woman passed through and, still without speaking, ushered me through another wooden door at the far end.

Then she departed and closed the door. It was an exact repeat of my last visit. From the bright sun outside, to this, all I could do was peer into the gloom. From it, exactly as last time, Nagi El Abdeen emerged from behind his large and ornate corner desk and walked across the tiled floor. He smiled and we shook hands.

Nagi is a small man, probably in his mid fifties. He wore a white, long-sleeved shirt and blue tie. Greyer than before, with his hair now receding badly at the front, he was neat, presentable and wealthy. Nagi was an effective middle man.

My Arabic is very basic. Fortunately, like so many Egyptians, Nagi's English is good. We sat around a low, glass-topped coffee table surrounded by an ornate, wooden framed sofa and two matching chairs. Nagi ordered tea and the woman brought it. I think she is his wife, but I have never asked and Nagi has never said. We briefly talked generalities as if it was where we had left off last time - business was, as last time, up and down, there were Egyptian troubles, there were European problems and the Arab-Israeli conflict was still unresolved.

180

Then: "It's good to see you again Ian," said Nagi. "I was pleased to hear about the successful prosecution. Your client must have been pleased. The arrogant rich should not be allowed to get away with such fraud especially when inflicted on the poor. What do you think?"

"I agree, Nagi. It was good to see a successful outcome."

We drank the tea and then Nagi sat back expectantly - it was my turn to explain the reason for my visit. "So, what is it this time, Ian? What can I do?"

I knew I had to be careful. Nagi operates behind the scenes. For all his outward appearances he is still, nevertheless, a powerful and influential man who is still well connected with various politicians of different persuasions and he also operates at unspecified levels within the Egyptian Military. He is a fixer and a man who earns commissions or fees from whoever or whatever he knows. But I know many other men like Nagi - some I trust, others I don't. Nagi falls mostly into the trustable category but there is always a need for caution and no chance at all of getting away with anything that might end up hurting Nagi himself.

"Let me say from the outset, Nagi, that I am here on what is my own private business. There is no client involved now although, I have to admit, I started off with one."

"It is unlike you to lose a client, Ian," Nagi laughed and leaned forward to pat my knee.

"On this occasion, they lost me, Nagi," I smiled back. "Sometimes I accept a challenge without the need for a fee." I then paused and spoke slowly to maximise the impact of what I was about to say.

"And the challenge is a big one, Nagi. It involves the pharmaceutical industry and research on infectious diseases. You will know that we have had many scares recently about the spread of viruses like SARS and bird flu. The world is densely populated, air travel is common, buses and public transport systems are congested and at breaking point. It is very easy for a lethal virus to spread very quickly. And when there is no cure or vaccine available it can have devastating results. Just think about Cairo, Nagi and how quickly an untreatable virus could spread?"

Nagi nodded philosophically.

"There is a new virus, Nagi. But the problem with this virus is that it is man-made. You see, it is not difficult with modern technology to create new viruses. It is a bit like designing a new car. You begin with deciding what type of car you want, what it will be used for, how big it needs to be, who it might appeal to. There are many laboratories that can design new viruses or change existing ones. And some of the laboratories are privately run. They all, whether public or private, get funded from somewhere. They often do this sort of research for academic reasons. Old, inquisitive, scientists used to like mixing things together just to see what happened. Many modern scientists do the same with viruses. It is called gain of function research. In other words you can create a novel virus that does something different or you design it to do exactly what you want it to do. If you wanted to create a flu virus that cannot be cured with current anti-flu drugs then that would be quite possible.

"I believe a private company now has such a virus. I believe it has already been tested and it kills. It is similar to influenza and so it could spread very easily and very quickly. This new virus could now be released deliberately into densely populated areas like Cairo. It would be like biological warfare - a war waged by a private company.

"But the creators of the virus, the people who run the business, will probably be immune because they also have a vaccine or a treatment. They can decide who gets the treatment. But add to that the fact that there may only be small stocks of this treatment available and its effectiveness is uncertain, it is not difficult to imagine that the outcome would be catastrophic.

"But why would a company want to do that? Most likely for profit but I suspect there are other motives as well, especially for the scientists involved. They want to deliberately reduce the world population in exactly the same way that bubonic plague, the black death, once killed millions."

I stopped. Nagi was staring at me. He had hardly blinked. I then finished what I wanted to say. "I believe that the company with this virus is probably based in Egypt."

Nagi blinked. "Why do you say that?" he asked calmly.

"I'm a private investigator, Nagi, but I'm also a businessman. An investigator investigates and a good businessman does his market research. You know that, Nagi. Then he uses logic, his past experience and a bit of intuition."

"So who is it?"

This was the tricky part. I wanted to be able to point my finger directly at someone or something but couldn't. Instead, I said: "I'm looking at three businesses. Two of them I know something about. The third one is less easy and that is why I need some help."

Nagi got up and wandered to his desk.

"You are making some very serious allegations, Ian. You are saying that there are three companies in Egypt that are escaping the attention of any inspections or other formalities that Egyptian companies need to comply with in order to trade locally or internationally." It was very well put.

"Yes," I said. "But there is a much bigger problem here, Nagi I am not pointing a finger at Egyptian authorities and saying you are failing to do your job, because they probably are. The fact is that there are no controls in place to stop a company doing this sort of thing whether they are in Egypt, America, Europe, Japan or China. Some people, senior scientists, have warned against lack of proper controls for years but no-one does anything. Some say the technology poses risks more serious than anything that has gone before, and that includes the risk of nuclear war. But unlike past arms races, no-one talks about it. The public are left in total ignorance.

"Organisations and companies who engage in this type of work can be inspected for compliance with good manufacturing practices, every conceivable official standard and every other part of their business that bureaucrats can dream up including checks on health and safety and employment law, their tax and even signs of bribery and corruption. Once they've got a product to sell they might need approvals and registrations which is more paperwork.

"But, in the meantime, no-one asks what the scientists and technicians in their white coats and nice clean laboratories are actually doing with their test tubes. Even if they did, they could be lied to and the boffins with their clip boards would write down exactly what they had been told. A box is ticked and away they go. Often, the only time anyone gets to know what's going on is if a scientist on an ego trip writes a paper or stands up at a conference or fills out a form to ask for a bit more funding.

"It's happening everywhere, Nagi, and I am not here to accuse Egyptian authorities of gross negligence or other failings.

"And another thing, Nagi. You might think I'm suggesting it's some big name international corporation like a pharmaceutical giant operating in Egypt. I am not. I am talking about small to medium sized businesses that you have probably never ever heard of. "

Nagi came to sit at the small table again. "More tea?"

CHAPTER 51

183

On the other side of Africa, Larry Brown was still feeling as angry with the system as he had been in London. He was equally angry that no-one, even Joseph, had noticed he had disappeared for three days. There was nothing from the Ambassador when he returned - not even a message to call the Embassy in Abuja. Larry decided to give him one more day. After that - well - the Ambassador might be the boss but Larry was none too enamoured with his job anyway.

But on the plane back from London, he had been reading the English Sunday Times - a thick newspaper with magazines and separate supplements - and there had been ample time to read it from front to back. What had caught his eye was an article in the "Travel" section on holidays in Thailand and a very short sentence pointing out that there had recently been a flu-type scare and tourists were warned to be careful. What they should do not to catch the bug was not made clear but if the British Foreign Office was issuing warnings to travellers then perhaps it would be a starting point to circumvent what he, as a persona non grata, was not able to get direct from the WHO.

Larry phoned the British Foreign Office in London and was told to check their website. He did so but got no further - just a repeat of the Sunday Times warning. So he phoned the British Embassy in Bangkok with a story.

"My name is Larry Brown. I'm a US citizen but my English girlfriend is on holiday in Thailand and I've not been able to contact her for several days. The last time I spoke to her she was in a place called Sukothai. She had a very bad cold and was running a very high temperature. I've just read about the recent flu outbreak and was worried."

"What is your girlfriend's name Mr Brown?"

"Emily Sinclair," said Larry," In fact I am a doctor, so it's Doctor Brown."

"I see, Doctor Brown. Hold the line while I check."

Larry held on for less than a minute.

"Doctor Brown. Sorry to keep you waiting. There are two pieces of advice. Firstly we suggest you talk to the American Embassy. The US Armed Forces Research Institute of Medical Sciences - AFRIMS - is based at the Embassy. They are apparently surveying influenza A outbreaks with a Thai laboratory. You need to speak to them. Secondly, speak direct to the Thai laboratory."

Larry was given the phone number of a laboratory in Bangkok who had been keeping a record of recent incidents of respiratory infection sent in from all across Thailand. The fictitious Emily Sinclair was not on the list. But half an hour later Larry knew where the outbreak had started, that all the known deaths except one were males and that they had all come from the city of Ayuttaya north of Bangkok. By saying he was an American doctor doors seemed to open everywhere. He was then put through to the doctor in charge, a Doctor Vichai.

"But my girlfriend, Emily was in Ayuttaya a month ago," Larry said, "Could she have been in contact with someone with the infection?"

The Thai doctor spoke good English. "All the patients were truck drivers," he said. "They all slept in the same building in Bangkok when making deliveries. We think this was where they contracted the infection."

"So was one of them a carrying the virus?"

"I cannot say for certain, Doctor Brown but my laboratory is concerned about something that was found outside the building where they were sleeping."

"What did you find?"

"Inhalers, Doctor Brown. Similar to those used by asthmatics. But the pressurised canisters were missing. It is very strange."

"Are you suggesting they were infected through using an inhaler? "

"I can not speculate, Doctor Brown but we have had cases of people taking drugs in various strange ways. But the fact is that amongst the hundred or so cases of respiratory infection we have tested since the outbreak we have found no more trace of that particular virus. It's good news but we cannot explain it. Something happened but we don't know what. We have, of course reported it to the WHO as a matter of course but have heard nothing."

For Larry this was enough. Aerosols, he decided, were being tested as a method of spreading the virus - and very effectively too it seemed.

He then further checked out the US Armed Forces Research Institute of Medical Sciences - AFRIMS as the girl at the British Embassy had called it. Larry had no idea it existed but, according to its website, it developed and evaluated products and collected epidemiologic data to protect soldiers and citizens from infectious diseases. It did clinical trials, had equipment for sample collections and worked with the Thai laboratory.

Larry phoned Colin in London.

Colin then emailed Daniel in Cairo and Daniel recognised the name of Doctor Vichai from the Bangkok conference. He also remembered seeing the Thai laboratory at the trade show at the conference. He had picked up a leaflet that was probably still in his black case. When he had a moment he'd check out its website.

But for Daniel it posed another obvious question. Someone was, or had been, operating in Thailand. But who? As far as he knew neither Shah Medicals, Livingstone or Al Zafar had a company in Thailand. So was this an individual? One of the scientists, a technician perhaps But the question was not going to be answered from where he was, in Cairo.

CHAPTER 52

"So, Ian, can you tell me the name of one of the companies you are interested in?" Nagi asked me.

I resorted to the tried and tested strategy of nothing ventured, nothing gained. I had to start somewhere. "Shah Medicals," I said. "Have you heard of them?"

"No," said Nagi.

"You see, Nagi? But what would you say if I told you there were links here with other small, and not so small, companies in USA, Hong Kong, Singapore, Kenya, Abu Dhabi, Dubai, Jordan, Syria, Turkey - I can go on."

"A network?"

"Precisely. It's certainly a viable distribution network and probably under the direct control of one or two key men with one or two key scientists running the technical side of things. Once they give the instruction, the distribution network starts distributing."

"What about the business records of the two men?" asked Nagi.

"In one case it's fraud, corruption, embezzlement. He's wealthy and he's not afraid of removing people from the scene if they get in his way. So far, he's been untouchable"

"Yah," said Nagi, "And the other?"

"Ambitious, wealthy and he enjoys power and influence. And he hates crowded places like Cairo. In fact, he seems to dislike crowds so much that his hobby is researching population control methods."

"Hmmm," said Nagi, and got up again.

I had forgotten how calm Nagi can stay. I'd noticed it before and put it down to his army days. Neither Colin or I had been able to work out Nagi's full background history but we both knew he was shrewd and had risen quite high - high enough to know when it was time to pull back and pull out."

The second pot of tea had arrived and he came over, poured each of us two more cupfuls and sat down again.

"Who is this second guy who hates Cairo so much?"

"An Egyptian by birth," said Daniel

"Hmmm," said Nagi again. "Name?"

"Mohamed Kader," I said and Nagi shrugged. I knew the name would mean nothing without the link with Kader's company, Al Zafar.

"And the murderous, untouchable embezzler?"

"An Irish American."

We sipped tea. Then I said, "I need to find out where they are operating from. It could be anywhere. It may well be a company operating under a completely different name to Shah Medicals."

I knew I needed a lead, names, anything and I thought for a moment. The temptation was there to say far more but I still did not want to divulge too much just yet. I needed to draw Nagi in slowly. "They are importing pharmaceutical manufacturing equipment into Egypt via Jordan." I said. "The Arab Bank is acting as consignee. Any help?"

"Can you get a copy of a Bill of Lading or something?"

"Not quickly," I said and kicked myself for not having thought of that one earlier. Clive might have been the answer. But too much had been happening.

"Who is the exporter?"

I knew Nagi was now pushing for details. Instead I said, "If you can get me some information either from the bank or any other source, I'll then point to a name."

Nagi stood up once more. "OK. Anything else you want? Whatever it is I'll be putting it on your invoice." He laughed.

"Yes," I said, "Someone I can work with for a few days - run around with me, not scared to get their hands dirty - good with locked filing cabinets - you know the sort, Nagi." It was my turn to laugh although I knew and so did Nagi that I was being deadly serious.

187

It was evening when Nagi phoned me with details of my helper.

"She is the daughter of a doctor from Alexandria and a graduate in pharmacy and business studies - well qualified technically and commercially, if that's what you want."

"She, Nagi? What does she normally do when not acting as deputy to a foreign sleuth?"

"Sleuth?" Nagi's excellent English suddenly failed him.

"An investigator."

"Ah, yes. She works in a pharmacy but wants to do something more interesting. She is thinking of joining the police but would also like to work abroad. What do you think?" Nagi also sounded less than enthusiastic. Perhaps she was all he could find.

"I thought you might have more of a professional on your books - someone like Khaled who helped me once before," I said.

"They seem too nervous of working with foreigners and you need someone who's not known."

That was undoubtedly true. "So, what is her name?"

"Maria Tawfiq. Her mother is Spanish, her father Egyptian."

My new assistant, it turned out, was the opposite of Jimmy.

Jimmy is tall, thin, athletic in his appearance. Maria was a short, plump girl in a long, brown-patterned skirt and white cotton top. Her hair was short and covered by a beige scarf. It was early evening, the day after my meeting with Nagi and we were sat in the hotel foyer. I was trying to get to know her.

"I am Maria Tawfiq. I am twenty five years old. My father is a urologist. My mother is a nurse."

Nagi was right about one thing. Maria was bored, bored with her life and bored with her prospects in Cairo. But a bright spark shone somewhere beneath the surface and I saw it. And she was a pharmacist. We talked a bit more but I still hadn't mentioned the job. It was deliberate. I wanted Maria to get impatient with my questions and ask me to get to the point. She did, more quickly than I thought.

"So, what can I do, Mr McCann?"

"I want to find an Egyptian company, Maria."

Then, nothing ventured, nothing gained, I told her about as much as I had told Nagi. Maria's eyes widened at every new revelation. What was more she understood drugs, medicine, vaccines, bacteria and viruses. I suddenly found myself defending my technical shortcomings.

Maria and I were still talking when my phone rang. It was Nagi.

"Shah Medical Centre," Nagi said and gave an address. "It's a small private clinic in Cairo owned, apparently, by a Doctor Ramses El Khoury. He ran a private clinic in Alexandria for a while, moved to Jordan and returned to Cairo a year ago."

I listened, unsure whether this was the Shah Medicals I was looking for. It didn't sound right and Nagi had been surprisingly quick. "And," Nagi then added, "He runs a regular family planning clinic."

I was still unsure where all this was leading.

"But hardly anyone attends any longer. According to information or rumour - I have never attended the clinic as you can imagine - the clinic strongly advocates a one family one child policy - Chinese style. The views are, what do you say in English, unconventional?"

I was not over excited. There are a lot of people with opinions like that. But then Nagi revealed the key bit. "And," he said, "The Shah Medical Centre is the one importing the equipment from Jordan."

This was better. "How do you know that, Nagi?"

"Contacts, Ian, contacts. I still have friends in the banks."

"So what's he doing with the equipment?" I wondered out loud

"Well, once the bank releases the goods with documents from Shah Medical Centre, someone else takes delivery. The consignments disappear somewhere."

"So, how to find out where, Nagi?"

"No idea, not unless you want heavy handed - like police involvement. But I thought you should know first."

I was well aware that I now needed to put even more trust in Nagi - a man I still didn't know as well as I should. I was asking Nagi - someone with obvious close links to some powerful Egyptian people - to please say nothing to anyone while I, Daniel Cappelli, a foreigner on Egyptian soil, delved into an Egyptian problem with potentially devastating consequences if things went wrong. It was not only a risk for me but a risk for Nagi.

"I need more time, Nagi?" I said. "I've got an idea but it will take a few days."

I then turned to Maria. "I think we've found your first job, Maria,"

It was midnight when my phone rang again.

I had not spoken to Jimmy since Bangkok. Neither had I been able to contact Jimmy from London. But Jimmy had called Colin and Colin was now phoning me.

"Looks like Jimmy has got himself a part-time job at Shah Medicals in Nairobi, Dan. Did you know?"

"Yes, he was saying something but it was a bad phone link. Tell me. I guessed something was up."

"He's the new cleaner," said Colin. "Not only did he know Jomo the salesman but Lucky the cleaner."

"Go on."

"You want it word for word? I recorded it - I do sometimes."

"Yes, please, I've not heard Jimmy's happy voice for several days." There was a clicking sound.

"Tell Mr Franklin that the cleaner's name is Lucky." said the recorded voice of Jimmy. There was a pause and Colin is heard to say, "Yes, anything more?"

"I went to see Lucky at his house and asked him if he felt ill. I said, 'Do you feel sick, Lucky?' Lucky said no. Then I said, 'How would you like to fall ill with pains in your belly?' Lucky said no - he was tired but he felt OK. But then I told him I wanted his cleaning job for a few days. Lucky was very surprised but said he could not afford to take time off. But I said he could easily afford it because I would pay him double to stay away from work for a few days. All he had to do, I said, was to phone and say he was sick with pains in his belly, but that his brother would do the cleaning. Lucky thought it was his lucky day - no work and double-pay. And guess what? "

"What, Jimmy?" Colin's recorded voice said.

"He agreed. But I would have to pay him four days double-pay in advance. So, you see my expenses are mounting."

"No problem, Jimmy. Anything else?"

"Yes, the Pakistanis are leaving. Jomo says they are going to work in Egypt. I watched them leave. All except one that is. I was sitting in my car. They wear white trousers, narrow at the ankles and long, white shirts hanging outside. Two of them wore small, white prayer hats and grey waistcoats over their shirts

In London, Colin switched the recording off.

"Another piece of your jigsaw, Dan?"

"Looks like it," I said. "A lot going on, Colin."

"There's not much more on the tape but Jimmy has only worked one evening. I hope his floor cleaning is as good as his ferreting. But it looks as if Cairo is the place to be, Dan. I thought you'd like to know. And there's one more thing, Daniel."

In London, I had asked Colin to check out the Dutchman, Jan de Jonge who had disappeared from Virex.

"We traced De Jonge's family," Colin went on. "His parents knew of his disappearance from the Dutch police. He is unmarried. His folks, mother and father that is, live in Utrecht. Mr and Mrs De Jonge are very concerned. He had run up a lot of debt in Holland for some reason. They wouldn't say what. He went to the States to escape the worry and to make some money. He had been back to Holland three times - once a year. Everything seemed OK on his last visit, which was at Christmas and New Year but he was still struggling to pay off the money. It sounds as though the money side was a real problem for the man. His parents did not want to talk about it. Finally, Dan, his parents said that he had told them he might one day join two British friends from another company who had also gone abroad."

It was just as I thought. I still believed they were all together somewhere. But where? Egypt?

CHAPTER 53

Jimmy was not the only one with a new job. In Cairo, Maria had started hers.

Arriving for Doctor Ramses El Khoury's evening family planning clinic at the Shah Medical Centre on the first floor of an old block in crowded, central Cairo she found she was already late. One look showed that all nine seats of the waiting room were occupied by mothers, some with young children crawling or playing on the floor. But Mr McCann's instructions had been quite clear. She was to be his last patient of the evening. Marie went back down the stone steps and out into the street to wait.

It was nine thirty before she tried again and found only one young woman still waiting. At nine forty five a buzzer sounded and a red light came on over Doctor Ramses door. It was her turn.

But it was not a middle aged man who sat there. Perhaps it was her pharmacy background but Maria had imagined a middle aged man wearing a tie that had seen better days hanging greasily from an open necked shirt. She had not prepared herself to meet a middle aged woman.

The room, office, clinic or whatever it chose to be was big, much larger than the waiting room. Maria quickly took in a cubicle surrounded by a green, plastic curtain in one corner, a wash basin, dispensers for antiseptic soap, a box of latex gloves, a glass cabinet of bottles, an open box containing stainless steel instruments and a grey metal filing cabinet. But the room had clearly seen a man's presence. There were dusty files, back copies of the Lancet and a strange stuffed bird in a glass box high up on a top shelf. Maria's sensitive nose also smelled man as well as woman.

But it was a woman who beckoned her to sit - a big woman with a long black skirt, a cotton blouse and her hair held back by several gold clips. Wide, gold rings some inlaid with blue stones sat on several of her fingers as she swung around in the man's swivel chair to face Maria.

"Sorry, but I was expecting to see Doctor Ramses El Khoury," said Maria.

He is away. I am his deputy. I am Doctor Fatima El Badry. How can I help?"

"Are you often here?"

"Yes, I am always here whenever Doctor Ramses is abroad. How can I help?"

"I need advice on contraception," Maria said.

"Your name?"

"Aqeelah,"

"Are you married?"

"Well, nearly."

"Then why don't you abstain until you are married?"

"My husband-to-be insists."

"Ignore him."

"But............"

"Do you want children?"

"No, at least, not yet."

"Then abstention is the best policy. Delay until you are entirely sure. Then restrict yourself to a maximum of one child. The world is far too crowded."

"I totally agree," said Maria as she had been told by Mr McCann. "Just look at the street outside and its quite late. It's so crowded and all you can hear is traffic. But what can I do?"

"Lead by example." the woman said. "We need to reduce the population not increase it."

"Yes," agreed Maria, "We discussed the subject at University just last week."

"You are a student?"

"Yes, of history and economics. Over half of the students agreed we needed to reduce the population."

"They are right. And simple contraception is not enough. That will take many generations. There is no time left. Governments should act before it is too late."

"Yes, that is what we agreed at the University. but what can we do? No-one had any ideas."

"There are solutions. We will see. Someone will do something."

"I so hope so," said Maria. " But what shall I say to my husband-to-be?

"Tell him to wait. Aqeelah. Live up to the name your father gave you, which means wise and sensible."

"But it is very difficult, Doctor. Are you married?"

"Yes."

"And do you have children?"

Maria recognised the hesitation. Perhaps it was impertinent to ask a doctor such a question. Nevertheless, she got an answer. "Ah, yes."

"Can I ask how many you have?"

To Maria's ear, it sounded even more impertinent but Mr McCann had said that whatever happened she should: "Push, push, push - you will not get much time with this Doctor Ramses El Khoury. Try to engage him in general conversation for as long as you can."

"Two. But we are a family who work very hard, we are educated, we are ambitious, we have money to invest, to provide education for our children at private school. There are many thousands who cannot afford children. We must deal with them."

"I so agree," gushed Maria, "And does your husband share your opinions?"

"Of course. They are his opinions."

Maria got up. "Thank you, You have been a big help to me in making my decision. I will tell my husband-to-be about your good advice."

As she shut the door, Maria looked back and noticed a faint smile on the face of Doctor Fatima El Badry.

For Maria, the name El Badry had meant nothing. For Daniel, it was perhaps the biggest piece of the jigsaw yet. He praised Maria for her night's work and asked her to meet him the following morning.

CHAPTER 54

Back in England, Kevin Parker had just bought himself a pint of best bitter and was carrying it carefully towards a vacant seat. He had not been to The Penny Farthing in Whiteladies Road for months and had just sat down when his phone rang. It was me.

"Kevin, it's Daniel. I'm in Cairo. Seen your MP yet?"

"Not yet, Daniel, his surgery is booked solid."

"Yes, on trivialities I expect. You need to try harder. Kevin. But, reason for my call - can you describe the woman you met at Doctor Mohamed El Badry's apartment in Chelsea?"

"Mmm - big woman, Daniel. Not my sort. Arab dress, black hair. But I was too taken by the apartment to notice - made mine look like a cheap hostel for down and outs.

"Anything else besides her being big and not your sort?"

In Bristol, Kevin scratched his head. "Gold rings, Daniel."

"Yes, go on Kevin. Were they on her fingers, hanging from her ear, stuck up her nose, pinned to her cheeks? Was she a punk?"

"On her fingers, big ones, blue stones. big bracelet as well if I recall."

That was enough for me.

"That's her. I've tracked her down, Kevin. She's coming to get you."

"Don't joke Daniel. Is it true you've found her?"

"Yes," I said, "But unless you get a move on, when I've tracked her husband down as well and found he is not Mohamed El Badry but Mohamed Kader as I suspect, it might all be too late and a pandemic will be upon us. What's more, Kevin, Mrs El Badry or Mrs Kader whatever you want to call her would also be a worthy member of the Malthus Society, Egypt Branch. Do you have a joint membership scheme for husband and wife?"

Kevin still failed to appreciate my humour.

"Have you ever been a burglar or a thief?" I asked Maria.

"No, of course not," she replied.

"Then the time has come for me to show you the rougher side of what I sometimes have to do," I said. "I hate doing it unless it's necessary. It's called breaking and entering with legitimate intentions, Maria. The intention will be to find something inside Doctor Fatima El Badry's clinic that might help us track down where her husband is and where the main Shah Medicals business is located. If the Clinic is the front for importing the equipment from Jordan then I hope we might find something. Are you willing?"

"I cannot do it alone, Mr McCann."

"No, and neither can I. I cannot read or write Arabic and this is where you come in. I'll do the breaking in part, you can do the translation."

For me, what I was planning was an extreme measure with huge risk. But time was running out. I had no wish to stay on in Cairo for any length of time knowing that I had shared what I knew with Nagi and, now, Maria. They both knew about as much as I did. But neither is it my habit to leave a job unfinished.

But, decision having been made, I phoned Colin, brought him up to date and told him what I planned to do.

"This is right on the edge, Daniel. Go careful."

"I know, Colin. Don't tell Anna." Then I said, "Please update Larry and ask him if he's managed to get a better description of the Doctor Mustafa from Kano."

Ten o 'clock in the evening and, on schedule. the old Mercedes taxi of Mahmoud drew up outside the hotel main entrance. I had already given him the destination. The Egyptian Pancake House in the Khan el Khalili night market was a busy, night-time venue for hundreds of locals and tourists and it was easy walking distance to the Shah Medical Centre. After eleven it would quieten down, but the roads and streets in the area would still be busy.

Mahmoud dropped us on Sharia Al Azhar with instructions to return to the same place when I phoned. We then walked over the pedestrian bridge above the traffic to the edge of the market close to the square. But instead of heading for the Pancake House, Maria, who knew the area better, led the way, first down one side street and then out onto another, wider road. Where we were heading was a street in an area that had probably, once, been an expensive and affluent place to live. The block that Maria finally stopped at was, in some ways, ornate - three floors high, built of large stone blocks with big windows and wrought iron balconies overhanging the street. At ground level most were shops - a tea shop, a florist - but all were now closed. Lights were off. Between each of the shops was a doorway leading to dark, stone steps to upper floors. To the side of one doorway there was a bronze plaque in Arabic.

Maria pointed to it: "Shah Medical Centre, First Floor, Doctor Ramses El Khoury - General Physician and Family Planning. 6pm to 9pm."

I stood back and looked up. Lights were on in some of the adjacent windows to left and right but directly above us it was dark and lacked the balcony.

""Any idea what goes on above the clinic, Maria?"

"Nothing, I think. The stairs go on up but there is a locked iron grill. Behind the grill there's rubbish."

"So it's empty above?"

"I think so. But there is also an iron grill on the first floor outside the clinic. It was open when I was there but perhaps it's now locked."

"OK, stay here, I'm going up."

"I cannot just stand here, Mr McCann. It does not look good in this area."

I smiled. "OK, come with me."

Maria followed me up the dark, stone stairs to the first landing where the steps then turned and went up to another level. It was pitch black. I switched on a torch I had brought and shone it up the steps to two iron grills. Both were padlocked shut but only the one ahead was cluttered with accumulated debris behind it. I shone the torch through the left side grill and picked out a well swept short corridor leading to a wooden door. On the door, another sign in Arabic.

"The clinic?"

"Yes."

I shone the torch up and down the grill. It was padlocked only at ground level. I then took a small piece of shiny metal from my pocket, pushed it into the lock, and twisted it. The well used lock opened with barely a sound. I took it off, shone the torch on it and showed Maria.

"How do you do that?"

"I made it from an empty Red Bull can," I whispered and pushed on the grill. It creaked and swung open. "After you," I said shining the torch towards the door.

"Another padlock," said Maria, "Can I try?"

"Sure, this is what you do." While I shone the torch on the lock, Maria picked it. It clicked and she turned the door handle. The door opened and we walked into the waiting room. It was hot and smelled of dirt and sweat and the torch picked out ten hard chairs, a scattering of magazines and a box of plastic children's toys.

"That is the red light." Maria pointed above the door to the clinic itself as I shone the torch at the door handle and turned it. This was also locked but not with a padlock but a key. I pulled up the leg of my trousers, withdrew three small screwdrivers from my sock and held them in the torchlight for Maria to see. A minute later and the push button door lock clicked.

"The filing cabinet," whispered Maria, clearly excited by events so far. "Shall we try that first?"

Minutes later, with files spread on the floor and with me sitting in Doctor Fatima El Badry's swivel chair holding the torch, Maria went through the files. And it didn't take long for Maria to suddenly hold something up.

It says "Al Zafar," she said. "Shall I open it?"

Minutes later, with Maria translating, I had what I hoped for - shipping documents for a consignment of stainless steel containers and piping, an invoice from a French company for "media for tissue culture" and then an invoice in English for two hundred thousand "pressurised metered-dose inhalers".

If there was a need for any more evidence of a link between Al Zafar, Shah and Livingstone, this was it - the invoice was from Livingstone Pharmaceuticals, New York. But there was more. As I tried reading the papers in the torchlight, Maria held up another file. "Majid, Mr McCan. What is Majid?"

Still engrossed in the shipping documents and invoices, I shrugged. "Read on, Maria."

"It's an invoice from a transport company for goods to be taken to Beni Suef."

"Where is Beni Suef?"

"South," said Maria, "On the Nile."

"Any more details of an address?"

"Majid, Nahda, Beni Suef."

"Enough, Maria. Let's take these with us. They won't notice anything's missing for a while. Tidy up and let's go."

It was Kevin who phoned Colin and broke the news that we might be too late.

"There was a posting on the Malthus site last night," he told Colin. "I think Daniel should know. It was Solomon. I'll read it to you.

'No-one can stop us now. We waited long enough for the politicians. But they were never likely to do anything and would always be too late, too disorganised, too self-interested. But in the end the people will be with us - the poor, the hungry, the economic migrants, the unemployed.

"The WHO can do nothing to stop us. The BWC and UN know nothing and can do nothing. We tested in Nigeria, we practiced in Thailand. We warned them and gave them ample time but time has run out. We are now ready - Solomon'

Colin called me.

I had only just returned from the break in at the clinic and it took a while for it to sink in. Then I said, "OK, I think we all knew we were running out of time. But I think we've tracked down the Shah Medicals HQ. I'm heading there tomorrow. Meanwhile, is it possible with all the technology at your disposal to track down where that posting was sent from, Colin?"

"Yes and I already did," said Colin. "It looks as if it may have been sent from an internet coffee shop in Bangkok, Daniel."

"Oh, Christ - and that'll explain the inhalers and the Thai cases. We need to move quickly, Colin. Bring Larry up to speed will you? And anything more on GOB? His role still bothers me."

It was Larry who broke more bad news.

"I've been looking into the marketing of asthma inhalers," he told Colin.

"Did you know that you can now buy them from supermarkets and, in some places, from dispensers along with your soft drink?

"So is this how their distribution network is going to work? Innocent-looking inhalers with counterfeit labels with a recognised company's name on and said to be containing salbutamol for asthmatics but, instead, containing a lethal dose of TRS-CoV? The distributors would not even know what they were distributing.

"Would this explain Daniels findings of new distributors being set up, including one who was once arrested for plotting population control methods against the wishes of the Singapore government?

"Or perhaps, their clever scientists are planning to release their treatment as an aerosol inhaler. After all, Relenza is a flu treatment administered via an inhaler and it's already on the market. They'd need some technical skills and the right equipment but methods for spreading a virus and then selling a treatment for it are endless.

"And let me try out another one on you Colin.

"How many counterfeit drugs get sold on the internet these days? I just Googled 'Buy salbutamol inhalers for asthma' online and up came pages of offers. Yes, you can buy openly or, as they like to say, discreetly. And who's to stop anyone stocking up on inhalers labelled as a recognised brand name like Ventolin but containing TRS-CoV from some cowboy outfit in India, Pakistan, or Egypt for that matter, and then putting them up for sale on the internet. And just think about Thailand where the aerosol canisters were found. Thailand has some of the best counterfeiters in the world. So is it all possible? You bet."

Colin had listened to Larry's passionate but entirely realistic scenario.

"Yes and it would tie in nicely with Daniel finding an invoice for a quarter of a million inhalers made out to Shah Medical Centre, Larry."

"Jesus," said Larry. "Where is all this heading?"

"I don't know but Daniel is going to what he suspects is the Shah production plant somewhere in Egypt as we speak. Stay close."

"And I'm going to Washington, Colin. There's no point staying here. I'll probably hand in my notice when I'm back in the USA.

But the next bit of news coming into Colin's red hot phone was from Jimmy in Nairobi.

"It's not just the Pakistanis who are leaving, Colin. I think they are moving everything out of the building. I arrived for my cleaning job tonight and two trucks were outside. They were loading equipment and boxes and many things into them. But Luther Jasman was helping them so I decided not to go to work tonight as Luther knows me.

"Instead I phoned him and asked when he needed his new students. He was very apologetic. He said they didn't want any now as they were closing down the Nairobi business and will use it as a warehouse.

"Luther is a very polite young man, Colin. I don't think he wanted to speak to me but I also think he is afraid he won't have a job soon. But I did get him to confirm that everything is going to Cairo.

"And another thing, Colin. The trucks were taking things out but a man in a small van was taking boxes in."

Colin phoned me and my response was swift.

"Ask Jimmy if he can find out what's in those boxes."

I know now that I was already starting to push Jimmy too far.

Deciding it was best to use a hired car from now on, I generously paid off Mahmoud and Maria and I headed south in a Toyota saloon towards Beni Suef. Maria was map reading.

Approaching Beni Suef the landscape was open, rural and flat with a scattering of high date palms. "There is a University, Nahda University, on the east side of the river, Mr McCann." said Maria. "But I still cannot find a place called Majid."

Passing the University on the right we approached a roundabout with a choice - either turn right over the river to Beni Suef town or carry on. But with the map showing nothing going further south, we turned right, over the Nile bridge and into the outskirts of the town itself.

Nothing ventured, nothing gained, I suggested a stop for tea or coffee and a few enquiries. Leaving Maria to talk to the coffee shop waiter, I relaxed. Ten minutes later we were on the road again, heading south.

The Majid Industrial area was a dusty, sand-blown area of small industrial units and untidy shop fronts, men in working overalls, dirty with grease and stray dogs watching the action. But driving on through we then found a better, more modern end of purpose built units with company names mostly in Arabic but some in English - Tobruk Tools, Hassan Engineering, Egyptian Confection, Majid Plastics. Then, as we rounded a bend in the road that seemed to run out into open countryside, a bigger, green painted building set behind a high wire fence came into view. The wire gateway, as high as the fence, was closed. Just inside on a stony, gravelled driveway was a small building of concrete blocks - a security man's shelter from the sun.

I stopped the car and Maria and I sat with the engine and air-conditioning running and took stock. The single storey front end had a smart-looking entrance of tinted glass, possibly a reception area. Two small saloon cars were parked directly outside on the gravelled driveway which continued around the side to a higher, two story rear end with plain, green metal cladding. There were no windows but a white van was parked next to a wide double door loading bay.

The building was big - far larger than I had imagined. I moved the car closer and pointed to the Arabic sign over the front entrance - "Shah Pharmaceuticals," in English and Arabic.

But around the back of the rear building was something else I had not imagined. It was a garden, a miniature oasis of bushes, palms and trees with yellow laburnum-like flowers. It resembled a small, artificially created garden of the sort found in some better hotels and I wondered if there might also be a swimming pool. But no-one seemed to be around - even the concrete security shelter behind the wire gate was empty. I took a few quick photos on my mobile phone and then we sat there. I looked at Maria, Maria looked at me. Maria asked the obvious question. "What do we do now, Mr McCann."

"We've found it. But we now turn around and go back to Cairo, Maria. I need to think."

CHAPTER 55

It had been a while since I had spoken to Walt Daniels at Biox, but there was still one thing I needed. Verbal descriptions of David Solomon and Guy Williams were one thing but good colour photos were something else. Somehow, I felt I was closing in on something and wanted to be able to recognise them. Back once more in Cairo and Maria having gone home, I phoned Walt in Boston.

With no questions asked, Walt obliged and by next morning I had an email with photos attached. Both photos, I decided, were trimmed, full face shots probably taken at a staff function somewhere. I already knew that Solomon was tall, six foot. The photo now showed him with short, very light fair hair and looking much younger than his forty years. Guy Williams I knew was short, stocky, five foot six or so and the photo showed him with a mop of thick black hair. With the photo of Jan de Jonge from Colin and a clear picture of Mohamed Kader and Greg O'Brian, in my mind it was enough.

I set off in the rented Toyota before dawn the next morning. I was alone this time but retraced the route back down south to Beni Suef. By seven thirty I was sitting in the car in the Majid industrial area with the sun rising behind clumps of palms on the flat, eastern horizon into a cloudless, pale blue sky.

I had already worked out where I would park. From the shade of one of the other smaller factory units, I had a good view of the whole length of the Shah building. With a pair of binoculars and a digital camera with a decent lens bought in the souk the night before and a 6 pack of water bottles, potato crisps and chocolate bars on the back seat, I was ready for the sort of day-long stake out I often use.

The two cars and van from the day before were no longer there, so several people must have been there and then left. But I didn't have to wait long for some action.

At eight thirty, a mini bus arrived, the driver unlocked the wire gate and drove in, past the reception area and stopped outside in the loading bay area. The driver got out and opened the sliding, passenger door. Three men emerged, one unlocked the double doors of the loading bay and all three went inside. But it was quite clear to me, from the way they were dressed that they matched Jimmy's description of those he had seen in Nairobi. These were also, probably, Pakistani.

Ten minutes later, three cars arrived and this time drew up outside the reception area.

I wound down the tinted window of the Toyota, picked up the binoculars and watched four men emerge. Three of them were white, of European or American appearance and one was black. All were casually dressed in trousers and open-necked shirts. They stood and chatted and one of the white men lit a cigarette. I switched to the camera, took a couple of shots, then watched them walk slowly to the main reception door. One of the white men unlocked it and all of them went inside.

No sooner had they gone inside when another saloon car drove in through the main gate - a white Toyota similar to mine. It stopped next to the other three cars and three men emerged. From my distance it was difficult to see detail, but these three looked Egyptian. I took a few more photos and then watched them go inside.

Then I settled myself once more, but the heat inside the car was building. With no wish to sit with the engine and air-conditioning running, I drank a can of Fanta, breakfasted on a bar of melting chocolate and looked at the photos I'd just taken. One might just have been Guy Williams and another Jan de Jonge but I was far from certain. None of them looked like David Solomon but that was to be expected - Solomon, from what we now knew from his Malthus posting, was probably in Thailand. As for the black one and the others, I had no idea who they were.

It was almost midday when the next vehicle arrived - a truck hauling a twenty foot container. All three of the Pakistanis emerged, one directed the truck driver to the loading bay at the side, the others opened doors and waited for the truck to reverse up to the bay. From what I could see through the binoculars, boxes were being unloaded. Then a forklift truck appeared and carried a large, shiny, stainless steel tank onto the driveway and left it there, glinting in the hot sun.

Now I can be quite masochistic at times. The painful, self punishment imposed by uncomfortable stake-outs is bearable to a point as it's what I sometimes need to do. But if I was an employee of some European or American company with health and safety posters stuck everywhere or an office worker with the Department Health and Social Security I'd have been quite entitled to say enough is enough, down tools and walk out. But I'm a self employed bloke who earns his crust doing this sort of thing. But I admit I was now very hot. My underwear felt as if I'd wet myself. But, the fact is, every drop of water I had drunk was seeping through my skin. It was never going to emerge through its normal exit point. The cars' temperature gage showed an outside temperature of 41C. Inside it was probably 141C. I was desperate for a long drink of cold water, but was hanging on to the last bottle of warm stuff just in case and was really glad I'd already eaten the chocolate. But I still did not want to attract attention by sitting in the car with its engine and air-conditioning running.

At one o'clock, though. there was, once more, action at the front. All the men who had arrived together earlier suddenly emerged through the front door, stood chatting for a while and the smoker lit up again. Three of them, two white men, including the smoker and the black man, piled into one of the cars. The other three went back inside.

I started the Toyota, felt the first waft of refrigerated air pass over my face in five hours and waited for them to drive past where I was parked. I followed them as they drove back in the direction of Beni Suef. But then they suddenly turned off the main road in the direction of the river. I followed them through a dusty village of flat roofed houses, a coffee shop, some small shops selling vegetables and general groceries and then into an area of big, new, more modern villas set behind concrete walls with high, iron gates. Suddenly, without warning, the River Nile appeared on my right. Between rows of palm trees, it shimmered in the still, midday sun. A boat with pure white sails drifted south close to the shore, but still the car in front kept going, northwards.

But then it slowed down almost to a walking pace. I stopped and pulled into the shade of a tree to watch The car then turned right between more trees and disappeared. I followed once again.

And there, laid out amongst flowering shrubs and green lawns with sprinklers casting rainbows of light amongst the greenery was The River View Hotel - a quiet place of unexpected luxury that I had certainly not expected to find.

A nice place to bring Anna, I thought as I parked the Toyota car almost next to the empty Peugeot that had just carried the three members of the Shah team.

I got out. First I checked the wetness still clinging to my armpits and groin, then I closed the car door and walked up some tiled steps into the cool, darker lobby. A young bell boy or porter in smart uniform asked if I had any luggage. I said no.

What I found inside was also a surprise - white marble, tiled floors, a wide spiral stairway and groups of American, Japanese and European tourists either stood fanning themselves, sat chatting or quietly reading travel brochures and books on Egyptian history and antiquities. It had not struck me that the area had become a stopping off point for luxury Nile cruises. But this, it seemed was where they came ashore before continuing on down to Aswan or returning to Cairo.

In my light grey slacks and white shirt I found I fitted in far better than I had feared although I probably looked as if I'd just emerged, full dressed, from a sauna. I stood for a moment, allowing my eyes to adjust to the relative darkness of the interior and my wet body to benefit a little from the hotel air conditioning. A curved, marble archway, edged by more ferns and flowers, marked the entrance to the restaurant. I walked through the archway and on my left was a bar and a waiter in a neat black and white uniform taking orders.

I spotted a seat by a corner table, wandered over to it and sat down. Then I ordered a gin and tonic and two glasses of ice cold mineral water. I gulped one down and then watched the twenty or so others who were sat around or stood at the bar.

The three men I had just followed were already relaxing at a table by the window overlooking the lawn. The black man was talking. The others nodded. The smoker talked. They laughed. The other white man, the shorter one had his back to me. The short black ponytail fixed high up on his head was held in some sort of band. He wore an expensive bright blue silk shirt with what looked like a flowery pattern. The black man was now looking around him - the bar, the garden outside. The third man, the smoker was listening to something the pony tail was saying. He nodded, took a drink from a glass of beer and sat back.

I knew immediately that I had found Jan de Jonge.

So who was the black one? Could it be Larry's friend, the French national from Nairobi who had only just gone missing?

And the pony tail? I needed him to turn around but it looked like Guy Williams with longer hair than in the photograph.

The waiter came and asked if I wanted lunch and I declined but ordered another glass of iced mineral water instead. It came and I picked it up and walked over to the three men. They saw me coming. Without asking I sat down on the empty fourth chair surrounding their table. They looked at me and then they looked at each other.

"Mr De Jonge?" I said and looked at the smoker. From this distance, a metre, I knew I was right. De Jonge stared at me but before there was time to reply my eyes moved to the black one.

"Philippe Fournier?"

I then looked at the pony tail. "Mr Williams? Guy Williams?"

The Dutch man had had a few seconds advantage over his colleagues.

"Who are you?"

"I take it you are Jan De Jonge?"

There was no reply but the pony tail had now had time to think.

"What's going on?"

"Yes, what do you want?" the Dutchman said again looking as though he was about to get up and run.

"Steady." I raised my hand. "Take it easy. Just a few questions."

They all looked at me and then at each other as if there was some unresolved mistrust between them. The Dutchman in particular looked at the pony tail. There was another short silence.

"You know him?" The Dutchman asked his two colleagues.

"Never seen him before in my entire life," said the pony tail in a distinctly English accent. The black one shrugged.

"I need some help," I said and leaned forward. Then I looked around the bar as if I wanted to share a secret. "I hoped you might all be able to help me."

"What sort of help?" The pony tail asked.

"I mean no harm assuming none of you have done anything wrong," I said, knowing full well that the Dutchman may well have been the one responsible for the theft of a million dollars worth of research material from his employer.

"So, how did you find me?" De Jonge said as if he was the only one I had just found.

"I followed you," I said and all three looked at each other again.

"The car that followed us from the highway?" the black one asked with a slight French accent.

"Further than that. From Shah Pharmaceuticals - your place of work."

"How do you know that? Who are you? Where are you from? Who sent you?" The pony tail was now getting anxious and his voice rose higher. His hands pressed on the arms of the chair, as if he was about to get up.

"As I said, just take it easy. I need to talk to all of you. I do not represent the law if that's what's bothering you." I paused and then repeated, "Can we talk?"

The waiter returned, looked concerned at the agitated state of the three potential diners, but told them their table was ready. The three men still seemed unsure of what to do.

"Can I suggest I join you at your table," I said. "I've already eaten." I was referring to the liquid Snicker bars and cheese and onion crisps.

They continued to look at one another but then the pony tail got up, followed by the Dutchman and then Philippe Fournier. All four of us followed the waiter in a line, into the restaurant, like ducklings to the pond.

Once seated, the waiter flipped white napkins onto their laps and asked if the fourth guest may now wish to order. I declined. There was an embarrassed silence. Then I started again. I looked at Jan de Jonge.

"Message from Mum and Dad," I said. "Zoe liked her necklace."

It was the test that Colin had suggested. Only De Jonge's mother and father would have known anything about a necklace and Zoe. I didn't have a clue about the significance but De Jonge clearly did. There was a stunned silence as he looked at me with his mouth ajar. "When did you see them?" he asked.

"I didn't," replied Daniel, "It's just a message."

"Do they know I'm here? How are they?"

"They don't know where you are. It's my secret. As far as I know I'm the only person in the world who knows the three of you are here." I said it as if trying to settle their nerves. Philippe Fournier looked embarrassed. The pony tail sat with his arms folded.

"But, just for the record. Am I right about your names?"

The Dutchman nodded without taking his eyes off me. The black Frenchman, Philippe Fourner said, "Yes, I am Philippe Fournier. I have only been here for a week. I am still learning."

The pony-tailed Englishman's response was different. "Clever of you, whoever you are. What do you want?"

"Help."

"Help? And what sort of help do you want?" Guy Williams sounded scathing.

"I'd like to know what you do at Shah Pharmaceuticals."

"That's invasion of privacy - industrial secrets - patents pending," Williams said. To me it was a scientist's response to a question that was, to all intents and purposes a business question. He sounded utterly naive.

"But why come out to this deserted spot to do research. Don't you get the resources in the UK or USA? Must miss a bit of the academic lifestyle?"

"None of your bloody business unless you give me a good reason. Anyway, how about coming clean yourself? Who the hell are you?"

"My name is Ian McCann. I'm an international commercial crime investigator. Private. Freelance, if you prefer the expression. English by nationality just like yourself, Mr Williams. Anything more you'd like to know?"

De Jonge's worried look grew more visible. Williams appeared sceptical and he sniffed. Philippe Fournier scratched his head as if it was all too complicated.

The Dutchman needed to double-check. "Commercial crime?"

"Yes. Why did you come out here, Jan. May I call you Jan?"

De Jonge looked away and was saved by the arrival of three prawn cocktails. All three looked at the food. Conversation ceased again.

"I don't have to sit here with some bloody, interfering stranger who's just walked in. I'm going back." Guy Williams stood up.

Philippe Fournier had just picked up his fork ready to tuck in but it hung there as if he was waiting for a decision.

"Where are you conducting your clinical trials?" I said and looked at Guy Williams.

Williams was visibly taken aback. "What clinical trials?" He sat down again.

"The trials on the treatment for the virus now known in some circles as TRS-CoV."

"I don't know what you're talking about."

"You don't know about the outbreak of TRS-CoV?"

"I'm a virologist. Sure I know. But what clinical trials on what treatment? "

"Let's start with the trials in Nigeria." I was testing him.

"We're not doing any trials. It's far too early."

"What about the trials in Thailand?"

"Thailand? There aren't any trials. What the bloody hell are you talking about?"

"OK, then let's start at the very beginning," I said. "Where did TRS-CoV come from?"

"And what the bloody hell do you know about respiratory viruses?" Williams said sneeringly.

"Enough to know that it's possible to engineer them for research purposes - so called gain-of-function - GOF - research. I understand this sort of research is done to identify combinations of mutations that could, for instance, allow an animal virus to jump to unprepared humans. By understanding the mutations, the thinking goes, you can prepare against a possible threat. Some say that GOF research is high risk."

"Yes, but there are strict controls."

"So such viruses can never escape?"

"No."

"Could someone steal a virus created by GOF research, nurture it, build huge stocks of it, release it?

"It's laughable."

"Do you have any TRS-CoV here?"

"No."

"Any other viruses?"

"Yes, but we know what we are doing."

"OK. The new antiviral treatments you are working on. How are they progressing?"

"Slow but we are making progress."

I was surprised I'd got an answer without a question about how I might know that was what they were doing. But Jan de Jonge suddenly got up. He was sweating. "Excuse me," he said. "I need the bathroom." I watched him go and turned to face Guy Williams again.

"You see, Guy - can I call you Guy? - I've become a bit of an amateur expert on viruses in the last few weeks. I can even explain how Tamiflu and Relenza work on influenza viruses, how drugs for HIV work. I've started to understand how clever you are at changing viruses just for the fun of it."

"It's not for the fun."

I knew I was being provocative. "OK," I said, "Then how about for the huge profits you can make out of it?"

"How about for improving health and wellbeing?"

Philippe Fournier was already finishing his prawn cocktail.

As this was going nowhere, I changed the question. "Why did you leave Biox?" I asked Williams..

"Opportunity knocked. Money was good. Nice location and improving every day. Look around you."

Then I changed tack again. "Where is David Solomon?"

I could immediately tell I'd touched another nerve.

"I don't know," Guy Williams said, more calmly. He came out here to help set it up. But he was closer to the management side than me. He moved on."

"To where?" I tried again.

"I really don't know,"

"Forgive me, Guy, but I think there are things going on here which you are totally unaware of. You are being used, exploited."

"Rubbish," said Guy Williams. "We're given a lot of freedom."

"What are the aerosol inhalers for?"

Williams now looked shocked. Was there no end to what this man knew?

"Tests," he said. "We need to improve our engineering for filling the pressurised canisters aseptically. It's not simple technology."

"And once you're happy with the engineering what will the inhalers be filled with?"

"Our new antiviral drug - the one we are developing here."

"And who is helping with the engineering side?"

210

"We have a small team of engineers from Pakistan."

I sat back in my chair and swallowed the final drops my third glass of mineral water. The waiter was clearing two dishes of untouched prawn cocktails and one that had been empty for several minutes.

"Lost your appetite, Guy? And where has Jan, gone? Did I touch a nerve?"

The waiter returned and asked if they would like their main course now. I was still sitting back. Guy Williams looked at the waiter, "Sorry but something has cropped up. We need to go. Please put the bill on my account."

"Yes sir."

"So shall we sit and talk, Guy?" I tried a comforting tone as if I was the man's psychiatrist.

I led Guy Williams out of the restaurant and back to the lounge bar. Philippe Fournier followed behind and Jan de Jonge re-emerged from the hotel foyer. He still looked unsettled and nervous.

We found a corner table, I ordered coffee and started with an apology for interrupting their lunch. Then: "Philippe, can I ask you something first."

Philippe Fournier visibly jumped. "How long have you been here?"

"Ah, nearly two weeks."

"Who recruited you?"

"I don't know."

Guy William's look was one of incredulity. "You don't know, Philippe?"

"I never asked. The man phoned me, asked if I was interested in a better paid job. I said yes. Anything is better than working for a charity. I met him for an interview. I was offered a job. He said pack a case, bring my passport. I thought it was for security or I was going to Paris for training. Next minute I'm on a plane with him bound for Cairo. We got met in Cairo by a woman. I was given five thousand dollars in advance of my salary to cover what she called 'settling in expenses.' I was brought here by car. I started work on the virus cultures. Nice research laboratory, nice garden, nice villa we stay in. Better than the job in Nairobi. So far I like it."

"What did the man who interviewed you look like, Philippe?" I asked.

"I don't remember faces too well."

"Christ almighty," said Guy Williams.

"Did he look like this, Philippe?" I said and flicked open my mobile phone.

"Yes, that's him."

"His name is Dominique Lunneau," I said and looked at Guy Williams. "He works at the Shah Medicals site in Nairobi but he once worked in Lebanon. My information is that he has close links with the company's owner."

"What Shah Medicals site in Nairobi?" Guy Williams asked.

"It's similar to the Shah Medicals operations in Hong Kong and Singapore but bigger," I said. "Just wait, Guy, there's so much you don't know."

Guy Williams rubbed his chin and looked at me. I then turned to face Jan de Jonge. But I had no wish to go around in circles just to arrive at the one question I wanted to ask. I just asked him straight. "Jan, did you take some research material from your previous employer, Virex, without permission?"

Jan de Jonge looked at Guy Williams, then back at me. He took a deep breath.

"Yes," he said and the relief on the man's face was visible. "Am I likely to be prosecuted if I return to the US?"

I deliberately avoided the question for now. "Who did you give the material to?"

There was just the slightest hesitation. "David Solomon."

Guy Williams muttered, "Christ almighty," again.

"Did he promise to pay you for it?" I asked.

"No, but he said he was now working for a company in Egypt and could guarantee me a job with double the salary and better conditions."

"Anything else?"

"He'd pay a lump sum so I could settle my debts but only after I'd moved to Egypt and if......"

"If what?"

"If I could also obtain a virus sample from the Virex bio-safety laboratory.

"What?" cried Guy Williams. "Bloody hell, Jan."

"What was the virus?" Daniel continued.

"A modified Influenza virus we'd been working on."

"And you gave it to him?"

"Yes. I trusted him and he was only a kilometre away at Biox and Virex and Biox were working together, or so I thought. And David is an international expert in that field - written papers on the subject - lectured on it."

Guy Williams stood up. "Jesus Christ. What the fuck is going on here, Jan?"

For a moment, I deliberately downplayed it. "Are you happy here, Jan?"

"No. Frankly I want to go home but I've still not had the money Dave Solomon promised. I owe money - a lot - back in Holland. You didn't know that either Guy - sorry."

"Do any of you know who actually owns Shah Pharmaceuticals?" I asked and glanced at all three in turn.

"Yes," said Guy Williams, "An Arab company called Al Zafar. They have a chain of pharmaceutical businesses in the Middle East."

"And do you know the owner of Al Zafar?"

"A man called Mohamed Kader. He came here a year ago when we were just starting up. Rich man."

"Have you heard of Livingstone Pharmaceuticals?"

"The name rings a bell," he said.

"How loudly does it ring?"

"I've heard of them - people in the States buy Livingstone indigestion tablets."

"Hardly a high tech biotechnology company, then. Did you know that Livingstone and Al Zafar, alias Shah Medicals, work together, co-operate, maybe have shares in each other's businesses? They have a network of distributors right across the Middle East, South East Asia and Africa. Then there is the Nairobi site and an office in Cairo. Do you know who owns Livingstone?"

"No bloody idea," said Williams. "Tell me."

"I'm not going to tell you his name but he's known to the FBI and other law enforcement agencies as a crook, a fraudster, an embezzler and worse. He's one of your three, ultimate bosses. The others are Mohamed Kader and David Solomon."

"I can't believe it. I've known Dave for years," Guy Williams said, "There's nothing wrong with him."

"How well did you know David Solomon, Guy?"

"Very well, we worked together for a long time."

"Did he have any hobbies, political leanings, strong opinions on anything in particular?"

"Yes, environmental issues. A lot of us shared the same type of views. As a biologist you get hung up about the destruction of the environment."

"Did he feel strongly enough about anything to want to actually do something?"

Guy Williams didn't need much time to think about it. "Yes, population control. He was an admirer of the biologist Paul Eyrlich and others but he thought Eyrlich had weakened his stance and wasn't determined enough to pursue his opinions into positive action. We often talked about it. We both belonged to a debating society at Boston University."

"The Malthus Club?" I asked.

"Bloody hell. Yes."

"So what would you say if I told you that I suspect David Solomon has created a new Influenza virus that could kill millions and that he plans to release it as part of a campaign deliberately aimed at reducing the world's population in numbers not seen since the Black Death?"

All three men, professional virologists in their own right, fell silent.

It was Jan de Jonge who spoke first.

"Warnings have often been made of an accident. But a deliberate campaign? Yes, he could do it," he said. "The virus I gave him, suitably altered, is probably capable of it. We'd created it at Virex and Biox were also involved."

That comment was hugely significant. It answered my one main lingering question - the one I'd not got from Charles Brady. It explained the business relationship between Charles Brady of Virex and Josh Ornstein of Biox. And Larry would like this one. It would explain Josh Ornstein's questions to him about the Nigerian deaths.

"But no-one could do it alone," said Guy Williams, "Certainly not on that scale."

"But that's the point, Guy, he could. He has funds, he has access to an international network of distributors in just the right places to start such a campaign - in Africa, the Middle East, South East Asia - just the places he believes are overpopulated, overcrowded trouble spots. And there is someone else who shares David Solomon's views and this person is in the perfect position to deliver it. That person is your other boss, Mohamed Kader."

"Are you serious?" Guy Williams asked, at last showing signs that he was beginning to realise the feasibility of what I had been describing."

"I'm deadly serious," I said. "So let me describe your other boss for you. The boss of Livingstone is a man whose sole interest is making money - lots of it. He's already made millions out of fraud and embezzlement. Funding David Solomon's little project and your place here in Beni Suef is small change. He'll then find ways to stash the profits in the Cayman Islands or somewhere else that's untouchable. But don't ever stand in his way. He's a nasty piece of work."

"But he can't make money by spreading a virus." For the first time, Philippe Fournier had asked a question and the question made sense. The other two nodded. I shook my head.

"Oh yes he can, Philippe. Your third boss has got something that he can sell at a huge profit margin - a treatment. First you spread the virus, then you sell the treatment. And if you get fed up selling the real thing or can't cope with the huge demand for it or it proves to be only marginally effective, what do you then do? You start selling counterfeit medicines."

Jan de Yong's complexion turned from sunburned red to an anaemic looking white. I went on:

"And how can they administer the treatment or spread the virus? Can I suggest the use of controlled dose inhalers? And who's working on the technology for these inhalers?" I spread my arms wide inviting the obvious answer. "You are all implicated."

CHAPTER 56

When in Lagos, Larry had tried to fix a meeting by email with New York Senator Joe Fisher but, just as Larry landed at JFK, New York, the news from his office was that he was in Washington. So, too, was the other New York Senator, Mary Collis.

He emailed both of them again telling them he was a doctor working for the US Embassy in Nigeria. He said he had evidence that the hundred recent deaths in

Kano were caused by a new strain of influenza virus and that he believed it was part of a deliberate plot to spread the virus as a form of population control. He had spoken to the US Ambassador to Nigeria but had got nowhere. Would they please check with WHO Geneva for further evidence about the virus.

As he clicked 'send' he knew he had made it sound as if he was a crackpot.

And even if they decided to check him out by contacting the US Embassy in Abuja they'd have got nothing except confirmation that Doctor Larry Brown worked for the commercial services section in Lagos, had only been there for two months and had gone AWOL.

He thought about contacting the press with the story but decided against it thinking that it needed to stay within circles that could do something not circles that fed on sensation or sought live interviews and quotes.

Larry did not even go outside JFK Airport. Instead, he flew to Washington.

In the UK, Anna had not heard from Daniel for two days. She phoned Colin to say she was worried and to ask if he had heard anything. Colin said he hadn't but that if he did he'd not only tell Daniel to phone her but tick him off. "Daniel is well known for going quiet when he's working, Anna. Otherwise, are you OK? Finding your way around London?"

"Yes," Anna said. "Too many Thai restaurants in Queensway. I already have many friends."

In Bristol, Kevin had finally fixed a day and time to meet his Member of Parliament. Not having voted for her he was none too enthusiastic, but he had promised to start somewhere. He met Tom Weston for lunch and brought him up to date. Tom listened to Kevin's tale of his meeting at the Cumberland Hotel with Larry from Nigeria, Colin from London and Daniel and by the time he had finished, Tom had drunk two pints and finished off a ploughman's lunch.

"So," Kevin finally said, sitting back to drain his glass. "What the fuck do I do?"

"Bloody hell," Tom finally said. "All hell breaking loose. As for our local MP, I wouldn't hold out much hope there. She's only interested in re-election. Why don't you speak to the Chair of the House of Lords Science and Technology Committee - Lord Peterson."

"But I don't know him," said Kevin.

"I do," said Tom. "I'll call him."

CHAPTER 57

At the River View Hotel, I was now encouraging a discussion on where David Solomon might be. To me, Thailand looked the most likely place and it was Jan de Jonge who, without any prompting, confirmed it.

"He back-packed in Thailand when he was younger and still had a girlfriend - half Thai-half English - a lecturer in microbiology and biotechnology Her name was Pim."

It was something that I thought Colin might work on but this wasn't the time or place to phone or email Colin. I sat back and glanced at my watch. It was now well into the afternoon and since my unannounced arrival at lunch, I think I had slowly persuaded the three men of my integrity. A kind of trust based on some common sense had slowly taken over. Jan de Jonge in particular seemed willing to do anything to help.

"So what do we all do?" The question from Guy Williams was exactly the same as mine but I daren't admit it. I wanted to return to Cairo - in fact I wanted to go back to UK to see Anna - but I really had no idea what to do next. I hoped Larry Brown might have managed something. Was he still in Nigeria or had he gone to the USA? And what about Kevin? And Colin would be waiting for the next call from me. More importantly, so would Anna.

In the past, I have often found that the next move would be forced upon me. And so it turned out.

We were just finishing an exchange of phone numbers and I'd ordered a last coffee as a prelude to the three Shah Pharmaceuticals men going back to work and me returning to Cairo when I saw, from where I was sitting, a man walk through the hotel foyer and go up to the receptionist.

I had seen the man earlier that morning from the car as I watched the movements at Shah Pharmaceuticals. The Pakistani man was now dressed not as he had been that morning - all in white - but in grey trousers and a blue shirt. The dusty shoes, socks and dark beard, though, were the giveaway.

"How good are your Pakistani engineers?" I asked.

Guy Williams laughed, Jan de Jonge shook his head. "I have to tell them everything," he said, "What screw to put where, which way round a filter goes. Fortunately the equipment comes partially assembled otherwise we'd struggle."

"So who sent them?"

"Al Zafar. We got an email from someone called Ahmed in Jordan saying they were on their way."

"Don't all look at once but is that one of them?" I asked. "He's stood by reception."

Philippe clearly misunderstood. He turned around. "Yes," he said, his name is Rahim."

Rahim saw Philippe and then the three others. With not the slightest sign of recognising work colleagues, he turned and walked quickly out of the hotel. I turned, looked out of the window behind and saw him in the car park on a phone. A sense of genuine unease now stirred inside me. I suspected that not all the Pakistanis were engineers. I have seen this before but if you are running a dodgy business then you need one or two trustworthy spies working inside.

I hit dense evening traffic as I was driving back into Cairo and had come to a grinding halt when my mobile phone sounded. It was a text from Colin: "Phone me ASAP."

I was tired, hungry and very thirsty but still desperate for some news and so I stopped the car and phoned.

"Message from Jimmy, Daniel. I recorded it but, as usual, it's long. I'll give you the gist. He's moved into his brother's house near the Shah factory - I tell you this only because he is now able to watch things at night without being too far from his bed.

"Mmm," I said, "Please get to the gist."

"Firstly, he is no longer the cleaner and neither is Lucky. Lucky was made redundant yesterday. Luther Jasman has had two week's notice. It looks like the whole place is winding down or rapidly going over to a different function. But he says there isn't much night security now - only movement-sensitive security lighting.

"The Frenchman, Dominique Lunneau still runs the place. Two different Pakistanis and four Arabs of unknown nationality have moved in. All the original Pakistanis except one have gone to Cairo. You may know that. That means Lunneau now has a staff of about eight. None are Kenyan.

"Now Jimmy wants to wander around inside the whole place, not just the small part he had been cleaning for two nights. But he wanted some clarity on what he was actually looking for. I said anything suspicious - that's usually enough for Jimmy. But I told him to go bloody careful.

"But all that was two days ago, Daniel. Jimmy has been very busy since.

"He met his friend Jomo again - the redundant salesman. I don't know what the hell Jimmy told Jomo but, suffice it to say, Jomo spoke to Luther Jasman and they agreed to meet for coffee.

"Lo and behold, of course, Jimmy turns up for coffee as well.

"Hello Mr Jasman, remember me? I'm the one who offered to find you some students. But I am an imposter, Mr Jasman. I lied. In fact I'm a private investigator, part of an international team based in London looking into a possible case of germ warfare.

"But it's jolly good news that you've been fired Luther as all hell is about to break out at Shah Medicals. CIA, MI6, Kenyan Security Forces are all about to descend. But you'll be safe now as long as you keep your mouth shut. Your new wife is also safe now so don't worry. Don't tell her anything. But listen, Luther. I need help."

Colin paused. "Following it so far, Daniel?"

"Yes, Colin. Keep going."

"Can you steal me a set of keys, Luther, says Jimmy. I need access to all parts of the premises. Once you've stolen them write and say you've found a job in Mombasa and then run away for a few days. You and your wife can stay with my Auntie Bahati - she runs a B and B by the beach. But don't tell anyone, including your wife.

"Believe me, I'm trying to shorten it, Dan. Just bear with me.

"Luther does his bit - steals keys, hands them to Jomo who hands them to Jimmy. Luther, scared stiff, gets on the train to Mombasa. Jimmy even buys him two tickets. Then the exciting bit. Jimmy breaks in using the keys at two o'clock last night. And what does he find? Let me find my list. Ah, here it is.

"Boxes of inhalers like the ones used by asthmatics. Twenty boxes labelled as - wait for it - "Breath Easy" - it's a well known brand name of an asthma inhaler made and sold by one of the top six pharmaceutical companies - label looks identical to the originals - lovely counterfeit job apparently.

"Next - ten boxes simply marked "Vaccine" in black marker pen on the outside. Inside? Hundreds of unlabelled ampoules with a clear fluid inside. One box carelessly left open next to a machine - possibly a labelling machine but no labels found. Quality control would normally have a fit, but there is no QC.

"Finally sixty cardboard boxes of what Jimmy described as 'tiny aluminium cylinders the size of cigarette lighters.' They were inside boxes labelled - and you'll love this, Daniel - "Malthus A Respiratory Virus."

"Jimmy took photos, re-taped the boxes and says they looked as good as new. He was in bed by 4am but wants to go back again tomorrow night to look in Dominique Lunneau's office. That's it Daniel - a precis, a summary, the gist."

For a moment, sitting in my hired Toyota on the side of a noisy main road on the southern outskirts of Cairo I did not know what to say. Colin helped me out.

"Where are you, Dan?"

"In my car on a congested highway in Cairo wondering what to say."

"You need to phone Anna, Dan. She's worried."

"Yes, I'll phone her as soon as I get to the hotel. Phone her now for me Colin - tell her you've spoken to me. OK?"

"Sure, anything else?"

"Yes," I said, "Check out the following: Thammasat University, Bangkok, National Science and Technology Centre. See if you can find a lecturer in microbiology and biotechnology. Her name is Pim. That's all I know. I need anything on her - emails, phone numbers anything and if you need to talk to anyone in Thai, ask Anna."

"Pim?"

"Yes, Pim something - like Anna is not really Anna but something longer."

"But you've already got a Thai girlfriend, Dan."

"Yes, I know but I'm too tired for your jokes, Colin. Fact is I think she might be David Solomon's girlfriend."

"Christ. Well done. And when are you coming home to see yours?"

"Soon. But any news from Larry? Any news from Kevin? Gut instinct is telling me we're too late. By the time the wheels of international bureaucracy and diplomacy start to go around, we could be in the middle of a pandemic - a

Malthus A pandemic. So I think I'll head for Nairobi and join Jimmy. I've done all I can here."

Back at the hotel, I phoned Nagi and deliberately played down what I had found at Beni Suef.

"It's a bunch of innocent expatriate scientists doing research and development work for the main company. Yes, the main company is Al Zafar but they are so naive they hardly know who they are working for. Scientists Nagi - give them a microscope and a few test tubes and they do as they're told. By all means get someone in to inspect their premises and ask a few questions if you like but the main problem is elsewhere. That's why I'm off to Nairobi tomorrow morning. And thank Maria for me, will you? She' a natural and if she wants a regular job ask Colin to put her on his list."

Business side over, I settled myself for a long talk with Anna.

CHAPTER 58

Until very recently I've never seen myself as a man who smiled a lot. Lurking behind the mask is a good sense of humour and my own thoughts often make me chuckle inside, but it rarely shows externally.

I suppose I take things seriously but I've always likened life to running a business. Seeing the many pitfalls ahead before falling into them and planning a course of action to avoid them altogether is a skill I have nurtured. Only if the way ahead becomes very murky and the pitfalls impossible to see do I resort to 'nothing ventured, nothing gained' and 'muddle through'.

I was on an Egypt Air flight from Cairo to Nairobi and spent most of the time staring out of the window and thinking whilst watching the ground and clouds far below move slowly backwards. I don't think I smiled at all. Lone travellers don't smile. But I was thinking about everything. Flying on your own is a good time to get your life into perspective. It's an even better time to analyse the state of your business.

This job had been different to all others I had taken on. A finished job usually meant a verbal report back to whoever was paying my fee followed by a written one if requested.

In this case, I already felt I'd done more than enough to earn a fee from Charles Brady at Virex. In fact, despite the vaguest of briefings, I felt I had far exceeded his remit and my own expectations. I knew who had taken Virex's lost material and I was right in thinking Brady had been a bit short on what he'd told me.

Jan de Jonge had spilled far more beans than I'd expected. In fact it sounded as if he had stolen not one thing but two - something they were testing as an antiviral drug and a lethal virus. The man should be locked up. So should Charles Brady for his security lapses.

I supposed I could, right then, have been flying back to UK. The next day I could be reporting to Brady about what I knew and then sending him an invoice. But, together with Larry Brown in Nigeria, Kevin and Colin in the UK and Jimmy in Nairobi, what I had uncovered went way beyond a simple case of theft of a company's property. This was a global problem that could now affect the lives of millions, if not billions. I looked around the half full aircraft. Half of us could be dead in a year's time. And why? Because of insufficient security by one organisation and the lack of international rules and controls placed on virus research.

But I could also understand some of the problems that would be posed for anyone wanting to introduce rules and controls. Monitoring and policing was the only way. But virus research, unlike nuclear or other weapons research, did not need concealing in remote spots or hidden inside mountains away from satellite surveillance. Given the funds and resources, this research could be carried out in a space no bigger than a teenage computer hacker's bedroom.

I was about to meet Jimmy for the first time for a few years. Jimmy was the only one of our small group that consisted of me, Colin, Kevin and Larry who was not fully aware of the enormity of what we had found and this was something that I intended to put right as soon as I could persuade Jimmy to sit down and listen for a while.

But none of us, on our own or together, was in a position to do anything to stop it.

Report it? Yes. But to whom? The World Health Organisation? The Biological and Toxic Weapons Convention which, as Larry had discovered, seemed to rent office space at Bradford University? Was there an international system in place that could detect and deal with criminality of this sort? What we were uncovering was criminality that operated so secretly and so far below the radar that it was completely undetectable. Not only that but it respected no national borders.

And what could anyone do? Make arrests? Close down the companies, the factories? And where was David Solomon? The man who, whilst not holding the purse strings, certainly held onto the technological strings and the ideological ones. And how many others were in on the plot. The Frenchman Lunneau? Were some of Livingstone's and Shah Medicals agents and distributors part of it? Were some going to hold stock of virus or of vaccine in the hope of making money? And even if they had managed to put a halt to the main Shah Medicals operation, how many others were out there and in on the act?

And as for Kevin's optimistic hope that his long list of population control fanatics would see sense and not join in the fun, then I was not at all convinced. I was already worried that some may have already been primed ready to act when the time came.

And this would also explain Mohamed Kader's visit to London and his meeting with Kevin. It was my view that that meeting was for Kader to check Kevin out in the same way he'd already checked out Kevin's Nigerian friend Tunje Fayinke. Kader, I felt, had wanted to see how radical Kevin was and whether he could be persuaded to be more actively involved in what was being planned. For some unknown reason, it seemed that Kevin had not passed the Kader test.

And Kader seemed able to travel the world freely and frequently perhaps using the El Badry cover. In the past year there was evidence he had been in Jordan, Egypt, Hong Kong, Singapore, Pakistan, Nigeria and Kenya - and that was just the places I knew about. And if Kader was also the fictitious Doctor Mustafa in Kano then he must have been in Nigeria for many weeks, if not many months. It didn't make sense unless there was another high profile figure out there. And one possibility now high on my list of suspects was Doctor Ramses El Khoury from the Shah Medical Centre in Cairo. This man was missing. Who was he? Where was he? At the very least, he seemed to have a very cosy relationship with Fatima El Badry who also seemed to double as Mohamed Kader's wife. No, this part of the organisation still needed unravelling and I just did not have the time or resources to deal with it.

On the flight from Cairo, sat not far from me, was a small team of Kenyan athletes - tall, slim, black-skinned men in smart blazers who smiled politely and signed autographs for a few younger Kenyan boys and girls. It was the athletes that had got me thinking about pitfalls and hurdles again. I knew there were a few more I had to jump over - and fast - before going back to London.

As I watched them I suddenly wanted Anna with me.

Kenya has always been my favourite African country. For all of its many differences to Thailand, I knew Anna would like it. And yes, Kenya had its problems too, like so many other African countries - corruption, health, poverty - but Nairobi is improving year by year. The number of cars on the roads is an indication of economic success. Like Thailand it relies heavily on a thriving tourism industry and the Kenyans, like the Thais, are good at it, recognising that a visible desire to give proper service to paying customers was paramount. Compare that to the English and it's clear who are the best at it. I know South Africa well, but there is still something that troubles me about South Africa but, then, perhaps it is my own personal experiences of dealing with businesses there.

Compare then Kenya to Nigeria where, until just a few days before, I thought I might go to join up with Larry Brown. My experiences in Nigeria had always been the worst of all - anywhere. Nigeria is still a mess. And what were the statistics that Kevin Parker had rattled off when we had met up at the Cumberland Hotel? Kevin had been in full, passionate flow about Thomas Malthus, Paul Ehrlich and others. Larry, Colin and I just sat and listened until he'd finished. But I will never forget what Kevin said.

"Fucking mess, man. You ask my Nigerian friend Tunje up in Barnet. He knows and he's Nigerian. Why are there so many living here? Yes, it's part of the old British Empire but the reason there's so many here is because there's so many there. Do you think if their lives were better there that they'd want to come here? It's the same with all economic migrants.

"Do you know that the current population of Nigeria is some 166 million and that figure is expected to reach 390 million by 2050. 390 million for Christ's sake!

"Even at 166 million it's unsustainable. And with the increasing ethnic and religious conflict up in the north where you were, Larry, it's complete madness. That population needs to come down urgently to a more sensible figure like the 45.2 million figure it stood at in 1960. But is anyone standing on a bloody soap box, holding up a finger, pointing somewhere and shouting about it? No. No-one has got the balls to do anything.

"And look at the unemployment figures in Europe and elsewhere. We just don't need vast numbers of people to sustain an economy any longer. Yes, we've got mass consumption but it's now mass over consumption. People don't need half the stuff they buy. Christ sake, look at the bloody shopping trolleys coming out of Tesco. They pack the stuff into the boots of their oversized cars, unpack it in their oversized homes, eat half of it and then throw the garbage and packaging away. Mass production is done by computerised machines unless local labour is still cheap. And as for all the hard, physical work like construction, building roads and canals that was once done by hundreds of labourers it's now done by machines.

"Just look at your favourite place, Thailand, Daniel. How many Thai farmers now use buffalos and hand plant their rice and hand harvest it. They don't. They sit and watch a man with a machine. Meanwhile, as the population increases they gradually use up more and more land space to house a growing population. The space to grow rice gets less and they then start encroaching on the jungle.

"Malthus saw this happening two hundred years ago. No-one was unemployed once. You needed to do something just to stay alive. But the millions of unemployed or underemployed able bodied people should not need to be kept alive by state handouts. For one thing it does nothing for their self esteem or quality of their lives. It merely keeps them alive. Quality of life comes from being a contributor. If an economy was working properly there would be jobs for everyone. Everyone would contribute and contribution is the bedrock of human contentment. We have the ability to control birth rates, maintain populations at sensible, viable levels and provide enough jobs to share around. So why not use it? But can you name one single politician who states the bloody obvious?

"Meanwhile, while we wait, look at poor old Malta - that tiny little patch of rock stuck out in the Mediterranean is sinking under the sheer weight of economic migrants. And what does the EU say about it? 'Stop complaining - it's their human right to come and stay.' 'But we don't have the space or the resources,' say the Maltese. 'Never mind,' say the big fat EU Judges sat in their robes and high chairs. 'Just pile them up one on top of the other behind barbed wire fences - that'll satisfy their human rights.'"

How Kevin manages to avoid his passionate opinion spilling over into the lectures he gives his students I don't know. He must have continued his lecture to the small group sat in my London flat for twenty minutes or more. He ended with more statistics and yet another of his strong arguments.

This one was about the human population expected to peak at 11 billion or so in a hundred years and about another of his fellow academics whose presentational style and opinions he was firmly against. The influential and convincing Swedish Professor Hans Rosling was well known for brilliantly presenting complicated statistics. But his facts about population seemed to suggest there was nothing to worry about. According to Kevin, this was Rosling's deep flaw. Rosling always failed to factor in resource depletion, environmental degradation and climate change.

"Even the Global Footprint Network and WWF knows that humans already consume resources at a rate 50% higher than can be produced sustainably," said Kevin. "Living standards are already going down in the West. Belt tightening is the message from politicians struggling to cope with ever increasing demand for services with less and less resources. We are already seeing the early signs of less affluent lifestyles. Nothing angers people more than taking away what they

225

think are their God given rights. They'll blame politicians and take things into their own hands. Mark my words - we've not seen anything yet.

"And don't expect technology to come to the rescue. The green lobby want wider use of green technology for fuel power and power generation but they are pissing into the wind. Nothing that satisfies them will keep up with the insatiable demand for more and more electricity and that demand is now coming from places like Africa, China and India. It's not just Europe or America,"

All of us, myself included, agreed with Kevin but we also agreed with the other side of his argument - that decisions about what to do could not be made by individuals like David Solomon or Mohamed Kader with support and financial backing from a criminal like Greg O'Brian. But, as Kevin also said, this is what happens when politicians fail to provide the leadership we expect.

But Kevin concluded by saying something I will never forget.

"The green lobby are a spent force," he said. "They will never win their battle by attacking big corporations and talking about carbon emissions. They should urgently get to the root cause of their grievances and change their focus to what the Malthus Society has been advocating for years - direct action on population control."

I think Kevin should be given a wider role with an organisation promoting population control. But does one exist, other than his own Malthus Society?

The plane landed at Jomo Kenyatta Airport exactly on schedule and I was in a queue for immigration ready to hand over a passport that said David John Franklin, Company Director, on the inside page. So the serious looking photograph on the inside was a good match with the serious looking face of the man in the queue. On the outside I didn't appear to be smiling, but inside I was thinking about Anna and smiling. The quicker I could get back to London the better.

Still occupied by my own thoughts, I hardly heard the Kenyan Immigration officer handing back my passport and smiling "Have a nice stay."

"Mr David!"

I did, though, hear the shout from somewhere as I emerged into the arrivals hall. Deep in thought and forgetting momentarily that I was David Franklin, I ignored it. But then I heard it again. Jimmy Banda was walking, if nor running, towards me. Tall, lanky, just like the athletes, Jimmy had a broad smile across his face and his hand was outstretched.

"Good flight, Mr Franklin? Did you see our Olympic athletes? Not raining today. Sunny. Booked you at the Best Western where you stayed last time. Not that you'll get to sleep much, we're going out tonight."

Jimmy looked around him. There was no-one within several metres but he still whispered, "Surveillance operation. Still got the keys. How's Colin? Ah, yes, you've not seen him. How's Cairo?"

I had no wish to quell Jimmy's unique energy and enthusiasm. The priority now was a serious face to face chat with him to explain more about the investigation, how it had started, where it had led and how difficult it was going to be to actually do anything with what we had found.

We were sitting in my hotel room and I wasted no time in telling Jimmy I wanted a serious talk and no discussion, at least for now, of Jimmy's plans for yet another night-time raid on the Shah Medicals site.

"It's difficult to know what we can do with our evidence, Jimmy," I said. "I am beginning to think it may be impossible to do something without some sort if international co-operation. And who is going to drive that co-operation? How many cases can you point to where there has been an instant international response to a problem on this scale? It can take months, if not years to organise debates of this magnitude. And then we'd need decisions on specific action. And how many times over the years have you seen nations coming together and actually agreeing unanimously on anything? Politics will raise its ugly head. National security matters would need to be put aside and there would be the usual pushing and shoving for the right to lead. I can't see it happening quickly. Neither can Colin or Kevin and neither can Larry who's currently in Washington trying to get someone to sit up and take notice.

"The least that could be done is for virtually every country to agree to a system of urgent inspection of suspected businesses and individuals. But who should be suspected? We have our own small list of possible candidates but the chances are that there might be hundreds, if not thousands more out there.

"So we are faced with a problem that has never been properly discussed in the past. But we are proving it is possible and that it is happening under the noses of governments despite all their business regulations and their surveillance technology. The closest comparison to what we have uncovered is to imagine hundreds of individual cells of terrorists - individuals not on any current databases held by the security agencies - individuals who could operate from home or small businesses hidden within communities. But they would be armed with sophisticated biological weapons just like the tiny metal canisters you found."

Jimmy had sat throughout with one long leg resting on the coffee table that separated us. He had said nothing until:

"Why Kenya? Why Nairobi?"

It was a good question but I threw it back at him.

"Why not? It's a great centre for the sort of terrorism being orchestrated. It's a big and sophisticated city with good communications. It has plenty of traffic going through - tourists, individuals, business people. Because you have already seen terrorism here, it is now as secure as somewhere like London or New York. It has good links with the rest of Africa - Nigeria, West Africa, South Africa, North Africa where the population control freaks might be looking to go first. Unlike Kano in northern Nigeria, international flights come in here from right across the globe. And Nairobi is not the place that first comes to mind as the sort of city associated with this sort of plot. For what my opinion is worth, I'd say that whoever decided on Nairobi as the centre was being very astute."

Jimmy nodded. I had just quelled all the enthusiasm he had started the day with.

"So," Jimmy said, "Shall we talk to the Government? The Minister for Trade?"

As I look back now, perhaps we should have gone straight to the Kenyan Government. I think now that it was a mistake not to. But hindsight is a useless tool. Instead I went for 'nothing ventured nothing gained' in the belief that the more evidence we had, the stronger our case would be.

I have to live with that mistake.

So, in reply to Jimmy's question, I said, "Yes. But we'll need to be very careful and diplomatic. It would be very easy to appear alarmist. And don't forget, Jimmy, that a lot of the evidence about Shah Medicals, Nairobi has come from you breaking and entering their premises in the middle of the night and posing as a cleaner. We'd need to present the Minister with a much bigger picture and so we'd need a properly organised and well prepared hearing. I wouldn't want a five minute lecture on government trade policy and tourism."

I stood up and went to look out of the hotel window, down into the road below and east towards the Kenyatta Hospital where Philippe Fournier had said he'd worked.

"My name is not really David Franklin," I said, turning to face Jimmy again. "My name is Daniel Capelli."

Jimmy removed the foot that had been on the coffee table and put both feet neatly on the floor side by side.

"It's the sort of work I do, Jimmy. Sometimes it can get a bit fraught. Aliases help preserve my independence and don't leave a trail. Colin keeps track of me. But I need to settle down. I've lived out of that suitcase for too long." I pointed at the black bag propped in the corner by the TV. "Ideally I think I'd work out of London or Bangkok and cut down on the travelling if I can. But I want to see this one through first." I then added, "You've done brilliantly, Jimmy."

Looking back I'm so glad I said that and I know Jimmy liked it.

He suddenly sat up much straighter in his chair with his hands on the armrests. I smiled at him. "Let's try just one more of your night-time safaris shall we? I need to see the Shah Medicals stuff with my own eyes. Then we'll decide how to deal with your Minister."

But I could sense that Jimmy now wanted to say something. Not surprisingly, he probably had a lot to ask. He rubbed his chin and opened his mouth ready to speak but, as he did so, my phone rang. It was Colin.

"I'm with Jimmy," I said after Colin had asked where I was. "We're going on a night safari tonight. Then we'll try to see the Kenyan Minister of Trade. Then, if all goes well, I'm coming home."

"There are things you need to know urgently Daniel. Listen to me.

"First, news from Kevin. His Nigerian friend, Tunje Fayinka, had a phone call. It was from a man who Tunje said sounded Arab but wasn't Mohamed El Badry. He said his name was Ramses. Would Tunje like to meet him in London tomorrow night? The Nigerian project that had been discussed with him before was now ready to launch. People were already in place elsewhere. Would Tunje like to help co-ordinate the Nigerian end? Big fee offered - five thousand pounds mentioned and flight paid to Lagos. Question. Was he up for it?"

"Is he going?" I asked already suspecting that this might the Ramses El Khoury from the Cairo Shah Medical Centre.

"He asked Kevin what he should do. Kevin spoke to me. I suggested he go along, check it out. That's what he's planning to do I think."

"It's just as I thought, Colin, we're rapidly running out of time."

"Agreed. Now the next thing. Following your suggestion, Anna has been helping track down David Solomon."

I smiled to myself. "And?"

"We are almost one hundred percent certain we know where he is."

"Thailand?"

"Yes, and your tip off about the girlfriend Pim was spot on. We tracked her down to the University. After I'd explained to Anna what we needed to know, Anna phoned her with some made up story that she was in England - true of course - and was trying to contact a fictitious woman called On who worked at the University.

"And?"

"You know what women are like, Dan. They talked and talked. Upshot was that after Anna told her she had an English husband, Pim seemed to want to share the fact that she too had an English boyfriend - such a co-incidence - laugh, laugh - and what does your husband do and where do you live and this and that. My phone bill soared, Dan, but it was worth it just to sit and listen. Prompted by me, Anna's story was that her husband was called David. They lived in Bristol and David was a lecturer in Economics at Bristol University - a University, another amazing co-incidence, natter natter, natter - are you getting the strategy here, Dan?

"That's Anna," said Daniel. "Once she starts there's no stopping her. But thanks for deciding not to call me Kevin. I've never seen myself as a Kevin. Go on."

"David was very handsome and they had a very nice apartment but David spent a lot of his time talking to the government about the effects of immigration on the economy and so on and so on.

"Well, what a surprise - another co-incidence - Pim's boyfriend was also called David and he also talked about immigration and population but that was not David's main job. David was a very clever - and of course very handsome - virologist from Boston in America and David was an adviser to a Virology Research Unit in Thailand. Pim was a lecturer in microbiology but viruses were not really her speciality. But David was an expert - so expert in fact that he had his own laboratory. But Pim didn't know where the laboratory was although Anna pushed her so hard it was almost embarrassing. So, are we getting closer, Daniel?"

"Yes," I agreed, "But I also think it's getting more complicated. My original idea of where this virus might be located was either Cairo or Nairobi. Perhaps it's Bangkok."

But there is only one laboratory in Thailand that fully matches the description," said Colin, "And it's not in Bangkok. It's the one that Larry identified and you already have the details. But what do you want to do, now?"

"Normally, I think I'd probably head back to Bangkok. But besides everything else I've got another Thai commitment already waiting in London."

CHAPTER 59

Kevin and Tunje Fayinka were lunching at a McDonalds in Finchley, north London. It was Saturday morning and it had been raining almost nonstop since Friday. Kevin was not in a good mood.

For one thing, Colin had now phoned him three times in two days to ask how he was getting on with contacting his MP and the other tasks he had been set at the meeting with Daniel and Larry Brown. But Kevin knew he had been doing badly and had had no confidence at the outset. Being a proponent of direct action because local politicians were a known waste of time, he had long abandoned existing systems and was no good at it.

And his recent experience was only hardening his opinion. The system of so-called surgeries for constituents to discuss matters with their MP seemed totally antiquated. It was hardly his fault if his Member of Parliament seemed to think that a constituent trying to help her pregnant teenage daughter claim housing and other benefits warranted more attention than his need for advice on where to go and who to speak to about biological warfare.

So it had been a welcome distraction from Kevin's increasing frustration when Tunje phoned to say that he'd had an invitation to meet another Arab in London. But in immediately phoning Colin to report this, he now realised it must have sounded to Colin that it was he, Kevin, who was trying to take the credit for progress.

Kevin had, earlier that week, met Tom Weston for lunchtime drink and only after an hour, as if it was an insignificant piece of news, had Tom announced that he had spoken to a member of the House of Lords, Lord Peterson, and fixed a meeting on Monday in London. Tom had assumed Kevin would not have a problem if he failed to turn up to deliver a lecture on Thomas Telford that he had been preparing for two days. It was a difficult decision but Thomas Telford lost.

So Kevin was in McDonalds in Finchley, it was grey and raining and Tunje was sat opposite him munching on a sesame bun that contained something brown, something yellow and something green. After this, he'd need to either go back to Bristol or hang around in London until Monday. Neither appealed. For now he was listening to Tunje's tale of his meeting with the man called Ramses El Khoury.

"Not a word, Kev. Just tell your new mates, OK? This is strictly conf OK"

"Conf, Tunj? Conf?"

"Confidential."

"Of course. Go on."

"Guess where I got to go, Kev?"

"Was it somewhere nice? The Zoo? Madame Tussauds?"

"Inter-Continental Hotel, Park Lane. He phoned me Wednesday. I met him in the lobby. He was definitely not Mohamed El Badry, Kev. This was a big bloke, six foot, all the genuine Arab gear, red and white spotted hanky the lot. Nice brown beads, gold rings, couldn't help notice the shiny shoes underneath. He said it was very private so would I mind a discussion in his room. Didn't see a twinkle in his eye so I accepted. Fifth floor. Big double bed. I thought aye aye, here we go but no, orange juice from the mini bar, sit in big soft sofa, thought I'd bloody suffocate. Then he gets out a brief case. Flips a bundle at me - looked like a few thousand but I didn't like to ask how much. I thought aye aye, here we go again but no, down to business. Want the gist, Kev?"

"Please," said Kevin.

"He'd heard good reports about me from Mr El Badry. We shook hands at that point. He laughed. Big man, big laugh. Was I still an active member of the Malthus Club? 'Course I was. Did I really want to do something that would make a difference? You bet. But what did I have to do? Oh, nothing much. Fly to Lagos on expenses. Fly to Abuja, then to Kano, then to Maiduguri, then to Port Harcourt. Meet up with people who would be expecting me. Hand over sealed boxes. Fly back to UK. Job done."

"That it?" asked Kevin.

"Yes, man. Simple. I was there twenty minutes, not even time to finish my orange juice. He got up, I got up, he saw me to the lift and I was back out on Park Lane."

"So did you agree to do this, Tunj?"

"Yes. He gave me the bundle. It was five grand but I have to pay for my own air tickets. I'm now expecting an email with further instructions."

Kevin could hardly believe it. "So why didn't I get an invite, Tunj?"

"Just not got the style, Kev. And you aren't Nigerian."

"You think there are Nigerians out there who would do it for money?"

"Too right they would. And the chances of them understanding exactly what they're doing is limited. You don't know Nigeria, Kev, but people do anything for dash. And I reckon that's what these clowns are relying on. Just do the sums. A thousand quid to infect a thousand or more people. Then have a thousand doses of something claimed to cure it in stock selling at two pounds a dose - that's a hundred percent profit. And it could just be sugar and water, useless for all the people would know. It's got nothing to do with a proper system of population control that you and I believe in, Kev. This is bloody fraud. Fraud on a massive scale."

"So will you go to Nigeria?"

"Yes, but only if you and your mates think it'll help to catch these bastards."

For the first time ever, Kevin recognised a sense of serious concern in Tunje's tone. He seemed apprehensive, worried. What he said next proved it. "We all know it's a fucking mess and overcrowded there, Kev, but this isn't the way is it? My mother lives in Maiduguri."

Larry had tracked down New York Senator Mary Collis enough to know she was at a meeting in the Federal Mediation and Conciliation Service (FMCS) in Washington DC. She might be free to talk after four in the afternoon but he needed to be there waiting or she'd be gone again. Larry, not having slept or washed since leaving Lagos, checked in at the Quincy Hotel, showered, changed out of his jeans, tee shirt and sweater, put on a crumpled suit and shirt, fastened a tie around his neck and went straight to the FMCS office block.

At four fifteen, his name was called and he was escorted by a young woman to an office on the sixth floor. Larry, although a New Yorker, had never met Senator Mary Collis in person. He'd seen her on TV of course and had liked what he'd heard. And she was black, a lawyer and with similar roots to Larry's. Smartly dressed in a light grey suit and white blouse she was sat at a coffee table with two other men in dark suits. She rose. The two men did the same.

"OK gentlemen, let's take it from there," she said and held out her hand. "I'm back in New York tonight so just keep me in the loop and I'll do what I can. OK?"

Larry stood for a moment as the two men departed. The young woman who had brought him there, opened and then closed the door behind them and then stood alongside Larry. She smiled up at him.

233

"You're Doctor Brown?" Mary Collis asked. She walked towards him and glanced at something on an IPad in her hand. Larry spotted it and realised he'd need to grab her attention right from the start or he'd lose it. He held out his hand.

"Thank you for seeing me Senator."

Mary Collis was shorter and smaller than Larry had imagined. Her hair was short and straightened. She looked neat and smart and when he shook her hand it felt small, soft and cool.

"Take a seat. Colette here will listen in and take any notes, OK?"

Larry had been practicing his opening sentences for hours.

"I've just flown from Lagos, Nigeria, Senator. I believe that tests on a biological weapon have been carried out on a community of Moslems in the north of Nigeria. The tests were successful. The agent used was a virus similar to the Middle East Respiratory Virus but was artificially and deliberately created in a laboratory. There is no vaccine or drug immediately available to deal with it."

Larry stopped. Senator Collis raised an eyebrow.

"You're not suggesting that the USA is responsible are you?"

"No, Senator. A similar successful test was carried out in Thailand using the same artificially created virus and miniature, asthma-type inhalers as the delivery mechanism."

"So are you suggesting Thailand, of all places, is developing biological weapons."

"No, Senator. My belief, and I am not alone in this now, is that a group of privately owned companies one of them owned by a man already known to the FBI is behind a plot to deliberately spread the virus because they already have a treatment to sell."

Mary Collis sat back in her chair and looked first at Collette and then at Larry.

"You're a medical doctor, right?" she said. Larry nodded. "Is this possible?"

"Too right it's possible, Senator," said Larry. "There are no tight controls on biotechnology that involves artificial creation of new viruses. It's called gain-of-function research - GOF for short - and it's perfectly legal and very common. Some say it's out of control. And in the wrong hands........" Larry stopped, allowing the Senator's imagination to start running.

"Mmm," she said after a pause. "So who runs checks on these companies?"

"As far as checking on what they are actually doing, no-one. And before you ask, Senator, I'm not talking about American companies. I'm talking about a motley group of small, Arab, African and Asian businesses that operate way below the normal radar. That being said the guy I mentioned is American."

"And this virus could be released in the USA or spread to the USA?"

"Of course, Senator, all ready to move." Larry knew this might be a slight exaggeration but if there was one sure way to get a politician to jump it was on the grounds of self protection.

"And no treatment? No vaccine right?"

"Correct, and you can add in a very high cross-infection rate and a very high mortality rate."

"So where might this motley group of Arab, African and Asian companies as you call them suddenly acquire such high technology?"

"Easy, Senator. Just tempt a few American or European scientists with money, give them a nice lab to work in and keep them in the dark about the real motives of the company that employs them. Scientists and technicians don't ask too many commercial questions - it's not in their DNA."

"These sorts of guys exist out there?"

"Yes."

"Where?"

Larry wasn't sure he was ready for this. He was desperate to catch up with Daniel again. He ignored it and decided to throw in some more scenarios to move things in a different direction.

"Ask WHO - the World Health Organisation - if they have systems in place to monitor this sort of thing. They don't. Ask yourself what international checks are placed on this sort of research - there aren't any. Then throw in a huge pile of subversive politics, idealism and views on the need for governments to stop talking about the risks of war and talk about the risks of unchecked population growth instead and you'll find you're into a whole new ball game."

"Are you saying this virus is also linked into a plan to kill millions just to reduce populations?"

"Yes I am," said Larry. "Ask yourself. Other than two world wars what has been the most reliable way of reducing human populations? Answer - disease. Bubonic plague, Spanish flu, Malaria, HIV - they've all done their bit. They've achieved far more in wiping out millions than Hiroshima and twentieth century terrorism added together.

"Now add together a commercial organisation financed by a few rich guys with no ethics and out to make a fortune from first spreading a disease and then selling a vaccine or a treatment with a few scientists who are world leaders in research on infectious diseases and viruses and who have also got a bee in their bonnets about the world being totally overpopulated to be any longer sustainable.

"Not only will these guys quote statistics about destruction of the environment and lack of resources but figures on economic migration, illegal immigration and mass unemployment to back it up. Their case is a good one and it may surprise politicians to know that their views are surprisingly popular. And you know what they're on record as saying, Senator? We've waited too damn long for politicians to face up to unsustainable population growth and provide a solution. We can't way any longer so we'll deal with it ourselves.

"And, Senator, they've already named their virus - 'Malthus A Respiratory Virus.' Have you heard of Thomas Malthus, Senator? Check him out and you'll find he was an English proponent of action to control population growth two hundred and fifty years ago. For some, that's two and a half centuries too long to wait for action."

Larry knew Senator Collis had been staring at him throughout. Was he getting a message across or had she already concluded he was an idiot? Larry had no idea. He watched her get up from her chair and wander to the window. Collette had been listening with a serious look on her face throughout but no notes had been taken as far as Larry knew.

Mary Collis was still standing by the window looking down and spoke without turning around.

"What actual evidence have you got for all this, Doctor Brown?"

"I have been working with an English private investigator of corporate fraud, Senator. He was originally engaged by an American biotechnology company to look into the disappearance of some research material. The company has since lost a scientist - he's disappeared - vanished. Evidence suggests he has linked up with two other scientists that disappeared from a separate American company a year or so ago. All of them are virologists. One of the three also has extreme views on the need for population control. So if you asking if America is

236

implicated, Senator, then the answer is yes. Where is my private investigator colleague at present? Kenya. Where was he before that? Egypt. Where did he start off? Thailand. Where did we meet up? London."

Larry at last felt he was getting somewhere. He kept going on this track.

"Have I researched my facts? Yes. Have I spoken to WHO Geneva? Yes. Were they able to clarify procedures for controls on gain-of-function research to safeguard against dangerous viruses escaping into the community? No. Have I visited the place in northern Nigeria where the field tests were carried out resulting in over a hundred deaths? Yes. And have I been able to find out who I should talk to who would actually be in a position to do anything? No.

"I've drawn a fucking blank, Senator, because I can't get past the first person who picks up the phone whether it's in Homeland Security or the US Army Medical Research Institute of Infectious Diseases - USAMRID - the Federal Drug Administration or the Environmental Protection Agency - who, by the way, wanted to know if I was talking about a virus that kills tomatoes.

"And have you looked at the Biological and Toxic Weapons Convention website recently? It's nearly two years out of date, there are no contact details for anyone and, if you don't already know, it is run from an office at Bradford University in England. Do you know where Bradford is?

"But that's why I'm here, Senator, and I'm hoping that you will listen to what I'm saying, believe what I'm telling you and then either do something yourself or point me in a direction that you think I should go."

Mary Collis walked back to her chair and sat down. Then she turned to Colette.

"Colette, please cancel the next appointment."

CHAPTER 60

Jimmy was explaining the layout of the Shah Medicals site to me as I drew a rough plan on a sheet of paper. He was also explaining each of the six different keys he had obtained from Luther Jasman.

"That's it, David - I mean Dan. We use that key to open the main gate. The light here comes on. We use this key to unlock the rear entrance there. Inside we'll probably find a fork lift truck and a van. This key then unlocks the cupboard where Lucky kept his brushes and mops. It is not interesting and I know it very well. This key opens the door leading into the big room with the boxes of

237

medicines and machinery which I found. It is where I found the boxes marked 'Malthus A Respiratory Virus.'

"This key opens the office where Luther and the Pakistani men worked - the room I cleaned. I think this key opens the second office where the Frenchman works. I've not been in there."

"OK," I said, "You go home, Jimmy. Come back to fetch me at 2am. Let's see what we can find."

"Uh, can I suggest something very important?" Jimmy sounded a little embarrassed.

"Of course, what is it?"

"Wear some black clothes. There is no moon tonight but white people make everything shine."

After Jimmy had left, I lay on the bed and phoned Anna.

When we had been together in Thailand and Singapore I had found myself constantly looking at her - the way she dressed, the way she walked, the way she would glance over her shoulder and smile when she knew I was looking at her Now it was the sound of her voice and accent that was affecting me. Something had clearly happened to me. But it was her final words on the phone that caused me to choke a little. "Don't worry, I have many friends already, Daniel. Too many Thai people live here. I talk all day long. But please come home soon. It is not good for a new husband and wife to be separated for too long."

Lying on the bed and knowing I needed to be up again at two, I couldn't sleep. But around midnight, just as I was dropping off, the phone rang. It was Jimmy.

"Daniel?" Jimmy whispered.

"Yes, Jimmy. What's up?"

"Shhh! I am already outside Shah Medicals. I couldn't sleep so I came here to check. The lights were still on. Then I saw three people working outside. They are using the forklift truck and putting boxes into the van. But that's not all, Daniel. There are three other men here as well. They arrived in a big Mercedes. Two were white and one was not - I think he is Arab. One of the white men is the Frenchman, Dominique Lunneau but I don't know the other one."

I got off the bed.

"OK, stay right there, Jimmy. I'll get a taxi and join you. If any problems I'll let you speak to the taxi driver by phone and you can direct him to where you are. OK? I'll get the taxi to drop me somewhere close but not so close to attract attention."

Twenty minutes later, my late night taxi stopped with its lights still on, beneath a lamppost on the outskirts of the Shah Medicals industrial estate. A minute later Jimmy was tapping on the car window. I got out, paid the driver and followed Jimmy down a dark side street and through even darker gaps between other small business units.

"I told you to wear something black, Daniel. I can still see you and there's no light here."

"Sorry, Jimmy. Live and learn," I said trying to follow Jimmy through a pile of wooden pallets.

"There," Jimmy suddenly stopped and pointed, "See the lights? Shah Medicals. Come."

As we headed towards the lights through gaps between two other buildings, Jimmy stopped again and pointed at a dark shadow. "My car," he said. "As you can see it's a black car." He opened the door and we both got in. It needed no further explanation but Jimmy then pointed towards the lights on a building behind a high wire fence. "Shah Medicals," he explained. I nodded. The building was lit by three lights fixed high up on the outside walls. Windows along the side wall were brightly lit by strip lights from inside. A big Mercedes was parked outside the front entrance. Alongside it, a smaller car that looked like a Toyota.

"Whose car is the Toyota, Jimmy?"

"Lunneau's. See the van at the back and the fork lift? It must be full, Daniel. I think it's the boxes I saw. They've been working for an hour. There are only three of the Pakistani men left here. The others have gone."

"Are you sure they're from Pakistan, Jimmy?"

"Oh yes, it's the white trousers and waistcoat."

The driver's door was opened and a man got in. Two men closed the rear door of the building, walked around the van and got in on the passenger's side. The van's engine fired and it moved slowly around to the front entrance and stopped again. The driver got out and went up to the front entrance. A light came on inside.

"Binoculars." Jimmy said and handed me a pair that had been lying on the floor.

"Thanks," I said and trained them on the building. Jimmy may have been right about the nationality of the men but shadows were not making it easy to see detail.

"Camera." Jimmy said and put a cheap Sony digital camera on my lap. "Keys," he added. "Do we go in later?"

"Not sure, Jimmy. Let's hang around a bit. What time is it?"

"Twelve forty-seven."

"Describe the Arab looking guy, Jimmy."

"Medium. And he was on the other side of the other two. I was really focussing on the white man."

"So, not much to go on there then Jimmy."

"Sorry, Daniel. But he was medium, not big not small."

"Wearing a suit? A dishdasha? A kameez? A Hat? Swimming trunks?"

"Suit, Daniel."

"The other white guy, Jimmy. Describe him. Was he wearing sensible black?"

"Looked like a light suit - the sort they used to wear on safari."

"He's another one who didn't take your advice then, Jimmy. Do you think he's on holiday?"

"No. he didn't have the matching hat. But white head, black hair - bald I'd say."

"Tall, short, fat, thin?"

"Tall - like you and me."

"But fat, thin?"

"Big man, bigger than you, Daniel. Taller and bigger than Lunneau."

"Did you watch him through these?" I pointed at the binoculars.

"Yes, but he was moving around."

I fished in my pocket for my mobile phone. As usual I'd downloaded a few essential photos onto it from the laptop. Experience often pays a few dividends.

"Change the dark blue suit for a light one. Could this be him?" I held the phone up in the pitch blackness for Jimmy to see.

"Could be," said Jimmy.

"How about this one?" I pulled up another shot of the back of the same man.

"Yes. That's his shiny, white head. If the moon had been out there would have been no need for the security lights."

I had to smile at Jimmy's use of words. He was often very funny but never laughed at his own humour.

"I last saw this guy in Bangkok, Jimmy. Unless I'm badly mistaken this is one of the top two guys - Greg O'Brian - come to inspect his warehouse stock at one in the morning. Nasty piece of work, Jimmy. Just as well you weren't inside when he turned up. If there was a garden fork handy you might have got it straight through your chest."

"There is a gun in there, though, Daniel. I saw it when I looked through the keyhole of Lunneau's office. It was lying on the floor underneath his desk. I forgot to tell Colin that."

"So perhaps they are planning to go on safari after all, then Jimmy."

In the darkness, I saw Jimmy grinning. Perhaps he liked my jokes better than his own. "But what do we do, Daniel? Wait till they've gone?"

"Are we going to learn any more by going inside, Jimmy? You've already found enough."

"Yes and I also forgot to tell Colin I'd photographed the boxes."

"Good man. Are the photos on this camera?"

"Yes."

"Can I borrow the camera to transfer the photos?"

"Uh," Jimmy suddenly looked embarrassed. "Yes, but let me delete some first." He grabbed the camera and as I watched he flicked through a backlog. The camera bleeped about twenty times and he then handed it back, his eyes looking at me out of their corners. "My aunty in Mombasa," he said.

"Instead of going inside again I think we'll follow them, Jimmy. Find out where they're staying and get some more photos. Build ourselves a photo album about Shah Medicals, Nairobi. What do you think?"

241

CHAPTER 61

It was Monday. Kevin had reluctantly postponed his lecture on Thomas Telford that he had been looking forward to giving to first year students. On the advice of Tom Weston he had also not attended his MPs so-called "meet the constituents" evening on Friday.

"I warn you, Kevin. She's a waste of space. You'll get nowhere. She won't even understand what you're talking about. If you're having a problem getting IVF treatment on the NHS she's red hot because she's had it herself, but don't expect much comprehension of what you want to talk about. In fact, she'll probably phone social services mental health team after you've left and ask them to come and check you out. Not only that, but she'll time you, and her PA listening outside the door will phone her mobile just as you're getting going to deliberately ruin the flow.

"No, you come with me, Kevin. We'll do things proper, like, and have a chat with Lord Peterson. If there's anyone who might know where to go or what strings to pull it'll be Bill. Meantime I'll do a spot of reading."

So Kevin was feeling highly dependent on an eighty year old second hand book shop owner and retired biology teacher to carry out the few responsibilities he had agreed to take on at the meeting with Daniel, Larry and Colin. It was doing nothing to improve the mood of despondency he had been suffering from for nearly a week. He hadn't even checked his Malthus website for days. Not only that but Tom had brought a large pile of science papers to read on the train up from Bristol and barely spoke for the whole journey. Instead, as he read the papers, he casually handed them to Kevin as if Kevin was interested in the latest improvements to genetically modified oil seed rape. Kevin was glad when they arrived at Paddington Station when he suddenly found a use.

"Give me a hand, Kevin. Bloody steps. Why don't they have floors that lower like on the buses?"

Kevin had only been to the Houses of Parliament once and that was with a group of students. But Tom seemed to know where to go and what to do. Walking surprisingly quickly with his stick in one hand and a buff coloured folder in the other, Tom made a few enquiries, asked someone to phone Lord Peterson to say they had arrived and then they waited. Tom was given a seat to sit on. Kevin was left standing.

As the current Chairman of the House of Lords Science and Technology Committee Lord Peterson was much younger than Kevin had imagined. Perhaps

242

it was the mental image of hereditary peers he still harboured or the fact that even politicians had started to look young these days, but Kevin cheered up a little. Introductions over, Peterson led the way.

"I've reserved us a space over in Portcullis House," he said as they walked. "You look as sprightly as ever, Tom. How long is it since we last met? Don't tell me, two years. I was in Bristol - couldn't possibly have missed visiting the bookshop."

Security and other time consuming formalities over, they finally sat in a corner of a large room clearly meant for large scale committee meetings. A tray of coffee and biscuits was ready waiting. Kevin looked around. Tom put his folder on the table.

"So, science and biology is still running thick and fast in your old veins is it Tom, and what's all this about research on viruses needing better controls. Don't we do enough these days?" Peterson said.

"No," said Tom abruptly, "nothing like enough." Then he sat back in his chair and placed his hands firmly on the table in front of him, the folder, at least for the moment, irrelevant.

"Malthus Society, Bill," he began. "Remember we once chatted about it? We're the dedicated followers of a fashion that never really died out - innocent fans and groupies of Thomas Malthus, Paul Eyrlich and others who once spoke the truth and nothing but the truth. They got ignored then and they still get ignored now because political leaders are only interested in getting re-elected and are afraid to both discuss and act on any of the biological challenges facing the human race."

Lord Peterson, Bill, smiled and sipped at his cup of coffee.

"I'm a founder member of the Malthus Society, Bill," Tom went on. "Kevin here runs the website. Now don't ask me about websites because I haven't a clue, but it's got a membership now running into thousands across the globe. Naturally it has attracted its fair share of nutcases over the years but there's one nutcase that's causing us a big headache and making Kevin here look more than a bit depressed at present.

"The nutcase is called David Solomon. He's a Brit but he once worked as a senior scientist for an American biotechnology company and his hobby was very similar to Kevin's and mine - studying the effects of population growth on world economies and the environment - the sort of stuff I've researched since the fifties and sixties.

"But Solomon is also one of those clever virologists who, with their modern technology, can pick up a virus as if it's a piece of Lego. They pull out a couple of bricks, replace them with a couple more with a different shape or colour and then sit back and play around with it. In the trade they call it "gain of function" research. As a biologist I call it bloody dangerous if it's in the wrong hands. And this is where the question of adequate controls comes in.

"In my opinion, and I know I'm far from alone here, virologists are going down a blind alley and the powers that be are blindly letting them go down that alley, which is tantamount to acquiescing. The end game could be viruses far more dangerous than the Spanish flu strain or anything else we've experienced before.

"But Solomon not only has a particular interest in gain of function research but he seems to have spent all his spare time slowly radicalising himself into becoming what I would call, for lack of a suitable word, a bio-terrorist. Solomon is hell-bent on taking direct action to reduce the human population. His plan is to use a highly infectious virus created by himself in the laboratory. His argument is that we've waited too long already for politicians to act, that there are still no signs of the problem being discussed let alone taken seriously and so someone has got to do it.

"Also, like all good terrorists, his whereabouts are currently unknown. He disappeared along with a few other virologists a year or so ago. That alone should have been enough to ring alarm bells."

Tom removed his hands from the table and then lay them firmly in his lap. His eyes had barely left Peterson's face.

"Now terrorists, from what little I know of them, Bill, do not usually act alone. To do anything significant they normally need financial backers and a way to deliver their weapon to the chosen targets. My friend Kevin, along with some colleagues, is gradually building evidence about who these others are."

Peterson fidgeted slightly. Tom noticed and did his own fidget. There was a slight pause.

"We're into a very long and complicated scenario here, Bill, so please hear us out and stop fidgeting. Let me summarise the current situation:

"One - evidence exists of a group of businesses operating in Africa and the Middle East who intend to release a new virus that causes a fatal, flu-like illness. Why? Because they also have a unique drug that they claim is a treatment. They want to spread the virus to sell the drug. They see huge profits. Evidence suggests that one of the companies is run by a wealthy man on a number of wanted lists for fraud and worse. Then there is a dubious sounding

Arab company with money and networks. The technical expertise comes from David Solomon.

"Two - the virus has already been spotted by WHO because there have been a few localised outbreaks. But WHO have said very little. Evidence through Kevin's contacts suggest these outbreaks may have been field tests carried out by the company or Solomon. There is also evidence that someone somewhere with a sense of humour has decided to call the new virus 'Malthus A - Respiratory Virus'.

"Three - what we have here is mounting evidence of a conspiracy to spread a lethal virus created artificially by a scientist with known extreme views on the need for direct action to reduce the world population using a group of companies with international networks of distributors run by a man who sounds to me like a mafia Don."

Tom sat forward and placed his hands back on the table.

"Now," he said, "Who will sit and listen in depth to the growing amount of evidence? Is it you, Bill? If not who, in the official UK political order of things, should know about all this? Does the UK have a system in place for dealing with this sort of terrorism? Is it MI6? Does the EU have anything? The EU stifles most bits of commercial ingenuity by regulation so what piece of EU legislation will stifle this ingenious plot? Who can do something to stop this virus coming into the UK on board a British Airways flight from Nairobi tomorrow morning hidden in an asthma inhaler? And who is responsible internationally for dealing with a situation like this?"

Peterson leaned forward and smiled.

"If I didn't know you better, Tom, I'd have thought you were the nutcase and thrown you out."

Tom interrupted immediately. "That's precisely why I'm here with Kevin, Bill. You know me but if it was Kevin who had wandered in here straight from a lecture on Thomas Telford and dressed in his usual Liverpool FC sweater or even his best House of Lords suit you'd have thrown him out. Right Kevin?"

For the first time, Kevin said something.

"Too bloody right, Tom."

"So will you give Kevin and perhaps a few of his friends - one of whom is a private investigator of international business crime and one a doctor working for the USA Embassy in Nigeria - a chance to explain what is known so far? Because I'm damned sure that someone in the government should know. Once it knows it can then decide what to do and who will deal with it. Perhaps it's a challenge for your House of Lords Science and Technology Committee, Bill. But don't hang around too long trying to organise a proper Committee meeting with a pre-circulated agenda. Why don't you go and speak direct to the Prime Minister?"

Then Tom laughed. "The PM might actually be quite pleased to hear of an impending flu pandemic. With the Chancellor looking to make yet more budget cuts and with the virus killing off two and a half million unemployed and six million elderly people like me on state pensions it could be their salvation."

CHAPTER 62

It was now almost 3am. The van parked outside the Shah Medicals front entrance was still there. The driver who had gone inside the building was still inside. His two colleagues who he had left in the van had got out and got back in several times as if bored with waiting. Both of them were smoking cigarettes. In the cool and still night air the smoke was drifting up towards the outside lights.

But then all of the lights at the rear of the building suddenly went out, followed by several of the strip lights along the side the building. Then the front door opened.

"Lunneau," said Jimmy. The Frenchman was also smoking a cigarette. He walked to the van, opened the passenger door and spoke to the two men inside. They got out and followed him into the building. Two more strip lights went out behind the side windows. The building was now in complete darkness except for the lights in what Jimmy called the "reception" office.

Until that moment it had been completely silent. Jimmy and I had heard nothing except a few normal Nairobi night time sounds - distant cars and trucks, dogs barking, a cockerel crowing well before its due time and some chirping from hidden insects. But then there was a sound that clearly came from the Shah Medicals building. Jimmy lifted his finger to his ear. I nodded. I had heard it too. It was a muffled shout. Then another, louder this time. Then silence again.

Jimmy pointed at the front door. Someone was moving behind it. The outside light was switched off so that the only light now was coming from inside the building - behind the door and the two front windows. I had the binoculars, but it was becoming difficult to see the van, the Mercedes or the Toyota except with the reflections of the inside lights.

The door opened and Lunneau appeared. He went to the smaller car, the Toyota and opened the boot. The boot light came on. He took out something that might have been a tool box. He put it on the ground. Then he pulled out a long sheet of what might have been plastic and lay it flat on the ground close to the van. Then he pulled out two other sheets and lay them next to the first sheet. Then he picked up the box and went back inside.

There was more movement behind the door - two men, perhaps three.

Then Lunneau's back appeared as if he was carrying something with the help of a second man. He was. A body was dragged out of the door, across the ground and rolled onto one of the sheets.

A third man then appeared at the door. He was a big man with a light suit and he stood with his hands on his hips as if giving instructions. He pointed.

"Mister O'Brian?" whispered Jimmy.

"Yes, that's definitely him," I said peering intently through the binoculars. I then trained them on the other man helping Lunneau but it was far too dark to see detail. But as O'Brian continued to watch, Lunneau and the third man wrapped the sheet around the body, tied it with something and then lifted it with a struggle into the open boot of the Toyota.

I looked at Jimmy who did not have the advantage of the binoculars but he had clearly seen what had happened. His mouth was open. He nodded at me and I handed him the binoculars to watch.

"Have they finished, Daniel?"

"I suspect not. Keep watching."

"They've gone back inside. O'Brian has gone inside. No, they are bringing out another. Your turn, Daniel."

The whole process took ten minutes. The second body was put in the boot with the first. The third body was placed on the back seat of the Toyota. Finally, O'Brian emerged completely from the front door from where he had seemingly been giving instructions. He stood, taller than Lunneau and several inches taller than the third man. But he was much bigger and broader than both of them.

"So how did they die so quickly, Daniel?" Jimmy whispered, clearly troubled by what he had just seen.

"No idea, Jimmy, but O'Brian could easily have done it himself.

"And why?"

"When you run an operation like O'Brian's there are only a very few people who are entitled to know what is going on. The others do their job and are then dismissed before they get to know too much."

"So lucky Lucky - and lucky Luther."

"Yes, you might well have saved Luther's life, Jimmy.

"So what now? We follow them?"

"We can't follow three vehicles with just your car, Jimmy. Let's focus on the car that GOB takes - obviously it'll be the Mercedes."

"GOB?" asked Jimmy.

"Colin's nickname for Greg O'Brian. Let's see which of Nairobi's smart hotels GOB is staying at."

O'Brian appeared once more and got into the Mercedes. It's headlights came on and floodlit the area where they had just wrapped up the bodies. Then the second man emerged and got into the van. Finally all the lights in the building went off and Lunneau came out, locked the front door and climbed into the Toyota. All three cars, led by the Mercedes, then drove off. It was almost 4am.

As the two cars and van - the big Mercedes containing Greg O'Brian, the smaller Toyota with its cargo of bodies and the white van loaded with boxes drove off, Jimmy started the engine of his own car and, without any lights on, edged along the side road towards the main road.

We quickly caught up with the van, overtook it, and then came up behind the Toyota. But as we did so, the Toyota, indicated left and turned off.

"Shall we still follow GOB or the hearse?" asked Jimmy.

"GOB," I replied, "that looks like his Mercedes in front."

At a discreet distance we followed O'Brian's Mercedes along Waiyaki Way and into the Westlands area of Nairobi.

"Sankara Hotel, Daniel. Nice hotel." Jimmy announced and stopped the car on the roadside near the entrance to the five star hotel.

"I told you, Jimmy. The Best Western could never match GOB's needs. But I assume he'll now sleep for a while. Let's do the same and meet for breakfast."

CHAPTER 63

Rightly or wrongly, Larry felt his meeting with New York Senator Mary Collis had gone much better than expected. Having extracted what he took to be a firm commitment to ask a few questions and then get back to him, Larry thanked her and walked back to the Quincy Hotel. Hoping he could now snatch a few hours sleep, he had only just picked up his key and stepped out of the lift to his room when his phone rang.

"Doctor Brown? It's the US Embassy, Abuja. Would you please hold the line, the Ambassador wants a word."

Still holding the phone, Daniel clicked open the door to his room and sat on the bed. "Well, whatever," Larry thought to himself. "I gave him the best part of a week to get back to me. Perhaps he's done something."

"Larry!" The voice of the Ambassador boomed out of Larry's phone as if he was sitting next to him on the bed. "Been trying to get you. Office in Lagos said you must be out and about. They hadn't seen you for three days but your phone was off. Had a problem with it or something?"

"No, sir, it's OK " said Larry. "Just been out and about as the office said."

"Well now, I promised to get back to you on this virus thing. But we've had a whole bunch of Nigerian politicians here this week, including the President himself - Boko Haram giving everyone headaches, the oil pipeline fire down south, you name it - not at all sure US wants any involvement but we got to give them some air time. Now, we've done a few checks on your virus as promised. Laura in the office here has worked wonders. I'll get her to call you but here's the gist.

"You need to speak to USAMRID - the US Army Medical Research Institute of Infectious Diseases, Fort Derrick, Maryland, Larry. They are the experts."

Larry interrupted him. "I already did, sir. I got nowhere."

"OK, I see. Well you need to speak to the Biological Weapons Convention people."

Larry sensed he was using a crib sheet given to him by Laura, whoever Laura was.

"Useless, sir. There are no people. It's a website and even the website is out of date."

There was a pause. Larry thought he could hear someone next to the Ambassador. Perhaps it was Laura. But Larry had already had enough. "Look, sir, this needs someone with genuine clout at US Government level - like a Senator - to sit up and take notice. That person needs to sit and listen properly, hear me out, give me a chance."

I hear what you're saying, Larry. Let me chat to Laura again and we'll see where we go." Larry very nearly pressed the off button on his phone.

"But hang on, Larry, Laura now wants a word. She's stood right next. Try to sort this out between you...........yes, let's get together........." The Ambassador's voice tailed off and Larry was sure the Ambassador had been in a simultaneous discussion with someone else - and it wasn't Laura.

But it was Laura who spoke next. "Hi, Larry, it's Laura. How are you? Been trying to find you. Sorry about all this research turning up nothing but if there's anything more I can do, let me know. Oh, and by the way, there was another guy on the phone looking for you yesterday. His name is........let me see...........yeh, here we go................. Abdouleye. You want me to spell that? No? But I got a note here saying he met you in Kano. He's a doctor so you must have clearly got talking doctor stuff sometime. You want his number for another chat?"

"Yes," said Larry with belated enthusiasm. .

"You want to fix a meeting, Larry? Anything we can do for you right now?"

Larry didn't have the courage to admit he was in Washington DC because he had got nowhere in Nigeria. But perhaps, he thought, he'd delay his resignation for a while. "No thanks," he said, "I'll sort it."

CHAPTER 64

At six thirty, barely two hours after Jimmy had driven me back to his hotel, there was a knock on my hotel room door. Dripping wet from the shower and with my face covered in shaving foam, I opened it. It was Jimmy.

"Couldn't you sleep either, Jimmy?"

"No. You want to know what I did instead?"

I looked at the lanky Kenyan who clearly hadn't washed or changed recently.

"Tell me."

"After I dropped you I went back to the Shah Medicals site. Using my keys I went inside. It's empty, Daniel. Nothing is left. Everything in the office is gone except an empty filing cabinet. The packaging equipment is gone, the boxes are gone, everything is gone. Dawn was breaking so I locked up and came here."

Jimmy was sat on the bed. I was standing by the window still holding the razor.

"They've decamped. Jimmy. Used the site for what they wanted, brought in a few temporary staff to do a few jobs under Lunneau's supervision, used them for a while, then sacked them and finally killed off the remaining three. Nobody can deny that GOB isn't efficient. And scattering their operations around various locations across Africa and elsewhere also looks deliberate to me. That way they become virtually untraceable. GOB is an expert in just this type of operation."

Jimmy nodded. He then lay back with his head on the crumpled pillow. I was still talking. "Well, we know where GOB is, or was, three hours ago. The bodies will probably have been dumped somewhere outside Nairobi and the hundreds of boxes of inhalers and ampoules that you saw and photographed have been moved. But where? They can't be too far away at present but they could be flown out and sent anywhere within hours. "

I pulled the curtains at the window and looked out. The sky was turning a mixture of grey and pink. But what Jimmy had just told me was my worst fear. By knowing where at least some of the virus, vaccine, drug treatment, or whatever it was, was being stored, it would have been easier for whatever law enforcement bodies we could involve to deal with. Now? Other than Jimmy's photographs and some other possible forensic evidence that could be gleaned, we were back to square one.

"Let's go and see if GOB has woken up yet, Jimmy," I said and turned around. Jimmy was fast asleep.

Leaving Jimmy to sleep on my bed, I resumed my shower and shave. Then I checked my mobile phone. There was a text message from Colin. "Please call me for an update asap. Also Virex Boston are looking for you."

I checked my watch. It was still the middle of the night in London, late evening in Boston. I'd do my catching up later. For now, GOB was on my mind. Leaving Jimmy where he was, I left him a message, "Gone to find GOB - Dan." Then I took a taxi to the five star Sankara Hotel.

One look inside the hotel was enough to convince me that Greg O'Brian, GOB, travelled in style. From his big, rented Mercedes to the best hotel in the heart of Nairobi's Westlands district surrounded by the best shops, restaurants, bars and big international businesses, this was the place to be for a wealthy businessman who wanted to be seen to be doing well by the rich and famous. But it was unlikely that O'Brian was there to chair a board meeting of Livingstone Pharmaceuticals at its African headquarters. No, Livingstone was deliberately kept low key - just high enough to warrant a bit of respect in the right places but low enough so that he could still use it as a screen for whatever other money making schemes he was involved in. So GOB would be enjoying the opulence but ignoring the opportunities it provided to rub shoulders and socialise.

As far as I knew, Livingstone had no official presence in Kenya except through a very loose arrangement with Shah Medicals, and Shah Medicals had, as Jimmy had just reported, been closed down overnight. Perhaps that had been his sole reason for coming to Nairobi - to oversee the final closing ceremony complete with three murders.

I strolled in off the street with no plan on my mind other than to have a look around and see what turned up. But it was a good time to arrive. There was the usual breakfast-time flurry of check-out activity around the reception area, breakfasts were being taken and trolleys of baggage were being wheeled around. Two mini buses were parked outside and a loud party of Chinese tourists took up a large space just inside the entrance.

I walked in amongst them and went straight to the reception desk.

"I understand there is a meeting booked for today - Livingstone Pharmaceuticals?"

The smart receptionist checked his list. "No, sir, I don't see that."

"It might be in the name Shah Medicals?"

"No, sir."

"Al Zafar?"

"No sir, sorry sir."

"I see. Is Mr Greg O'Brian a guest here at the moment?"

"Sorry sir but I am not allowed to give out the names of guests."

"Sorry to trouble you. Perhaps he'll arrive very soon. If I may, I'll wait here for a while."

"Of course, sir. If you need breakfast, the restaurant is open to non residents."

I decided to find a seat somewhere. GOB had definitely gone into the hotel four hours earlier. I'd just sat down when my phone rang. It was Jimmy. "You want me to join you, Daniel?"

"Yes" I said, "It's lonely sat here waiting just to see what turns up. But don't ask me to buy you breakfast - it's too expensive."

But no sooner had I pocketed the phone and picked up a newspaper to read when a tall, white man in a blue, open-necked shirt caught my attention. He had taken a seat not four yards away and was sat with a brief case on the floor by his feet. I knew I had seen him before and it soon came to me. This was the Livingstone Pharmaceuticals manager I'd seen in the Bangkok bar with Walt Daniels - the same man I'd spoken to next day on the Livingstone trade stand. His name was Sam Marshall so if Sam Marshall was here, the boss must be too. I took a chance, got up and walked over. "Sam Marshall?"

The tall American looked up from his paper. "Uh, yeh," he said but remained seated.

"Ian McCann. We met at the Bangkok Infectious Diseases Conference."

"OK. Yeh, I was there," he replied, clearly non too interested and he'd probably forgotten anyway.

"I spoke to your boss Greg O'Brian about some students looking to work in Kenya. I'd heard Livingstone were setting up here."

Sam Marshall still didn't stand up. "Is that right?"

"So, how's it going? Up and running?"

"That's why I'm here. You'd need to speak to Greg." Sam Marshall then picked up his newspaper as if he had no wish to be spoken to. Hmm, I thought. Either I've touched a sensitive nerve or the man merely possesses an unfriendly streak.

"Is Greg here?" I asked.

"Should have been here at seven thirty," he said looking at his watch.

"Any chance I could have a word?"

"Unlikely," Sam Marshall eventually looked up from his paper. "You can always try."

"My appointment hasn't turned up yet either." I said. "If Greg turns up before mine, I'll be sat right there." I tried smiling and pointed to the chair I'd been sitting in. Sam Marshall nodded.

But it was Jimmy who turned up next and knowing Jimmy's style, I decided to intercept his chatter before he had a chance to open his mouth. We were only a few metres from Sam Marshall - easy hearing distance.

"Morning, Jimmy. Did you get my message? The appointment with the university is at ten and I've got six students lined up for interviews. They've been told to ask for me, Ian McCann. We should be finished by midday."

Jimmy scratched his head and looked at me. "And I've just bumped into someone I met in Bangkok at the Infectious Diseases Conference - he's sat just there waiting for his boss to arrive - guy called Greg O'Brian. Small world."

Jimmy glanced in the direction that I had nodded. "Sorry I'm late," he said, "Late night. I overslept."

"Shall we get a coffee?" I said and ushered Jimmy away - not far but just out of earshot.

"OK, you're Jimmy Banda from the University, I'm Doctor Ian McCann from Malaysia. Let's just hang around, Jimmy. See what transpires. Take a seat."

It was half an hour before the lift opened and Greg O'Brian emerged. Hardly dressed to impress in a crumpled white shirt and dark trousers, he looked as if he had just got up. This was my first daylight close-up since Bangkok. O'Brian sauntered past, in the direction of where Sam Marshall was still sitting. Marshall stood up, they shook hands. O'Brian slumped into the chair next to him but they hardly looked at one another. O'Brian yawned. There was little in the way of obvious conversation. Marshall opened his case and came out with a writing pad. O'Brian said something and pointed with his hand. Marshall wrote something down. Then O'Brian got up, sauntered back towards the lift, pressed the button and disappeared again. Marshall stayed seated, slid the pad into his case and stood up.

"Stay here, Jimmy," I said and went over to intercept Marshall.

"Did I see Greg O'Brian just then?" I asked.

Marshall, still fastening his case, looked up. "Sure. I got a glimpse of him myself."

"Is he coming back?"

"No idea, man. I got my instructions and that's it."

"Will you be seeing him again?"

"Shouldn't think so. He's heading off today."

"I'd better be quick then," I said.

"I wouldn't bother, my friend, he's always in a fucking hurry."

"Ah well, if you see him tell him you met Ian McCann from the Bangkok Conference will you?"

"Sure," Marshall said and walked away.

I returned to Jimmy. "Follow Marshall, see where he goes. I'll wait here."

It was a mistake.

Yes, I make them. This was a bigger one than most. But that's the business I'm in.

CHAPTER 65

Larry finally got a call through to the Nigerian doctor Abdouleye in Kano.

"You left a message at the US Embassy for me to call you," he said.

"Yes. You wanted to know more about Doctor Mustafa, who ran the Kofi Clinic - the one who ran the tests on the new medicine."

"Yes," relied Larry. "Have you got anything more?"

"Yes," Abdouleye said. "Can you meet me?"

"I'm in the USA at the moment," Larry said. "And I'm not sure when I'll be back."

"So, you lost interest in one hundred Nigerian deaths?"

"Definitely not," Larry said, "In fact that's why I'm here. I'm in Washington."

There was a pause.

"I think I told you there was also a white man here," said Abdouleye. Doctor Mustafa arrived first. He set up the clinic and the white man joined him just before the tests started. Because people saw a white doctor they trusted Mustafa."

"Do you now know the name of the white man?"

"Doctor Suleiman He stayed about one week then left."

"How do you know this?"

"The wife of one of the patients who died. She says her husband was healthy but they needed money. They had heard about cash being offered to help test a medicine for coughs. Her husband attended the clinic and was given, from what I can make of her description, an asthma inhaler. Several men, including her husband then got sick. They were told they would be moved to hospital for more checks. More money was paid out. After a month, the woman and several others had heard nothing. They went to the clinic but no-one was there. They reported it to Kano State Government. They inspected it and then closed it. The woman then heard about many other men."

"Are you sure the white man's name was Suleiman?"

"Yes."

"Could it have been Solomon not Suleiman?"

There was a distinct hesitancy from Abdouleye. "Yes," he said. "According to the woman, he did not look Arab. Mustafa spoke Arabic. The white man only spoke English."

"If I send a photo to your mobile, can you check it out for me? Let me know by text if it's the same man?"

"But what are you going to do?"

"That is why I'm in Washington. Please stay in touch as we may need you to provide evidence in due course."

CHAPTER 66

Jimmy had left the Sankara Hotel to follow Sam Marshall. Meanwhile, I sat to wait for O'Brian to re-emerge. And it wasn't long before the lift door opened and O'Brian walked out with a mobile phone clamped to his ear and a small overnight case in his other hand. He had changed, not into a suit but into casual black trousers and a bright, check shirt. He went straight to reception, put his phone in his back pocket and checked out. Meantime, I walked outside, ordered a taxi and told the driver to wait on the road outside until the Mercedes came past.

Forty five minutes later, I was at the airport. I had watched as O'Brian returned his Mercedes to the car rental and then followed him as he checked-in for a

Vietnamese Airline flight out. But it was his destination that now bothered me. O'Brian was heading to Bangkok.

I suddenly felt exhausted. If this had been the start or even the middle of a typical investigation for an aggrieved client then I would probably now be on the phone to Colin in London asking if he had someone in place in Bangkok who could perhaps pick up O'Brian on arrival and track him somehow. Then I'd probably have bought myself an air ticket and followed. But this was no longer a typical investigation and there seemed no point in carrying on with what was becoming an international goose chase. I had not even spoken to Colin, let alone Anna, for three days. What I needed now, above all else, was a chat with Anna and then a complete review of where each of us - Larry, Kevin and Colin - now were. I slumped onto a seat and closed my eyes. But then my phone rang.

"I'm at the airport," Jimmy said.

"That's odd, so am I," I said. "I've followed GOB as far as I can go at the moment."

"I'm outside a freight-forwarder's warehouse," Jimmy said. "Marshall took a taxi to the Oakwood Hotel - Dominique Lunneau was there - but they hardly spoke. I don't think they had met before. Lunneau approached Marshall. Marshall gave Lunneau some paperwork. Then Marshall left. I stayed to watch Lunneau. He made some phone calls and then he also left. I followed him here - Ace Logistics Africa. Lunneau is inside and.............no, wait, he's coming out."

"I suspect he's organising a Shah Medicals shipment to somewhere, Jimmy. See what you can find out."

The phone went dead but I continued to sit. Then I sent a short text to Colin, "Coming home. Tell Anna. Will call later." I went for a coffee, ate a ham sandwich and then had another coffee. Then Jimmy rang again.

"There are two containers here, Daniel. They are being shipped by sea to Jordan. But there are also three big boxes marked "Livingstone Pharmaceuticals - Pharmaceutical Supplies." The paperwork accompanying them says and I need to spell this, Daniel -"SALBUTAMOL Inhalers." They are being sent by airfreight to Shah Medicals, Singapore."

So, I thought, as Jimmy continued, the distribution network was getting organised. Shah Medicals, Singapore and David Chua - the man I had already met and who Caroline had described as a wiry little chap - was involved either wittingly or, to grant him at least some justice - unwittingly. And what else had Caroline said about him? 'Chua, has history - his family were criminals - Chinese mafia - before the clampdowns.' And he had once been arrested for being involved in a far right wing group - Singapore 2100. And it was Kevin Parker who had confirmed that Singapore 2100 was an action group committed to a reduction in the population of Singapore. So could it be that it wasn't just the crowded, underdeveloped, trouble spots like northern Nigeria that were at risk but highly civilised and ordered places like Singapore?

"How did you find all of that out in the space of 30 minutes, Jimmy?" I asked him.

"Easy, Daniel. I said that I was from Shah Medicals and Dominique Lunneau had sent me to check on the paperwork."

"Are you sure that was safe, Jimmy?"

"Yes, anyway, the man in the office is the cousin of Lucky's brother in law."

"That should be OK then, Jimmy," I said, smiling to myself. Then I went on. "Can you get over here to departures, right now? I'm thinking I need to get back to UK to meet up with Colin and others and decide where we go next."

I booked a flight back to London for that afternoon and then, with more than half an hour gone and still no sign of Jimmy, I phoned him but got no reply. I waited another twenty minutes and phoned again but the phone had been switched off. Unsure what to do but needing to return to my hotel to collect my bag and laptop and check-out I decided to take a taxi. But I didn't like the fact that Jimmy's phone was off. It was unusual. Concerned but confident that Jimmy would be in touch very soon I left and was back in the hotel in thirty minutes. I went to my room, packed my few things in the case and, with several more failed attempts to phone Jimmy, checked out and took a taxi back to the airport.

It was now after midday and my direct flight to London was in two hours. I checked in but instead of going through passport control, stayed outside and tried, once more, to phone Jimmy. Again, his phone seemed to be switched off so I sent him a text message.

Then I phoned Colin in London.

"I'm booked on a flight due into London at 10.30 tonight," I said. "Please tell Anna. And we need an urgent review on this job. I've got so much to report. Is there anything from Larry and Kevin? Can you get them to meet us again? If Larry can't make it, a conference call or something. But, unless they have already succeeded, then we need to engage some real big hitters now - politicians first, then any international law enforcement bodies that could cope -

that'll probably mean Interpol. But how quickly can they get themselves organised?

"And there's another problem, Colin," I continued. "I'm worried about Jimmy. I think he might have overdone his adventurous streak this morning. Now I can't get him on his phone. He was supposed to meet me here more than two hours ago and he was only a few minutes away from the airport. I fear something has happened. We witnessed three murders last night, Colin, and your friend GOB is in the thick of it. GOB's gone to Bangkok this morning but Dominique Lunneau is still on the loose here in Nairobi. And neither of them is on any wanted list - and that includes Interpol's - I know because I checked."

"Christ!" Colin said. "I'll phone Jimmy's office right now, see if they know anything. You might be worrying unnecessarily. Perhaps it's as simple as a dead battery."

"But he could still come here, phone or no phone. I'll feel very responsible if something's gone wrong."

"There's not much more you can do anyway by the sound if it, Dan. And I agree, we're running desperately short of time. Just get back here."

With Colin continuing to persuade me to leave immediately as there was nothing I could do about Jimmy and with my flight having been called, I went through passport control and headed for London.

CHAPTER 67

It was Anna who spotted Daniel first as he emerged with his black bag into the arrivals hall at London Heathrow's Terminal three. Colin stood back as she ran forward and tried to grab his bag as if to relieve his load. But Daniel dropped the bag and, instead, wrapped his arms around her. Then he kissed her. For the first time in his life, Daniel felt as if he was coming home.

"So much to tell you, Daniel," she said as they walked with Colin to the car park. "I have so many friends already and Colin has been so good to me. He even showed me how to use the London Underground."

"So do you like London?" Daniel said, still holding her hand.

"Yes," she said, looking up at him, "But so much better when you are here."

In the car, driving into London, it was Colin's turn.

259

"No news from Louise in Jimmy's office, Daniel. I phoned twice today. She didn't know where he was. She's not worried though because it often happens with Jimmy. So stop worrying for a while."

Then it was more questions and answers.

Had Daniel contacted Virex's president, Charles Brady, yet because Brady had phoned Colin's office, Asher and Asher, twice and was angry that he didn't have contact details for Daniel.

No, he hadn't yet reported back. He'd do it tomorrow. Remiss of him, perhaps, but it had been relatively unimportant.

Had Colin heard from Larry?

Yes, Larry had met New York Senator Mary Collis in Washington. It had been a good meeting and Larry had spoken to her twice in the last two days. Problem was he was beginning to run short on fresh facts as he hadn't spoken to Daniel for a while. Daniel needed to speak to Larry urgently or the Senator would go cold far faster than it had taken her to get warm.

And what about Kevin?

Kevin just didn't seem to know how to deal with his few agreed tasks. Colin had found him frustrating and defeatist to talk to. But Kevin had brought in an old friend of his with connections - someone called Tom - and, good news, they had already had a meeting with Lord Peterson who chaired the House of Lords Science and Technology Committee. They thought the meeting went OK but Tom also wanted to meet Daniel. Yes, it was to be another meeting.

"But time is fast running out, Colin."

Agreed. And there was movement on the Nigerian front. Larry had got more details about the disappeared doctor. He had had an accomplice - and here's the interesting fact, Daniel - he was white and his name? Solomon.

And the other movement on Nigeria was with Kevin's Nigerian friend Tunje. Tunje had met with an Arab who had offered him money to go to Nigeria and help with the, so-called, project. Last information, two days ago, was that Tunje was willing to go, check it all out and report back.

"They are using networks, Colin. Buying some, stitching up others and leaning on those whose sole motive is to make money. It's becoming very clear to me now. From what Jimmy found out this morning, Singapore is also on their lists. And I know who is involved, how he'll operate and probably why. But the one big question remains. Who can stop it? That's why I need to stop running around chasing geese. We need to regroup and identify the best way to getting international law enforcement to do something."

From the back seat of the car, Anna then asked her question. She leaned forward. "And what about the boyfriend of the Thai lady I spoke to - Pim?"

In the front passenger seat, Daniel turned around and held Anna's hand. "Yes, and we've not even started on finding David Solomon yet, Anna. Do you want to go back to Bangkok so quickly?"

"Well, no - but perhaps yes. But only if we go together and I can help."

Daniel looked at Colin. They were in heavy, late night traffic on Hammersmith flyover, but Colin was looking out of the corner of his eye. "Anna would make an ideal partner, Daniel," he said quietly. "You need to formalise things, get a contract signed urgently, make it watertight so that neither party can get out of it."

CHAPTER 68

It was Larry Brown's third night at the Quincy Hotel in Washington and as there was little hope of his expenses being paid for by the US Embassy in Nigeria or any other organisation he could think of, he was beginning to wonder if he should downgrade.

But Senator Mary Collis's PA, Collette, had phoned him three times with requests for more information. The problem now was that he was running out of evidence. He had started to repeat himself too much and it was now becoming embarrassing.

At Daniel's Queensway apartment in London it was past midnight. Anna was making coffee. Colin and Daniel were sat either side of the stained coffee table that was the centre piece of Daniel's living-room.

In Washington, Larry was lying on his hotel bed in his room wondering if he could afford to eat in the hotel or whether he should go and get something outside when his phone rang.

"Larry, it's Daniel. I'm back in London. So much to tell you. Any chance you could fly over for an urgent recap and to decide where we're going."

"Jesus, I was just thinking of you, Daniel. Yeh, I'm running out of steam here. You'll know from Colin that I've got Senator Mary Collis interested - but she's a busy woman, Daniel and I need to give her far more. Passionate opinion and argument is no substitute for written evidence and facts."

"So what's she done so far?"

"Not enough, Daniel - that's my honest opinion. But that's partly my fault. I'm well aware from what Colin has told me, that you've been chasing around trying to piece together the commercial side and I've given her bits on that. But all I've really been able to do is explain the risk of a deliberate plot to spread a flu virus and it sounds so weak and implausible when you start to describe it.

"Yes, it worries the shit out of her but she's having the same problems as I did in trying to get anyone to listen and take action because no-one knows what action to take. She gets asked too many questions that she can't answer and the scientists say that modifying viruses for research purposes is perfectly legal. Yes there's a risk of it escaping but it's such a small risk that it'll never happen.

"And who the hell, they ask, would want to do it deliberately?

"But if we could add in the commercial element with questions about fraud and corruption then I think we can start to have an impact. And that's where you come in, Daniel."

"So far, who has she spoken to in USA?" Daniel asked.

"She started by checking with the WHO - it's the obvious place. Yes, they admit to knowing something but she's clearly hit a wall there. Then she spoke to all the other bodies I'd already spoken to - Homeland Security, USAMRID and so on. More fucking brick walls. Today she got back to me through her PA, Collette, to say she'd spoken to the US Department of Defence to ask about this risk being classified as bioterrorism. Of course, they needed more like something from the WHO or specific evidence about the virus. She asked them about the definition of bioterrorism and then, according to Collette, got mad with them after they started quoting chapter and verse about the need to define terrorism. You really don't need to know, Daniel.

"But, for your information, the definition is - and here I need to read out what I wrote down - 'the calculated use of unlawful violence or the threat of unlawful violence to inculcate fear, intended to coerce or intimidate the government or society in the pursuit of goals that are generally political, religious or ideological.'

"I said to Collette that that is exactly what we've got here - the threat of unlawful violence by using a virus as a weapon. Collette laughed. And I know why she laughed."

In London, Daniel was past laughing. He was tired, still worried about Jimmy and desperate to spend some time with Anna without Colin, dear friend though he was, sitting there listening in to the conversation.

"So, Larry, can you get over here? If that's not possible or you think you can do more by staying in Washington then we'll talk on the phone or Skype or something. What somebody needs to do, Larry, is to take a few key people out of circulation very quickly. We know the names and roughly know where we can find them. But that means international arrest warrants and, as I see it, Interpol is the only organisation capable of doing this. What can Senator Collis do on this?"

"I checked Interpol as well, Daniel."

"And?"

"Yes, Interpol's Washington Liaison Office can instigate something. But as a private citizen I'd have to start from scratch with the local police here. If you get time, Daniel check the US Department of Justice website and you'll see what I'm talking about. Senator Collis might swing it but we then come back to the lack of evidence once more."

Sat alongside Daniel in London, Colin was listening in. He nodded. "He's right," he said. "It's the bureaucracy and it's understandable. Without it you'd get every Tom, Dick and Harry phoning in asking for help in tracking down their ex wife."

Larry clearly heard Colin.

"That's right, Colin. Senator Collis could do something but she still needs the evidence, a clear plan of action, names, lists of crimes."

"And we might even struggle with the name of the crime. What is a crime called that involves a plot to decimate a population by the deliberate spreading of an infectious virus? If it was a government doing it, it could perhaps be ethnic cleansing. But a private company? An individual? To me, this is clear-cut bioterrorism but, believe it or not Daniel, bioterrorism is a dull subject since nothing ever came of past threats to explode bombs full of anthrax and smallpox over New York and London.

"And even Senator Collis would probably find the form-filling a chore. Forms in duplicate and triplicate, case numbers, statements of the precise crime, description of the exact help needed, full background details. In urgent circumstances Interpol Washington will accept telephone requests but will do nothing internationally without paperwork.

"I think she is taking me seriously but she can't do much with the information I'm able to give." Larry paused.

In London, Anna was pointing at the cup of coffee she'd made Daniel. He hadn't yet touched it. He picked it up.

"Yes, I'll come over, Daniel. I'll see if I can get a flight out tonight. But what I'll do first is speak to Senator Collis or Collette and tell them what's happening. Maybe we can even get the US Embassy in London to help. But I've also probably become a persona non grata within the US diplomatic service so perhaps that's being optimistic. I understand the Embassy in Nigeria have found out I've gone AWOL. Tough shit, I say. Anyway, I hope to see you tomorrow."

It was one thirty in the morning and Kevin Parker was the next to receive a phone call from Daniel.

"Fuck off, Tunje. I've had enough of your late night calls."

"Kevin? It's Daniel."

Kevin sat up amongst the tangle of duvet, pillows and damp towels that constituted his bed.

"Christ, sorry Daniel. I was sound. Thought it was Tunje."

"No problem," said Daniel. "I'm in London. Can you get up here tomorrow afternoon?"

"What time is it?"

"I don't know. But no need to set off right this minute. Question is, can you get to London this afternoon? Larry is flying from Washington, I've just got back from Cairo via Nairobi. My Bangkok agent is sat right next to me and Colin started off earlier today from Edgeware Road. Can you make it?"

Kevin untangled himself and put his bare feet on the floor. "Uh, yes. But Tom is the main man at the moment. I'd need to speak to him, see if he can close the bookshop for the day."

"Tom runs a bookshop?"

"Yes, didn't Colin tell you? Second hand books."

"I hear he's well connected at Government level, though."

"Yes, he was once. He's a retired biology teacher."

"But he's got his head around this problem of ours, Kevin?"

"For sure, not only is he a biologist but a founding member of the Malthus Society who has followed David Solomon's career quite closely over the years. He also knows Lord Peterson."

"Sounds like you need to bring him, then Kevin," said Daniel.

"What time is it?" Kevin asked again.

"Well, if Larry gets here from Washington by early afternoon, I suggest we meet mid or late afternoon."

"No I meant what time is it now?"

Daniel looked at his watch. It was still on Nairobi time. "5.15 am he said. And another thing, Kevin? Where is your friend Tunje at the moment?"

"Tunje? Probably at a party in Watford."

"I meant has he gone to Nigeria yet? Clearly he hasn't. Any chance you could get Tunje on the phone and ask him to make himself available for a meeting with all of us before he gets on the plane to Lagos?"

"Yes," said Kevin, smiling to himself. "I'll phone him right now."

CHAPTER 69

In Nairobi, Jimmy was in trouble.

He had followed Dominique Lunnea and watched him go into the Ace Logistics Africa office. He had then been on the phone to report to Daniel when Lunneau came out.

Then, with his usual brazen approach, he had waited a few minutes before marching into the freight-forwarder's reception office and saying that he worked for Shah Medicals and that Mr Lunneau had just been in but had phoned almost immediately to ask him to double-check the paperwork he had only just presented.

It had worked like clockwork. Somehow he had recognised the clerk in the reception office, had had a quick look at the paperwork that was still sat in a pile on the desk, saw there was one sea shipment for Jordan and an airfreight consignment of the aerosols for Singapore, told the clerk that it looked OK and then gone back outside to phone Daniel again. It was then that his problems started.

He was just putting the key in the lock of his car when he felt a hand on his shoulder. It felt heavy. When Jimmy looked around the first thing he saw was the long sleeve of the dark green shirt. It was exactly the same colour he had seen Dominique Lunneau wearing earlier and Jimmy was about to get his first real close-up of the man.

As he looked at the face, the North African, Algerian or Tunisian features were now obvious. There was a fine, black stubble on his, Lunneau's, lightly tanned face, an incongruous looking ear-ring in his left ear and his hair had a slight curl with grey streaks. He looked about forty. But it was what Jimmy felt and saw in the other hand, half covered by the long green-sleeves that bothered him. The gun that he had seen through the keyhole in Lunneau's office door was now held firmly in Lunneau's hand and was digging into Jimmy's ribs.

Jimmy had parked his car on the road outside, not in the wired off area that was Ace Logistics' car park and for a moment there was silence as Lunneau looked up and down the road as if checking if anyone was looking. It seemed not.

Jimmy was standing perfectly still as the gun was pressed further and further between his ribs and it was becoming painful. Lunneau eventually spoke.

"I don't like people following me, OK? There is no-one around and it'll only take me one second to shoot you and three more to get your dead body in my car. Move!"

Lunneau pointed to the car behind - the Toyota that Jimmy had followed earlier and the car he knew had already held three bodies the night before. But it was now parked right behind his own car and Jimmy hadn't noticed. It was a big mistake, but too late now.

"OK," said Lunneau, opening the rear door of the Toyota. "Get in."

Jimmy did as he was told. Lunneau, still pointing the gun at Jimmy through the open door then opened the driver's door. He then shut the rear door and got in the driver's seat, swivelled round and pointed the gun directly at Jimmy's head.

"Now," Lunneau said, "Who are you? And what's the name of that fucking white friend of yours?"

Jimmy said nothing but looked down the barrel of the short pistol. The gun clicked and Lunneau's finger seemed to move on the trigger. Jimmy, thinking his time was up, closed his eyes and tried thinking of the beach in Mombasa. But nothing happened. When he opened his eyes, the gun was only two inches away but Lunneau was holding a mobile phone in his free hand. He then spoke into the phone.

266

"Yes, got him. He's in the car. Get over here now. I'm outside Ace."

Jimmy wondered if he could make a run for it but it didn't look promising. If anything the gun was now touching his forehead. But he also felt he needed to say something. It wasn't in his nature to stay silent for too long.

"Sit," said Lunneau as if Jimmy was trying to get up. "I ask again. Who the fuck are you?"

Jimmy said nothing.

"OK, put your hand inside your shirt pocket and remove the mobile phone."

As the gun was now making a dent in his forehead, Jimmy decided to comply but knew it was going to be a giveaway. Daniel had warned him once before about mobile phones and the information lying on them. That's why Daniel constantly changed his. But it was too late now. Another mistake. He took out his phone. Lunneau grabbed it.

"OK, now take out the wallet in your back pocket."

"Oh, my aunt," thought Jimmy. "Now he'll see everything." But with the gun poking him in the right eye, he leaned forward to access the back pocket of his trousers, pulled on the wallet that contained nearly all his personal details and handed that over as well.

"OK, " said Lunneau. "Now pull on the seat belt."

Jimmy obeyed.

"Now twist it and put it around your neck."

Jimmy had seen this done in a movie once and so he knew what to do, but he hadn't liked what happened next in the movie.

"Give me the buckle."

Jimmy tugged on the seat belt and handed it over. With his free hand, Lunneau twisted it a few more times and pushed it into the seat belt point of the front passenger seat. Then he tugged on it, almost choking Jimmy."Now lie down facing the back of the car."

Jimmy already feeling trussed like an oven ready chicken, pulled up his long legs, put his feet onto the seat and rolled over.

It was then that he heard and felt what seemed like the shattering of his own skull. For a second he thought he'd been shot. But then it happened again, louder this time. Jimmy lost consciousness.

When he came to, he found he was still in the back seat of the Toyota with the seat belt tightly wound and tied around his neck. He was in a sitting position but with his head drooping forward onto his chest. This time his hands and feet were also held together with a rope that threaded itself under the front seats. Jimmy could not move. If he had, he'd probably have strangled himself. But as his brain slowly began to function again he could also feel a coldness coming from a crack somewhere in his skull. He wanted to touch it but couldn't. So he just lay there wondering how deep it was. Then he slowly raised his head.

In the front driver's seat, where Lunneau had once been, sat a man he'd never seen before. He was peering around the head rest with a strange grin on his face and the same gun was again pointing at Jimmy's head. The man was not North African French Arab like Lunneau but Middle Eastern Arab. Jimmy could not have placed him on a map but he could place him as the third man who had driven the van away from the Shah Medicals site the night before.

Either way, Jimmy didn't like his sense of humour.

"So, Mr Jimmy Banda. Accountant and part-time office cleaner. You are very lucky that I am a doctor. Do you need some paracetamol?"

"No thanks," muttered Jimmy.

"That's good to hear. Doctors always overprescribe. That is because they have a duty to keep people alive, you see. Even when there is no longer any will to live left in the patient they are still required by law to do something. And because people now live so long, doctors are so overworked. Is it any wonder they prescribe without carrying out a thorough diagnosis. But they don't have time to think any longer, you see. The queues at their doors get longer and longer."

"Yes," Jimmy said, hoping that a conversation about medical ethics might yield positive results. But as he couldn't think of anything more to say, he repeated himself. "Yes," he said again.

The mysterious doctor was playing with the gun. One minute it pointed straight at Jimmy's head, the next it pointed out of the car window. And so Jimmy tried to look out of the window although his vision now seemed flawed. But he could tell they were no longer outside the Ace Logistics building. In fact Jimmy had no idea where he was. There were short, thorn trees all around the car and the ground looked red and dusty and it had potholes. A small round hut with a corrugated roof was just visible through the trees. Unfortunately, though, there did not appear to be any other human beings close by.

"Where are we?" Jimmy asked, thinking it best to adopt a friendly tone with his doctor.

"Somewhere quiet." the man replied. "But if you want to go back to your office or go home then you'll need to tell me something very quickly as I haven't got long. I am very busy and we are expecting a flu epidemic."

There was a short pause, the man's grin disappeared and the tone of his voice suddenly changed.

"So," he said, "I understand you are not just an accountant. Mr Banda. You are also a private detective. Am I right? You have a nice office, Mr Banda. Louise was very co-operative when we spoke to her."

Jimmy's interest in the view outside the car window ceased.

"Now, before I lose my temper, Mr Banda, tell me something. Who is this man you phoned? The number is entered twice on your phone - once in the name of Franklin, the next as Daniel. But it is the same number. You phoned him just before my colleague apprehended you. He then tried to phone you several times and then sent you a text. In the text he says he's flying to London and will get Colin to phone you. He signed off as Daniel. Who is the man called Daniel?"

"I don't know," said Jimmy.

"Well I think I do," said the doctor. "Because the other man, Colin, called from a company called Asher and Asher in London and spoke to Louise in your office to ask if she knew where you were. I think we'll know sooner rather than later who he is, Mr Banda. It'll be very easy to hunt him down."

Happy go lucky Jimmy, trussed up on the back seat of a Toyota with two gashes in his sore and thumping head and a gun in front of his eyes was in no mood for any humour. But he tried it nevertheless. "So, are you here on safari, Doctor?"

"No, Mr Banda. But we don't really need you do we? You are like so many millions of others - superfluous."

Jimmy stared at the grinning face of the man still peering around the side of the driver's head rest. He was still grinning as Jimmy conjured one last vision of the beach in Mombasa.

CHAPTER 70

I had never entertained more than one person at a time in my small Queensway flat but, with Anna organising tea and coffee, there was now six. It was late afternoon. Larry had just flown in from Washington, Kevin and Tom Weston had come by train from Bristol and Colin had been there since early morning. Kevin had not managed to contact Tunje.

I instantly liked Tom Weston. He is my sort of ex teacher, academic and second hand book seller. If all school teachers end up like Tom once they'd retired the world will be a much more interesting place. And it was plain to see that Tom like Anna. She immediately became "my dear".

I was trying to pull together a complete summary of what each of us already knew.

We had all started at different points but, completely unknown to each other, had all arrived at the same conclusion - that something needed to be done urgently on a huge and co-ordinated scale at international level.

But, as separate, private, individuals it was proving difficult to persuade anyone to listen, let alone act. Larry now felt he might be getting somewhere but Tom and Kevin were already frustrated and had heard nothing from Lord Stevenson for two days. We agreed it was because we were lone voices, offering private, individual opinions and relating just a few recent experiences. It was not enough. It was certainly proving time consuming and time was running out.

"It's as if we weren't convincing enough, Daniel," Tom moaned. "And I've known Bill Stevenson since his days at University College, London. Perhaps it was because we'd just walked in off the street looking like a couple of fools trying to sound off about lack of adequate controls on virus research - Kevin being a mere lecturer in Social and Economic History and me an old codger who runs a book shop."

"Exactly," piped up Kevin. "What do the bastards want? Aren't they supposed to listen to the people who vote for them?"

"But there are just too many people trying to grab their ear," said Tom. "Just too many people. Sound familiar, Kevin?"

Colin and I had agreed the night before that the first thing we needed to do was produce a complete summary of what each of us already knew. And with Colin, and now Larry, convinced that any concerted international action to make arrests or to carry out forced inspections of suspect companies would, despite the digital age, require a mass of hard copy paperwork, we decided to produce some sort of formal report that would be ready and waiting once we'd established exactly who could instigate some action. It needed to be strong on facts with as much independent evidence as possible - evidence from third parties such as Kevin's friend Tunje, Abdouleye and the Nigerian doctor Larry had met. And Jimmy's photos of the inside of the Shah Medicals factory would be invaluable.

With Colin in his organisational element with the flip chart from his office, I began the summary.

"There have been three separate starting points for what we now know," I said. "And there are also two quite separate but inter-linked sides. On one side is the development of the influenza virus tailor-made to use as a population control method and on the other side is the commercial exploitation. This is what has made Larry's job of persuasion so difficult.

"So let's first look at this artificially created virus called, by its creator, Malthus A. We know there are plans to use it as a tool to reduce the world's population. But it needs to be released in a controlled and systematic way.

"For me, it started with my investigation for Virex in Boston. This was a very vague request to find out where some valuable research material had gone. It's unlike me to take on a client with such a vague remit but I admit I needed an excuse to go back to Bangkok where there was some other private, unfinished business waiting for me."

Despite my attempt to keep my summary serious, Anna suddenly clapped her hands and smiled. I blew her a kiss, smiled and continued.

"But that investigation got me looking at scientists that had recently gone missing. One of them was David Solomon."

"Simultaneously, there was Larry's discovery of the hundred Nigerian deaths from an influenza-type disease. He reported these to the WHO.

"Thirdly there is Kevin's Malthus Society website. The website occasionally attracts some extreme views but is otherwise well monitored by Kevin. But this led him to a meeting in London with an Arab called Mohamed El Badry. El Badry claimed to have a solution to world population control that was ready to launch. It looked as if Kevin was being invited to take part.

"Then Kevin discovered that another Malthus Society member, Tunje Fayinka, a Nigerian and close friend based in UK, had also met El Badry. Tunje reported all this to Kevin. Tunje has since met another Arab who, he says, was not El Badry but a different man. This man has offered Tunje money to help with what appears to be the spread of the virus in Nigeria. Tunje has promised to keep us all posted.

"Now, we are still unsure about this man Mohamed El Badry. It is possible he is using two or three different names including Mohamed Kader. The name

Mohamed Kader also crops up on the other side - the commercial side. And there are at least two other men of Arab origin - one is possibly Egyptian. We have possible names but it is a weak point for us. There is a definite link to an Egyptian doctor going by the name of El Khoury and we have an address in Cairo. This man is linked to Fatima El Badry, at the same Cairo address. In most Arab countries, women keep their full birth and family names and do not change their family names to their husband's name. So have we got a case here of Mohamed Kader also using his wife's name of El Badry when it suits him? But Fatima El Badry is certainly involved somewhere as she seems to harbour the same hard-line views on population control as Kader's. But this is definitely a weak area for us.

"Now, alongside the Nigerian deaths were the reports of deaths in Thailand and a single Kenyan death. All these got reported at the Infectious Diseases Conference in Bangkok so they are already on record. There are now other links to Thailand and Kenya that we have uncovered.

"Subsequently WHO got involved but there is very little information from them that has been made public.

"It was Larry who got more detail on the Thai deaths from the virology research laboratory in Bangkok and it was from here that we learned of a link with the use of mini aerosol canisters either to spread the virus or to administer a genuine treatment or to sell as a fake treatment for profit. We'll also come onto that in a moment.

"But let's look at David Solomon. When I started the work for Virex I was never told precisely what the lost material was. It turned out to be a potential drug to treat several types of influenza and it was nearly ready for clinical testing. But it had clearly been stolen and we now know who the culprit was - a Virex scientist called Jan de Jonge. We know where he is located. He had passed the material to David Solomon. But that is not all he stole. He also stole a modified virus from their so-called secured stocks

"No-one else knows where Jan de Jonge is yet. I suppose I have a duty to inform Virex as part of my very loose contract with them but I am reluctant to give them any chance to cover their tracks and reduce their liability for their lack of adequate controls.

"Biox, David Solomon's former employer, and Virex appear to co-operate whenever it suits them. There has to be some shared responsibility here. But the question is, who could deal with that?

"So something that Larry can take up in the USA is the lack of adequate controls put on biotechnology companies and any other organisations working

272

with viruses. If USA sit up and then act then maybe other countries will follow suit. These companies and research organisations are all funded from somewhere. If their funding is limited until proper controls are put in place then I think we will have made a very positive contribution.

"But David Solomon is a British citizen and he is no longer an employee of Biox. He is a leading expert on virus engineering. He is basically freelance. He is a loose cannon and his funding seems to come from a company or companies already associated with fraud and embezzlement.

"Thanks to Tom, we have written evidence of his extreme views about direct action on population. He is, to all intents and purposes a terrorist hell bent on ignoring the rights of others or democratic government in the same way as a bomb maker is for Al Quaida or the Taliban or Boko Haram.

"We do not know David Solomon's precise location. This is classic terrorist behaviour. Thanks to Anna, we suspect he is in Thailand but he may be moving around. And we have evidence from Larry's contact Abdouleye that someone called Solomon was in Kano in Nigeria around the time of the tests on the new virus. All this needs recording."

Finally I stopped. Colin was still busily trying to catch up by writing names and drawing lines connecting them on his flip chart.

"Can we agree that that is a rough summary of the situation on the virus and the key people involved?" I asked.

"Yes," said Larry, "But we could add in details of the virus structure, which, by the sound of it, the Thai laboratory is working on. And the symptoms of the infection."

Colin drew a line to 'symptoms' and another line to "virus structure."

"Yes," said Tom, "And I also have copies of other papers and articles written by Solomon. They are self incriminating and would add weight to the case and be invaluable in re-enforcing the argument."

"OK," I said. "Let's come back to all that. Can we now summarise what we know about the commercial side because this is what I've been trying to piece together for the last few weeks and you'll need to bear with me on this - it'll be a bit like trying to describe a ball of knotted string."

I looked at Colin. "Are you making sense of all this?" I asked.

"I think so. Shall we have a coffee?"

"Good idea."

Anna got up to make coffee. Tom tried to stand up. "My back gets stiff if I sit for too long," he groaned.

"Well, that's the first time I've heard you say that, Tom." said Kevin. "You know, he'll sit for hours reading his books and barely notice his back - and he never complains in the pub."

"It's the chair," explained Tom. "Perhaps Larry can give me something for it."

"How about a beer instead of coffee, then Tom?" I suggested. "We have a few in the fridge." Then I turned to Colin again.

"I can't stop worrying about Jimmy," I said quietly. "Something has gone wrong. Can you try phoning Louise in Nairobi again?"

As Colin picked up the phone, I went into the kitchen to help Anna and fetch some beers.

"You are worried about your friend, Jimmy." she said to me.

"Yes. It's unlike him to be silent for so long. But he often worries me. It's not so unusual. But Colin calls him a ferret - it's a long, slender animal that runs very fast and burrows down into tight holes to find things. It's a good description of Jimmy but he also takes risks. He's very enthusiastic but he sometimes runs first and thinks later. It has always worried me that he might, one day, get caught out. In this case though I blame myself. It was me who suggested he take a risk. If anything has happened to Jimmy I'll blame myself."

Colin joined us in the kitchen. "No news. Louise is now getting worried. Jimmy has not been home, phoned her or come to the office."

Still trying not to think the worse, I rejoined the others and we continued.

"OK, let's look at the businesses involved here. Putting Virex and Biox to one side we've basically got two companies - Al Zafar and Livingstone Pharmaceuticals. But we've also got several smaller businesses who have either been bought out by Livingstone or Al Zafar or are distributors.

"The main trade name you will hear mentioned is Shah Medicals. Companies with the name Shah who are also linked to Livingstone and Al Zafar operate in Hong Kong, Singapore, Egypt and Kenya. Colin's research has thrown up many more with the same name but they are almost all Indian and have no connection with this. However I suspect we might find a number of other companies that have business relationships of one sort or another with Al Zafar and

Livingstone. It is just that we don't have the time or resources to do thorough checks.

"And another clever thing about the Shah Medicals set up is its apparent ability to attract highly qualified, American and European trained scientists - virologists. I think that's David Solomon's influence but we have three working apparently innocently on viruses and antiviral therapies in Egypt. It's pioneering work, but Solomon is probably the guiding hand. They have no idea about the other, shadier side of Shah Medicals, of Livingstone or even Solomon himself.

"But Jan de Jonge is one, a guy called Phillippe Fournier from Kenya is another."

Larry jumped. "So that's where he is."

"Yes, you see how it all ties up? But the third guy working in Egypt is an ex work colleague of Solomon's from Boston, another Brit, Guy Williams. Yes, they are allowed to get on with their work, enjoy the facilities and the big villas and the pool beside the River Nile that they live in But I do not envy them. Someone is keeping a close eye on them and one false move or some argument about the direction of research might not be to their advantage.

"But the main guy that concerns me is Greg O'Brian - Colin calls him GOB. Colin will confirm that GOB's background is sinister. He came from Northern Ireland, had links to the IRA and is now an American citizen. But, as far as we know, he has not entered the USA for several years. He is a rich man with most of his cash stashed in the Cayman Islands although I suspect he is astute enough to have scattered it around elsewhere.

"How did he make his money? Well, fraud, embezzlement and insurance scams rank quite high and he hates people getting in his way. Colin will confirm that garden forks are one tool he uses to rid himself of anyone who causes him a headache.

"We believe he bought Livingstone for a knock-down price when no-one else really wanted it with the intention of using it as an ethical-looking front for far less ethical pursuits. He has staff whom I suspect he is not the slightest bit interested in. They might suspect something about their owner but it'll only be company gossip.

"So Livingstone, the company, gets on with running itself while GOB sits back and has dreams lit up by dollar signs and pound signs. He is not the slightest bit interested in David Solomon's political views on population control because he is using Solomon. But Solomon is also using him. So when Solomon says he has created a virus that can kill thousands and has a treatment that will work, GOB sees three big opportunities for himself.

"One. He wants to cause trouble. GOB is still just one, big, street-wise hooligan. He is also a frustrated small time politician who has a few scores to settle. He operates in a kind of underworld and, if the whole truth ever came out, I suspect he's still deeply involved in other rackets. So he still has a few old friends around that he wants to impress. That's how pathetic some of these guys can be.

"And what really turns him on is when he can show these old mates that no-one can touch him. He'll adopt a can't catch me approach, stick a middle finger up and put a thumb to his nose. And he'll stay out of the limelight under a different name in a big villa in the Caribbean or some other safe haven and remain untouchable unless..........well let's discuss how we might get him in a minute. But as far as we know, and Colin has checked, he is currently not on any wanted lists anywhere and that includes Interpol. That is despite his record.

"So on to GOB's second big opportunity. GOB wants Livingstone to be the distributor of an effective treatment for the influenza epidemic he has deliberately created. Just think of the profile that would give to Livingstone. He'll enjoy that but don't expect him to stand up at an annual shareholders meetings and pronounce on expected dividends. The only person likely to be benefitting, other than the innocent, hard working staff he employs to work nine to five in total ignorance of who their ultimate boss is, is GOB himself.

"And don't think GOB will let a little thing like USA Federal Drug Administration - FDA - or UK NICE approvals get in his way. The world is a big place. If America or the UK don't want to approve his treatment while a flu pandemic rages then so be it - others will probably rush approvals through. The public will demand it.

"Finally, I believe, and we have some evidence from Kenya of this, that GOB wants to make and sell large quantities of counterfeit products not just for influenza. They'll cost almost nothing to manufacture but sell at an extortionate price to innocent victims through pharmacy stores. And with Livingstone's new profile it'll be easier to exploit because this is where Livingstone's and Al Zafar's international distributor network fits in. These distributors are scattered right across the Far East, Africa and the Middle East. They are all small businesses often run by local guys who are just after making a quick profit and they will instantly blame suppliers for any problems over product safety.

"But just look at what drugs you can buy online these days. You can even buy asthma inhalers in supermarkets. Now just imagine the implications if some of these inhalers contained not medicine for asthma but a flu virus? And it struck me on the flight over from Nairobi as I watched a woman use a breath freshener. It was like a miniature deodorant spray. What controls are there on these things? Are counterfeit breath fresheners on the market?

"Apart from improving controls on research on viruses, the so-called gain of function research we talked about earlier, I think we need to scare the pants off politicians with possibilities like this."

I stopped once again. "Any questions so far?"

"No, keep going, Daniel," said Larry. "This is exactly what I needed before talking to Senator Mary Collis. If we can get this into some sort of report form all the better."

"OK," I said. "Then let's look at the other commercial organisation, Al Zafar. Colin has dug out a lot of information on this organisation. Mohamed Kader is its owner. Basically it's an importer and distributor of pharmaceutical products. It started in Jordan. Mohamed Kader is an Egyptian. But here we have the problem referred to earlier. I've got a photo of Mohamed Kader but it does not resemble the descriptions of the other Arabs we seem to be encountering. Is Mohamed El Badry another name used by Mohamed Kader? We suspect it is.

"Kevin's description of the woman at the Chelsea flat where he met Kader fits perfectly with the description of the woman working at the Shah Medical Clinic in Cairo - Fatima El Badry. There is also the mystery surrounding an Egyptian called Doctor Ramses El Khoury who seems to own this clinic but travels a lot. Who is he? What we do know is that he, too, appears to have very similar views to the Mohamed El Badry that Kevin met.

"What I'm saying here is that it is impossible to pull this complicated picture together on our own. We have, I believe, uncovered a plot technically masterminded by a skilled virologist to kill millions of people using a biological weapon for ideological reasons and a network of companies run by some highly unethical people one of whom already has a record in international fraud. It's terrorism working hand in hand with international commercial fraud.

"Now what makes everything so urgent is what we have learned in the past few days mostly from Jimmy Banda working in Nairobi. Jimmy infiltrated Shah Medicals Nairobi. This business was, up until a few days ago, fully functional but it suddenly started to lay off people. This is where Jimmy photographed the aerosols.

"Who was running Shah Medicals, Nairobi? Well, here's another name: Dominique Lunneau, a French Tunisian or Algerian once worked for Al Zafar and was production manager for a small pharmaceutical company in Lebanon.

"Jimmy and I were sat outside the Shah Medicals site long after midnight two days ago when guess who turned up - GOB, Greg O'Brian himself, with another unidentified man and Lunneau. There were only three employees left by this stage - all Pakistanis. Ramses El Khoury Was the unidentified man Mohamed Kader or Mohamed El Badry or Ramses El Khoury or someone else? We don't know. What we do know is that Mohamed Kader has some sort of relationship with Pakistan that needs checking out. But it just shows the international spread of this organisation.

"So, yes, there were only three employees left by the time Jimmy and I got there - all were Pakistanis But how many employees were left by four o'clock in the morning? None. The last three were killed somehow, their bodies stuffed into the back of a Toyota and driven off."

Tom sat up straight.

Kevin said "Bloody hell."

Larry said "Jesus."

Anna looked shocked. "Oh!" she cried, "You saw that?"

"Yes, Anna. Jimmy and I were hiding in Jimmy's car outside. But the Toyota was driven off, presumably to dump three bodies. A van carrying the last remaining boxes from the warehouse went in another direction and Jimmy and I followed GOB in his black Mercedes to a hotel.

"Next morning, I watched GOB hand over some paperwork to an employee of Livingstones. I'd met this man at the trade show in Bangkok and think he is probably completely unaware of what is going on. I then followed GOB to the airport where he got on a flight to Bangkok. Jimmy, meanwhile, had followed Lunneau to a freight forwarders warehouse at the airport. I spoke to Jimmy twice while he was there. But then....." I broke off. "I think something went wrong. We've been unable to talk to Jimmy since."

There was a moments' silence before Larry spoke.

"You are right, Daniel. Time is running out or has already run out. O'Brian flew to Bangkok you say?"

"Yes, and we think David Solomon is also in Bangkok. Question is what do we do now?"

Tom, Kevin and Larry all sat back in their chairs. Anna was sitting cross-legged on the floor with her head resting on my knee. It was Larry who again spoke.

278

"Let's get this report written, Daniel. Paperwork seems to be what they need to take any action. A conversation and opinion, however passionately conveyed by a few people just walking in off the street is just not enough to get anything started."

Colin had been half sat, half standing by his flip chart for an hour. That was exactly what he had been saying to me for the past two weeks. He said:

"That's exactly it, Larry. I've been in this business a while now. Even the way private investigators operate has been the subject of a lot of debate in the UK over the last few years. Politicians, the police, whoever they are, require more information and evidence before they'll even get out from behind their desks.

"For instance, in the USA, the FBI and CIA should be involved. They need to be made aware of what we know urgently. What they do with it afterwards we can't say.

"But why the CIA? Well, their top three prime functions are gathering information about foreign governments, corporations and individuals. And why do they do this? For reasons of national security. So does the risk of bioterrorism fit the bill here? Of course it does. Are the risks of uncontrolled tampering with viruses a risk to national security? Many voters in the USA will say yes. So what are the CIA doing about it?

"And what can the CIA do with the intelligence they acquire or we give them? Well, they could carry on or take over what Daniel has been doing for free with the help of Jimmy. They can carry out further covert activity and then, once enough evidence is there - and I think we've got enough already - they can oversee tactical operations by their own CIA employees, by the US military or by overseas partners. In other words put a stop to it.

"What I'm saying is that, unless I'm totally misunderstanding the way US security operates, I think the CIA should deal with this - certainly as far as ensuring security for US citizens is concerned. But don't imagine the CIA's Directorate of Science and Technology sounds like just the body you need to talk to. Science and technology in the CIA is about satellite surveillance and electronic gadgets. The only viruses they know are computer ones. And if you talk about designer viruses with the CIA they'll think you're talking about a way to hack into or block the Russian or Chinese internet.

"So who do you need to speak to, Larry? Well, ideally the President, after all he's the man in charge. But if you can't get that far up then get as close as you can like the Director of National Intelligence. Nobody will want another run in with the way the CIA about how it's run. There has already been criticism of CIA work relating to security failures and intelligence gathering and they won't

279

want another probe into the way it operates. It's timely, Larry, but you are right. Senator Mary Collis has probably done all she can with what you've told her verbally. She needs more, and that is why we are sat here.

"Now let's look at the UK. What have we got here in the way of an organisation that could deal with this? We've got the equivalent of the CIA, the SIS, the Secret Intelligence Service - MI5 and MI6. And if you look at the SIS you see something very similar to the CIA. Its priorities are dictated by politicians. If politicians think that stopping more bombings of the London Underground by disgruntled Moslems are a priority then that is the SIS's priority. If you ask them this evening if they are keeping watch on a British virologist called David Solomon as a potential terrorist threat then they will ask you who David Solomon is.

"And while their intelligence gathering doughnut, GCHQ, in Cheltenham, has a list of key words it looks for in all our emails I suspect the words 'engineer', 'virus' and 'influenza' seen together in a sentence won't flash a red light.

"SIS functions are just like the CIA's - to obtain and provide information and perform other tasks, in this case relating to the UK Intelligence Services Act 1994. This includes national security, the economic well-being of the country and the prevention of serious crime. Terrorism is so-called Tier One risk and so you would assume the SIS remit fits what we want like a glove. But ask them exactly what their priorities are within this Tier One and they'll say Al Qaeda. They won't say Shah Medicals, Greg O'Brian or David Solomon.

"And then in the UK we have SOCA - the Serious Organised Crime Agency - who's remit is to describe and assess the threats posed to the UK by organised criminals and to consider how these may develop. What are SOCA's priorities?

"Well they do, at least, recognise that criminals are entrepreneurs at heart, that they spread their criminal, commercial activities around and that they move around. But their priorities are, as ever, decided by politicians. So in the case of SOCA we see drugs - by which they mean Class A drugs not counterfeit medicines - money laundering, fraud, human trafficking, identity crime, cyber crime, kidnap, extortion and so on. But I know from experience that their intelligence is woeful. I often know more about certain individuals than they do. That's because they are not a single force but work in partnerships. Not their fault but that's the way it is.

"But is GOB known to SOCA? I doubt it. SOCA is a bit like the CIA. It's a bureaucracy fixated largely on protecting itself. So, like the CIA, it spends half its time navel gazing and trying to fend off attacks that threaten its own survival.

"So what have we got that crosses international boundaries?

"Clearly there is the UN, the European Union and the other global partnerships like ASEAN in South East Asia and the African Union. The EU is bad enough but how long do you think it would take to get the African Union to do something about a small pharmaceutical company making counterfeit medicines and selling them on the internet through small distribution outlets scattered across the globe?

"Interpol is the only body I think could react quickest and make a few arrests to get a few people out of circulation. Getting GOB onto its wanted list would be a good move. But we still can't just wander into the London liaison office of Interpol and ask them to stick a few photos of GOB and Solomon on their lists and ask for help from police forces in all the other signed up members. There are procedures.

"But Interpol concerns itself with just the things we need - public safety, terrorism, organised crime, corruption and illicit drug production. And Interpol agents do not make arrests but call upon the law enforcement agencies in other countries. That would make it easier to ask, say, the Egyptian police to check out Shah Medical Centre in Cairo or the Shah research operation down the Nile at Beni Suef and take a few people in for questioning.

"There is a secure 24/7 communications network, an incident response team on hand and a Terrorism Watch List which we might be able to lock into to track down Solomon - that is if we can get him classified him as a terrorist.

"To me, Interpol is probably the best solution to our immediate needs. But the challenge remains that we need to convince certain people with our evidence so that they will activate the system. We can't just march into a police station and expect a response. In the UK the National Central Bureau which acts as the focal point for enquiries is based at SOCA. So we are back to SOCA again. And in the USA, Larry, Interpol Washington makes it quite clear what the process is and its bureaucracy, paperwork, statements, reports and full details of the alleged crime - and you can't do it yourself. The least you'll need is Senator Collis at your side.

"So, if we agree that Interpol is the best option, we then need to decide who to talk to in order to guarantee some action.

"In the UK, I think it's no lower than the Home Secretary. If we can get the ear of the Prime Minister all the better. And, yes, Tom is right to be concerned about Lord Stevenson. He has probably done little more than carry around the few notes he scribbled on a pad while Tom and Kevin were talking, scratched his head a few times, perhaps spoke to another colleague on his Lords Science and Technology committee who dismissed it and then started to plan his next meeting on science funding for the next budget. I think our report needs to go straight to the top and somehow we need to make sure it's read properly and urgently."

Colin drew a breath. "So, the first job is to write this report with an opening paragraph or two that gets the attention. The second job is to get it read. The first job is easy. I'll have it ready by the morning."

The six of us had now been sat in my small apartment for four hours. With Colin's final summing up, I asked how long they were prepared to carry on.

"Until we've done all we can," said Tom. "Kevin and I can get the last train back to Bristol or we can sleep on the floor. I haven't done that for years."

"And I'm booked at a small hotel in Notting Hill," said Larry, "So no rush."

"Then I know what we'll do," said Anna. "I'll phone my new friend from the Tamarind Thai Restaurant and order some Thai food."

CHAPTER 71

It was early morning in my apartment.

Tom and Kevin had left to catch a late train back to Bristol the night before. Larry was expected to arrive at my apartment after breakfast. Colin had not left until after midnight but was already back. While Anna made coffee, he and I were sat side by side in front of his laptop going through the report he had worked on during the night.

"So, that's our conclusion, then, Colin," I said. "You'll deal with the UK Government, circulate the report to the names on this list and aim to get a one to one meeting with the Home Secretary and, if at all possible, the Prime Minister. See what reaction you get but recommend, with your ex police background, to engage Interpol as a priority and ensure the SIS also sit up and take notice. Because of the health implication, do you think the Health Secretary should know?"

"Let's leave that to the Home Secretary to decide," said Colin. "But I'll start this morning. I'll also phone Nairobi again about Jimmy."

Anna brought in two more mugs of coffee and sat down beside me. I put my arm around her shoulders and pulled her close.

"We are going back to Bangkok," I told her.

Anna put her hand to her mouth. "So soon? Are you fed up with me already?" She smiled.

"No," I replied, "I need you to help me. And we'll be together."

"So what are we going to do?"

"Colin is staying here to talk to the government. You and I are going to try to find David Solomon and Greg O'Brian."

"But when will we come back to London?"

"As soon as possible, Anna. I need a change of life. I need to slow down and I need to settle down. Colin agrees with me."

"Oh, yes," Anna replied. "I agree. You need some babies to look after."

Colin burst out laughing and got up. "Wow, Dan. You are well and truly hooked my friend. But Anna's right as usual. You need to throw that little black bag of yours away and buy a bigger one that Anna can fit some clothes into as well. I suggest you buy it today. If you're going to Bangkok tonight then you haven't got much time left."

"Tonight?" asked Anna.

"Yes, overnight British Airways flight. It's booked already."

"You know, he did this once before, Colin," Anna said. "One morning he came to my apartment and told me he was taking me to Singapore that night. I knew from that minute that he was going to be my husband."

I looked at Colin. "What can I say, man? She's right. I knew it myself."

I then hugged Anna even tighter. "Go and make some breakfast or something, Anna. The more you sit there, the more you embarrass me in front of my best mate."

"Colin is your only mate, Daniel," Anna said. "You told me that once as well."

"So what will we do when we arrive?"

Anna's question as she and I sat waiting to board the aircraft at Heathrow was, as usual, a good one. But I was also taken by Anna's use of the word 'we'. I knew she now wanted to be part of my professional life as well as my private life and I had found I was not at all phased by this. In fact, I already sensed she had a certain flair about her that was not too dissimilar to Jimmy. The way in which she had struck up a relationship by telephone with a complete stranger, the woman called Pim, Solomon's suspected girlfriend, was so reminiscent of Jimmy's style.

But then, of course, my thoughts turned to Jimmy.

Louise, Jimmy's business partner in Nairobi had also started to worry. Jimmy had now been out of contact for nearly three days. One or two days was not unusual but three suggested something was wrong. She had even phoned the local police to report his absence and to check if there might have been an accident or something, but nothing had been reported.

It was Colin who had been phoning Louise up until that morning. Finally, I had become so concerned that I had spoken to Louise himself. But I had never spoken to Louise before. Jimmy was Colin's man in Nairobi and so all my previous contact with Jimmy's office had been done through Colin. Louise had not known about a Daniel Capelli until I introduced myself.

"Ah yes," Louise had said. "Someone telephoned three days ago to ask if Daniel was here. I said no, there was no-one of that name here. He then said did I know Colin. Of course, I said yes, he's from Asher and Asher in London."

That was enough for me.

Someone had got Jimmy and if they had Jimmy then they also had his phone and Jimmy's call and text log. Whoever had Jimmy now also knew about Asher and Asher, about Colin and about myself. The likelihood was that the person who had spoken to Louise was Dominique Lunneau. And if Lunneau knew, Greg O'Brian would know. And if GOB knew it was likely that David Solomon might also now know.

I had told Colin. Colin's reaction was, "Oh, Christ. GOB's been aware of Asher and Asher for five years. This could now make him very, very angry. I'd better make sure my garden shed is locked."

I had told Colin but hadn't yet told Anna.

So, when Anna asked, 'So what will we do when we arrive?' I said, "Well, the first thing is that, as a precaution, I'm going to use a different passport when we arrive in Bangkok."

We were sat side by side with my old black bag between my legs. Anna's hand had been resting on my knee. She looked up. "So, now I begin to understand you even more. You want to be Kun Look Lap again?" she asked.

"No, I'm going to be David," I said. "And that's your fault. You told Solomon's girlfriend you had a husband called David and that you lived in Bristol. Do you remember?"

"Oh, yes," Anna replied sheepishly.

"Well, luckily, I've got a David Franklin passport down there," I said pointing at my black bag. "In private you can call me Daniel but otherwise I'm David. OK?"

"Yes, David."

CHAPTER 72

It was the start of our first full day in Bangkok. Anna and I had arrived in Bangkok late afternoon the day before and checked in to a hotel off of Sukhumvit Road in the name of David Franklin. As usual I bought myself a new phone and a local SIM card. This time, though, I also bought a new phone for Anna.

We had rehearsed the plan on the plane.

While Colin, Larry and the others were trying get their report read and acted upon back in UK and the USA, I would try to track down David Solomon and Greg O'Brian. But our only hope of finding GOB was to first track down Solomon.

Anna was on her new mobile phone. She had spent an hour trying to contact Pim, Solomon's girlfriend. I was listening in but had to wait for the translation afterwards to know what was said.

"Hello, its Anna from England. Do you remember me? I have come to Bangkok with my husband for a holiday," was how Anna had begun. "Yes, we are going to visit my family in Kanchanaburi."

Pim was not working today. She was shopping in Bangkok with her friend. They were in Siam Paragon. Did Anna know Siam Paragon?

Yes, but it was expensive. Not that that mattered to husband David. Had Pim managed to get the phone number of On as she said she would when Anna had called from England two weeks ago?

No, there are many Ons, but no-one who has a friend called Anna living in England and married to a man called David.

So is your boyfriend, David, in Thailand now?

Yes he's in Thailand but very busy.

I just wondered if your boyfriend David would like to speak to my husband David. I told my husband David about your boyfriend David and he thinks he might know him. My husband David is a member of the Malthus Society. Have you heard of the Malthus Society? He thinks your David is also a member and thinks his last name might be Solomon. Is that right?

Yes, that's right. But my David is a very busy man. And I have my friends here. They want to eat now.

Do you have your boyfriend's mobile phone for my husband to call him?

I don't know the number. He phones me. He doesn't give his number to anyone. But I'll tell him you called. What is your husband's number?"

Anna had given her my new phone number and said goodbye.

"I don't think she likes me anymore," said Anna disappointedly. "What do we do now?" she asked, clearly concerned that she had not got what I really wanted.

"We wait, Anna. He might phone. On the other hand we've got several other directions we can go. It's my turn now."

I contacted the US Armed Forces Research Institute of Medical Sciences - AFRIMS - through the American Embassy. Saying I was an epidemiologist from England doing research on Influenza. I asked if there was any other laboratories in Thailand besides the one I already knew about - the Kamphaeng Phet-AFRIMS Virology Research Unit - KAVRU - doing similar research. I was put through to an American accent.

"Yeh. Hi, I'm Captain Karen Thompson, how can I help?"

I explained again who I was - David Franklin - and what I needed to know.

"Well, we work with KAVRU on stuff like that," Karen said.

"Yes, but are there any other similar laboratories doing the same sort of thing? Influenza testing, virology research, that sort of thing."

"Well, there's the Virology Association, there's several HIV centres around, you got the Thailand Science Park and you got other Universities doing some. What are you looking for?"

I wondered whether to spill the beans completely and tell all but it didn't feel right just yet. We still needed to prove a few things.

"Any private laboratories?" I asked.

"No, not as far as I know."

"Might the Thailand Science Park know more?" I suggested.

"Yeh, why not give them a call."

"You know a guy called David Solomon, a virologist from USA? Have you come across him?"

"David Solomon you say?"

"Yes. He worked for a company called Biox in USA. He's a world authority on influenza viruses. I heard he was working here in Thailand."

"Hang on, sir. Let me ask."

I waited.

"Mister Franklin? Sure. He's known. I understand he sometimes teaches at Thammasat University. He's visited KAVRU a few times."

"Any idea where he is now?"

"Sorry.........hang on again. My colleague says he is still here. He has a girlfriend at Thammasat. He lectures on bio-safety. Seem like the guy?"

"That's him," I said. "I'll bet his girlfriend is called Pim. Thanks for your help. I might be in touch again soon."

"Sure, you take care."

I switched my phone off and looked at Anna. "We're getting closer," I said. "Let's try Larry's friend Doctor Vichai."

I knew from Larry Brown that KAVRU - the American Armed Forces Virology Unit based in Kamphaeng Phet in central Thailand was where Doctor Vichai was based. It was Doctor Vichai who I had watched speaking at the Infectious Diseases Conference and who had revealed the possible implication of asthma inhalers to Larry when Larry had enquired about his fictitious English girlfriend Emily Sinclair. If anyone knew about a foreign virologist working in Thailand it must be Doctor Vichai.

It took me an hour to reach him on a mobile phone but it was worth it.

287

"Ah, yes," said Doctor Vichair after I had introduced myself as an epidemiologist and said I'd attended the recent Infectious Diseases Conference. "Yes, Doctor Solomon, he has visited us several times. He stayed with us for a month to teach some of our technicians."

"Do you know where he is now?"

"Ah yes, I expect he is in Bangkok. He travels abroad but he also has connections with the Thailand Science Park. He is very experienced and well known internationally for his work on influenza viruses. We are very lucky to know him."

"Yes, he has become very well known to me, " I said looking at Anna again. "Do you have a contact phone number or email address or anything?"

"Ah yes, but I am in a taxi. But if you call KAVRU and ask for Sarapee, she might know."

"Sarapee," I repeated. "Thank you so much Doctor Vichai. Perhaps we will meet again soon."

Less than five minutes later I had a mobile phone number and an email address. "We don't normally give out phone numbers but as you've spoken to Doctor Vichai I'm sure it's OK."

Clearly, there were circumstances when Solomon wanted to be contactable. But this was the lead we needed.

It was midday in Bangkok, 1am in Washington and 6 am in London. Colin had been in his office since 3am and was still trying to phone me. When he finally got through to me he could not disguise his excitement.

"Thank God, Daniel. I've been trying you for an hour. I was beginning to think you'd given me a duff phone number.

"Listen. I've been up all night. We've got Washington buzzing, Daniel. The report has made all the difference. Senator Mary Collis has pulled strings and Larry's been at it non-stop since he got back.

"Not only that but I've now spoken to Lord Peterson, myself. Basically threatened that government policy on bio-medical research was in tatters if they allowed uncontrolled research on flu viruses and that the government response to signs of a potential flu pandemic would be seen as totally inadequate unless they took notice. I emailed him the report. Then I spoke to the Home Office -

the report went straight in and was backed up by Peterson. All of a sudden Peterson had nothing but praise for Kevin and Tom for raising it - strange isn't it? The Home Secretary was briefed by a senior civil servant last night, the PM and Health Secretary were notified and, as a result we've got action, Daniel."

"Good, Colin. But before you tell me, any news about Jimmy?"

"No, sorry old man, but nothing. However from what is now happening we might get something on that as well. The good news, Dan, is that Interpol are being asked to help. The report enabled Senator Collis to cut through all the red tape within hours and instead of red tape we're getting red notices. And I've been told that GOB will go onto their wanted list.

"It transpires they've been watching him for years. It's all the stuff I was able to pick up - fraud and embezzlement and they've added in money laundering, He travels under different names - that accounts for the Nairobi hotel not having him registered. And if he's in Thailand then the Thai police will have a special interest in him. They already have an Anti-Corruption Commission and there's an initiative called StAR - the Stolen Asset Recovery Initiative. GOB's details are to be circulated probably within the next twenty four hours.

"As for David Solomon - it's more tricky. They are working on it. He can't be classified as a terrorist without more facts. He's also a British citizen. He could easily slip through the net if we aren't careful.

"Now, listen, Daniel. This is important. I'm sat here trying to get the Thai Police to understand your role in all this so you can work with them. But, fact is, I suspect you entered Thailand under a false passport yourself. Am I right? This makes it tricky. You, too, could, be arrested under Thai Immigration rules. But the British Embassy in Bangkok have been told by the Foreign Office here about the case. They know that Interpol are being engaged and that David Solomon is a British citizen. I'm not sure how fast things work but I've asked someone at the Foreign office here to speak to the British Embassy about you, tell them you're in Bangkok working undercover on the case. It might help."

I was sitting next to Anna on the bed in our Bangkok hotel room. If to Colin sitting in London I sounded frustrated, then I was.

"Christ, Colin. I'm here as David Franklin because I'm probably known by GOB as Daniel Capelli working for your company, Asher and Asher. Anna has also spun this yarn to Solomon's girlfriend that I'm called David. And, what's more, every phone call Anna and I make as we sit here, the closer we're getting to Solomon. I'm about to try phoning the guy - he's that damn close."

"Yes, but you must see the little issue we've got, Daniel."

"Yes, Colin. I understand," I said. "Leave it with me. The solution might, in fact, be sat right next to me though I didn't want to involve Anna to that extent."

"OK," Colin said, "But, my advice is go into the British Embassy, ask for assistance and come clean. I'm sure, under the circumstances, they'll help."

"So do we have any idea where GOB is?" I asked.

"Thailand?" It was a question not a statement.

"Bloody big country, Colin. He could be sat in the next room for all I know. On the other hand he might already have come and gone - flown off somewhere. My guess is he came here to see Solomon but that he might go to Singapore to catch up with his consignment of inhalers."

"Well, that's what the Thai police and Immigration will look into. They'll check photos, ID, passports, hotel registrations. Thanks to you they will know what flight and airline he came in on. The Thai police are good, Dan. That's why it would be good for you to work alongside them. But they also have their procedures to follow and I don't want them to be speaking to you from behind bars at Bangkok police HQ."

"And I'm still worried about Jimmy," I said.

"Yes, and the Kenyan Police will also be working with Interpol. So Dominique Lunneau will be on their list as well as an inspection of the Shah Medicals factory site that you and Jimmy know so well. And they will track the two shipments that went out - including the one to Singapore. So Singapore Interpol will be involved. Have we been busy, Daniel?"

"Yes, very good, Colin. And what about Egypt?"

"Yes, Interpol Cairo as well. They will have the names El Badry, Al Khoury and others and two businesses to look at - the Shah Medical Centre and the site at Beni Suef. So your friends down there including Guy Williams and Jan de Jonge might get a rude awakening. The net is closing, Daniel. I just hope we are in time to stop the release of this virus."

"And our net is closing on David Solomon. I just hope he's still in Thailand. Just tell me, what's the Interpol take on Solomon? As there is no international consensus regarding the definition of terrorism or a terrorist what can the Thai police do?"

"Interesting question. But I believe the plan will be to arrest him on suspicion of plotting to make a biological weapon. They can certainly bring him in for questioning. And another thing, Daniel, Virex phoned again. You still haven't contacted them."

"No, because I haven't finished the investigation for them. But we're getting damned close to identifying their problem right now. If they phone again just tell them I'm working on it. But they and their industry are partly to blame for all this. So have the US and UK authorities woken up to that issue yet? Virex and Biox should be held partly responsible for this. Fingers need to be pointed somewhere and so long as the fingers don't point at themselves, politicians are usually pretty good at that. I wouldn't want to be Charles Brady or Josh Ornstein just at this moment."

"Meanwhile, do I wait until all the red tape is complete and replaced by red notices to Interpol? Or do I carry on as if nothing has yet happened? Do I ask the Thai police to help now because we're closing in on Solomon and GOB and so risk my own arrest? Or do I delay it a while longer until they've got their red notices in place? Do I wait until the local police chief has decided on a plan of action, then given instructions to their army of police officers to act? Or do I carry on as if nothing has yet happened and wait until we've got him cornered?"

"Your call, Daniel. You decide."

"OK, I appreciate the speed you're working at Colin. It's fantastic. We're a good partnership. But, meanwhile, here's my high tech solution. I'll give you what I believe to be Solomon's phone number. I'm not sure if you can track a phone that's not switched on but if Anna phones you to say that I've got Solomon on the phone right that minute, could you see if, with all the high technology at your fingertips these days, you can track where he is?"

"I know a man who can," said Colin. "Let's try."

CHAPTER 73

It was late afternoon in Bangkok.

In an air-conditioned coffee shop not far from Daniel and Anna's hotel room, two men were huddled around a small table. Their coffee cups were empty, the dregs already dry. The younger, fair-haired man was leaning forward, playing with the empty cup. He was dressed in black shorts and a white tee shirt printed with a bright green and red apple and the words "An apple a day keeps the doctor away."

The older, bigger man was leaning back in a chair that was far too small for him. He was dressed more formally in a dark grey suit and open-necked white shirt. He swiped at a fly that was, perhaps, trying to settle on the back of his neck and then ran his fingers through the thinning black hair. Then he scraped his chair back and stood up ready to go. As he did so, the younger man put a hand into the pocket of his tee shirt as he felt his phone vibrate.

Daniel had delayed phoning Solomon to give Colin a chance to set up some sort of track on Solomon's mobile phone. He had no idea how it worked or who it was had the technology but Anna was now phoning Colin to tell him to get ready.

"Yes?" said the younger man abruptly. Then: "Just a moment."

In the background, Daniel heard a metal table or chair being moved, perhaps a cup rattling. "OK," he heard the man say. "See you later.............Yes? Who is it?"

"Doctor Solomon?" Daniel asked.

"Who is it?" he repeated.

"My name's Ian McCann. Sorry to bother you but I was given your number by Miss Sarapee at KAVRU."

"Hmm. I see. What can I do?" The English, Oxford or Cambridge accent was obvious.

"I'm a lecturer at Bristol University but here in Bangkok - just a short stay with my new wife - we're on our honeymoon. I teach British and Social Economic History - a particular interest in population control - in fact I help run the UK end of the Malthus Society. Can I ask if you're the Solomon who occasionally puts a message up on our site?"

Solomon sounded unsure. "I have been known to."

"Then - it's just a big co-incidence - but I was talking to a virologist a week ago and he mentioned your name. Said he thought you might be working in Thailand where we were heading. Name of Guy Williams. Know him?"

"Ah, yes," Solomon still sounded as if he really wanted to switch his phone off. "Uh, how did you meet Guy?"

"On the Nile, we were on a cruise. Jumped off at a place somewhere down river. We were having lunch at a hotel where the cruise boats stop. Seems he works close by. We got talking over gin and tonics. I told him about my interest in population control. He said I should speak to you - you were the expert."

"Did he now? Did he give you this phone number?"

292

"Oh no, as I said I got it from KAVRU but I knew you were a virologist like Guy and the only place I could find on the internet was KAVRU. Sheer chance." Daniel tried a short laugh.

There was a definite pause from Solomon. It sounded to Daniel as if he was moving about. He heard what he thought was a waitress saying how much a bill was and then Solomon mutter something as if he had just paid.

"So - I'm so sorry to bother you," Daniel continued in an apologetic, English sort of way, "But I'm writing an article on Thomas Malthus and Paul Eyrlich for a magazine. Nice way to spend a honeymoon you might say. Ha! But Guy said you were an expert - especially on the environmental side of the argument. Any chance of a quick cup of coffee if you're in Bangkok? I'd really appreciate it."

"Sorry, I'm far too busy just at the moment. "

"Shame," said Daniel. "Are you in Bangkok?"

"Yes, but I'm just too busy."

"But you're an expert. Why the hell aren't population control methods enforced. No-one even wants to talk about it. The world is grossly overpopulated but I can't even get my MP back in Bristol to raise it in Parliament. Look at Bangkok, for Christ's sake, you can hardly walk on the footpath out there for traders trying to scrape a living and a million tourists from God knows where. The place is packed."

"Yes," Solomon said, "I agree. Malthus saw it coming more than two hundred years ago. But you're right. If a politician even raises the subject of enforced population control it's a quick route to political suicide."

"But something's got to happen," pursued Daniel with a sudden passion for the subject. "Look at Africa, look at world food and water shortages, the fighting over land and mineral resources. You ever been to Cairo? It's worse than Bangkok. And just look at the unemployment rates in Europe now. There are no jobs, there is no hope, there is no......."

"Yes, you're right," interrupted Solomon and Daniel thought he heard a chair being scraped up as if Solomon was sitting down again. "The UK Science Minister once said that synthetic biology could fuel us, heal us and feed us. He might be right but it's not the full solution - there are still too many of us."

"So what can be done?" asked Daniel.

"Enforced population control. We can tailor make living cells to act like electronic circuits, we could make synthetic plant leaves to produce fuel, we can

293

do anything we like with bioengineering. But everything is pointless if the population continues to grow like it is. There will be no quality of life for those that biology itself gives birth to."

"You are so right," said Daniel. "But it's all back to politicians again isn't it?"

"Of course," said Solomon, "The problem is self-interested politicians and their short-term thinking. They do not understand science and they survive on maintaining total public ignorance. They deny them the facts and do nothing because they are too afraid of infringing the modern laws they've invented. Human rights is a good example. But is it a human right to live like overcrowded rats in a cage. And even when science can resolve the problems of food shortages, they deny scientists the right to exploit what they know. The EU has not even approved a new genetically modified crop for cultivation for nearly twenty years. What sort of message does that send?

"As you will know as a lecturer in economic history, economists such as Thomas Sowell and Walter Williams have argued that poverty and famine are caused by bad government and bad economic policies, not by overpopulation. They are right but the two go hand in hand. Overpopulation makes political and economic management totally impossible. The people themselves are selfish - they expect improvements in their own lifetime not in the next generation."

It was already clear to Daniel that Solomon was on a roll. He had touched a nerve. The one thing that was driving Solomon's daily thoughts and daily actions was just this subject. He needed to keep Solomon talking for as long as possible.

"Yes," Daniel said, "I recently re-read the old Henry Kissinger reports for the National Security Council. You recall it?"

"Sure," Solomon said, "And much more recently than that was David Pimentel's research at Cornell where he states that the Earth can support a population of two billion individuals, but only if all individuals are willing to live at a European standard of living and use natural resources sustainably. They also stated that reducing population from today's 6.8 billion to 2 billion would take more than 100 years and that was if every couple, worldwide, agreed to produce an average of only one child. Direct action is absolutely necessary. We cannot wait for politicians."

"I totally agree," said Daniel. "Even in the UK we've got people like David Attenborough and Jonathan Porritt saying exactly the same. Did you know that the Malthus Society website now has several thousand signed up members?"

"Yes, I know," said Solomon. "We need to use these members to help us spread the message."

Being done, thought Daniel, wondering how Kevin's friend Tunje was getting on in Nigeria.

"In 1968, Garrett Hardin proposed relinquishing the freedom to breed," went on Solomon. "He said we are breeding ourselves into oblivion. How right. But still we see no action."

"And what about Jeffrey Sachs?" asked Daniel, now rapidly reading some notes he'd made over the last few weeks. "Didn't he call his 2007 Reith Lecture, 'Bursting at the Seams'?"

"But then look at the opposition - the Roman Catholic Church," said Solomon seemingly now getting quite angry. "Each of the Popes talks about solving poverty and yet they argue against contraception. But if they checked their accounts instead of cooking them and had a genuine understanding of what it means to be poor, they'd find they've got enough money to help solve all the problems they get so upset about."

"Yes, it's all about money, "agreed Daniel wondering how long he could keep this up.

"Money and technology will solve the problem, mark my words," said Solomon. "But we need more scientists as political leaders. We urgently need to reduce the population by around fifty percent. What did you say your name was?"

"Ian McCann," said Daniel.

"Listen, I've got to go. Nice speaking to you. Have a nice honeymoon."

"Thanks," said Daniel, "I hope we meet sometime."

Seven o'clock, Bangkok time and Daniel and Anna were eating at the roadside close to their hotel. Daniel was still desperate to know if Solomon's phone had been tracked. Finally, Colin phoned with the news.

"We've tracked it to Soi 11, Sukhumvit. I don't know Bangkok, Daniel, but I've looked at a Google map of the area and it looks like a busy area. Am I right?"

"Oh yes," said Daniel and looked at Anna. They were sitting in Soi 11. Their hotel was also in Soi 11. They had just walked the full length of Soi 11 looking for somewhere to eat. "It's busy - bars, cafes, restaurants, hotels. I can vouch for that. And where are we with Interpol?"

"I'm expecting to hear that a Red notice is going out within the hour for GOB. That was requested by Washington. That means that, if he is in Thailand, then the Thai Police can issue a formal arrest warrant and begin the search with a view to extradition. It's paperwork, Daniel but things are moving fast - frustrating but fast."

"And Solomon?" asked Daniel.

"Mm," said Colin. "He's proving more difficult. Interpol action hinges on the problem you already highlighted - what's he actually done? The definition of his crime. Has he committed one? Is he a terrorism threat? I'm getting asked for real evidence all the time. This is the head scratching that's going on. But, believe me, Daniel, it's our report they're using. They no longer suspect we are cranks. And someone has spoken to Virex and Biox and discovered what we knew all along - Solomon worked for them and disappeared along with more of Virex's research material. They've come clean. They've had to. And I suspect you might not get chased by Charles Brady for a while. He's both embarrassed and worried about his company's reputation and the implications for him personally."

"So, for Solomon, until we get more information, I suspect we might end up with a Blue Notice - a so-called request for additional information about a person in relation to a crime. Virex might press charges but, without much more evidence, I don't see that as on a scale needing Interpol."

"So, yet another reason why I need to continue to check Solomon out, Colin."

"Yes," agreed Colin. "And WHO have also sprung to life which might help to nail him. This is all Larry's doing. He's been putting pressure on them through Senator Collis and the US Department of Health. Pressure is being applied to clarify the source of the outbreaks in Thailand and Nigeria. But they are struggling because, without direct evidence that this is a laboratory engineered virus that has either escaped or has been deliberately released, they are unwilling to say. Larry thinks they are beginning to suspect that what he's been telling them for several weeks is true. And I suspect the WHO are fully aware of our report as well - it's gone that high.

"And if you've not had enough different colour notices for one day, how about an Interpol Orange Notice? We're trying it. This warns police and other international organisations about potential threats from disguised weapons or other dangerous materials. No-one knows whether lethal Influenza viruses being shipped around under uncontrolled conditions fit into this category."

Colin stopped. "So - enough to go on with? And, by the way, where are you?" he added.

"Soi 11, Sukhumvit, Colin. It's where half the world seems to hang out. Co-incidence or what?"

"Christ," said Colin. "I call that convenient. Just you go careful young man."

CHAPTER 74

Daniel had been listening to Colin but also watching something on the other side of the road. A small hotel opposite that Daniel knew specialised in short stays for those frequenting the many bars nearby had a terrace that faced directly onto the narrow street and mostly served beer. Two men were sat at the back, both facing the hotel so only their backs were visible. But one of them, the younger one had just turned around.

"Colin, thanks for the advice but something has just cropped up. I'll phone you later."

Daniel only had time to hear Colin in London saying, "Daniel - think what happened to Jimmy," before he switched the phone off and turned to Anna.

"Anna, go back to the hotel. Stay there until I call you. Any problems, call Colin. OK?"

"But what is it, Daniel?"

"Over there," Daniel said, pointing only with his eyes. "That's David Solomon and if I'm not mistaken the back of the head belongs to Greg O'Brian."

"But Daniel, what are you going to do?" asked Anna.

"Just watch them - see where they go."

"Then what?" It was, as usual, a good question. Daniel looked at her.

"I don't know," he admitted, "It's what I always used to do before I had you sitting beside me. I need your sensible questions, Anna. I said it before, you are good for me. But it's what I still do. It's my job. At the moment I can't get it out of my system, but I'll change. I want to change."

"Then change now. I am afraid for you, Daniel."

Daniel was not familiar with public demonstrations of affection and such a thing was rarely, if ever, seen on the streets of Bangkok. But Daniel suddenly wanted to reach out to Anna, pull her towards him and kiss her. Instead, he held out his hand, pulled hers towards him and held her warm fingers to his lips. It was enough. Anna smiled. "OK, I'll go back to the hotel and wait. Please don't be long."

With that she pushed her chair back, got up and walked away.

Daniel continued to sit and watch the two men. Unnoticed by anyone, he took a few photos on his phone. The phone flashed but was lost amongst the people, the myriad of coloured lights, motorcycles, taxis, shops, sounds and night-time mayhem that was Sukhumvit Soi 11.

The two men were too far away for any detail so Daniel decided to get closer. He paid for Anna's and his meal, got up and walked across to the open air bar, mounted the two steps and was welcomed by a girl in tight jeans and tee shirt. She beckoned him to sit at the front overlooking the street but Daniel declined, ordered a beer and moved into the darker area at the back, two tables away from Solomon and O'Brian. It was clearly O'Brian. There was no doubt about it. The same refusal to wear anything too casual. It was the same dark suit and although the tie was now missing, the same white shirt. But Daniel needed to be careful. O'Brian had seen him twice now. Daniel may have changed his name but not his appearance.

Solomon was wearing a white tee shirt with an apple printed on the front with some words that Daniel could not read. Two half-full bottles of beer lay on the table between them.

GOB was talking, quietly almost inaudibly. Perhaps, Daniel thought, he could detect his deep voice, and the Irish American accent but it was still too far away and the noise from the street too loud. Solomon was nodding, gesticulating. Then he seemed to demonstrate something - he opened his mouth, put something imaginary to his lips and moved his thumb. To Daniel it could only be a demonstration of how to use an asthma inhaler. GOB looked around. Solomon sat back. Solomon then sat forward again and pointed down the street. GOB nodded and said something. Then he picked up his bottle of beer, drained it and wiped his mouth. Solomon did the same. They got up, pushing the two chairs back. Solomon beckoned the waitress in tight jeans, spoke to her and handed over some money. GOB had meanwhile sauntered out onto the street where he was waiting.

Daniel then beckoned the same waitress, paid his bill and watched, ready to move.

Solomon and GOB started to walk up the road away from the main Sukhumvit Road. Daniel followed, one minute on the crowded pavement, then between parked motorcycles and then back into the middle of the road. At 8pm Soi 11 was, as usual, crowded, busy and noisy. At the end of the street the two men turned right and then left and the sound of Soi 11 became fainter, the street darker and the pavement rougher and narrow. But tuk tuks and motorcycles still passed by, short cutting from somewhere to somewhere else.

As Daniel slowed to stay further back, the two men disappeared to the right. Daniel quickened his pace and found a hidden entrance to an apartment block and a concreted parking area surrounded by grass, shrubs and trees. The block was much lower in comparison to others in the area and looked older. Daniel slipped between two shrubs and watched as Solomon and O'Brian walked up to a glassed front door that opened automatically. Behind the tinted glass, Daniel could now see a hallway and a reception desk on the left. A man stood up from behind the desk and said something to Solomon. Then the door closed.

Daniel retraced his steps to the street outside again, looked back and saw lights come on behind blinds covering two windows on the top floor.

Beside him, half hidden by the shrubs, was a sign in English: "Apartments for Sale or Rent" with a phone number. It was an idea he'd used before if he needed to go inside somewhere and have a look around. But not now. He decided to hang around a while to see if there were any movements. There was a small gathering of tuk tuks touting for business at the end of the road if he needed to go anywhere in a hurry. And so it turned out.

As Daniel watched the windows on the top floor, the lights behind one of them suddenly went out. A minute later, Solomon and O'Brian appeared at the doorway. Solomon was carrying a large, heavy-looking cardboard box. The two men then walked to a Honda car parked under the trees in the corner and Solomon put the box in the boot. O'Brian stood, watched and lit a cigarette. Solomon then returned to the apartment and, after a minute or so, the second light went out and he returned with a an identical box, which he carried to the car and put in the boot. O'Brian just stood and watched.

Assuming they were about to drive off somewhere, Daniel glanced in the direction of the tuk tuks to see if he might need to use one. But instead, the two men stood alongside the car as if waiting. Solomon was using his phone. The call lasted just a few seconds. O'Brian was now on his second cigarette.

Less than five minutes later, another car drove along the road past the tuk tuks, and past where Daniel was standing in the shadows. It drove into the apartment car park and stopped right next to Solomon and O'Brian.

In poor light or complete darkness, the one colour that shows up, as Jimmy had once reminded him, was white. The man that got out of the second car was an

Arab, dressed in a long white gallabiya. In Thailand, the sight of Arabs and Africans in traditional clothing had once been rare. But in Sukhumvit Road between Soi 1 and 11 it was now a common occurrence. One or two streets now resembled Cairo with shoe shops, clothing, crafts, money changers and Lebanese and Egyptian restaurants. But could this be the Arab connection that had been missing?

Little or nothing was spoken between the three men. Solomon raised the car boot lid, lifted out the boxes he had only just put there and, as the Arab held the rear passenger door of his car open, the boxes were transferred. Then there was a brief hand shake, the Arab got into the car and drove off past Daniel. Daniel walked quickly towards a tuk tuk and asked the driver to follow the car.

But the distance it travelled was short and quick. It took less than ten minutes for the car to find its way into another congested and busy street running parallel with Soi 11. They were now in the heart of the Arab quarter, a street Daniel knew well and the one that had blossomed into something resembling Casablanca or Cairo.

The car stopped right outside a fully lit Arab pharmacy. Daniel paid off his tuk tuk driver and watched as the Arab abandoned his car where it was, got out, went around to the passenger door, opened it and then beckoned to someone sitting just inside the pharmacy doorway. A teenaged Arab boy came out and, one by one, carried the two boxes inside as the man watched. Job done, the Arab got back in his car.

But it was the boxes themselves that now caught Daniel's eye. Standing, less than ten metres away, he could see they were specially designed boxes marked with the words "Clinical Samples - Refrigerated - Do not open until final destination," printed in red.

Daniel was no novice in the business of transporting cargoes of every conceivable type whether by sea or air. His business often depended on understanding international shipping regulations. By understanding them he could then recognise attempts to bypass them. And he also knew it was easy to mark boxes so that they scared the living daylights out of handlers, whether they were customs and excise officials or your local mail delivery man. But the survival of good, legitimate businesses sending hazardous materials by air or sea was always at stake. They were often overly cautious.

Not so rogue companies. And this was a rogue organisation with everything to lose by compliance with regulations. They would break every rule in the book to ensure their illicit goods got through. So Daniel did not believe that the contents of the two boxes were simple, clinical samples. But by labelling them "do not open until final destination" it virtually guaranteed security until the goods were handed over to whoever was expecting them. Paperwork, however false, that accompanied the boxes would see to the rest.

So what sort of biological materials needed constant refrigeration? Vaccines? Live viruses? And where had the boxes just come from? An apartment block.

Daniel, unsure whether to follow the Arab or watch the pharmacy, decided, for the moment, to follow the Arab. And by the time the car had been turned around in the narrow street to face the way it had just come, Daniel had already re-booked the same tuk tuk driver.

"You want to follow that crazy Arab again?"

"Yes," said Daniel. "Don't lose him."

"This a crazy road, Mister," the tuk tuk driver said as he revved his engine. "Many things go on here. But good business. Lot of money here."

They followed the car out onto Sukhumvit Road where it had to turn left. It went past Soi 11 and, according to Daniel's estimate, turned up Soi 17 or 19 and almost immediately disappeared into the underground car park of a hotel.

Daniel paid off his driver for the second time, walked into the hotel, picked up a copy of the Bangkok Post and sat down. And he didn't have to wait long for the door to the hotel's underground car park to open. The Arab walked in, his car keys in one hand, beads in the other. He went to reception, took a key and then headed for the lift. The lift stopped on Floor 6.

It may have been pure luck or professional instinct, but Daniel put his newspaper down went to the reception and said. "I think I just saw Mr Mohamed Kader arrive. I was reading my paper and didn't notice. He is on the 6th Floor. Can you just tell me if that was him?"

"Yes sir, room 604."

Daniel thanked him and returned to his seat to ponder on his next move.

With all three main characters currently in Bangkok it was looking almost certain that Thailand was the centre of operations. And it was looking more and more certain that Solomon had some sort of facility in Thailand that he was using for his work. But where was it? It was very unlikely that KAVRO was the place although he may well have access to certain of its facilities, especially if he was regarded as an expert who was welcomed to the unit from time to time to lecture or teach its technicians. And it was also unlikely to be a University or the Science Park although, again, there was a possibility he had access to some facilities there. Perhaps this was his reason for keeping the innocent girlfriend, Pim.

And the apartment? Was this Solomon's Bangkok home that also served as a storage facility? Or even a laboratory?

And Kader? This was what made Daniel smile behind his newspaper. At last, he had found him. Questions still remained about the other Arab names but at present, Daniel wasn't sure how to solve that one.

And O'Brian? Where was he staying tonight? Daniel felt he needed to be in three places at the same time. And what was in those boxes? Despite Mohamed Kader being upstairs, there was no point in sitting there. He decided to return to the pharmacy and maybe ask a few questions. He'd walk. The walk would do him good and Anna was only two blocks away. He wouldn't be long.

It was nearly 10pm but the Arab Pharmacy with its illuminated Arabic sign above was still open. From outside, Daniel saw the teenage boy still sitting on a stool talking to an older, Egyptian-looking man behind the counter. Daniel wandered in and went up to the counter. The teenage boy got off his stool and nodded politely.

"Is this Mohamed Kader's Pharmacy?" he asked.

"Yes," said the older man behind the counter. "Mr Kader owns it but it is called Shah Pharmacy."

"Ah, yes," said Daniel "I was not able to read the Arab sign outside and I have not been here before."

"Can I help you sir?"

"Yes, I was looking for a man called Mohamed El Badry."

"Mr El Badry is in Egypt."

"Doctor Al Khoury? Is he here?"

"He is also in Egypt. Can I help you sir?"

"No, never mind," said Daniel. "Thank you for your help." He turned to go but then turned back. My friend David Solomon told me Mohamed Kader was in Bangkok."

"Yes, sir. He is here. And Mr Solomon was here earlier. Are you in the business as well?"

"Yes," Daniel said wondering if he could now engage the man in a longer conversation with a string of plausible lies - lies that he had been inventing during his short walk along Sukhumvit Road. "My name is Ian McCann. I arrived here this morning from Singapore. I am with Shah Medical - Mr Kader's Singapore company."

"Oh yes, sir. Mr Kader is going to Singapore tomorrow afternoon."

"Yes," said Daniel, as if he was well aware of this. "Do you know if he delivered the two boxes here this evening?"

"Yes, sir. We will be sending them to Shah Medical Singapore tomorrow morning."

"Thank you," said Daniel. "That will save me asking Mr Solomon." Then, as if as an afterthought he added, "And Mr O'Brian, from America, is he here?"

The older man looked confused. "Mr O'Brian? No sir, we have no-one of that name."

That proved another suspicion. That GOB either operated under different names or kept himself well separated from the monotony of routine, day to day business.

"Bloody nerve if he keeps changing his name, though," said Daniel to himself. "Thank you very much," he said aloud and walked away wondering whether any Thai policeman or any other policeman on an Interpol investigation could have got away with what he just had.

But, while he waited for the Interpol process to catch up Daniel wanted to stay ahead and if that meant going to Singapore, then that is where he intended to go. But, times had changed recently. In the past, if he decided to do something, then he just went ahead and did it. Now? Well, just telling Anna what he was going to do would probably not be enough. Anna would need a better explanation.

And so, too, would Colin. Colin had already advised him to back off and let the process of international policing take its course. But he already had another bit of work for Colin. Tracking and intercepting a small cargo of refrigerated biological specimens that might well be live Malthus A virus ready to distribute around the world was going to be an interesting challenge and especially so if Interpol Singapore or Thailand still hadn't received their red, blue or orange notices.

Daniel rejoined Anna in their hotel room and told her what he'd just found out and what his plan was.

"But Daniel, what are you going to do when you get to Singapore?"

It was the second time she had asked a similar question that evening. The first time, Daniel had eventually admitted he didn't know but he had since thought about it and now knew why. "It's the way I am, Anna. I always finish a job. I cannot leave a job unfinished."

"But you promised you'd change, Daniel. For me. You said it. "

"Yes," Daniel said, "I will change. But I'm still in the middle of a job that started before.....before I said we'd....... I need to finish it, Anna. Then we'll go back to London and start a different life."

"But I am still very afraid, Daniel."

"Yes, I know, Anna. But you can help by staying here. I'll phone you and you can always talk to Colin. And there's a job you can do to help if you are willing."

"What is that?"

"Go and check out the apartment that Solomon uses. It's got a sign outside saying Apartments for Sale or Rent. Go and have a look. See if you can find out anything."

Anna gave a small smile. "OK." She said, "But don't be long. What time are you going to Singapore?"

"First thing. I need to be there before Solomon, Kader and GOB arrive."

CHAPTER 75

Daniel was in the arrivals hall at Changi Airport in Singapore when his phone rang with the first piece of bad news. It was Anna.

"Daniel, please listen. I went to the apartment where Solomon lives as you asked me to. You said everyone was going to Singapore. But they are not, Daniel. Solomon is still here. I saw him in the car park at the apartment block. He was with GOB and an Arab man, maybe it was Kader because he was wearing a long white robe like you described to me. And..........."

Anna's breathless voice tailed off. "What is it Anna," Daniel said.

"There were two other men in our hotel this morning. They both looked Arab to me but they wore normal clothes, so I don't know. When I got back from the apartment, they were standing at reception. I heard them ask if Daniel Capelli was staying at the hotel. The receptionist checked and said no. But they didn't go. They stood by the reception desk talking on the telephone. Then I heard them ask if Ian McCann was staying here. That's you, Daniel - sometimes. The receptionist said no. Then they asked if David Franklin was staying here. That's you again, Daniel - sometimes. The receptionist said yes but she wasn't allowed to tell them our room number. They then stood and telephoned again. I immediately went up to our room, packed everything and moved out. I didn't pay the bill, Daniel. I am very worried. "

"Don't worry about the bill, Anna. That's the least concern. We'll sort it. But......." he paused. "Where are you?"

"I am in a taxi. I am going to my old apartment to leave our things, maybe stay there a while. Why don't you come back, Daniel. I am very worried. They know about you. Somehow they know you are in Bangkok. What name did you use at the pharmacy last night? I think that is it. I tried to phone Colin but it is night time and his phone is not on. What shall we do?"

"Stay in the apartment, Anna. I'll come back as soon as I can."

Daniel swore at himself. Then he got up and walked in circles. He'd made a mistake. No question about it. The luck had run out. Colin and Anna had both been right. He should have handed everything over to the authorities to deal with. After all, he, Colin, Larry, Kevin and Tom had all done enough. Let Interpol, the Thai police, the Singapore police or whoever deal with it. But he was an impatient person. He made his own decisions, sometimes they were hasty because he disliked officialdom and bureaucracy. He had always been like that but had always been successful. Daniel Capelli always did things himself - alone.

So where were the police? Had they got their Red Notices yet? And what was the decision on Solomon and Kader. Had they been red noticed as well? So had it been a bad decision to go to Singapore? Yes and no. If he'd stayed in Bangkok at that hotel, the consequences for both himself and Anna were unknown. Who were the men who had turned up? For a few minutes, Daniel was unsure what to do.

But then he phoned the British Embassy and asked to speak to Caroline Mason.

"Caroline, it's Rupert."

"Rupert, dear, back so soon. Missed me?"

"Yes," admitted Daniel to avoid any of the usual, time-wasting female analysis if he'd said no. "Listen I'm in a spot of bother."

"Mm, that's not like you, Rupert. Always in charge. What's up and where are you?"

"Changi. The airport. I arrived an hour ago but I may have to fly back to Bangkok again on the next available."

"Busy man, eh?"

"Yes but this morning I'm a man with a problem, Caroline. I didn't know who else to turn to."

"So you immediately phone Aunty Caroline. What can Aunty do?"

"You remember Shah Medicals?"

"Yes, naught little David Chua. Did you meet him last time?"

"Yes I did and he's involved in something big and very complicated - so complicated that Interpol have got involved. It'll take me hours to explain everything Caroline so you'll just need to listen to me and believe what I'm about to tell you. But we've got everything here - counterfeit medicines, fraud on an international scale and a plot to deliberately spread a flu virus that has been engineered specifically to kill - some would call it bioterrorism. It's all being run and financed by a small group of rich individuals - relative unknowns operating like the mafia."

"Good Lord, and you are involved?"

"Involved in as much as I'm trying to stop it, get people arrested and mostly intercept a consignment of what I think might be live flu virus coming into Singapore this morning destined for Shah Medicals."

"That'll explain Singapore 2100 then, Rupert. I checked them out - it's an underground group committed to reducing Singapore's population before the island suddenly becomes so top heavy with high rises it tilts over and topples into the sea."

"Yes, and make a tidy profit to those that survive a pandemic, Caroline. Have you had your Malthus A vaccination yet?"

"Never heard of it, Rupert. Is it like bird flu?"

"Well put it this way, Caroline, and in a nutshell. Tests by what, for want of a better name, I'll call the Malthus gang in Nigeria gave rise to one hundred deaths. The guy behind the technology is British, a world renown virologist and whose hobby is to see the world population reduced by fifty percent. And his financial backers are the New York and Egyptian mafia."

Daniel knew his description was colourful but it was not inaccurate and it was said to ensure Caroline took him seriously. And neither did he give her a chance to respond.

"Now listen, Caroline, the UK and US governments have become aware of this. I assume someone in the British Embassy here knows. The Ambassador? I don't know. Whoever it is, I need you to talk to them and tell them you've spoken to me because of the commercial link. Tell them to take it seriously and let me know what's going on. WHO are also starting to wake up. But as far as Interpol is concerned the Singapore police should by now have received a red notice to arrest at least one individual - a guy called Greg O'Brian. But there are several, if not many others involved here as well, including - wittingly or unwittingly - your little friend David Chua.

"But the immediate priority, Caroline, is to intercept a couple of boxes that are being air-freighted into Singapore today. They may even be here already. They are marked as hazardous and not to be opened until final destination. That final destination is Shah Medicals.

"Have you got all that, Caroline?" He ended. "Because I need to get back to Bangkok right now."

"Yes," said Caroline. "I always said I'd drop everything for you, Rupert. But, seriously, yes, I understand. I now see what you were up to a few weeks ago when you were here and I know you well enough to realise this is serious. I'll try to speak to the Ambassador and others right away and we'll check with the Singapore police. How can I get hold of you?"

Daniel gave Caroline his mobile phone number and also the phone number of Colin in London. Right now, he needed to book a flight back to Bangkok and speak to Colin.

By the time Daniel got through to Colin he was in the departures lounge ready to board a Thai Airlines flight back to Bangkok. But before he could speak, Colin had a lot to say.

"You should be proud of that new wife-to-be of yours Daniel, my friend. I've just spoken to her. She's worried about you. She's updated me on your antics last night. Yes, good news about finding Solomon's hide-out and the two boxes going to Singapore but clearly something's gone wrong because we're all being targeted now."

"What do you mean?"

"Well let me give you the first bit of bad news. Wait for it.......... Jimmy's dead."

"Oh no. Oh Christ," said Daniel and put his head in his hands. There was a pause from both men. Then: "How, where, when?" asked Daniel.

"His body was found hidden in a hut at a campsite in the National Park outside Nairobi. He had been shot. It was Louise who told me. Since then I've been onto the Kenyan police direct. And, by the way, the red notice for GOB has gone out. It went out a few hours ago. That still leaves half a dozen or more on the loose out there - Lunneau, Kader, Solomon amongst them. But for Jimmy it's too late."

"I'm so sorry," said Daniel, "I blame myself for pushing him right at the end."

"Yes," Colin said, "You push everyone, including yourself. Don't push Anna. Do you hear me? She's too good to be tied up in all this shit and yet you have involved her. You asked her to do something this morning."

Colin was right. Daniel knew it.

"And you know what, my friend?" Colin continued, "Right now, she's scared. But she's standing by you because, for some reason, she only sees the good side of you. I've seen all your sides - the good, the bad and the downright foolish risk-taker over the years. Now let me give you another bit of bad news." Colin paused.

"They got too much out of Jimmy before and after he was shot - his mobile phone, his wallet and even his note book. Did you not know that Jimmy, despite his style that always reminded me of Will Smith in a comedy role, was very well organised - too well organised. I told him many times not to carry it around. But the notebook had a lot of names in it including two versions of you, the David Franklin one and the Daniel Capelli one. So GOB knows about you. And they already knew about Asher and Asher, of course, which means me. Now, as you know, I've crossed swords with GOB before. I do not want to be garden forked just yet - do you get my drift?"

"Yes," said Daniel feeling as if he was receiving an Anna-style lecture.

"And the third big problem, my friend, is Anna. Unfortunately, she was seen in the car park of Solomon's apartment block by three people and, from her description, I guess the three people were Solomon, Kader and GOB. They definitely saw her because she had a little accident in the car park and broke a heel on the shoe she was wearing. The concrete needed repairing.

"Now ladies do not always make the best detectives, Daniel, unless properly attired and properly briefed. And Solomon, despite his desire to eliminate half the world population, appears to have a very old-fashioned, gentlemanly side because he rushed to her aid. But he was not quick enough because Anna fled into the street and jumped into a tuk tuk. If that wasn't enough to ring alarm bells with GOB and Kader then I don't know what was.

"So, as a previously successful, self-employed, one-man-band small business for the last fifteen years - I suggest you either stay like that or remember all of this when you next decide to employ others - whether black African male, Thai female or any other nationality. Got it?"

"Yes."

"Now. Next thing. Anna told you she only saw two people at your hotel but there was a third sat outside in a car and I have a horrible suspicion that it was GOB. How do I know this? Anna told me. She roughly described this third man to me, but bear in mind she'd only seen the back of his ugly neck as you sat having dinner last night. She didn't tell you because she didn't want to worry you and because you were already in Singapore. Are you starting to understand this woman of yours Daniel?"

"Yes," said Daniel.

"Now, you need to get back to Bangkok ASAP, right? Go straight to see Anna. You are no longer a sad creature, a lonely, single item who thinks only of himself. You are a partnership. So no bloody detours because of a sudden whim or because you've had another of your bloody hunches - accurate though they often are.

"My concern is, and knowing how GOB operates, he may already have seen Anna exit the hotel in a hurry carrying your new, larger, shared suitcase. He may have had her followed. He may have followed her himself. He may, with luck, have lost her taxi in a Bangkok traffic jam and so still be looking for her but.....are you getting my message, Daniel? If he can't get you, he'll get the next best thing."

"Yes," said Daniel, "My flight has just been last-called."

"Then call Anna and me as soon as you get back."

"Thanks, Colin. And I really am so sorry about Jimmy. But - just one other thing from my side - I've spoken to the British Embassy and they now know about Shah Medicals. They are going to try to get the Singapore police or customs to intercept the two boxes."

"Yes, I know. Well done, Daniel. But I've already spoken to someone called Caroline Mason. She phoned me. Now fuck off."

CHAPTER 76

Anna was busy in her apartment that she had not lived in for several weeks. It was just as she had left it to fly to Singapore with Daniel. Cobwebs had already appeared and, as always when the apartment had not been lived in for a while, the tiled floor was littered with dead bugs that had found their way through the loose fitting mosquito netting. She swept it, mopped it and folded clothes that she had left to dry weeks ago. But she had not touched the suitcase she shared with Daniel and had rushed to pack at the hotel. She thought that when Daniel arrived they might move out again, perhaps into another hotel so she needed to be ready.

Anna had felt safer after her second long phone conversation with Colin and had tried phoning Daniel again but his phone was engaged.

By early afternoon she was feeling hungry and knowing that Daniel would be back in Bangkok in a few hours, she decided to venture outside and buy something to eat on the street. Wearing just the pair of shorts and tee shirt she had put on to clean the stiflingly hot apartment, she picked up the small handbag that held little more than her purse, passport and ID card, put on a pair of cheap rubber flip-flops, shut the door, pocketed the key and then made her way down the double flight of stairs to the ground floor.

It was a shadowy movement by the main entrance that stopped her. The stairwell she had just come down was dark, sometimes too dark, but the outside was bathed in bright, hot sun. She had already past the bottom step but had not yet reached the empty office and store room for brushes, mops and buckets that were used for cleaning the communal areas when she saw the man. He had been looking in at the entrance but as soon as Anna appeared from the darkness, he vanished. Anna stopped, her heart pounding.

Then she turned and started to run back up the stairs. As she reached the first landing she heard someone coming up the stairs behind her. Anna ran up the next flight and by the time she reached the top corridor, she knew the person following her was already on the first landing. Anna ran as fast as she could, past her own apartment door to the end of the corridor and the rusty fire escape. She pushed open the metal fire door and slammed it behind her still hearing the person behind her. She ran down the steep spiral steps, jumped over the iron gate at the bottom and raced around the side of the apartment block. Then she ran, still clutching her handbag, towards an alleyway lined with refuse bins that she knew led onto the main road. There she stopped just momentarily to look behind her. A man in jeans and tee shirt was already at the bottom of the steps, over the gate and standing on the corner of the apartment block. Seeing Anna, he started running towards her.

Anna turned and ran into the main road. Without checking for traffic she ran straight across the road, jumped over the central traffic barrier and ran further up on the other side. She stopped again and looked. The man was waiting to cross the road but he clearly saw her. He suddenly dashed across between a taxi and a truck and jumped the barrier. Anna didn't wait any longer. She ran, without once looking back, she headed for a junction, ran left, crossed that road and totally out of breath, stopped and stood in a shop doorway. There was no sign of the man now but that was not enough for Anna. She was now very frightened. She waited there until she saw a taxi coming with a red light in its windscreen, came out from the doorway, beckoned the taxi to stop and jumped in.

An hour later, Anna was still sat in the same taxi but now in the Bus Terminal where buses headed north and west out of Bangkok. If need be, Anna had decided, she would head home to her parent's home in Kanchanaburi and wait for Daniel. Nothing was going to keep her in Bangkok until it felt safe.

She was worried about Daniel and whether someone might be waiting for him when he stepped off the plane from Singapore in the next half an hour. Should she wait until he had landed and she could talk to him or head for Kanchanaburi right now?

Anna sat there, with only her handbag and some money and still wearing only shorts, tee shirt and flip flops. She was also, now, increasingly confused - not about Daniel but about what this whole investigation was about. She had enjoyed parts of it. She had loved her visit to London and had made many new Thai friends. But other parts still confused her because she didn't fully understand everything.

She trusted Colin and had liked Larry from America and Kevin and the old man Tom. She had listened to the discussion and had followed much of it but not all. And she didn't feel as if she was alone in that respect. Kevin had looked particularly confused. He had hardly said anything but mostly listened.

She had read about and watched movies about the mafia and Chinese gangs and so on, so it was not the discussions about fraud and murder by the man called

GOB. The part that confused her still was the discussion about Flu. She had no conception of what a virus looked like. It was a tiny thing that got stuck in your nose and throat and gave you a cold. That she understood. But she did not understand Daniel when he started taking about virus engineering, about changing and designing viruses. It seemed impossible. And when he used phrases like - what was it - gain of function research, it was way beyond her. Daniel had tried to explain but she still didn't fully understand.

But that, according to Daniel, was what David Solomon did. The English man who had wanted to help her when she broke the heel of her shoe, the handsome man with the fair hair and blue eyes, was a clever man who looked down microscopes and picked viruses up, moved them about, changed them and made them do things they were not supposed to do. Many clever scientists could do this but Solomon did it to kill thousands of people because he thought the world was overcrowded. Daniel had tried to explain it simply.

"A virus is like joined up pieces of Lego, Anna," he had said.

"But a virus is very, very small and it looks like nothing you've ever seen before with your eyes. Viruses come in thousands of different shapes and sizes and they grow inside you and make millions and millions of copies, identical to themselves.

"But Solomon plays with these viruses just as if they were pieces of Lego. He picks out one brick, puts in another or changes its colour, then he looks at it and sees what this new piece of Lego can do. If you want to and you are clever enough you can make a piece of virus Lego that causes diseases for which there is no medicine, no cure. Someone who catches this virus will die.

"That is what Solomon is doing," Daniel had said. "It's called 'gain of function' research and some people say it should be stopped or at least properly controlled. Gain of function means you can change a virus to make it do something it was not naturally designed for.

"Solomon has changed an influenza virus into a new one that he calls Malthus A. Malthus A can kill millions of people just like past diseases like plague killed millions. Why has he done it? Because he thinks there are too many people.

"You might ask why not just use big bombs instead like other terrorists? Well, the police are always looking for terrorists with guns and bombs. They don't look for viruses."

Anna thought she understood but she definitely understood why GOB and Kader were involved. Daniel had explained that as well.

312

"Solomon's work takes time and money. He needs a place to work and special equipment. GOB and Kader are giving him the money. But GOB and Kader will get all their money back again when the virus is released and people fall sick because they will then sell medicines - medicines that work and medicines that don't."

As Anna sat there on the hard concrete seat wondering what to do, she felt a sudden longing to be with Daniel. She wanted him there with her right now. It was Daniel who had discovered this problem. It was Daniel who had persevered with it and taken the risks and it was Daniel, with Colin, Larry and the others, who had made the governments in America and the UK sit up and listen. And what was it Daniel had been waiting for before he decided to wait no longer and go to Singapore? Interpol.

Instead of catching a bus, Anna decided to get a taxi to the nearest police station.

She had only just arrived when her phone rang. It was Daniel. Relieved to know he was back, she rapidly and breathlessly told him what had happened at the apartment, what she had done, how far she had run, where she had gone and that she'd now decided to go to the police. Daniel, trying hard to keep up with what she was telling him, was shocked.

"Where are you now?" he asked. Anna told him.

"Stay there, Anna. Don't move. I'll be with you as soon as I can," he said as he walked quickly towards the taxi rank. Colin had been right. He had also been right to get annoyed with him and to tell him, in no uncertain terms, to get back to Bangkok.

An hour later, in the Thai police station close to the British and American Embassies, a senior policeman confirmed that a red notice had been received from Interpol for the arrest of Greg O'Brian, an American citizen following a US request for his deportation to face charges of fraud, embezzlement and money laundering. That was the formal announcement.

"And Mohamed Kader and David Solomon?" Daniel asked. "They are all involved and all three were in Bangkok less than eight hours ago."

They were in an office with a uniformed senior police officer and two other officers. Daniel and Anna were sat on one side of a long table facing the senior man. The other two officers were on either side of him. All three policemen now looked at one another. "No sir, we have nothing."

"Nothing?" Daniel almost shouted. "They are all involved in this. Has no-one read our report?"

"Sorry, sir, but we only have the request from Interpol to arrest the American, Greg O'Brian."

Daniel looked at Anna and shrugged. But it was Anna who then spoke.

Facing the senior officer across the table she spoke in Thai. Daniel listened as Anna spoke rapidly and increasingly loudly. He could already tell from her face that she was not going to be treated like this and was warming up to a full blown tirade. Not understanding what was being said, Daniel listened and watched the face of the senior police officer as he fidgeted and squirmed. Then Anna stood up. Her chair almost fell over.

"Give me that report, Daniel. I know it is in English but I am now so fed up with people not listening to you and me."

Daniel put his hand inside the old black bag lying at his feet and pulled out a copy of the report he'd taken to Singapore earlier and brought back with him. He handed it to Anna and she snatched it, hardly noticing him giving it to her. She was still standing but now talking in Thai again.

She threw the report down as Daniel tried picking up words and phrases Anna was now using as she threw in bits of English - American President, Senator Mary Collis, British government, biological warfare, viruses, bird flu, Influenza, Solomon, terrorism, everyone sick, laboratory, my husband, Shah Pharmacy, Egypt, Singapore, Nigeria. Then he heard 'Jimmy, Kenya'.

Daniel put out his hand to stop her for a moment.

"Anna - Jimmy is dead. He was shot. Colin told me this morning."

Anna had never met Jimmy but it was as though she knew him as a close friend. Her hand went to her mouth to stifle something, then tears came to her eyes. Daniel leaned over and put his arms around her. But Anna shrugged him off.

"You see?" she said in English pointing a finger straight at the police officer. "Somebody is dead. With gun. By this man Kader and this man Solomon. You want me to die? My husband to die? Do you want to die? Your family to die? You want them to get sick, then die?"

She stopped suddenly and sobbed, the tears running down her cheeks. Daniel pulled her to him and she almost fell from her chair and collapsed into his arms.

"Sir," Daniel said, looking at the officer. "Anna is right. That report has gone as high as it can go. We can translate it into Thai if you wish. I can have it ready by tomorrow. But the man David Solomon was in Bangkok this morning. I saw him last night. Anna saw him this morning. He was with Greg O'Brian and Mohamed Kader. The least you can do is raid the apartment off Sukhumvit road and check it out. I believe that this is where Solomon works. If it was a bomb factory you would raid it. But it is not a bomb factory, it is more dangerous than that. Your officers need to be very careful."

As Daniel was speaking another police officer came in with a sheet of paper. He handed it the senior one who glanced at it. He then stood up.

"OK, sir," he said. "We now have the other paperwork. If you give us your report, we will translate it but other officers of the Royal Thai Police have already seen it. We already have police out ready to arrest these men this evening. We know where they are. The man Solomon is the only exception. He took a flight to Kuala Lumpur earlier. But we are working with our Malaysian colleagues on this and we have officers already outside his apartment.

"If you would like to stay here for a few moments," he continued, "I can confirm everything. We will also provide you and your wife with any security you feel you might need until this process is complete. Please excuse me, one minute while I report what you and your wife have just told me. This will support the action we are already taking."

Then he bowed politely, put his hands together in front of his face and nodded and spoke to the other officers.

Daniel and Anna were served coffee within five minutes.

Within two hours, they had checked in at a hotel almost opposite the British Embassy and police guards were provided. Neither Daniel or Anna had eaten all day so, with an armed policeman stood outside the hotel restaurant, they ate supper and retired to their room.

But Daniel could not resist a phone call to Colin. He thanked him for the earlier ticking off.

"You were right, Colin. I needed you to tell me to fuck off. It did me good. And I could not have done any of this without Anna. She was brilliant tonight. You should have seen the tears. She nearly had the three police officers in tears as well."

Daniel looked at Anna, who was already half asleep, her head on the pillow. But she raised her head and smiled. "Good wasn't I?" she said. "We make a good man and wife team. Can I speak to Colin?"

"Sure," said Daniel and kissed her forehead.

"Good night Colin." Anna said. "See you in London."

CHAPTER 77

Kevin Parker's routine had returned to relative normality since the get together at Daniel's apartment in London. So, being nearly midnight, he had just returned to his Clifton flat from the pub. Unexpectedly, that night, Tom had also been there so they had sat together in the corner discussing the most recent update from Colin.

"The Egyptian police visited that place down the Nile and then took away that Dutch bloke, Jan de Jonge and Guy Williams," said Tom.

Kevin already knew this so he added in his own snippet. "Yes and they raided the Shah Medical Centre in Cairo and arrested El Badry's wife. I've been sleeping better since I knew that she and her husband are out the way. I wonder if his Chelsea apartment is up for sale."

"And Greg OBrian's been flown to the States to face charges," added Tom.

"And what about that laboratory that Daniel found in Bangkok - in Solomon's apartment. Surprising that no-one knew what he was doing in there." said Tom.

"But where is he?" asked Kevin. "Colin said they lost him in Malaysia or somewhere. But at least they got that bugger who shot Jimmy Banda. We never got to meet Jimmy but he sounded a bundle of fun."

"And Singapore 2100 was in the paper again. Did you see that, Kevin? Must have scared the shit out of the Singapore government. But they only arrested one guy. Is it still operating? Do they post on the Malthus site?"

"I'll check tonight," said Kevin. "I haven't checked anything for a few days. I've been so busy."

"And what about Larry?" asked Tom.

"Resigned from his job at the Embassy. He's got so much spare time now he's coming over to see Daniel and Anna. Perhaps you and I will get an invite to a wedding, Tom?" Kevin laughed and drained his glass.

Kevin was now sat on the edge of his bed and had just opened his laptop to check the Malthus Society website for the first time for a week. As he logged on, his phone rang. It was something else that hadn't happened for a week.

"Tunj. How are you? Just going out? It's nearly midnight - time for your social life to begin."

"I'm feeling tired, Kev. And my head and eyes are hurting. I think I'm sickening for something."

"Too much hard work and attention to detail, Tunj. You need to relax. You should have used that money you were given to go to Nigeria and gone somewhere where normal people go to relax. And that's not Lagos, Tunj. People avoid Lagos like the plague. When was the last time you heard of package holidays to Port Harcourt or Maiduguri? No, I'm talking Tenerife or Ibiza or somewhere in between like Brighton."

"Please don't mention the plague, Kev. My head and eyes hurt."

"Wear sunglasses, Tunj. The sun in Barnet is too strong and bright for a man of your complexion."

"Now I've warned you before about your racist comments, Kev. If you don't stop it I'll tell you a story about a white Englishman and his favourite hobby."

"I'm a white Englishman, Tunj, but my hobby is a very private matter. "

"Well, I know one who thinks his hobby is a very public matter."

"Who's that Tunj?"

"David Solomon. Haven't you seen his message on the Malthus site?"

"No," said Kevin, suddenly pressing keys on his laptop. "I was just about to check it."

"Well, call me back when you've seen it and tell me if you also feel as if you've got a headache and a bout of flu coming on."

Kevin logged on and there it was. A posting from 'Solomon'.

"Well, they closed down one laboratory but they were, as always, too late. Unlike the politicians we saw it coming. We had a plan in place. It has already been said by others but democracy cannot survive overpopulation. Common sense will always stay a step ahead and will, one day, rule over democracy. But we cannot wait. Thomas Malthus was always right. The Malthus A virus is now ready and we will release it."

CHAPTER 78

I started this by venting my frustration with the system of governance in the West. Whether this is a symptom of the impossible challenges imposed by trying to manage a world that is already overpopulated is, perhaps, a subject that Kevin might like to take on. For me, this is neither the time or the place. But I'll finish with a short and true story that might go some way to explaining my original rant.

In the hillside village of Nah Noi in Kanchanaburi, Thailand, Pah heard her father shouting as she crouched over the clay cooking pot and fed fresh lumps of charcoal into the embers. As the smoke and sparks from her small fire rose high into the still air, she had been quietly humming to herself as the distant, orange and blue glow of dawn broke over the far off hills. Until then, the only sound had been the early morning calls of birds, the croaking of frogs in the rice field and the familiar but faint whimpering from inside the wooden house as her five year old son, Lek, woke to the reluctant realisation that it was probably school today and that he did not feel well.

Pah's house stood on wooden stilts just out of sight of the others, down the track and over the slope where her mother and father also lived.

On hearing her father's call, Pah stopped humming and stood up, wiping her hands on the sarong around her waist. Little Lek, tottered outside onto the platform of the house, shrouded in his sleeping blanket. He crouched near the top wooden step, rubbed his eyes and coughed. He had been feverish for two days. "Meh!" he cried, and coughed again.

"Go - wash your face. Meh's cooking your rice for school. You want fish?"

She then heard her father shouting her name. "Go, wash your face," she called once more to Lek. "Meh will be back in a minute."

She ran passed Boon-Mee's house where six year old Suchin, and in the same class at school as Lek, lay outside on a blanket. Suchin, too, was coughing. Her grandmother, Sinee sat alongside her, fanning the child's hot and feverish face. Sinee said nothing but pointed to Pah's parent's house.

Pah's mother had also had a high fever for three days. Last night she had started coughing. When Pah arrived, her father was crying and holding her mother's limp hand.

Pah is Anna's sister.

THE END

OTHER NOVELS by Terry Morgan

AN OLD SPY STORY (published 2012)

The old spy in **"An Old Spy Story"** is octagenerian, Oliver ("Ollie") Thomas. During a long career spent trying to earn an honest living with his own export business, Ollie was also, reluctantly, carrying out parallel assignments in Africa, the Middle East and elsewhere only loosely connected to British Intelligence. But, by using threats and blackmail, his controller, Major Alex Donaldson, was forcing Ollie to help run his own secret money making schemes that included arms shipments to the IRA through Gadaffi and Libya, money laundering in Africa and assassination. Now aged eighty six, recently widowed and alone Ollie still struggles with guilt and anger over his past and decides to make one last attempt to track down and deal with Donaldson.

STIGMA (due to be published in 2014)

After making public accusations that high level government bureaucrats and politicians were involved in criminality through organised theft of International Aid money, ex businessman and newly elected Independent Member of the UK Parliament, James (Jim) Smith, rapidly becomes a political outsider.

Hounded and ridiculed by sections of the press for naivety, for making accusations without proof, for a lack of political finesse and for his blunt, no-nonsense style, he then endures a deliberate campaign of harassment clearly intended to silence him. But with his long marriage also under strain a newspaper then publishes doctored pictures of him with a nightclub hostess and he is unable to stop his wife, Margaret, from leaving him.

Determined not to give up he is sure the campaign to stop him is being well orchestrated and funded from somewhere but feeling there is no other option for the time being, he deliberately flies abroad to escape the stress and publicity.

Three years later he is living alone in very basic conditions in rural Thailand and still struggling to come to terms with a failed marriage and his short but bitter incursion into politics. A growing appreciation of Buddhism and his new found skill as an artist helps with the lingering anger and the stigma of failure he still feels but throughout that time he never gives up looking for ways to renew his campaign.

He eventually finds it through an English business consultant, Jonathan Walton, who specializes in international aid, a Dutch mole, Jan Kerkman, operating inside the system and an ex Irish newspaper reporter, Tom Hanrahan.

What they uncover is a highly sophisticated fraud that has already netted millions of Dollars and Euros from economic development and humanitarian aid funds and the mastermind is a strange and illusive Italian calling himself Guido.

But with beneficiaries of the fraud at all levels - from the bottom to the very top - and the danger for Walton and Kerkman increasing, the problem remains: How to get the fraud recognized and dealt with by a system that does everything to cover its own weaknesses and uses threats and bribery to ensure silence.